Praise for *Of Kings*

'A clever and exciting collision of space opera, high adventure, and devious politics. Insightful and highly entertaining!'
Jonathan Maberry, *New York Times* bestselling author of *Relentless* and *V-Wars*

'Political and prophetic, comprising battles and betrayals, bourgeoisie and brutes, and the persistent hum of bees, Of Kings, Queens and Colonies *is a masterful epic of exploration and exile. A cautionary tale for citizens of the Old Earth. Sure to be on the award lists.'*
Lee Murray, Bram Stoker Award winner and author of *Grotesque: Monster Stories*

'Worthen shows himself a master of style and substance.'
Michael R. Collings, 2016 World Horror Convention Grand Master

'The worlds of Coronam, with their mixture of old and new technologies, create a unique setting for an ageless story about humanity.'
Daniel Yocom (Guild Master Gaming)

'Johnny Worthen is a bold and imaginative writer; his Coronam *work is a fascinating look at our troubling history through the lens of tomorrow.'*
Bryan Young, author of *BattleTech: Honor's Gauntlet*

JOHNNY WORTHEN

OF KINGS, QUEENS AND COLONIES

Coronam Book One

This is a **FLAME TREE PRESS** book

FLAME TREE PRESS
6 Melbray Mews, London, SW6 3NS, UK
flametreepress.com

US sales, distribution and warehouse:
Simon & Schuster
simonandschuster.biz

UK distribution and warehouse:
Marston Book Services Ltd
marston.co.uk

Publisher's Note: This is a work of fiction. Names, characters, places, and
incidents are a product of the author's imagination. Locales and public names
are sometimes used for atmospheric purposes. Any resemblance to actual
people, living or dead, or to businesses, companies, events, institutions, or
locales is completely coincidental.

Thanks to the Flame Tree Press team, including:
Taylor Bentley, Frances Bodiam, Federica Ciaravella, Don D'Auria,
Chris Herbert, Josie Karani, Molly Rosevear, Mike Spender,
Cat Taylor, Maria Tissot, Nick Wells, Gillian Whitaker.

The cover is created by Flame Tree Studio with
thanks to Nik Keevil and Shutterstock.com.
Map design © 2021 Johnny Worthen,
map illustration by Sean Nathan Ricks.
The font families used are Avenir and Bembo.

Flame Tree Press is an imprint of Flame Tree Publishing Ltd
flametreepublishing.com

A copy of the CIP data for this book is available from the British Library
and the Library of Congress.

HB ISBN: 978-1-78758-598-0
PB ISBN: 978-1-78758-596-6
ebook ISBN: 978-1-78758-599-7

Printed in the USA by Integrated Books International

JOHNNY WORTHEN

OF KINGS, QUEENS AND COLONIES

Coronam Book One

FLAME TREE PRESS
London & New York

Dedicated to: Ursula K. Le Guin, Naomi Klein, & Lee Miller

PART ONE
COLONY

'History doesn't repeat itself, but it does rhyme.'
Mark Twain

CHAPTER ONE

The invention of the Focused Fusion Wormhole Engine in the late twenty-third century was largely ignored even after a successful test in 2278. It was seen as a waste of resources at a time when the planet was in continued economic, social, and environmental chaos. The promise of interplanetary colonization was a shallow idea, a solution for a select few at best, and of course ultimately a pipe dream since no other habitable planets had been identified. This changed in 2310 with the discovery of the Coronam System.
Jareth, *A New Beginning: Prospectus for Coronam Colonization*
June 17, 2325

21, Fifth-Month, 937 NE – Aboard the Hopewell, *Western Trade Corridor*

Fifteen-year-old Millicent Dagney, known as 'Millie' to her family, sat beside her father and feared her world was ending.

They were on the seventh deck of the *Hopewell*, two months into a journey to Tirgwenin, also known as Jareth's World. Their little family living space was a four-meters cube shipping container made of composite carbon and crystal thread. The smell inside it was fetid and sickly, dried blood and disease, bleach and incense to cover the worst of it.

One side of the cube had been removed for a door, a sheet draped over it for privacy. Forty-four other identical cubes cluttered the rest of the convex deck interior and served as quarters, offices, and church. The Dagney cube was distanced from the others. Even in the cramped deck of the *Hopewell*, they'd allowed fifteen meters between it and the next cube. There was a latrine between it and the next house on one side, and a ceiling-high wall of sail silk on the other. The Dagney cube was quarantined because they had the pox.

"Trees," said Henry Dagney. "Trees and trees."

"I know trees, Dad,"Millie said, stirring a thin mushroom broth over a heat stone.

"Forest," said her father. "Wild forests. Can you imagine it?"

"A group of trees? Aye, Father. I've seen wood farms."

"Wood farms are not forests," he said too forcefully and began to cough. It was a short fit, over after a dozen hacks, but it was raspy and raw and it tightened Millie's back like a wrench. She tensed, expecting it to go on and on like it had last night. On and on. Her father finally spitting up yellow-tinted blood, the color of pus from the sores on his back.

She found herself holding her breath. The broth bubbled for lack of stirring when her father spoke again.

"Enskari had forests once. A long time ago. Real forests filled with scaled beasts and flame birds."

"I know, Father."

"Of course you do." He spat into a stained handkerchief. "But have you imagined it?"

"It'll be great. Aye." She tried to sound enthusiastic. "Real trees. What we'll make with those trees."

"New trees. Unnamed and unfound. A new world," he said over a broad smile.

Millie smiled back, ignoring his swollen gums. At first when he spoke this way she'd assumed it was a pep talk for the benefit of Dillon and herself, but as the months on board stretched on and his enthusiasm grew with each day, she had to admit that he either said these mantras of new beginnings as a nostrum for his own worry or, as unlikely as it seemed for an educated man, he actually believed in a waiting paradise.

"It'll be great," Millie said. "I only wish we all felt better."

"We'll be fine by the time we get there," he said and winked.

She forced another smile and stirred the broth. She gathered a handful of bitter trap lace leaves that would soothe his sore throat and ease his pain, but her hands shook as she crumbled the dried herbs into the little pot. She turned her back so her father wouldn't see them, though his eyes were now closed and his head heavy on the stained pillow.

She'd not felt right since the day the peddler came.

He'd come to the back door of their carpentry shop. He wore a dark rayburned rash over his face, lightning scars up his arms. Scars that hid his pox scabs.

"I have for ye thimblewood, good lass," he said, counting the boards like a deal had already been struck. His confidence had impressed Millie, who was there alone then.

He mumbled to himself and squinted as if calculating in his head. "Aye, I'll make it an even hundred dollars."

Millie laughed at the audacious figure. It was twice what it was worth and he didn't have papers to show that the wood had been legally gathered.

He'd smiled and coughed into the crook of his arm and then scratched his leg. She suspected it then. She should have sent him off, called the police for the poaching, and disinfected everything in sight just to be on the safe side. Instead, she'd talked him down to a reasonable price, more than he deserved, but still a good deal, wood being as scarce as it was. She'd paid him in real coin after he unloaded it into the workshop.

"Might you know of a free clinic nearby?" he said, wiping sweat from his face with a tangerine cloth, blinking against the shop's dim light.

"You can find one down the cobble road there, past the butcher," she said. "Ask for the nurse not the doctor. She is nobler."

"Thanks to you," he said and fell into a coughing fit that bent him over.

"Is it the pox?" she said.

"Couldn't say."

She gave him a bottle of water and he took it gratefully with a low bow and a tip of his hat.

"You barter like a merchant," he rasped between gulps, "but blessed ye are, young lass. Blessed ye are."

That night she had a cough. In a week she had fever. In a fortnight Morgan came to their home and invited them to Tirgwenin.

*　　*　　*

Millie lifted her father from the bed and stuffed a duffel behind him for support.

"Comfortable as a king," he said and coughed. He'd fallen asleep. Millie had woken him for the broth.

Her father tried to take the spoon and bowl from her, but she shook her head and insisted on feeding him.

"Darling Millie, brighten your eyes," he said.

"I will if you eat all your broth."

He sighed, nearly coughed, and then nodded.

"It's not so much," she said. "It'll settle your stomach and cool your throat."

"Don't waste all the trap lace on me," he said, turning away from the spoon. "Your mother needs it more—"

"She's doing much better than you are, Father. She can go to the latrine. You can tell me how much trap lace to use when you can do that."

He blanched in embarrassment.

"Trees and trees," Millie said. "Remember? We'll have fields of trap lace, right? Orchards of starch apple and red grape; mountains of gold, rivers of nectar."

"Darling Millie, it will be hard, but it will be wonderful. Be grateful. Be optimistic."

"Eat your broth," she said sternly.

He raised an eyebrow but opened his mouth and swallowed the offered soup.

"I'm sorry," she said. "I'm being disrespectful."

"Mind your temper. The way of our family is not the way of the world."

She nodded and hid her mind behind a face of sweet womanly calm. She knew it as a mask women used to hide among strangers and men. Though in her home she was not required to 'keep sweet' as was the Saved doctrine for her gender, she knew the accustomed mask and wore it now for her ailing father.

"No," he said. "Don't do that. Show me your true face. Show me your worry so I can assuage it. Bury it not or it will germinate and grow."

"You sound like a planter," she said and let some worry into her voice.

"That's what we are now. Or will be. We'll be planters first, then merchants, then nobles. Now we're cargo." He coughed. "Where's Dillon?"

"He's with Mother at the latrine."

He took spoonfuls of broth, swallowing with difficulty, grimacing at the act, but quick to smile when it was done. "What did the governor say this day?" he asked.

"Governor Morgan said that we're coming up to Dajjal. We'll be able to see it in a day or two. Then a week or so to Freeport Station to take on supplies."

"Good. Any word of the *Sebastian*?"

"No, but the *Mallow* is nearby. Five days behind is all."

"That's very good." He reached up to scratch a sore under his eye but withdrew his hand when Millie glared at him.

"Don't scratch," she said.

Millie put the bowl aside and wetted a cloth for her father's brow. The act made her cringe. It was not the sickness or the sores but how the water splashed so unnaturally. It clung too long to the sides of the bowl, lingered in slow-motion surface tension. The unreal lightness of things on the spaceship upset her. It made everything unfamiliar and suspect. Like a fever sickness, it made her nauseous and tinged her waking mind with hallucinatory visions of impossible physics that her instincts rejected though her mind supposedly understood.

It was by design. The spinning ship created depths of centrifugal force, from nothing at the core, to 1.8 Enskari Natural at the edge of the *Hopewell* where the thick ablative armor shielded the craft from Coronam's fiery moods.

On their low deck, the gravity was a mere .5 Enskari Natural. It was a cargo deck filled with eighty-three pilgrims en route to a wild planet far from the civilized worlds. Their leader, Minister Morgan, now Governor Morgan with Sommerled's Royal Patent for the colony, led frequent trips to the upper decks for the fit pilgrims to feel greater gravity so they wouldn't be atrophied when they arrived. Millie went with them as often as she could. She'd gone that day, careful to keep far in the back, partly for having had the pox, but mostly because she was a girl and would likely be sent away to do chores rather than exercise. She'd been gone but an hour, but she'd felt bad for going. Her mother was just getting over the disease, her father starting into it. She should have stayed with them to help, watch Dillon at least, but her legs had cramped and she'd longed to feel her weight again.

"What's the talk among the parish? Get any gossip on the walk?"

"Same as ever. They talk of war as if we have a stake in it anymore. Prince Brandon is cursed along with the prophet. New epithets and fears because of the *Sebastian*, and though I would not say there is love for the queen, there is still a decided sympathy for her."

"Lesser of two evils," he said. "Brandon has Temple purgers, the queen has Connor and his Guard. I say, what's the difference? Homegrown or imported thumbscrews hurt all the same."

Millie wrung the rag over a bedpan and waited for the water to squeeze out. Finally, impatient with the resistance, she shook it to get the water off.

Her father back on his pillow said, "God help us if Brandon got the *Sebastian*."

"They'll be along," Millie said. "We are not at war with Hyrax, though all still believe Brandon intends one. There've been no storms. Coronam is quiet. All is well. The ship is only delayed."

"Delay is death," he said. "If we're late for the planting season...."

Her father's change in mood, dour and worrisome now, told Millie that the trap lace had hold of him and would soon soothe him to a quiet sleep.

"Father, you worry about things you cannot influence. Trust in your ministers."

"You sound like Connor." He laughed. "Well, I guess it fits."

"Sleep now. I should see to Mother. She's taking a long time."

Henry Dagney coughed once and scratched his leg under the blanket. Millie glared at him for it but he did not see.

"I'll rest for a while." He closed his eyes. "Bring me a fever pill if you can find one. Everything seems weird to me."

"Trap lace," she said. "And the fever, don't forget that. Oh, and it could have something to do with us being inside on a spinning metal cone somewhere deep in space halfway around the sun."

"A quarter," he mumbled, his speech thick. "We'll be halfway when we're done."

"Get some sleep. I'll find you a pill."

"Darling Millie," he said and slept.

Millie stood up, wound the key on the glowglobe, and adjusted the light. The deck would be dimmed for evening soon and then shut off for nighttime.

She ruffled her skirt and adjusted her blouse and bonnet. She knew how she looked. Sick and starving. She was too skinny, sharp cheekbones. She'd been called gaunt and malnourished even before the trip. Here it was worse. She hadn't eaten well on the ship, no one had, but her cheekbones made it look so much worse. Her red hair leaned to the burgundy, a color unnatural on Old Earth she was told, but now becoming common on Enskari due to its particular refraction of Coronam's radiation. She tucked as much of it under the bonnet as she could, the womanly way. Her skin had the reflective nature of all the Saved who had made Coronam their home after the Unsettling of Old Earth. Something about crystal absorption and again, radiation. She was told that the natives on Tirgwenin had it the worst, or best, depending on your perspective. They were said to glitter in the daylight and glow at night. Millie heard there was one aboard, a man named Mathew, but she hadn't seen him.

Properly modest to be seen by non-family, she stepped out of the cube to search for her mother.

The concave deck sloped upward, always upward and away.

Beyond the bank of latrines, she saw women doing washing in the low gravity, fighting surface tension with more patience than she had.

Her brother, Dillon, sat with his back to her squatting over a pile of garbage by the overflowing cans of rubbish. The smell was terrible but better than the stench from the latrines.

Dillon had turned eight years old onboard and still hadn't had the growth spurt his parents kept promising him. Millie saw his shoulders jerk in a cough and noted the sores on his shaved head.

Millie said, "Don't pick at your— Don't touch that!"

Dillon jumped and dropped a length of plastic tubing he'd been using to poke at a dead rat by a can.

He turned and looked at his sister, shame and embarrassment on his face. He opened his mouth to speak, but coughed and then bent over with it. Mille knelt beside him and held him until it passed.

"Dillon?" she said.

"It's dead," he rasped. "It can't bite me."

"It's not something a little boy should be playing with," she said. "It's disgusting."

He scratched the rash on his neck. "I'm bored."

"Don't scratch," she said.

He dropped his arms to his sides like a soldier at review.

"Try to enjoy having so little to do right now," Millie told him. "Mark my words, we will wish for more days like this when we're arrived at Tirgwenin. We'll pine for days like this, we'll have so much to— Don't scratch!"

He pulled his hand back as if it had burned. "Mom's taking a long time in there," he said, pointing to the latrines.

Millie looked up at the wall of plastic doors and felt a cold chill run up her back.

An imagining touched her mind. A fear. A worry.

She told herself it was the lingering disease, a memory of the fever she'd endured and recovered from, but she did not believe it. The idea tarried too long and seeped into her mind like a venom. She shuddered and shook and her breath caught in her throat.

"What, Millie?" said Dillon. "What is it?"

Millie closed her eyes and listened. Dreading. She listened past the murmurs of the nearby pilgrims, the under-thrum of the ship's pulse engines, Dillon's raspy breathing, and then her own quickening heartbeat. She listened for her mother. She listened for plumbing noises behind the door, for movement, a rustling of petticoats and bonnet. She listened for coughing, for breathing, for song. For life.

"Millie?" Dillon's voice was low and fretful.

She opened her eyes and stumbled forward. She knocked on the door. Millie prayed it was not a dark premonition but a fever-echo dread, a hallucination, a nightmare. A lie.

"Mother?" she called. "Emma? Are you all right?"

No answer.

"Mother," she called again. Then louder, "Mother. Mother!"

"Mom," added Dillon. "Mah'om!"

Millie took a penknife from her pocket, opened it, stabbed it in the door lock and turned it.

For hope's sake, she called again. "Mother. It's me, Millie. Are you all right?"

Silence in the room; cacophonies in her mind.

Millie looked inside.

In dim light and deep shadow, Millie saw her mother's body slumped against a wall. She lay twisted in the folds of her handmade dress, her face turned to the floor. Her cold, glassy eyes lifeless and lost.

She was wrong, she thought, they would not wish for more days like this.

CHAPTER TWO

This Holy Writ and Most Noble Command to all the Blessed Saved comes from The Holy Word and The Sacred Will of His Eminence Eren VIII, Supreme Minister of the Saved, Anointed Prophet of God.

Be it hereby known and effected by all the Holy and Saved, that Zabel Genest, the pretended Queen of Enskari and the servant of crime, by bell, book, and candle is cast out of the Saved, declared a known heretic and enemy of God.

We charge and command all and singular the nobles, subjects, peoples, and others within her influence that they do not dare obey her orders, mandates, and laws. Those who act to the contrary shall be included in like sentence of excommunication.
The Pretender Bull, Prophet Dictate CCMXIV
25, Second-Month, 925 NE (New Era)

30, Fifth-Month, 937 NE – Vildeby, Enskari

Sir Nolan Brett, Second Ear of the queen, arrived at his private office in Kent Castle before dawn. He slipped in unnoticed using one of the nondescript side entrances and ascending a servants' stairs to arrive at his upper floor. He greeted his guards in the anteroom after sending one away for coffee and bread, letting them know to send his secretary in when he arrived. He slid his key into the door, turned the complicated lock until the heavy blast door swung open and let him in.

The sky outside was already a mauve glow, the planet's crystalline atmosphere warming as Coronam peeked over the horizon. Waves of blue and red auroras skittered outward across the sky like fleeing phantasms chasing the darkness. Thunderclaps from distant lightning heralded the day while waves of radiation, seen and unseen, churned up storms of clouds – ionic, electric, and dry, to harass the wet ones of sleet and much-needed rain, as Coronam, their sun, would have it.

On Old Earth, Nolan was led to believe, daybreak and sunset had been pleasant times, beautiful, soothing, and serene. He could not imagine it. All his life – for the lifetimes of all his known ancestors, the changes of the day had always been terrible and awesome. Many would call them beautiful, but only the mad would call them serene.

He looked out to Government House across the Reedy River and confirmed by the flags that the queen was not there this day. She was out of the city, away from Vildeby. She'd be at her northern estates in Upaven by evening if her train wasn't delayed. He'd telegraph her later with warm wishes and any news that wouldn't keep.

To his left down the river a few miles, closer to the sewers, was Gray Keep, its dungeons filled with criminals, Connor's captives, traitors. Problems. Nolan had his own suite of cells there for his problems. Discreet, effective, and if necessary, permanent.

Connor – Archbishop Ralph Connor – was the highest-ranking cleric of the Enskaran Church. Queen Zabel led the new church, like the prophet ruled the Orthodox from Temple, but Connor ran the day-to-day operations on her behalf. Those operations, since the rise of Zabel, had centered on exposing and eliminating Her Majesty's enemies who threatened the new church.

Off to his right Nolan could see the ocean, and there at the port, reaching into the clouds of crystal and smoke, was the Vildeby space elevator thread connecting the city to an orbiting spaceport. He couldn't see the cable, it was too thin from this distance, but he saw a climber launch and ascend it with increasing velocity. In a moment it was out of sight above the clouds, but still days from the connected platform.

Thin pillars of smoke appeared over the city skyline as Vildeby came awake. The black sooty columns were a sign of wealth and prosperity across the civilized worlds. Though it would make lightning clouds by noon and color your spit to pitch by suppertime, it was a good sign. It signaled commerce as factories started up and homes cooked breakfasts over heated hearths. Though Nolan had read the alarming environmental reports, he still took comfort in the rising smoke. It looked like home to him.

He turned from the window when the ticker tape machine in the corner turned on and clattered away at exactly 6 a.m. It spat out a ribbon of paper in short code with official reports and news condensed by the Royal Signalmen for three minutes. As quickly as it began it stopped.

He set his watch and sat down at his desk to look over the stack of letters. He sorted them by the crests of the wax seals into piles of importance. The nobles he put in one pile: the Earl of Dawnray, the Duke of Ellsworth – again, and the Dowager Combs. That could be interesting. Merchants with their new crests, overly expensive wax, and fine paper he put in another pile. Most of these were scented. Whoever started the rumor that scented letters were fashionable should be executed, he thought. He pushed these letters to the end of his desk. Then he looked through the important ones, the unassuming notes without crest or seal, often scrawled in charcoal across a penny envelope, his title only on the front, tobacco and sometimes blood smearing the page. These were the currency of his trade.

There was a knock on the door.

"Come," he commanded.

The door swung wide and Jim Vandusen, Nolan's personal secretary, entered carrying a breakfast tray.

"Sir," he said, putting it down on a sideboard. He poured a cup of steaming coffee and added sugar and cream before bringing it to Nolan's desk. "Sir Nolan, the other Ear wishes to see you."

Nolan sighed. Sir Edward Kesey, the First Ear of the queen, would take up his entire morning.

"Won't he be put off until tomorrow when I'm in Government House?"

"No, sir. He says it's urgent."

"When?"

"Presently. His page just left."

Nolan shook his head. "I need a new office."

"To hide from Kesey?"

"Aye."

Vandusen smirked. "I do believe he's the only one in the court who knows specifically about this office."

"The queen."

"Nay, I don't think even Her Majesty—"

"The queen," Nolan repeated.

"Oh," said Vandusen. "Sir Edward told her?"

Nolan nodded.

"Would you like me to inquire about other rooms?"

"No, it's not important. We'll keep on with this one for a while. Until it's too known." Nolan opened a grease-stained letter and read it. He said,

"Jim, I want you to hold Sir Edward off until after lunch. Then I probably should see him."

"I'll try, sir," Vandusen said.

"And Jim, there'll be a sailor here in a few minutes. Send him straight to me."

"Yes, sir."

"After he's disarmed."

"Of course."

Nolan read the note again and waited for Vandusen to take the hint and leave the office. When he was gone Nolan opened his safe and examined his accounts. Making note of the week's expenses, he tallied the numbers and sighed.

★   ★   ★

Twenty minutes later Vandusen peeked his head around the door. "A sailor, Sir Nolan."

Nolan put down his pen, cracked his knuckles, and nodded.

A tall rayburned man still in his sailor reflective vest shuffled into the room followed by Vandusen with a sheaf of official papers.

The sailor had the short-cropped hair and stocky upper body build of men who worked in low gravities. He held his hat in his hands at his waist and kneaded the worn felt with his fingers. His eyes were cast down. To the floor, he said, "Sir. I've been sent to you."

"I just received word," said the Ear. "I make you welcome."

The man flicked his hand up to his forehead in an instinctive salute of an order received.

"Partake of coffee?" said Nolan.

"I'd not trouble ye."

"Nonsense." Nolan crossed to the table and poured a cup for the man. "Sugar and cream?"

"Not my usual, but aye, if it's no bother."

Nolan handed him the cup. He took it with unsteady hands, still standing awkwardly two steps from the door in the middle of the room.

"What is your name?"

"McCabe, sir. Freeborn from Southland. Able-bodied seaman aboard the *Starlight*."

"And you come from Lavland this day?"

"Aye, sir."

"With news."

"Aye, sir." He fumbled with his hat and cup to free a hand for his pocket. He finally tucked his hat under his arm and removed a folded envelope from inside his vest. He passed it to Nolan.

Nolan took it, noting the smell of diesel emanating from the paper, and thought of the perfumed letters at the edge of his desk. He put the envelope in his pocket.

"Aren't ya going to read it, sir?" asked McCabe.

"Later," he said.

"I see." The sailor shuffled his feet. Then, as if suddenly remembering that he held a cup of coffee, took a sip. "Most excellent, sir," he said. "I'd expect nothing less from the Ear of the queen."

"Is there more, McCabe?"

"Aye, sir. Aye, that there is." He swallowed and took a deep nasally breath. "I'm supposed to report that I have myself seen none less than twenty-eight ships of arm, including eight of-the-line in shadow behind Hyrax. And a big 'un, I don't know what to call it."

"It's not uncommon to see ships in shadow behind Hyrax."

"Aye, aye this is the truth, upon the Saved. That is true, but these are grouped, sir, and waiting. They do naught but wait and assemble."

"Twenty-eight at arms?"

"Aye, and more a-coming, sir. They fix to overthrow Her Majesty."

"You have the ear of the prince? You know Brandon's mind?"

McCabe blushed. "Nay, sir. Nay. I am Enskaran, sir. I am loyal to the queen. Never a rebel in my family, sir."

"No, McCabe, of course not. I speak only of your knowledge of Prince Brandon's designs with his lingering fleet."

"Begging your pardon, I am speculating. Aye. I speak only from the rumors of the docks and taverns."

"And rumors say the fleet has designs on our fair world?"

"Aye, sir." He nodded emphatically.

"Eight of-the-line?"

"Warships? Aye, sir, I counted. Eight of-the-line. And something bigger."

Nolan's stomach turned but he hid it behind a knowing smile. The number was twice what he expected. It wasn't nearly enough to breach their defense, but the number was growing.

"Anything else?"

"Aye, sir. I heard a trader say he could not get a ship tended on Claremond because the yards were all a-use in shipbuilding, for Hyrax, he said."

"I see," said Nolan, calmly sipping his coffee.

"Begging your pardon, sir, don't you see? If Hyrax is hiring Claremond for ships, that means their own yards must be a-busting at capacity."

Nolan shot a glance and the man blushed for forgetting his place. He shifted his weight from leg to leg and mumbled to the floor, "Begging your pardon, sir. My manners are rough."

"But your loyalty is noble," said Nolan. "Speak not of any of this to anyone. Do you understand?" The last question carried a threat and McCabe, blushing again through his burned skin, nodded emphatically.

"When are you shipping out again?"

"Eight days," he said. "I must catch the climber on the morrow or be AWOL."

"Worthy McCabe, you have done a service to your queen and empire."

"Just a messenger, sir."

Nolan removed a leather pouch from a drawer in the bureau and weighed it in his palm. He took the unfinished coffee cup from McCabe and replaced it with the pouch.

"Take this from a grateful planet. Know you have a friend in this office. Loyalty is rewarded."

"Aye, sir." His fingers went up in salute again.

"The *Starlight*, you say?"

"Aye. Captain Faraday."

"I'll put in a good word for you," Nolan said. "See if I can't get you more shore time."

"I'd love to see Southland again."

"I mean on other worlds. Docks and taverns. You have bright eyes and sharp ears."

McCabe nodded and squeezed the bag. The clink of rubbing metal coins was faint but solid inside the leather. "Aye, sir. I'm your man," he said.

"Something else to remember, McCabe. If you fail me, it won't be just you I'll be angry with. Your sister, Rachel, and your brother, Paul, and his two promising sons, would suffer for your mistakes." No need to be subtle, not for a man like McCabe.

The color left the sailor's face. "No sir," he said. "I'll not fail ye."

"I know you won't, McCabe. Blessed be, and safe travels."

"Blessed be to thee, sir. God save the queen."

"Quite."

Vandusen was at the door, holding it open. McCabe left the room scurrying backward in an awkward half bow.

When he was gone, Vandusen said, "Sir Edward will arrive in half an hour, sir. It was the best I could do."

Nolan shot him a disapproving look. "All right. Leave me until then."

The secretary nodded, gathered his pile of papers back in his arms, and left.

Nolan closed the door and locked it before fetching a cypher book from his desk safe. He set it beside the diesel-stained letter and went to work.

★   ★   ★

"Sir Edward, sir," said Vandusen, peeking in the door half an hour later.

"Send him—" He was cut off as the First Ear of the queen pushed his way in. "Sir Edward," said Nolan.

"You may leave," Sir Edward said to Vandusen.

Vandusen looked to Sir Nolan, who nodded. The secretary retreated, pulling the door behind him.

Nolan knew the old man did not mean disrespect by his forceful intrusion or by ordering his servants. Others would take offense, but he knew his peer from decades at court and understood his directness toward him was a compliment.

Edward paused for a moment and collected his thoughts as was his way before beginning an interview. Nolan took the chance to look over his old colleague. Like the sooty smoke pillars outside his window poisoning the world, the sight of Edward comforted Nolan with a certain timelessness that connected the present to the past, a long line of kings and councilmen to the very founding of Enskari.

Sir Edward Kesey was an old man, portly and gray, a leftover from the Privy Council of Zabel's father, King Theodore the Thrice. Edward's loyalty and pragmatism had survived the Enskari Reformation, which put a woman on the throne and broke the planet from the Orthodox Saved, and out of the grip of the prophet on Temple. Theirs had been the biggest rebellion but hardly the only one. Many such rebellions still burned throughout the civilized worlds in a thousand different sects. Splinter groups of splinter groups popped up like hot spots after a wildfire, with the prophet's men and purgers in quick pursuit addressing each in bloody turn. The Enskaran rebellion was most egregious since it removed an entire planet from the fold. Though in doctrine there was little to differentiate the Orthodox from Enskaran churches, the one thing that made the break necessary, the ascension of a woman onto a noble throne, was enough to threaten the peace of the entire system.

Brett had to admire Edward's loyalty to the House Genest over the house of the prophet. Sir Nolan Brett had been the newest of the Privy Council when the king died without heir. He'd not been sure where to put his loyalty then, but Edward, to everyone's surprise, supported the rise of the princess, Zabel, just a child then, to the highest throne on the planet. Brandon on Hyrax had planned to marry Zabel and unite the worlds, or if not him, his half-witted brother. Barring that, a suitable courtier from Temple or one from the loyal continents of Claremond would have been appropriately blessed by the prophet. But the Enskari were a stubborn people, proud and isolated. The Hyraxians were too hated, the Temple ministers too corrupt, the House Genest too loved to be lost by marriage.

Amid swarms of rebellion and reformation, as Lavland burned under Hyraxian fire directed by official Temple purgers, Enskari made a queen. When Zabel would not be married or moved, the prophet issued the Pretender Bull, which far from frightening the people, reinforced their love of queen and empire and hatred for Temple and Hyrax.

For eighteen years they tried to remove the queen and failed. There was little left for them to try now but war and assassination.

McCabe brought Nolan word of both.

"Sir Nolan," said Edward, finally ready to commence their meeting. "We must talk."

"Sit down, Edward. No need to be formal here."

"I am – I am vexed," he said and paced the room.

"What have you heard?"

"Heard? Me? No, that's you, spymaster. What have you heard?"

Nolan waited.

Edward went on. "It's Connor, sir. He's gone too far. He's to execute Ellsworth for heresy against the queen."

Brett glanced at the unopened scented letter from that house on his desk. "Indeed?"

"He claimed first that he is a Mumbler but now maintains he is in fact Orthodox Saved."

"Either could cost him his head," said Sir Nolan. "The latter faster than the former."

"He's a noble!"

"Since when has nobility been a guard against treason?" said Nolan. "In my experience, far from being a preventative, high birth is a stimulant for sedition."

"The plague of the age!" Edward roared. "No one knows their place."

Nolan knew Edward meant the nouveau riche who had risen to courtier class and some to noble rank, but the same sentiment was at the heart of Temple's quarrel with Enskari. The irony was of course lost on the old man.

"Ellsworth, Nolan. What are we going to do?"

"Does Connor have proof?"

"What difference does that make?"

"Might let us sleep easier one way or the other."

"Damn sleep! A luxury for the weak and simple-minded. I haven't slept in fifty years." Edward looked out over the city. A wind had come and the sky had cleared, a bright glowing canopy instead of the usual dark shifting lightning storms.

"He has his supporters," Nolan said.

"That's why I'm here."

"Not to vary far from the subject," said Nolan, "but have we given any thought to what will happen to Ellsworth's holdings should he fall to Connor's Guards?"

"You think of money now? We are nearly at war, sir. Prince Brandon rattles his saber, conscripts from three worlds. It is a time for queen and empire."

"I have expenses," Nolan said. "They're not the kind of thing I can submit to the treasurer."

Edward turned on him, his face flushed with temper.

Nolan cut him off. "I will take the measure of the court," he said. "Is Connor set on his path?"

"I could not turn him."

"But you did not use all your influence?"

"No, of course not. The man still breathes."

Nolan remembered Ellsworth, his snidely inbred features, his chronic bad breath and grating laugh. He once visited his large estate on Dorothia and knew an estimate of the annual income from his two plantations on Southland. "Ellsworth is no Mumbler," said Nolan. "But to the other thing, I think there is credence."

"Damn these traitors," Edward said. "Damn them all."

Nolan glanced at his safe, calculating costs and income. "Yes," he said to agree.

CHAPTER THREE

Coronam, the name of our sun, comes from an Old Earth word meaning 'crown'. It was so named because of the ring of habitable planets circling it. These are like the jewels of a crown.

Coronam has a very unusual solar system. The eleven planets circling Coronam all share the same orbit and travel around the star in a line, like cars on a train. More unusual still, the orbits keep the planets at a specific distance from the sun, within what is called 'Goldilocks Zone'. The Goldilocks Zone means that the planets are neither too hot nor too cold to support life. This is why the Coronam System was chosen for the Unsettling of Old Earth. It was lucky we found it!

People have wondered about the origins of Coronam since it was first discovered, but no one knows for sure how this strange arrangement came about. Maybe you can solve this mystery when you grow up.

Lavlandian Third Grade Science Textbook, 'Chapter 8, Astronomy'
Seized and sequestered by holy purgers under the Heresy Dictate, 929 NE
Evidentiary/Apocryphal Vault 92, Section 87A:55, Temple Record Archives

4, Sixth-Month, 937 NE – Aboard the Merry, *Eastern Trade Corridor*

"That was from the *Astro*, sir. Rail grapeshot."

"Get me a damage report," barked Sir Ethan Sommerled. "And keep on her, Mr. Kyle."

"Aye, sir."

Sir Ethan Sommerled, commodore and knight, stared through the periscope at the fleeing ships. "Where's my firing solution, Mr. Paul?"

"Nearly done, sir."

Sir Ethan glanced above him to the strapped weapons officer and listened to the clicks of mechanical computing devices.

Mr. Paul swore under his breath and reset the machine for another try.

As his hands fell to the keys, his pencil floated serenely out of his hand, jerking back to his board only when it reached the end of its tether.

The zero-grav battle bridge at the center of the *Merry* was spartan and close-quartered. It had room for just seven officers and the commander. They were arrayed at odd angles to take advantage of communication links and optics tunneling through the ship. Clattering teletypes and computer mechanics competed with the sound of the plasma pulse engines at the end of the ship.

"Damn," said the weapons officer.

"Mr. Paul, the *Astro* is firing upon us. Let us return the favor."

"Aye, sir." Another reset of the machine and the weapons officer went back to work.

Ethan knew the strain the man was under, knew the complicated maths needed to send railshot across thousands of kilometers of space into an enemy ship from the gun platform. He watched Mr. Paul work the sums longhand, tracing vectors with rulers and scribbling lines of calculus with a pencil stub, at any moment expecting to have to start again for movement or storm. The command staff stayed as quiet as they could, letting him work, waiting for the word, excited for the hunt.

No one on the bridge could feel otherwise. Though they'd taken a volley from the Hyraxian convoy, Sir Ethan's exhilaration was contagious. He wore his thoughts openly, his emotions on his sleeves. He was quick to smile, anxious to share his pleasure, and likable to a fault. He knew this because he'd been told so by many at court. Some had told him this in praise, in an effort to garner patronage because he was high in the queen's esteem, others had told him the same thing in warning, for the same reason. He was a favorite.

"Damage report, Sir Ethan," said Mr. Andrews.

"Go ahead."

"Three-meter ablative armor scar in sixth quadrant," said the damage officer.

"Latitude?"

"Eighteen."

Ethan visualized the place on his ship where they'd been struck.

By necessity, ships that flew between Coronam's planets had the same general design. The main hull, which carried crew and cargo, was a spinning cone pointed ever at the sun. The hull was stacked with reflective ablative armor, composite layers of radiation shielding – gold, steel, lead, crystal fiber, and carbon thread at least ten meters thick. Warships had more than this, often much more, but this was the minimum to get men around their angry spitting star with any degree of safety. Like hellfire hurricanes Coronam bred on the oceans of the worlds, the star itself shot out unexpected flares of radiation and debris, cinder-light and gravity quakes that could tear even twenty meters of armor and turn dense mass to molten slag in the flash of a flare.

In the shadow of the hull, behind the ship, extended the utility decks. These housed a thread weaver for docking and planetary work. Depending upon the type of craft, the gravity-less deck could hold extra fuel pods, landing craft, cargo bays, or in the case of the *Merry* and the *Astro*, gun platforms.

Behind the utility decks, extending kilometers outward, was the mast, which ended at the plasma core engine used for direct thrust.

The mast supported the solar sails. When turned up, the silks would ripple and sway in the plasma, stretch to the length of the mast, several kilometers or more, like flower petals arrayed around a central stalk. Smaller navigation sails – navsails, wider and much shorter than the mainsails, caught the runoff from the hull and were likened to leaves beneath a blossom.

From a distance, with the sails filled and the hull a shiny little button beneath the glistening white florets, interplanetary ships had not a little resemblance to dandelion seeds and were oft called 'seed-ships' because of it.

Ships sailed by balancing Coronam's solar winds with the erratic and deep gravity well of the star itself. Beyond propulsion, the sails collected plasma to fuel the core which allowed ships to slow and maneuver as needed.

Coronam's storms and radio disruptions meant that even under the crystal shielding atmosphere of the habitable worlds, electronics were a thing only of history books, a memory of a magical technology that had allowed the Unsettling but which Coronam had taken in quick sacrifice for human survival. Sails were raised and lowered, angled and tacked, by pulley, winch, and wire. Carbon filament, plasma-absorbing sail silk, and grease were the basis of space technology.

"Quadrant six, eighteenth latitude," Ethan repeated. "Three meters?"

"Aye, sir."

"That's nothing!" He slapped his hands.

"Wait, I'm getting reports of tears."

The bridge fell silent except for Mr. Paul's mechanical calculator.

"Sails twelve, thirteen and fourteen. Navsail two," said Andrews.

"Extent?"

"Sail thirteen and nav two total loss. Others reparable."

"Jettison thirteen and nav two," ordered Ethan.

"Aye, sir," repeated the chief mechanic. "Jettisoning sails thirteen and nav two. Confirm?"

"Confirm," said Ethan.

"Away."

"Don't be down, chief. I think the sails on the *Bandima* will fit our mast."

"That they will, sir," beamed the mechanic. "Aye, that they will."

"The *St. Silangan* is running," called Mr. Kyle. "Z positive."

"She's the fat one," Ethan said. "How fast can she run?"

"She's emptying tanks."

"So if we take her we'll have to sit to refill?" Ethan asked. "Give the fleet a chance to come back for her?" He turned his scope to the orbital plane, checked the level, then panned upward. There it was, the big fat *St. Silangan*, loaded with Hyraxian loot from its namesake colony. Full of gold and spice, silks, Saved and slaves, flying for its life, burning its plasma stores in a long glowing streak of orange, like a hell-bent meteor.

"Signal the *Cuffly* to pursue her. We'll stay with the *Bandima* and *Astro*."

There was a pause before the communications officer said, "Aye, sir."

"Relax, boys." Ethan wrung his hands in anticipation. "We'll make it a fair fight. The *Bandima* has a few plasma cannons at most, lads, close range. And the *Astro* can't shoot worth snot."

"Aye, sir."

The comms officer tapped out the signal. It would show in lights along the dorsal rigging as a message to the *Merry*'s escort, the *Cuffly*. "Message alight, sir."

"Begging your pardon, captain, sir," said Mr. Kyle. "But it's not a fair fight."

"Why's that, Mr. Kyle?"

"Because they're sons of godless whores."

"You mean Hyraxian?"

"I believe that's what I said, sir."

At that, the officers laughed. It was an old joke, one told first by Ethan himself in his first battle, and now part of the ritual that brought luck and bounty to the entire privateer fleet. It'd been picked up by other captains aboard other ships, and like a prayer for the profane, it was said to harden hulls and align firing sights.

"I have a solution, sir," said Mr. Paul.

"Call it out and look sharp, Mr. Kyle."

"Aye, sir."

The weapons officer called coordinates and vectors to the navigation officer, who steered the ship's nose into proper alignment, bringing the gun platforms to facing.

"Vector set," said Mr. Kyle.

"Alert crew," Ethan called.

Chimes and klaxons echoed through the ship, alerting the crew that they were in battle in case they didn't know, and that the main gun was about to fire. Men secured metal objects and braced themselves as best they could.

Within the bowels of the ship, plasma batteries topped off magnetic rail cells and a half-ton projectile of composite steel, diamond shards, and Enskaran hate, waited for a signal.

"Thirty seconds to solution...mark!" called Mr. Paul.

"Fire at alignment."

"Aye, sir."

Mr. Paul counted down while Mr. Kyle kept the ship aligned, struggling against the loss of the navsail.

"Steady, Mr. Kyle."

"*Astro* is slowing. Looks to be coming around for the *Cuffly*."

"Adjust solution," Ethan ordered.

"Twelve degrees X of Y," came the correction.

"I got him."

Ethan felt the plasma engine fire and was shaken to his right.

"True to new alignment," called Mr. Paul.

Kyle picked up the solution countdown: "Five, four, three, two, one, aligned."

The ship jolted. Men were either pushed into their seats or yanked out, jostled as the ship was flung by magnetic recoil.

Ethan found his scope and adjusted the optics to locate the *Astro*. "She's pretty," he said. "Brand new. Not a scratch on her."

He saw the flash of phalanx guns as the Hyraxian corvette tried to intercept the shot with a cloud of projectiles. Its plasma engines fired, pushing its hull downward to Ethan's angle. The ship shifted but not enough.

The shell impacted the *Astro* aforeships and cut a shiny twelve-meter furrow down its side.

"It's scratched now," Ethan said.

The officers cheered. A signal went out to the crew, reporting the hit.

Ethan watched debris scatter like fireworks from the tear. It burst in orange light close to the ship where decompressing atmosphere gave it fuel.

"Nice shot, Mr. Paul. Nice shot indeed."

The weapons officer's smile was broad and toothy. "Reload?"

"Aye, Mr. Paul."

The signal went to reload. It would take a quarter hour to prepare another center railshot.

"While we wait, let us put holes in their silk," Ethan ordered. "Man the batteries. Freedom for the man who cuts a sail."

The communications officer signaled the crew.

Gun batteries were situated on the edge of the spinning hull where gravity approached 2 Enskari Natural. Unshielded and exposed, a scant meter of armor between man and space, it was the most dangerous job on the ship. Be it shrapnel, debris, grapeshot, or solar flare, men died in the batteries. It was so common that they had a space hatch, not for escape, but for quick disposal of bodies to make room for replacement. No sane sailor would volunteer for such a detail, so slaves were used.

Using weaker railgun mechanisms, grapeshot gun batteries flung debris across the kilometers of space, trying to destroy sail and rigging and peel away the metal hull in centimeters. Once a ship was stopped, relatively speaking, an attacker could move in with the plasma cannons and literally melt the ship into submission.

"*Bandima*'s running Z negative."

Another volley of grapeshot struck the *Merry*'s hull. The rattle and boom echoed like drums across the decks.

"Multiple twelve-meter rents," called the damage officer. "Quadrant two, latitude twenty and twenty-one."

"They're after our navsails," said Ethan.

"Damage to utility deck. Decompression. Main gun offline, sir."

"There's a lucky shot for ye, men. We'll burn 'em for that." Ethan beamed a wide grin and tried to put a glint in his eye that would ease the tension. The lucky shot was not only on the gun. Multiple twelve-meter rents could mean serious damage to the primary hull. "Target the *Bandima* with odd batteries. Keep the even on the *Astro*. We'll get *even* with them."

That drew a nervous chuckle from the officers.

The batteries fired in turn, sending vibrations through the ship like thrumming guitar strings.

"Do you smell smoke?" Ethan said.

A clatter of code to the damage officer.

"Fire in central armament," he said.

"Damn the prophet!" Ethan said.

"*Bandima* is four sails down and slowed," announced Mr. Paul. "Fouled rigging."

"Mr. Paul. Firing solution for the *Astro*."

"But sir, we have no—"

"Firing solution!"

"Aye, sir."

"Mr. Kyle, bear down on her. Close in. Close in tight."

"Aye, sir."

The pulse propulsion shook the ship. Navsails tilted and aligned. Within the ship, howls and creaks echoed between hull and man, as winches pulled and loosened, metals flexed carbon and tested their strengths.

Another volley of grapeshot like hail skittered across their hull.

"Multiple, ten-meter—"

"Shut up!" yelled Ethan. "Communications officer, turn signal to *Astro*."

"Aye, sir."

"Solution plotted."

"Mr. Kyle, aim the ship."

Mr. Andrews spoke. "Sir, even if they don't know we can't fire, they'll know we haven't had time to reload."

"One more word of mutiny and I'll space the lot of ye. Aim the ship, Mr. Kyle."

"Aye, sir."

"Message to *Astro*?"

"Signal 'Remember the *Pempkin!*'"

"Aye. Message alight."

"Keep sending."

"Aye, sir."

"Are we close enough that they know who we are?" Ethan asked no one in particular.

"Aye, sir, they should," said Mr. Kyle.

"Central Armament evacuated. Twenty-two casualties, fifteen lost."

"Ship coming onto solution," Mr. Kyle said.

"She's running, sir! The *Astro*'s pulsed down the well. They're running!"

"Ha!"

Ethan clapped his hands and floated back into his seat. He strapped himself in and aligned his scope to see the escorting Hyraxian corvette heading starward, full blaze, plasma engines burning behind it like a streak of cowardice. "Turn on the *Bandima*. Order them to stop."

"Aye, sir."

*　　*　　*

Without their armed escort the two Hyraxian cargo ships surrendered quickly. They were practically unarmed, far too slow to flee Ethan's nimble raiders, and terrified of the threat evoked by the mention of the *Pempkin*.

Though closer to her quarry, the *Cuffly* was out of position and needed an hour of maneuvering before it could board. The *Merry* was in position in only twenty minutes.

Keeping the *Bandima* targeted with battery and plasma cannon, the *Merry* spun out a nanocarbon thread and attached it to a grapple before launching it at the *Bandima*. It caught the mast behind the utility deck and Ethan ordered boarding operations.

"I'll come along," he said.

"Aye, sir."

Twenty marines and able-bodied sailors donned spacesuits with Ethan.

Tethered to the grapple, they made their way across the open expanse of space to the waiting ship, marines in front, guns ready.

They made their way to the rear hatch and knocked. No need to forget our manners, thought Ethan.

One of the marines unscrewed the hatch wheel and pulled the door open. The airlock was small, large enough for only some of the company. Half the men were held back. Ethan and the marines entered the hatch and sealed it before recompressing.

When the light was green, the marines took up positions around the door, floating weightless, their rail muskets, crossbows, and a flamer at the ready. Ethan drew his sword.

With a nod from their commander the inner door was spun and pushed open.

Three men waited inside. Ethan recognized the uniform of a captain and a first mate beside the black garb of an Orthodox Saved minister. The two sailors were Hyraxian, sable hair, sharp features, dark eyes and a half meter shorter than the average Enskari. The minister was a Templer for sure, pasty skin, white-blond locks, weaselly eyes. Seeing the men without pressure suits, Ethan removed his helmet before floating inside. The marines followed but kept their gear on.

The *Bandima*'s captain saluted. "I am Captain Bartholomew of the—"

"Is that a purger?" Ethan said, looking over the minister's black-and-red checkered sash.

"I am Minister Carlote, Mid-Minister to his Holy Prophet Eren the Eighth, who speaks for God from His sacred throne on Temple, Arch Minister of the Saved. I know you. You are Ethan Sommerled, murderer, thief. Lowborn usurper. You are a pirate and heretic and you sin against God in your wickedness. You're a disgrace to the true Saved who are God's own seed cast upon the—"

"It was a simple question, Minister," Ethan said, interrupting him with a finger to the man's lips. "A one-word answer is all I require."

The minister kept his chin up and looked down his nose at the boarders. The effect was surely not what he imagined it to be, since he was thirty degrees off the plane of the door and fighting to keep from floating away by wedging his foot under a pipe.

"I am a holy purger," he said.

"Space him," Ethan said, pushing past the three men. "Captain, I want to see your manifests."

"What? Wait. S-sir," stammered Bartholomew. "He's a man of God."

"He's a purger."

"You can't space him. We surrendered. That's murder."

"That's justice."

"Animal!"

"For your surrender, we'll not space the crew –"

"We were not there at the *Pempkin*," said Bartholomew. "I am not Clelland."

"– but," continued Ethan, "for Lavland – for Goffsted, the purger goes. I have – had – friends there."

"Captain Bartholomew, you cannot allow this," Minister Carlote said. His eyes flashed between the two captains, the pride that had been in them before evaporated now like a last breath in open space.

"Sergeant," said Ethan. "Remember to warn the others to stay clear as you open the outer door and send this filth to the fires of Coronam."

"Aye, sir."

Three marines moved forward and grabbed the minister.

He screamed.

They pulled him by his robes and flung him back to the other men, who caught him and tossed him into the airlock, where he floated in screaming circles. One marine went in with him to work the outer door.

"Manifests, Captain?" said Ethan.

The amber light over the airlock illuminated as the air was pulled out of it. The screams of the suffocating minister faded long before the sound of his pounding on the door. That stopped only when the red light came on signifying the outer door was open.

Bartholomew stared at the door as the light changed back to amber for recompression.

Ethan turned to the first officer. "Manifests," he said. "Remember there's plenty of space out there."

The man, already pale, blanched the more.

"The manifests!"

As if coming out of a dream, the Hyraxian first officer pulled papers from his tunic and offered them to Ethan.

"They met us prepared." Ethan laughed. "How civilized."

"Damn lowborn pirates," mumbled Bartholomew, still staring at the airlock.

"Privateers, my dear Captain," Ethan said without looking up from the papers. "We work under law. Consent of the queen."

"Parvenu," said the captain. "Haughty, uppity wench. She's a disgrace to her gender and the entire social—"

He was cut off by the back of Ethan's gauntleted hand across his jaw.

The Hyraxian captain spun around from the cuffing. He broke from his purchase on the pipe, flew to the rear bulkhead, bounced once and back. When he caught himself, his jaw hung loose on one side: blood poured out of his nose and mouth in zero-gravity bubbles that splattered like heavy summer rainfall on whatever it touched.

"Mind your place, sir," said Ethan.

The rest of the *Merry* sailors entered the lock and unsuited.

"Take the ship, men," Ethan said. "She's fat with treasure."

A cheer went up.

The first mate swallowed.

Bartholomew bled.

"And, men," said Ethan, "there's another minister on board. An apprentice. When you find him, reunite him with his master."

"Aye, sir."

Uppity. Parvenu. Ethan knew the insults well. Like his beloved queen, he endured them daily.

CHAPTER FOUR

During the early water wars in the Times of Strife, Old Earth world powers assembled into four main bodies identified along religious lines: Judaism, the Hindu Federation, United Islam, and United Christianity.

United Islam is said to have been formed to combat Judaism, which at the time had spread by force across areas formerly controlled by Islamic states. Though sworn and bitter enemies for centuries, United Islam and Judaism had much in common; they each claimed dominion over the same territory, claimed the same religious figures and icons, and each ruled by theocracy.

In response to the formation of United Islam, and in like manner of collecting the various branches of its faith by force and necessity, United Christianity rose as a central ideological body advising some of the most technologically advanced nations on the planet. Though powerful and closely aligned with government, United Christendom was not a theocracy as of 2345.

Also not a theocracy, the Hindu Federation's polity was a series of widening ruling councils advising a Lama, raised from birth for the duties of government. And unlike the other groups, the Hindu Federation was not limited to a single doctrine or dogma, but sheltered a myriad of beliefs (including atheism). Though Hinduism was by far the most popular organized entity within the Federation, it recognized within itself no fewer than five hundred other identifiable religions, branches, and sects, including many of those absorbed by the other powers and the other powers themselves. It alone of the four great united faiths never had an inquisition or forced indoctrination....

Footnote: [The Hindu Federation] was the first of the four to fall in 2433, a victim of an effective, albeit short-lived, alliance of the other three.

Old Earth History, Jareth's Lectures
(Date unknown; recorded in transit to Coronam, 2345-2395)
Footnote added afterward.

20, Sixth-Month, 937 NE – Freeport Station, Dajjal

Governor Alpin Morgan looked out through his porthole at the receding climber heading downward to Dajjal. He noticed a new tremor in his hand and covered it with his other.

"Could he be the prophet's man?" Roger Aguirre suggested.

"Nay, nay," said Morgan, shaking his head. His hair whipped in his face in the zero-gravity and caught in his mouth. He spat it out and tried to calm himself.

Morgan couldn't let the planters see him like this, not vexed as he was. Not angry and worried.

He'd summoned his assistants, Roger Aguirre, Nicholas Pratt, and Henry Dagney, out of the *Hopewell* for this meeting aboard Freeport Station so as not to be overheard and start a panic. Morgan's fourth assistant, in name at least, was Freddy Upor, pilot of the *Hopewell*. Ostensibly and by writ, Morgan was in charge of the entire expedition and Upor only the pilot, but Morgan was having a devil of a time convincing his fourth assistant of this fact.

"It's his ship," said Pratt, scratching a scab on his arm. "Surely he knows what's best. There are considerations we just don't understand. We mustn't be paranoid, Alpin."

Dagney coughed into a rust-stained handkerchief and then quickly put it in his pocket.

Morgan knew Dagney was over the worst of the pox but he still looked terrible. Morgan took in the scars on his skin, the dark circles under his eyes, his gaunt features, and his cold lifeless stare. The governor could accept all this except the lifeless stare. In that was more than sickness; that was heartbreak. He knew Dagney could recover from the pox, he'd counted on it, but he wasn't so sure about the loss of his wife. It had always been a liability. Henry Dagney was famous for spoiling his women, wife and daughter, and that weakness had now come home to roost in those darkly drawn empty eyes.

"Sommerled would not have sent Upor if there was a hint of a shadow, of a smell of the prophet on him," Pratt said.

"There is a bounty on Upor's head," said Dagney, coughing. "Hyrax would have him served as stew and send his scalp to the prophet for decoration."

"We are too small for Temple to be concerned with," Morgan said.

"The queen then? Connor?"

"Nor are we a concern to them," said Morgan, trying to keep his hair out of his eyes.

"No, not anymore," agreed Dagney.

They spoke calmly but as Morgan looked at his men's faces, he saw concern in their eyes. They were concealing it better than he was, he realized, and felt then not a little ashamed of himself.

"Aye, of course," he said. "I'm overreacting."

Pratt said, "We all feel the frustration, brother Morgan. None of us have slept soundly since the *Sebastian* went missing."

Morgan turned suddenly and lost himself in the null gravity, having to catch himself before careening off a wall. "Aye. Aye, and that," he said. "What of that?"

Three ships, the *Hopewell*, the *Mallow*, and the *Sebastian*, had left Vildeby port together with Sommerled's patent under the leadership of Alpin Morgan. Their charge was to colonize Tirgwenin with one hundred, five and twenty Saved souls. The *Hopewell* and *Mallow* were moored at Freeport Station now, had been – inexplicably – for eight do-nothing days. The *Sebastian* had not been seen since the third day from Enskari, twelve hours after a Hyraxian ship had been seen nearby.

The way was treacherous, the destination untried. Tirgwenin had been visited only a few times before by civilized men. Sommerled had directed five visits to the world. The first two failed to arrive and ended in disaster, Sommerled's own brother perishing in a storm. Of the three that made it, the first was a scouting expedition, the next dropped off a military contingent. The last removed it leaving a skeleton crew this journey would relieve. Sommerled had been on the first expedition only, but Upor had been on all three. Morgan had been on the first and second. Among the indentured crew, there were half a dozen sailors who'd been on one of the earlier voyages, but the bulk of them, like the colonists themselves, had never been this far away from home before. Everyone was on edge.

"Could not the delay here be but a wait upon the *Sebastian*?" said Aguirre.

Morgan rubbed his temples, telling himself to calm down. He had to be stronger than this. He was taking his people to an unknown planet to face untold terrors and challenges. He was their leader. He needed to lead. He needed to be an example, now and always. They were too far to turn back, had been for years. It was selfish of him to unburden his worries upon anyone now, even his assistants. Even they should not see his worry. Even they.

Morgan pulled himself to the window and looked out again at Dajjal, one of Coronam's victims. A dead world, misshapen and pockmarked, little more than a glorified asteroid, a shallow memory of its former self. Supposedly, like Ravan, its twin on the other side of the system, Dajjal was once habitable with a crystalline-aligning atmosphere like the other living planets. Coronam, in a particularly foul mood, had shredded its sky one day and then cindered the world beneath. It could have been worse. The Kanluran Cloud was supposedly once a planet too before a terrible and ancient storm from Coronam – possibly the same one that had wrecked Dajjal – destroyed it. Now Kanluran was a spreading mass of radioactive rock and debris, arcing plasma rings that spun off meteors and blocked the way between Dajjal and Tirgwenin, preventing the establishment of a western trade route, at least until Tirgwenin was occupied.

Without an atmosphere, millennia of storms had peeled Dajjal back to just iron and ore. Optimistic and enterprising traders from Lavland had set up Freeport on the dark leeward side of the tidal-locked planet for dense-metal mining. By all accounts it was a failing concern.

Lavland had Freeport but Claremond and Hyrax also had bases on the planet. These were too far to routinely use the Freeport elevator, so were resupplied by ship thread. A rail line had been proposed to link mines with Freeport Landing after gold was discovered, but that idea vanished as quickly as did the narrow vein and the Hyraxian invasion of Lavland.

Morgan had been to Dajjal twice before en route to Tirgwenin. Both of those times, he'd landed in Freeport and taken the short thirty-hour trip down the cable to the ground. He'd been impressed not by the deep mining shafts or smelted ore, but by the farms, the cattle, the stores of meal, and the water system that the inhabitants had built underground. It gave him hope.

Freeport Station was the last civilized outpost along this side of the system. Farther on lay the terrible Kanluran Cloud, wild Tirgwenin, and then around the arc over the Gap, before coming to Silangan and the start of the eastern route.

Morgan had asked to be allowed to land on Dajjal, but Upor, without explanation, had refused to let him go. To Morgan's knowledge only a few crewmen had been allowed down and their business, as near as he could tell, was shore leave and not related to the pilgrim enterprise at all. When asked about it, Morgan had been put off and frustrated. He'd been allowed off the *Hopewell*, but only as far as the port where he was just as powerless in the station as he was shipboard.

Morgan could just make out the dome beneath them, a glowing white speck against the black shadow of the world. There were people there. There were friends, or at least not active enemies like he now suspected he had here.

The light gave him comfort. It was a symbol of solidarity, if not for a people, then for the species. The infinite blackness of space filled a man with a yearning for company like nothing else. It was easy to imagine a grand fraternity of mankind when in space, away from politics and religion. One felt so small and alone there. It was a mystical and troubling feeling that Morgan knew well from his other trips. It was a profound soul-splitting loneliness that could only be cured by the voices of other men. But not on this trip. The feeling remained with him always. Even in the cramped decks of the *Hopewell*, surrounded by his congregation, Morgan felt the abyssal loneliness always. He told himself it was because he had seen so much space during this flight, so often visiting the upper decks and periscopes for exercise. He did not believe it though. He knew he'd done it to himself; he'd isolated himself from everyone because he feared he'd doomed them all, and the blackness of space around them reflected that doom in forever.

"Aye, of course, brother Aguirre," said Morgan, forcing cheer into his voice. "I worry like a woman. We have had fair weather and good company. We are blessed."

Dagney cleared his throat. "There is worry here, Governor," he said. "If I understand it, we are not halfway to our new home and the planting season is passing fast. There is worry."

"Fear not. With the supplies we gain here on Dajjal we should be able to quarter a winter and plant next year. It will be a lean time, but we will survive well." He punctuated his statement with an optimistic smile that he knew his eyes didn't reflect.

"And when will we take on these supplies?" asked Pratt.

"Soon," Morgan said. "When Upor has them. I'm sure he's checking on the cattle now."

The men nodded gravely.

The hatch at the far end of the room screwed open and a tall yellow man peered in. Even in the low orange light of the wound glowglobe, Mathew's skin shimmered like a reflective sail. The tribal tattoos around his eyes drew attention to them. He blinked at the assistants, an inner eyelid sliding diagonally across his irises before his lids clapped down and up.

The Tirgwenian scout didn't step into the compartment, only leaned in and said, "Governor. You asked to know. Now Upor is aboard."

Mathew spoke in an upper-class accent that belied his limited vocabulary. He was one of the treasures taken from Tirgwenin on Sommerled's last visit. Presented to the queen with another man they'd called Jacob, who later died of the pox, he was returned to Sommerled for this expedition.

Morgan had known the man for years and found him as inscrutable today as the moment he'd met him.

"Thank you, Mathew," Morgan said.

The Tirgwenian looked at the other men, nodded in farewell, turned, and left. He floated effortlessly down the corridor, his tall two-meter frame more graceful than the sailors who plied their trade in such gravity-challenged places.

"I'll go see the pilot directly," Morgan said. "Ye men return to the *Hopewell* and tell the people all is aright."

"As you wish, Governor," said Pratt.

Morgan put his arm on Dagney's shoulder. "Hold back a moment, Henry, if you would."

"Of course."

The other two nodded as Mathew had, and then floated out along the same corridor.

"I am sorry about your wife," said Morgan.

"Aye, a blow to my family."

"To all of us," the governor said.

"Aye."

Morgan cleared his throat, trying to find the right words to say. "I understand that Millicent now must take her place in the household. That is to be expected. You have little Dillon, who needs caring for."

"He's not so little."

"What I mean to say, Henry, is that though Millie is a fine young lady and is doubtless up to the task of your household duties…uhm, I understand she's a great little cook."

"Aye."

"Ah, aye. Good." Morgan wished he'd spent as much time thinking of what he would say to Henry now as he had planning his confrontation with the pilot. "What I mean to say is that though she must assume greater responsibilities, she is in fact not actually a matron of the community. She is but a girl – a fine young lady, but she is too willful and opinionated."

"Has she run afoul of some of the other women?"

Morgan nodded. "We have not that many women with us. By God's will more of us will follow after we, the first, have planted roots in our new home. But in the meantime, we must all get along to face the trials set before us. There must not be dispute or ill feelings. It will hinder us."

"Millie is a strong-willed—"

"You spoil her," Morgan said curtly. "She assumes a position she has not attained. Further, she voices non-womanly opinions. She speaks of politics and commerce, strongly and loudly."

"She used to help me run my shop. She—"

"Do not argue with me, Henry." Morgan sighed. "I have much on my mind. Control your daughter or she will have to answer before the congregation." Morgan couldn't read Henry's expression for his sickness and the dimness of the room. "There, I have told you. Deal with it."

"Aye, Governor."

Morgan turned back to the window and tried to find the climber along the cable for something to do while Henry Dagney floated out the door, down the corridor, and eventually back to the *Hopewell*.

He hated to get involved in such trivial matters as that, but to keep the peace in his own house as well as the community, he knew he was right to act. His own daughter, Daria, had told him of her conversation, the uppity way Millicent had talked to the married woman, far above her station.

No matter. It was handled now. Henry was a good man. He'd sort it out. Now he just had to deal with Upor.

He floated out the door and screwed it shut out of habit and then turned up, thinking he'd most likely find the pilot at the tavern.

Along the way he passed a framed map of the system. The map wasn't to scale, more of a fanciful rendition of the geometry of the worlds foreshortened to emphasize the limits and barriers of where he was now: Freeport Station over the words *End of the Line.*

Again Morgan felt small. One small man leading a small group far from home. No. He corrected himself. There was no home. Not now. Maybe soon, but not now.

They were pilgrims and outcasts, members of the small All Community Congregation of Ministers, dubbed the 'Bucklers' from their martyred leader, Sir Henry Buckley. They were separatists, and not just from the Orthodox Saved led by the prophet from his throne on Temple. They were a splinter of the Enskaran Revolution, which allowed a woman, Queen Zabel the First, to rule an entire planet from her throne in Vildeby. And while that act threatened to erupt in holy war among the planets of the Saved, the Bucklers had gone further; they believed that in the right circumstances, God could speak to and through not only a woman, but someone not highborn. This idea was so revolutionary that the Bucklers could be arrested for treason on sight because of it even on Enskari. For, as the prophet maintained and the queen reinforced with only a slight deviance to allow birth to trump gender in her case, the classes are set by God and must be maintained. Though all are Saved, God speaks only to nobles.

The queen had moved in the right direction but not far enough. The Bucklers were ahead of their time; Morgan knew it. He did not blame the queen for their plight. Society was not ready for them. Before the second stage of a revolution can take place, the first one must be secure. He understood her necessity. Enskari had to survive Temple and Hyrax. Tolerance was a luxury she could not afford in the face of such greater problems. Morgan understood this. His own major problem – the survival of his people, was paramount. He had not time to entertain distractions such as Millicent Dagney. He had given the problem to Henry not unlike the queen had given her problem to Connor, whose Guard were the Enskari equivalent to Temple's purgers, forcing uniformity and stability through whatever means. Henry Dagney at least shouldn't have to resort to whips and hot irons.

Connor was ruthless. He'd been stopped from destroying the Bucklers only because they had sympathizers within the court, particularly Ethan Sommerled. Their martyrdom had been forestalled long enough for them to receive exile. Sommerled's patent to start a colony on faraway Tirgwenin was the Bucklers' terrible salvation from Connor's Guard.

Morgan caught Upor's glance when he floated into the tavern.

Upor pretended not to have seen him enter, turning to talk with Mr. Hale, the first mate, who similarly pretended not to have seen him.

They sipped from sealed cups tethered to the table and laughed suddenly together right as Morgan arrived.

"What is our status, assistant?" Morgan said, wishing his hair was cut short and not waving into his face. "We are wasting time."

"Good day, Mr. Morgan," Upor said.

"Governor," he corrected him.

Upor raised an eyebrow but didn't meet Morgan's eyes. "Yes, we're waiting on supplies."

"What of the beef?"

"I'm getting in touch with my friend," Upor said. "He will supply the animals we'll need. Have no fear."

"*We'll* need more than we thought. And salt."

"We'll dig our own salt in the Cloud. Cheaper. We don't need the extra weight."

"Let us buy it here."

"Governor," Upor said slowly like he was forcing the word out from between two back teeth. "The price is too dear here. We haven't the money to buy it. Our money is better spent on things we can't get for free."

Upor's use of the plural 'we' used to be reassuring to Morgan, but now it sounded mocking and put his teeth on edge. He rubbed his temples and combed his hair back with his fingers.

"Freddy," Morgan said, using Upor's first name, "the delay is dangerous. We had a late start and we've lost more days. We cannot dawdle here."

"We need the supplies." Upor glanced at Mr. Hale, who sipped his drink and watched. "Think of the cows. Think of how they'll thrive on Tirgwenin."

"If we don't land at Placid Bay by midsummer—"

"We must not look hurried, Morgan," said Upor, an edge in his voice. "Hyraxian spies are watching. They must not know our enterprise. Relax.

Go pray. Do whatever it is you Bucklers do. We're in good time. We'll resupply and be on our way. Leave me alone now, we're busy."

Morgan tried to catch the pilot's eye but failed. He did instead catch Mr. Hale's watching him over the top of his drink. Morgan did not like what he saw there.

CHAPTER FIVE

It should not have come as a surprise that though unified at the time of the Unsettling, the subsequent isolation of the Saved upon their several worlds – seven hundred years without contact with one another – resulted in some regional and planetary cultural variance. What is most surprising is that there was not more of it.

Ministers of the Saved were found on all worlds working harmoniously within the adapted doctrine when communication was reestablished in 750 NE and confirmed in 800 NE when regular trading contact commenced.

The concept of a single reunified doctrine or 'Saved Orthodoxy' centered in Temple was first officially proposed to Prophet Hansen II in 816 NE. Though debated and discussed, nothing was put into practice until 843 NE when, under Eren I, the Orthodox Missionary Program was begun. This outreach effort sent thousands of Temple ministers to all corners of the civilized planets to reeducate and realign Saved teachings into a single unified creed.

These efforts have been largely unsuccessful and have led to a general distrust of Temple among the worlds. This has no doubt exacerbated the national protestant movements which we struggle against today.

The failure of the missionaries must be seen as the failure of a parent unable to wield a disciplinary switch on a misbehaving child. Stated bluntly, Temple has not had the power to bring the strayed back to the fold.
Proposal for Alliance of Hyrax and Temple
14, Tenth-Month, 872 NE

23, Sixth-Month, 937 NE – Goffsted, Lavland

The work was far from done and with such diminishing resources it might never be. The bureaucrats on Temple might think everything on Lavland was wrapped up, but High Purger Tarquin knew differently. Goffsted was still under condemnation. The entire continent had been sentenced to die, all the heretics who'd gone against the church and all those Saved who had let them.

The continents of Lithu and Holls had slipped the decree by some political maneuvering with their Hyraxian conquerors, yet those continents needed Tarquin's attention more than Goffsted. Heretics, protestants, and sympathizers alike walked freely there, openly. There were noble houses in those places who'd not taken the oath of allegiance to the prophet. They risked total destruction. They deserved total destruction, but Tarquin and his resources were cleaning Goffsted instead.

The day's cases were slid under the door of his little room with a scratch on his unswept floor. He'd been up for hours, watching the sky turn from clear, star-speckled black to white opaque as it aligned against the sun after the morning auroras. It was a spectacular sight, proof of God's glory and might, anger and wrath.

He glanced at the files but turned back to his little window. He could smell the fire but not see it from here. The smell of oil and flesh mixed in a holy sacrament of outrage, correction, and renewal. He'd feed the fire again this day, would for weeks, months. He'd decimated whole cities, lined up the people and taken one in ten for the fire – no trial, no appeal. Sacrifice. An example for obedience, for the church on Temple and for the conquerors from Hyrax.

That had been effective and powerful and in the early years after the uprising it was all he did. Now he was a judge and the work was surgical and slow. He was wasted down here when the upper lands had barely been touched by his holy office.

He was correcting peasants and slaves on Goffsted while the wealthy houses on the other continents bought favor in Temple and continued their apostasy in the name of commerce or politics. Or something. If only Tarquin could speak to the prophet himself, go around the corruption of his apostles, get to the great man, he could tell him how all of Lavland needed cleansing. Given the chance, Tarquin knew with God's help he could move the prophet to return the Hyraxian forces and complete the purge. The danger was not gone. It was not open to challenge like it was before when Prince Brandon had landed, but the disease was still here, festering, waiting to spring up again like a scab over a pox sore. He needed more men. He needed to test every man, woman, and child on the planet, cleanse them and save them.

Tarquin hated how politics got in the way of heaven's work. Prince Brandon had been insulted by the bitch pretender queen on Enskari and would hear of nothing but revenge upon her. That world needed cleansing too, but what good was putting out a new fire when coals were left to relight an old? The prophet knew this, but of course his counselors weren't as wise and fed him bad advice. Was it not one of the Twelve who had adjusted the execution decree? Now only the directly accused would come before his court. Picking nits off a condemned man's scalp. Better to take it off at the neck.

He fanned through the folders. They had the smell of pettiness: one poor farmer accusing another poor farmer of heresy, hoping to get him executed so he could take his land. There were a couple of minister accusations. In the early days the word of a minister would have been acted on immediately, no trial, no judge. Action. Now he had to hear the accusation like any other complaint. It suggested that a minister might be wrong. It went against everything Tarquin believed. A minister was God's hand in the material world and though men might think he erred, he did not, could not. God knew. Questioning his authority was heresy. God moved the minister and that was enough. It irked him to see those cases in the day's work but they'd be fast. He'd already decided those without opening them. He'd go through the motions as he was directed. Another order from Temple, like the decree, and the adjustment to the decree.

He would obey.

He shouldn't wonder at such things. He needed more faith. This was all part of God's justice.

He left his rooms and crossed the courtyard of the monastery, which he'd assumed as his capitol, and went down to the second cellars. The shouts and screams of the condemned were muffled but discernible on this side of the door. When he opened it, the terrible sounds washed over him like hell's own heat.

Tarquin pulled the door closed behind him and climbed down the stone steps following glowglobes and the smell of burned hair and torch smoke.

He turned the corner and passed a row of screaming cells. Hands reached out to him, garglings and moans. One man who still had his tongue called out, "Minister! I am Saved. There are lies against me. Stop this injustice! By the prophet, save me!"

Tarquin held a scented handkerchief over his face for the smell and pushed on to the inner chamber.

Three minister purgers saw him enter, stopped their work and bowed.

"High Minister," they said together. "Blessed be to thee."

"And to thee," said Tarquin.

One of the ministers held a branding iron, black and sooty, the scent of cooked flesh rising from it like an aurora in the evening sky. A man lay stretched before him suspended above a spike, an angry burn still smoking on his thigh. Another purger held a pair of grisly shears over a woman within a clump of rags at his feet, unconscious and bloody. The third purger was at a table eating a sandwich of cheese and the monastery's ubiquitous salted roast beef.

Tarquin removed the handkerchief. It wasn't doing much good anyway. He was accosted by the stench of burn and blood, tears and sweat, and it stirred him. He covered his smile with his hand and without another word or a slow in his step, moved down the corridor to the far cell.

He went in, wound the globe for light, and pulled the door shut behind him.

He found the barbed and knotted whip on the cot where he had left it.

He took off his black-and-red checkered sash, his high minister robes, his under-robe garments, and then his cilice; the latter opened scabs on his back as it fell to the floor.

Tarquin knelt down and prayed before taking up the scourge and opening the rest of the scabs.

★　　★　　★

An hour later Tarquin sat at his table on a dais as the crowd settled along the walls of the little church. He was about to begin the day's work when Baron Lupeysun strolled in. Tarquin watched him sidle up to the dais, walking stick clicking ahead of him every other step as he crossed the church's tile floor. Though the pews had been removed, it was still a church and Lupeysun's irreverence irked Tarquin.

"Good morning, High Purger," said the Baron.

"Blessed be, Lupeysun. I'm surprised you chose to attend today," Tarquin said.

"I might not stay for the entire docket." He slid a chair next to Tarquin and tossed his gloves on the table.

"As you wish," said Tarquin. It was the baron's prerogative to be a judge, his duty actually, but not his custom. Tarquin glanced down at the day's cases and wondered which one had brought out Lupeysun.

Secular politics in God's court. It chafed him, but he had to endure it. He shifted in his chair and felt the hair shirt stab his wounds and scratch open new ones. The shirt would keep the blood from staining his holy garments and keep his thoughts holy all day.

He clenched his teeth in sacred agony, dabbed a bead of sweat from his forehead, and nodded for the guard to bring in the first accused.

A man in Sunday dress and a shackled woman in rags were brought forth.

A low minister read the charge. "This bondswoman is accused of witchcraft, of seducing by spell Mr. Fernley, freeborn, devout Saved, married."

Tarquin glanced at Lupeysun. His interest was in his cuffs. He tugged at them, fluffed them, arranged the lace around his ringed fingers. He didn't even look up at the accused.

Tarquin scanned the people standing behind the guards. He noticed one woman he assumed to be Mrs. Fernley. Her eyes were fixed in rage at the bound woman, her cheeks blushed red. She'd been crying.

The notes outlined eyewitness reports of Fernley and the bondswoman being caught *in flagrante delicto* in Fernley's barn. If Fernley had gone to the woman of his own free will, he was an adulterer and could himself be charged before this court. If, however, he'd been seduced by magic, then he was innocent and the witch was to blame.

Tarquin scanned the documents, testimonials of the woman's unholy beauty, the man's family connections and charitable offices.

Tarquin put the papers down and spoke. "I decree Mr. Fernley shall receive nine and twenty lashes from a cat-of-nine after a full day and a night in the stocks for his weakness of soul. He is also liable for the remaining balance on this woman's term of servitude. Injured party may make petition. Put the witch to death."

"But, Minister," said the man. "I can—"

"No!" The woman made a break for the door.

An alert guard ran her through the back with his lance before she could even reach the crowd.

Seeing her killed, the man screamed, weak-willed that he was.

The impaled woman spun, pulling the shaft loose from the guard's grasp. Facing Tarquin and Lupeysun, who was then examining his fingernails, she tried to speak, but produced no sound. She looked down at the blade protruding from beneath her ribs, coughed once, then twice, and spat blood over the floor.

Tarquin signed his name under the order on the official form and passed it to a clerk on his right.

The woman crumpled to her knees, her eyes shifting unbelievingly from the blade in her body to Tarquin at his table.

The man fell to his knees facing the witch. He wept and wailed. Tarquin wondered if he hadn't been too lenient on him.

The guard yanked his spear out of the witch with a loud sloshy slurp and she toppled over on her side. Two slaves quickly came forward and carried her twitching body out a side door to the waiting fire.

Guards dragged Fernley away to the second cellar cells to wait his turn in the stocks.

No one bothered with the blood.

By rights they both should have been executed, but he'd been ordered, no doubt by a corrupt official, to show mercy to the Lavlanders.

Tarquin caught himself here questioning, complaining, being less faithful than he should be. He leaned against his high-backed chair until the stabs from his cilice sent his hands shaking and drove water to his eyes.

A low minister saw his tears and, surely thinking that Tarquin felt sorrow for the poor sinners, painted his own face with solemn sympathy.

Tarquin wanted to laugh. There was no sympathy. No sorrow. He'd sent a sinner to God. God would deal with her, as God would deal with everyone. Tarquin just had to send them on faster, so God's will could be done more expeditiously.

Two men were escorted into the church next. One was obviously noble: his clothes and manner made it clear. His skin was pale and uncolored, a man who seldom stepped out of the shade. His Lavlandian auburn curls sweeping above his ears in the style popular at court. He was steeled with a knightly sword that hung at his side. He wore a family crest on a sash over his left shoulder. Tarquin did not know the crest but saw the prophet's cross among the other devices. The man bowed to Lupeysun, who nodded recognition. So this was the case the other judge had come for.

The man brought in with the new noble was better dressed than he, costumed in more fashionable and newer clothes. He had the same Lavland auburn hair, but modernly cut. He had an air of haughtiness that contrasted with the confident demeanor of the hereditary noble.

The low minister read the charges. "Freeborn merchant trader Rynck, accuses Sir Wilburn of heresy, sedition, and rebellion."

Tarquin found the folder, opened it and read.

Rynck was a portsman, a dock owner of some wealth. He'd made formal lawful accusation against a noble, following the requisite curse of paperwork and evidence established for the class difference. His complaint was accompanied by shipping receipts showing Wilburn's attempt to smuggle weapons onto the continent for the Millers, a particularly nasty flavor of heretic born on Claremond and infecting Lavland now. The complaint outlined Wilburn's family ties to Claremond, included sworn witness affidavits attesting to Sir Wilburn's public support of the heretical sect, and also and most damning, his crested signature on the invoices.

Rynck had dutifully alerted the guard and the shipments had been confiscated. A letter from the chief constable attested to this.

Rynck's formal accusation sought summary judgment and the favor of the court to a share of the spoils from Wilburn's disgraced house, which was his right under the law. Rynck had included in his paperwork a detailed inventory of Wilburn's holdings, which were not insubstantial.

Tarquin read the reports and felt a headache rise between his ears, knowing the moment he looked up what would happen.

He swallowed, shifted in his chair and jumped as the shirt caught a nerve under his shoulder blade.

"Aye, most treacherous," said Lupeysun. "Have you ever seen such a frame-up?"

Tarquin looked at the two men waiting for judgment. Rynck stood tall and confident – proud even. A man expecting to be rewarded for doing good. Standing next to him, Wilburn looked no less confident, but Tarquin knew it to be for entirely different reasons. While Rynck knew he was right and awaited only confirmation, Wilburn knew he was safe and waited only the formality.

"Baron," Tarquin said quietly to Lupeysun. "What is he to you?"

"Wilburn is noble born," he said.

"Have you seen the charges?"

"I have no need to," he said. "Just look at the man Rynck, upstart like that whore queen. Lowborn, one generation out of bondsman. See – a cock with his feathers, vilely accusing his betters, seeking to bring down a great house, to put himself in its place. It goes against the order of things. It goes against society. It goes against God."

Tarquin bit his tongue lest he speak his mind and tell this popinjay what God surely thought of him.

"It is my court," Tarquin said.

"True, High Purger. I am but an advisor."

Tarquin dreamed of seeing the baron in the cellar, of tearing his flesh with wires, breaking him on wheels, and burning his flesh with iron stones. But he had his orders. "Do advise, Baron," he said.

"Wilburn's relations on Claremond will supply Hyrax with five thousand men-at-arms and two ships for the coming war on Enskari," he said. "These are trained men-at-arms and good ships. Oh, and of course Wilburn has offered ten thousand dollars to this court from his holdings here on Goffsted – Lavlandian dollars, to support this court."

"If I judge him, this court will have that and all he owns, lands and wife and dollars all."

"Aye," Lupeysun said slowly as if pondering the possibility. "But then Prince Brandon wouldn't get his men or those ships. His Majesty really wants those ships."

"Bribes?"

"That would be true only if Sir Wilburn were guilty."

"These reports are damning."

"Ransom then," said Lupeysun. "Think of it as ransom. An age-old tradition for the well-to-do when they step out of line."

The purger shifted in his chair and grimaced. He closed his eyes and said a silent prayer to find peace with what he knew he was required to do. For each man from Temple here there were easily a hundred from Hyrax. It occurred to him that the arms Wilburn tried to smuggle onto the continent were for killing Hyraxians more than Templers. Somehow that made Tarquin feel a little better.

Rynck no longer stood quite as confidently as he had. The crowd was fidgeting. Tarquin was renowned for his quick judgments and this one was dragging on. Wilburn brushed his sash and readjusted his stick by his foot with a sharp click that carried over the murmurs of the onlookers.

"But of course," whispered the baron, "there must not be any stain left on Sir Wilburn. That wouldn't do."

Tarquin looked out over the assemblage and spoke. "Sir Wilburn," he said, "you have been wronged and falsely accused. Mr. Rynck, for making false accusation your freedom is revoked and you are bonded to Sir Wilburn for a term of no less than ten years and ordered to pay a five-thousand-dollar fine to this court for wasting its time."

Tarquin signaled the guards to seize Rynck. The man didn't resist. He stood staring in disbelief as the guards dragged him away.

Wilburn bowed, turned on his heels, and with his walking stick clicking ahead of him, briskly left the church. Baron Lupeysun followed him out.

There was man's justice, and God's justice, and both were drawn in sacrifice. Tarquin's work was far from done; Wilburn's ten-thousand-dollar ransom would keep this court going for at least another year.

CHAPTER SIX

The life of this new world is not as alien as we thought it would be. There are mammals here, lizards and birds. Their species are of course unknown, their genus and classes unique, but on the surface they resemble creatures of Old Earth. There are oxen-like things and fast hoppers we've already called 'rabbits'. There are songbirds of a thousand different varieties and multi-legged insects. There are worms, whales, and fish, flies, spiders, mice, and deer. All are different. They are unique species to be sure, but still identifiable as a like thing from the history of our own lost world. Similarly, there are trees and grasses, flowers and thistles, ferns and mushrooms. Though they are all exotic, unknown, and unstudied, they are nonetheless familiar to our eyes.

The scientists are baffled by what they are calling this 'parallel evolution'. The United Christian clergy of course call it a miracle and like the Coronam system itself, a gift from God. They're insufferable.

Still, I am in awe. It is as though a previous planter seeded this world centuries ago and their crops have gone on to adapt to this place with weird armor and physiology to protect themselves from the burning sky, for that is the most alien thing of this new world – the terrible sun-beaten sky.

The native creatures are curious things. They come right up to us. Predator and prey alike they are easy to catch. Governor Genest believes it will be an easy matter to supplant them with the livestock we brought along.
Journal of Jonathan Yates, Enskari Colonist
8, First-Month, 1 NE

27, Sixth-Month, 937 NE – Upaven, Enskari

"These reports are disturbing, Your Majesty."

"You do not tell us to be disturbed, sir," said the queen.

"N-no," stammered Sir Aldo. "I meant only that it disturbs me."

The queen looked at the charts and not at her minister. Perhaps she had overreacted, but Sir Aldo was of the old order, raised before the revolution, still possessed of prejudices and assumptions that her very reign challenged. A reminder now and then of the new order was never out of place.

She turned to the maps of her world. Familiar and reassuring. She admired the cartography, the detail of the islands, the threads of roads and rails that linked Enskari together. The transparent overlay was a swamp of red gradients centered on the industrial centers. The next overlay was a spattering of black dots in differing sizes representing atmospheric violence – severe storms, lightning clusters, and radiation seepage. These too were centered on the industrial centers but spread beyond them in a predictable trail, like diminishing ellipses across her world.

Aldo spoke. "It's gone as far as Southland. The beef stockyards there lost five thousand head last year due to lightning alone."

"Their rods are insufficient," said the queen. "Have they forgotten where we live? This is not Old Earth. We are all transplants, cattle and people. We do not have the protection of the native species. It is stupid for them to forget this. It is not a royal problem; it is the stockmen who must act."

"Yes, that is true. But across Enskari this is a repeating pattern. Energy gets through. The rods even on Dorothia are not always adequate."

"Are they not improving them?"

"Yes, Your Majesty. Very aggressively. Forests of rods out to the horizon, to protect the pastures there." He pointed out the window. "Refineries with webs of wire to ground, but still some have taken damage. The explosion in Portown for example."

"We were told that was Hyraxian sabotage."

Aldo cleared his throat. "Not to contradict anyone, but the reports I've read suggest an act of God. Overheated rods and lightning."

"You speak to me of God?"

"No, Your Majesty." He blanched. "A figure of speech."

The queen smiled wryly. The informal pronoun easily put him off balance. It was good to have them off balance. Even Aldo.

Aldo was unique in the court. He was apolitical, not ambitious, honest, and well educated. He was also seldom at court. He was here today because he had requested to see the queen, been trying to see her for months, but she'd put him off. She'd finally relented and given him an appointment that required half a day on horseback and three days of train for fifteen minutes of her time.

She was surprised he'd kept the appointment. She'd have forgiven him not keeping it – had given him leave to miss it while arranging it in fact, but he'd kept it. He was a serious man.

Even so, it was difficult for Zabel to take him seriously, mostly because he took himself so. There wasn't enough seriousness left in her. He was reactionary and panicky, a man who'd never come to like the world he'd been born into, she thought, a man who saw enemies in the shadows and poisons in the water. This was a good attitude at court, necessary even. A requirement for survival, but Aldo saw it everywhere. If there was a sect of the Saved that believed that man had no right to exist at all and believed Coronam had it in for them, he'd be their prophet.

Queen Zabel looked out at her entourage. Since this was a private meeting, there were only half a dozen other people in the room. Beside herself and Sir Aldo, there were two pages, two ladies-in-waiting, a clerk, and a guard.

The ladies-in-waiting fanned themselves idly beneath the far window, whispering and giggling to themselves. The pages sweated by the far door, bouncing on their toes, awaiting orders that could come at any moment. The clerk shuffled papers and stood by Aldo ready to help with his presentation. The clerk, too, looked nervous. Only the guard and she hoped herself looked calm and cool. The guard looked bored. She tried not to.

Sir Aldo pressed on. "The problem is getting worse, Your Majesty, and it is but a symptom of a greater problem."

"Which is?"

"A compromising of the shielding atmosphere."

"I thought you said the problem was overpopulation?" said Queen Zabel.

"It is related." He wiped his forehead with a handkerchief. "Pollution caused by people is affecting the atmosphere."

"Like on Old Earth?"

"Nay," he said. "Well, aye. That too, given time. That too. But the problem, the immediate problem is different due to our unique world. The crystalline lattice that shields us from our star is being weakened. Energy storms, plasma leaks, that sort of thing."

"Smog is breaking the sky?"

"Aye," he said. "Aye, that is it exactly." He looked up at her excitedly then calmed down instantly when he didn't find the same enthusiasm in her face. "It's not people so much as the heavy industry," he said. "The factories."

"We understand," she said. "Is it an immediate crisis?"

"It c-could—" he stammered. "Nay, not at present. Just more lightning. At present."

"And the population?"

"It is the same. Uhm…uhm, let me…." He signaled the clerk to hand him his other stack of charts. He removed a large one and unfurled it over the map the queen had liked.

"This is a graph of the growing population of Enskari based on the Royal Census. That's in blue. In red, here, is the predicted growth based on those figures and our best calculations. As you can see our birth rate continues to rise aggressively."

"We were chosen for the Unsettling because of this trait," the queen said. "We are not surprised to see this, Sir Aldo." Zabel put an edge in her voice, a warning that she would not be condescended to. Woman she might be, but monarch she was. She was at least as well educated and surely better informed than anyone in court, with the possible exception of her two Ears, Edward and Nolan, whose job it was to be just that.

"Of course, Your Majesty." Aldo blushed. "I'm just putting my own thoughts in order."

She began to pity the man a little. He was terrified, she saw. Afraid of a misstep, sure he was making them, scared of sharing the fate of others who'd dared to cross her, their skulls over Government House to this day, lightning-burned and bird-picked. It had not been a bloodless revolution and memories died hard when it was your friends and family who died.

"Go on, Sir Aldo," she said. "Tell us why this is a bad thing."

"Aye, my queen," he said with gravity that seemed to calm him. "It is that our food production has not kept up. Our ancestors imagined a much less hospitable world for us, or perhaps misjudged our efficacy. They did not know the worlds. These planets were kinder than we imagined and we have not been the best stewards."

"We have no famine, Sir Aldo."

"Again, my queen, now all is well, but here I have another overlay. Behold."

Sir Aldo positioned a transparency over the graph. "This shows the food supply. We'll go from surplus to equilibrium to deficit in a very short time. Here is where we will have famine." He placed his finger on an intersection of the charts.

"Not to be crass, but it seems to us that this problem, *if* it were to happen," Queen Zabel said, "would solve itself."

"Eventually, but with a sudden deficit as I see here, the problem would last for a long time. Even when the population returns to addressable levels, the disruption in the society would prolong the famine and the crisis could stretch on. The loss of this many people would reverberate for decades if we are not careful. It would threaten all of society. Unrest would surely follow."

The queen looked at the date of the possible problem and scoffed. "This is a distant problem," she said.

"This is the best-case scenario," said Sir Aldo.

"As imagined by you."

He blushed again. "Aye, as *calculated* by me."

She regarded him and he held her eye, not backing down from his correction. He was a strong man, worthy of her court. She smiled.

"You have brought to us compelling science, Minister Aldo," said Queen Zabel. "We pray we shall have the opportunity to address them. But truth be told, we cannot even consider these issues now with the threats we face. Hyrax would conquer our bodies, Temple our souls. They would flay and fire us all. If we fail to safeguard our world, these problems won't matter. Now, as needs be, our people must be many, our industry strong and vibrant. If we give up these things now, hinder them or hold them back, we'll have nothing left. Take heart if you must, Sir Aldo, that Prince Brandon may yet solve all these problems; he would destroy our industry and save the air; murder our people and have surplus food."

"Aye," he sighed. "Sir Nolan said the same thing. Almost word for word."

"You've spoken with our Ear?"

"Aye, many times. Again this morning, in fact. His stance is much the same as yours."

"Naturally," she said.

He blanched.

"You telegraphed our Second Ear this morning?" she said.

"Nay, ma'am. I ran into him in the hallway."

"Sir Nolan Brett is here? In Upaven?"

"Aye, Your Majesty."

"You have discussed this many times with our Second Ear and yet you feel obliged to bring it to us personally. Do you not trust our counselor?"

"Nay. Aye – of course I do," he said. "I have no doubt that Sir Nolan has only the best intentions for the world and Your Majesty. But I know also he has been very distracted and he told me he has not communicated my science to you. I felt an urgency."

"Did he give you reason for not communicating these things to us?"

"Not specifically," he said. "I believe it was along the lines of what you have said, that there are more urgent matters to concern you."

"Quite."

"I hope I have not overstepped my bounds."

"Nay, Sir Aldo. You have not. We appreciate your candor, your enthusiasm, and your science. We shall speak of these matters again. We are grateful."

"Thank you, Your Majesty. I am always for you."

Sir Aldo collected his papers and turned to leave.

"One question, Sir Aldo. Perhaps two."

"Aye, Your Majesty."

"Is this science influenced by data from the other civilized worlds?"

"Aye, Your Majesty. Lavland and Claremond mostly. Some from Hyrax, and little from Temple. The latter two are under purger persecution and their science, old and new, is endangered."

"Are the other worlds facing similar problems as these you have shown us today?"

"Aye, Your Majesty. All the civilized worlds have the same issues. Hyrax and Enskari being most threatened, Temple the least due to its lack of heavy industry, but they all face these crises."

"Let us come through the current crisis and then we will most definitely speak again, Sir Aldo."

"Thank you, Your Majesty."

"Blessed be."

"And to thee," said Sir Aldo before bowing and leaving the room.

When he was gone, Queen Zabel folded her fan and said, "Apparently our Second Ear is in the palace. We'd like to know where Sir Nolan is."

A page turned quickly on his heels toward the door when one of the ladies-in-waiting said, "Your Majesty, I saw him in the south wing in the Lavender Suite."

The queen looked at the lady suspiciously, gauging her attractiveness.

She blushed. "No ma'am. Nothing like that," she said. "I saw him go in there with a Hyraxian girl."

"Hyraxian? Are you sure?"

"Hair black as coal, cheekbones you could cut bread with."

"We shall drop in." The queen adjusted her dress and headed for the south wing and the Lavender Suite, followed by her entourage.

The halls were filled with people on their way to lunch or back from breakfast, nobles and courtiers, ambassadors and functionaries, living at court draining the Royal Reserves.

She'd moved court partially as a financial decision to lessen the hangers-on. There was less to do in Upaven than Vildeby and the move had shed a good third of the people but still there were many. State solvency aside, she'd had her own motives for the sudden move. As Sir Aldo had pointed out, the smog in Vildeby was not nice and the heat would just make it worse. During the winter rains the capital was fine, but she'd already wasted the spring and didn't want to lose any more of the summer there. There were too many gossips besides, too many idle voices and pointing fingers trying to pick the queen's new paramour out of the current stock of contenders.

She moved with a practiced grace down the hallway, eyes fixed to the distance, ignoring the bows and curtsies that greeted her and closed behind her like a wave. She only glanced at the highest-ranked nobles she saw, recognizing their status as she was taught.

She took a shortcut through a gallery and paused for a moment before one of her coronation portraits. She looked at herself as she was a dozen years before, a sixteen-year-old abomination about to rule an entire planet, loved by the people for who her family was, and hated by other worlds for her sex.

The artist had not wholly concealed the terror in her blue eyes. He'd sharpened them, made them look regal and wise beyond her years, but he'd been unable to remove all the fear from them. Or was it sorrow? Thousands upon thousands of Enskari had died in the two-year civil war it took to allow for that portrait.

No. It was fear.

Turning from the eyes, she took in the dress, an ancient style older than the planet; ruffles and folds, jewels sewn on the garment with gold thread like veins of riches in a Southland mine.

Her skin was pale and pasty, a symbol of her class. She wore makeup now to accentuate it, a ghost in the mirror, the whitest of the white, but in the portrait there was still blood in her cheeks, a subtle reflection of the strawberry hair that distinguished her race and the curls that had come from her ancestors of the House Genest, founders and still rulers of Enskari.

"So young," she said to herself, feeling the years like centuries.

Before someone could fill the air with sycophantic banter, she started off again and crossed the gallery into the south wing.

She turned a corner and saw the door to the Lavender Suite, one of the palace's most comfortable and sensuous accomodations. She'd used it herself. Seated in a chair in front of it was Nolan's secretary. He started when he saw the queen, made to move toward the door, but the queen stayed him by raising a finger. He bowed and backed away from the door.

She threw it open, expecting to see Sir Nolan Brett, near sixty years old, in the arms of some underage off-world whore. Instead she found her Second Ear sitting on a desk by an open window thumbing through sheets of paper while a Hyraxian woman lay fully clothed on the bed with a book in front of her.

The Hyraxian shrieked when she saw the queen, jumped off the bed and nearly fell on her face rushing to bow. Sir Nolan looked up from his papers as if he'd expected the queen to walk in on him all morning and was a little peeved it'd taken her so long. He smiled and moved to make a slight bow in keeping with his high station.

"Your Majesty," he said.

"I didn't knock," said the queen, sliding into the informal parlance she was accustomed to use with Sir Nolan Brett.

"I noticed."

The Hyraxian girl kept in her low curtsy. It was a good pose, natural and beautiful, not something a commoner would do half so well.

"Who is this woman, Nolan?"

"Might we have a private audience?" he said, glancing at the string of people peeking in from the hall.

The queen turned and the door was shut.

"My queen, this is the Lady Vanessa of the Hyraxian House Possad."

"Hyraxian?"

"Aye."

"In my court? You best explain, Sir Nolan," she said. "This looks like treason."

"It is." He put down his papers. "Lady Vanessa is a friend. She brings me news from Brandon's court."

"How—"

"She is attached to His Excellency, Sir Temsil. The new Hyraxian ambassador."

"A new one?"

"You sent the last one from court."

"I nearly had him shot," she said. "I should have had him shot. How'd they dare send another?"

"I requested a replacement," Sir Nolan said. "Friends close, enemies closer."

The queen looked over the Hyraxian courtier. She was pretty, but hardly underage. A year younger than twenty. She had in her eyes a fear not unlike the one the queen had seen in her own portrait.

"To whom are you loyal?" the queen said to her.

"In what things?" answered the girl in a strong, clear voice.

"In politics."

"First to Sir Nolan," she said.

"To Nolan? Not to Enskari? Not Hyrax?"

"If Sir Nolan asks me I will be loyal to them."

Zabel laughed. "Really, Nolan. My spymaster makes a girl lovesick? I'd not heard you were so formidable in bed."

"Ma'am, your noble Ear has never touched me in that way," Vanessa said, scandal in her voice. Her tone and the impudence of speaking without being spoken to caused the queen to pause and slowly turn on the girl.

Vanessa shrunk back at her stare, but only a half step.

"Prince Brandon had her house purged," said Sir Nolan. "I helped secret her brother and uncle off-world."

"The Drusts killed the rest of my family," Vanessa said. "Tortured them to death."

"And you would be loyal to Brandon if Nolan told you to be?"

"Never."

"But you said—"

"I said I'd be loyal to Hyrax. I love Hyrax. It is my home. But Brandon Drust and his whole accursed family I would gladly watch die. Slowly."

"Believe it or not," said Nolan. "She's noble."

"Hyraxian manners are a little different apparently."

Vanessa blanched and began to apologize when the queen, again with but a raised finger, extorted her will and kept her silent. "You have spunk," Zabel said. "And I too have no love for Prince Brandon. Coronam's worlds would be very different if I had."

"Quite, Your Majesty."

Nolan nodded as if satisfied. It always unnerved her how her counselor, her Second Ear, always seemed to understand things she barely recognized existed.

"I'm surprised you haven't heard rumors about Vanessa and me," said Nolan. "I've gone to great lengths to spread them."

"My lady-in-waiting told me just this day."

He nodded, again with that farseeing, far-knowing gleam in his eye, the look of a man who'd just solved a math problem in his mind or saw the checkmate twenty moves away.

"You spread the same rumors on Hyrax?" the queen asked.

"Most assuredly, my queen."

She nodded. "And what is the bargain today? What do we get? What do we give?"

Sir Nolan grinned. The queen saw the admiration in his eyes, the look of a teacher well pleased with the progress of a pupil.

"Two Templer assassins are on Enskari now," Sir Nolan said. "They are among five mid-ministers who slipped by my men and are also on world. I'm not sure what their designs are."

"Slipped by your men?" she said. "Five?"

Another proud smile. "Two. The other three I have eyes on. We'll see where they lead us."

"And what do we give the fair Vanessa?"

The Hyraxian girl shifted uncomfortably.

"Did you not hear?" said the Second Ear of the queen. "There is a terrible epidemic of the pox in Vildeby. A new strain. We're keeping it hushed up. You fled north to escape it."

"Could spread to the whole planet, I suppose."

"Could weaken us terribly."

"Prognosis?"

"Touch and go."

"I hope Prince Brandon doesn't find out. He'll not need to attack us if he thinks we'll die on our own."

Nolan nodded gravely.

"Sir Nolan, what's this I hear about Lord Ellsworth?"

"What have you heard, my queen?"

"That he may be disloyal."

"I've heard those rumors." Nolan steepled his fingers, a gesture that meant he would be delicate. "From whom—"

"Connor. Is it true?"

He rearranged the steeple. "I know he's one of your favorites," he said. "I would not have breathed a word to you about it until the facts were all in. I'm loath to—"

"Out with it," she said.

He nodded and to his credit didn't put on a grieved expression, didn't cloud his eyes with sympathy for her feelings for a man she sensed he was about to condemn. "It touches upon the Templers I just spoke of. One of the ones I have eyes on abides now with him in his Vildeby home. He has a secret room under a pantry."

The queen felt her face flush in rage and embarrassment. Remembering Vanessa, she calmed herself and cooled her neck with a fan.

Vanessa averted her eyes.

"Harboring an enemy of the state is an executable offense, is it not?" said the queen.

"It is, Your Majesty," Nolan said. "Even for a favorite."

Vanessa looked up then. "I love you, Mistress," she said.

The queen was taken aback. "What?"

"I don't know you, but I love you. All proud women must love you. I am not your enemy."

Zabel stared at the girl for a moment, then regarded Nolan, who mirrored she was sure her own expression of wonder and surprise.

"Ha!" said the queen. "Ha!" And broke into a wide smile.

She looked at the girl as if with new eyes. She noted the controlled fear in hers, the stubborn manner, the pride. It all struck her as familiar. "We like this girl," she said, as an official pronouncement.

"I thought you would," said Nolan.

"See to Ellsworth," she said and turned away.

At the door, she said loudly into the hall, "Your tastes disgust us, Sir Nolan. Disinfect yourself before we see you again." With a rush of her dress she stormed away, followed by a long string of admirers.

CHAPTER SEVEN

A girl of fifteen is but a child
Sweet and caring, pure and mild.
But on the morn of her sixteenth year
She puts aside that childish cheer.
For on that day a woman may wed
And take a husband to her bed.
Child at dark, woman at dawn
Merry cheeks to woebegone.
Traditional Enskaran Folk Song

29, Sixth-Month, 937 NE – Aboard the Hopewell, *Freeport Station, Dajjal*

For the cargo of the *Hopewell*, there was no difference between the time spent in flight versus that spent waiting in port. Millie felt the same persistent wrongness with the gravity, the same sunless sky, which she told herself was actually beneath her feet somehow. The water washed her the same, the looks of the other colonists were the same – the boredom and waiting and growing hunger as they were already put on cut rations, were all exactly the same lingering in Freeport as they had been to travel there.

When they'd arrived at the station over Dajjal eighteen days before, the company had been excited and relieved. They'd celebrated and had a feast of sorts that first night. They'd made room for the cattle that would be collected, the seed and materials they'd pick up, the salt they needed. It was the first brightening of the dark mood that had come over everyone the day Emma Dagney had died. No, that wasn't wholly true. The mood was bleak before then, a steady fall of spirits with occasional plummets like when the *Sebastian* was lost, or the pox spread. The death of one of their number, even one of the unpopular Dagneys, had been a free fall for a while. The arrival at Freeport had buoyed the company if only by virtue of it happening without incident and, relatively speaking, on schedule.

But now that schedule was broken. The mood was again dour and they were still at Freeport. No one was allowed to leave the lower decks.

"Why did they stop the treks?" she asked. "We need the exercise. We need a window once in a while even if it's just to see the stars."

"I assure you there are reasons," her father said.

"What are they?"

"Several."

She couldn't tell if her father was being evasive because he was tired or for some other reason.

"Is it the same on the *Mallow*?" she said.

"They're about the same," he said. "They can go up decks but can't leave the ship."

"That's better than what we have."

"I don't like walking the other decks," said Dillon. "It's hard."

Millie ignored her little brother. "It's stupid to be stuck down here," she said.

Her father spoke into his breakfast bowl, fatigue in his voice. "Morgan doesn't think it's a good idea to let anyone off the ships."

Freeport was the last civilized outpost they'd encounter. It represented the last chance for anyone to change their minds. Realizing this, Millie understood why Morgan wouldn't want to give anyone the chance. "Why are we still here then?" she said.

Henry Dagney sighed and shrugged his shoulders.

"But why not the upper decks? We're turning to jelly here."

"Most people don't even like those treks, Millie."

"They're hard," put in Dillon.

"Was that Morgan's idea again?" she said.

"Pilot Upor's."

"Why?"

"Maybe he's busy. Governor Morgan is working on it."

"Well, that settles it then," said Mille. "If Morgan is working on it...."

"Watch your tongue, daughter."

Millie blew a lock of hair out of her eyes with a snort and sawed into the loaf of black bread like she was cutting bars of a prison cell.

Dillon watched her with a blank stare, his lip beginning to quiver. Mealtimes were always hard for him. Millie had yet to decide which upset him less, making it as much the same as when their mother was alive, or making it decidedly different. Her arguments and bread aggression put today's breakfast into the latter category.

"Don't cry, Dillon," she said.

"I'm not going to," he said with a sniffle.

Their father put his hand on the boy's shoulder and gave him a squeeze.

He'd spent a lot of time comforting Dillon after their mother's death. He was eight years old, and the concept of death was as alien to him as the idea of not having a mother. Millie was more worldly but still felt a tinge of resentment toward her father's attention to her brother. He'd hardly said a word to her about Emma's passing, offered her no reassuring promises or religious dogma of an afterlife. He'd given her no emotional leave to mourn. They'd barely spoken of the incident at all except about practical changes it brought to their household, chores, and women's meetings.

"Can I get special permission as the daughter of an assistant to go up decks?" she asked. "I'd rather go alone anyway. The men won't talk to me and the other women irk me."

"They're not letting anyone go up." Her father rubbed his eyes and yawned.

"Why not? I want a reason."

He'd been up late at the church with Morgan and the other assistants. Millie had given up waiting for him and fallen asleep well past midnight. She'd woken him with the smell of a burned breakfast. Lost in her thoughts, she'd let the meal boil over and nearly set off the ship's alarms.

"Honey, times are as they are. Do as you're told."

"A brave new world."

"What?" Her father scraped the last of the cereal into Dillon's bowl and split the piece of bread with him.

"Nothing," said Millie and cut herself another slice.

"What do you mean the women irk you?" he said.

"I don't like the way they look at me."

"What do they say?"

"Nothing. That's part of it."

"What about Daria Morgan?"

"She's too pregnant to do much more than sit around and look tired."

"I thought you didn't like talking to women," said Dillon, putting some bread on his butter.

"Save some of that,"Millie said, scraping some butter off his slice and back into the bowl. "And I don't like talking to women. They're stupid. Do you know half of them can't even read, Father? Nay. More than half. Much more than half."

"You're surprised?"

"Times are what they are," she said.

"Aye."

"I was mocking you."

"I know."

She snorted again.

"Millie, you're going to have to make peace with the women. We'll need each other on Tirgwenin. You're the woman of this family now. Much will be expected of you. It'll be hard. Let's not make it harder. Please."

"If we were home on Enskari—"

"It'd be worse. Much worse," he said.

Millie bit her lip.

"How, Father?" said Dillon. "How is it worse at home?"

Millie caught her father's warning glance but ignored it. She said, "He means that in Vildeby I'd be a despised not only for being a girl but also a Buckler, neither condition, I'd like to remind everyone, I chose."

"Maybe I have spoiled you." Her father coughed. "You'll be old enough to marry next year. Things might look different then."

Millie bit her bread and chewed.

He coughed again and then fell into a fit long enough and hard enough that Millie decided not to answer his challenge.

"Dillon," Father said when he'd caught his breath. "This day go to Mr. Browne. He has new pigs born."

"I heard." Dillon's eyes lit up.

"I told him you'd help him with his chores today. It'll be hard work, but it'll do you good. You'll learn a lot."

"Can I have a pig?"

"They're not pets, you know."

"I know. But can I have one?"

"That's between you and Mr. Browne. You can ask him, but mind you ask only after you've given him a good day's work. Maybe two."

"Aye, Father."

"Give me your washing," said Millie, collecting the breakfast dishes. "I'll go mingle with the women and clean your shirts."

"Thanks, honey."

"Can I go now?" Dillon asked.

"Go ahead," said his father.

The boy was out of the house and running up the sloped deck before Millie could even tell him to take a jacket. He probably didn't need one, but that's the kind of thing their mother always said and Millie thought it fell to her now to say things like that.

★   ★   ★

After putting their rooms in order as she'd done ever since her mother first fell sick, Millie collected the washing basket and carried it to the cauldrons.

She watched her feet to escape the vertigo of the ever up-sloping deck. She resisted making short jumps, skipping along as many did, taking advantage of the decreased gravity. She put one foot deliberately in front of the other and moved as she would if she were walking someplace real, someplace solid and open. A world. Any world at this point. Months aboard this spinning bucket and that much again ahead of her. No wonder Morgan had kept the people from Freeport. Even among the devout and indentured, the pledged and hopeful, they'd risk catastrophic desertion if given the chance. It was the Saved way to avoid temptation whenever possible, prevent it from happening. It was an ancient tenet embraced wholeheartedly by the Bucklers. Millie often thought that the Bucklers were in fact leaving Enskari not so much because they were forced to, but because they wanted to. Away from civilization, ideas and temptation could be better controlled. Too much worldliness and even the Bucklers could stray spiritually if not materially. She was the prime example of that.

Mrs. Archard was at a cauldron stirring clothes. The smell of strong detergent rose from the pot on clouds of hot steam.

"Blessed be to thee, Mrs. Archard," said Millie.

"And to thee, Miss Dagney."

Mrs. Archard was a stern woman. She was a hand taller than Millie, tight gaunt features, sharp judgmental eyes, a downturned mouth and needly fingers. Though not in evidence now, Millie knew Mrs. Archard's hair was a dark brown, nearly black. There might be some Hyraxian in her past, but Millie doubted anyone had ever had the courage to ask her. She looked over Millie as if measuring meat for the butcher.

"Your hair is come loose from beneath your bonnet," she said, pointing.

"Oh," said Millie and tucked it back.

Millie poured her basket into a warm cauldron and adjusted the fire. She scraped soap into the pot with the edge of a knife and stirred it with a length of plastic pipe. The heat and steam rose to her face and made her sweat instantly.

She looked over at Mrs. Archard and noticed her sweat as dark patches under her arms and down her back.

"Mrs. Archard, do you think we might not undress ourselves a little to better abide the heat? Our bonnets perhaps?"

The woman turned on her as if she'd blasphemed. "Child, propriety is at the core of godliness."

Millie, at least, wasn't wearing the entire 'proper' costume of her sex and class. She had only a light cotton day-dress on, no petticoat, chemise, or bodice. Though many, Mrs. Archard included, felt she should now dress more maturely as the female head of the household, Millie had deliberately kept to more juvenile and comfortable outfits. It served her well. If she, dressed as she was, was suffering now, Millie could only pity Mrs. Archard in her long black wool mantua. But of course, Millie didn't pity her. She thought her prideful and stupid. What else could she think about someone who refused to adapt to something as simple as washday? How would she ever survive on a wild planet like Tirgwenin?

The women worked in silence, pulling their washing out of the pot and scrubbing it on washboards before rinsing in a cool vat and returning it to their basket to be hung modestly back home. Mustn't see pantaloons even on a clothesline.

Millie had planned this chore poorly. She should have come on another day, a day without Mrs. Archard and her kind. A day with Daria. Then at least there'd be talk. As inane and gossipy as that woman's chat was, it was better distraction than the solemn silence of working beside Mrs. Archard. Millie had been to graveside funerals with less sorrow.

She finally took the last garment from the rinse vat, wrung it out, holding her temper as the water resisted her muscles, clinging to the cloth in the low-gravity suspense she'd come to hate. She did the best she could before tossing it in her basket. "Good day, Mrs. Archard," Millie said, feeling proud of herself more for tolerating the woman than for cleaning her family's clothes.

"Blessed be," said the woman.

"And to thee," responded Millie.

She put on her mask of sweet womanly calm and carried her basket away. She tried to keep it in place for the people she saw, nodding politely to the other colonists she passed as her mother had done, but a few moments into her walk home, her eyes were back on her feet and she didn't like herself. She felt unclean, as if she'd been lying for an hour when there'd hardly been a word spoken.

Looking up, she saw Governor Morgan walking across the deck. He looked as tired as her father, but moved with purpose and urgency.

He approached a hatch near the wall and pulled it open with a hiss of equalizing pressure. He propped it ajar and went downstairs toward the higher decks.

Without a second thought, Millie slid her basket behind a row of oil barrels and followed Morgan down the steps. She knew the way. The up-deck treks had used this hatch before. It led down to where things felt more normal.

Another unnatural thing about the ship was the deck designation. As you went downstairs the deck numbers increased. Zero deck was at the center, the gravity-less heart of the spinning vessel. The command deck was twelve. The deck numbers had minimum relationship to the distance; each deck was a different height. The engine decks were at the core controlling the rotation and working the cables. Then the low decks of cargo where she lived. The middle decks were mostly tiny crawlspaces of ducts and machinery, a labyrinth of tunnels through interior armor to keep Coronam out of the sensitive ship works. The command decks at the top were of a normal height, but they did not extend around the whole of the ship. For as big as the ship was, it was surprisingly cramped.

Four flights down, Millie could feel the strain on her body. Six flights and she felt heavy. Ten flights and she felt positively unfit. Just a week without this walk and already she felt more jelly than muscle.

Morgan's footfalls continued with the same paced click-a-clack and she, padding softly, followed. She heard him stop and turn a hatch on deck eleven. A few moments later, she saw the open hatch and slipped through.

The gravity felt thrice Enskari but she knew it was only a little over one. On the armored hull, it was 1.8 but that was still far out through the heavy metal and ablative shielding.

She'd never been to this deck before. The treks had stopped a deck or two below this one on a wide area where animals were kept. There they'd walk circles and exercise as they might and then returned up the steps after an hour.

This deck was furnished. It might once have been opulent but now sat in a state of sad careless decay. The narrow hallway the hatch opened to was carpeted, red-and-black paisley design, dusty, old and threadbare. Glowglobes were spaced evenly but only one in three were wound and these unevenly, two together then a stretch of eight dark and one lit. There was a polished wooden handrail running along the wall, broken in places, splintered and worn. There were wooden doors which led away. These, like the carpet, must have once been beautiful, intricately carved and stained, but they were now chipped and untended, in need of refinishing if not replacement.

Millie heard knocking to her right. The deck sloped up but not as drastically as it did on the lower decks and she could make out Morgan's legs at a door.

"Morgan," came a voice. "What brings you here?"

"Upor, this delay is intolerable," the governor said.

Millie saw Morgan enter the room and heard the door close.

Something in the governor's voice alarmed her. The delay at Freeport had been overly long. It was supposed to be only a day or two, but it had gone on for nearly two weeks. Still, there was something greater than that in his voice, something beyond impatience and frustration. Worry? Fear? Terror? She'd never heard that in his voice before.

She moved stealthily to her right until she came to the door where Morgan had gone. Pressing her ear against it, she heard Morgan speaking.

"Tomorrow?" His voice was shrill, nearly panicked.

"When the crew is sober."

"Tomorrow?" Morgan's voice incredulous, defeated.

"That's what you want, isn't it? To get underway."

"Aye, but what about the cattle? The supplies? What about your friend you said you had here?"

"My friend?"

"For heaven's sake, Upor, your friend. What about your friend who would supply us?"

"Oh aye. I don't think he's on Dajjal anymore. I seem to recall that he migrated back home a year ago."

There was a long silence. Millie's ears filled with the sound of her own pounding heart.

"Upor, what are you—"

"What have we here?"

Millie felt a hand on her neck. She turned and saw an unshaven sailor, his reflective vest stained with food and stinking of body odor and liquor.

His eyes wandered down her neck and she pushed at him and tried to run.

He grabbed her sleeve and yanked her back, tearing it, ripping her dress from collar to waist on the right side.

"No undies," the man said, running his tongue over his broken teeth.

She was bare beneath her torn dress, her flesh uncovered, her breast exposed.

She fumbled for her clothing to cover up, but the man held tight. He tugged at it again, pulling her toward him, ripping it down to her thigh.

"Mustn't bother with that," he said and reached for her chest.

Gripping her torn dress, she screamed and twisted to escape.

He held tight to her ruined garment and jerked her back. Again, she tripped and fell to the moldering carpet, raising a cloud of gray dust around her.

She screamed and kicked at the sailor.

He laughed and came closer.

She landed a heel to his knee that slowed him enough for her to place another where it counted. He doubled over.

"You'll pay for that, ye trollop," he snarled through gritted teeth. "I'll make you kiss it better, I will. Blessed be, I will!"

Another man moved behind the sailor. It was Governor Morgan. He slapped his hand on the sailor's shoulder and whirled him about.

The sailor took the momentum and used it to land a blow on the governor's jaw.

Morgan stumbled backward into the wall, catching himself with the handrail.

The sailor let go of Millie and went after him, grabbing him by the coat.

"Mr. Gordon!"

Another man was there. Millie recognized Captain Upor. He wore only a dingy nightshirt.

"Mr. Gordon, stand down or I'll have ye flogged."

The sailor, Mr. Gordon apparently, let go of the governor, who rubbed the side of his face.

"Beating up old men and raping children, Mr. Gordon?" said the captain.

"Begging ye pardon, Captain, but I found this lostling here in the hall, her ears up against your door. Listening. I grabbed her for ye, and she panicked like a scared rabbit and ran right out of her dress. Tore it by her own doing."

Shaking with shock, Millie could only stare at the three men and try to gather enough fabric to cover herself.

"As for the planter there, I apologize. The girl kicked me and I was up in arms, so to say. He put hands on me first."

Mr. Gordon looked at Millie. Unseen from the other men, he winked at her and licked his teeth.

"Millicent?" said Morgan. "Of course it would be you. What are you doing up here, child?"

Milled pulled her eyes from Gordon and fastened them on Governor Morgan like he was an anchor in a storm.

His face was red, a swelling already rising under his left eye.

"I followed you," she said. "I wanted exercise."

Mr. Gordon winked at her again.

She shuddered.

"That bastard attacked me," she said.

"Mouthy little thing," said Gordon with a grin.

Millie clenched her fist.

Captain Upor spoke. "You have no business being on this deck, lass." He wore an expression of bemused contempt. He'd come out the door wearing the same grin. Millie wanted to hit the smile from his face nearly as much as she wanted to smash Gordon's broken teeth in. "You really need to stay below where you are supposed to be. Both of ye."

Morgan shot Upor a cross look, but then, glancing at Millie, softened it.

"I'll take the child back to her family."

"Do."

Morgan helped her up and cover herself.

"What will become of that?" said Millie, making an obscene gesture at Gordon.

Morgan slapped her face.

The surprise of it more than the force made her stumble and stare open-mouthed at the man, the other colonist, her ally and friend, but then she remembered he was more than just another refugee, more than the governor of the still-far-off colony. He was a head minister of their congregation. He was endowed with power over her and all the Bucklers to discipline and correct. More so, it was his duty to do it.

"You make disreputable our entire band with your ill temper and foul manners, Miss Dagney. You must learn respect for your betters. You must learn obedience and modesty. Keep sweet. You must learn your place. Stop being a child."

"Looks like no child to me," said Gordon, not even trying to hide the wide amused smile on his face.

"Dagney?" said Upor. "Henry's daughter?"

Millie didn't dare speak. She choked back a rush of tears. She shook from anger and horror. Friendless and helpless.

"Aye, Freddy. This is Henry's daughter."

Millie kept her face downcast, but saw Upor from the corner of her eye. She saw his expression soften, turn from amused and irritated to soft and sorry.

"We'll be underway in the morning," Upor said, and without another word, he turned and reentered his room, throwing the bolt with a loud low click.

Mr. Gordon, chortling, wandered up the hall, leaving the two colonists alone to watch him go, huddled together in front of Upor's locked door.

CHAPTER EIGHT

Initial visitors to Tirgwenin had dismissed the possibility that that world's inhabitants were even of human descent due to it not being among the planets colonized during the Unsettling. This belief was compounded by the dramatic physical and cultural differences between the Tirgwenians and the Saved of the civilized worlds.

Sir Gael Aderyn's historic second circumnavigation of Coronam (919-923 NE) settled this question and solved the long mystery of the fate of Jareth's original Old Earth colony. Sir Gael showed that the primitive natives of Tirgwenin were in fact the direct descendants of that ancient lost expedition when he found the ruined landing craft on the plains of Aderyn. That planet is now often called Jareth's World.

Our best scientists postulate that the Tirgwenians' physical mutations are most likely due to an unfortunate radiation seepage at one time through their atmosphere. As for other differences, the worlds of Maaraw and Silangan can be seen as recent instructive examples of technological regression. Both of these worlds were colonized during the Unsettling, but neither fully recovered from the early loss of technology as did the five civilized worlds. Technologists estimate Maaraw remains a century behind the rest of us, Silangan three or four hundred years, and Tirgwenin, even though it's the longest inhabited world around Coronam, is millennia behind Enskari. These technological discrepancies have allowed the civilized worlds to parse Maaraw up between them, and for Hyrax to so easily dominate and subjugate all of Silangan.

As descendants of Old Earth, by common law dictate, Tirgwenin and its population of humans are subject to the laws of conquest, the same as claimed by Hyrax for Silangan. If we get there first, our claim to Tirgwenin must be respected by precedent.

Excerpt from 'Application for Tirgwenin Royal Colonial Patent'
Ethan Sommerled, 928 NE

6, Seventh-Month, 937 NE – Coebler, Maaraw

A dozen ships were anchored in the bay waiting to be filled with tomorrow's purchases.

Andre looked out upon the sails and counted one ship from Claremond, one from Temple, three from Enskari, two from Lavland and five from Hyrax. The other twenty or so were local ships and barges, Maarawan traders and transports.

Though he couldn't see the ships well enough to know which were pressurized for orbital insertion and descent, he could count the thread masts which were required for it.

The many anchored Hyraxian ships reinforced the rumors that Prince Brandon was buying troops today. The Temple ship had a thread mast too, possibly for the same reason, but he knew the *Juniper Berry*, the only Enskari ship with such a mast, was not taking anyone off-world. Once perhaps, but now, never. It was an old landing craft, broken and repurposed. It would hemorrhage air like a cut throat if taken up. Andre knew the captain, Billibe. He was a crotchety old man who drank gin instead of rum and passed out in the privy with some regularity when he drank. He'd bought the ship used and was just too lazy to remove the mast.

Andre could just make out in the distance a ship breaking through the high clouds, apparently floating but obviously descending along an unseen thread. It appeared to hover and then slowly move down. It was an illusion at this distance. The ship had to be falling at near-terminal velocity, but from where Andre stood onshore watching it kilometers out over the ocean, it looked as serene as falling clumpseed.

"You see that yonder there, Karl? Just there. See?" Andre pointed to the new arrival, a dark blip over the horizon.

"Another one?" said Karl, holding a hand over his eyes. "Hyraxian, I suppose?"

"Who else?"

"What they doing with all this?"

"Making a statement, I'd say," Andre said.

"But the Iquiani elevator is but a hundred kilometers yonder." Karl gestured that way as if Andre had forgotten where it was. "What's the point? They could sail up there with barges in a day and a half. Load 'em up and be away. What's the cost of a thread like that? What's their hurry?"

"Don't know for cost," said Andre.

"Ain't it dangerous?" Karl said. "Wind could take that one right now. Thread base could be in mud, pull right up, drop that ship a thousand kilometers. Kill everyone and everything. Don't make no sense."

"They haven't lost a ship on the threads here all week, so I hear."

"Who tell you that?"

"Heard it from a Hyrax sailor down at the kro. He could barely stand his legs were so weak."

"Drink?"

"Mostly," said Andre. "But I'd say it was a lot from being up yonder too much." Andre pointed to the sky for emphasis as if Karl had forgotten where that was.

"They ain't even got the legs to be down here," Karl said, spitting on the ground and then kicking red dirt over it. "What about all them dockers? Trying to put them out of work? We got freemen come a hundred kilometers to make that run up to Iquiani. Good men. Know the way. Know how to handle slaves. Got families to feed. Now there'll be barely work carting them off to those ships. And come all this way and can't buy a drink for Brandon's filling the bar seats with drunken sailors."

Andre tore into a length of cane with his teeth and sucked the sugar out of it watching the ship descend. "It's a pissing match, Karl," he said. "Doncha see? They're showing how big they are. Think of the threads as a metaphor for Prince Brandon's skinny little dick. He's compensating."

Karl laughed and reached for the sugar. "Gimme some of that."

Andre broke the cane in two and handed his friend some. "Nah, but really. It's gotta be a show," he said. "They want everyone to know they don't need us. They're showing they're too big to fight, making us afraid and all that."

"What do we care?"

"It's not for us. It's for them." Andre pointed at the anchored ships. "Them Enskari ships mostly."

"Billibe?"

"Nah, not him. I'm saying there are spies everywhere. Word will get back to everyone, Enskari, Claremond, Temple – everyone. Hyrax is making a statement."

"Don't make no sense."

"Does to them. It's not meant for you."

"But it is making me nervous," said Karl.

Andre sucked on the stalk and nodded. "Maybe it is for you then," he said.

"What?"

"They're doing it to intimidate folks before the auction."

"Ah, well that makes some sense."

"That it does."

Karl said, "Not for me. I'm here to get three maybe four good workers for my fields. They trying to scare me away from that?"

"Maybe," said Andre. "It ain't the time to buy. If I were you, I'd get all my slaves out here by tomorrow and sell the lot. I got a feeling money will be no problem for these Hyraxian fools. Pay top dollar for anything. They'll make a show of it. Buy the lot with Silangan silver before you can write out an IOU."

"What am I going to do with my fields?"

"Come on, dummy, there's always more slave and slave markets. Go inland where they ain't so many Saved. Buy local." Andre winked.

"Top dollar you say?" said Karl.

Andre sucked on the sugar and nodded.

The falling ship was nearly to the water now, the red-orange thrusters engaging to slow the fall. A low sonic boom cracked over the harbor and echoed off the foothills behind them.

"Eh, I don't know," Karl said, kicking more dirt.

"I'll tell you what," said Andre. "I'll give you a hundred dollars a head for men. Right now. How many can you have for me by tomorrow?"

"Wait. Uhm, what about women?"

"Nah. They'll probably go too, but I'm not so sure there. How about it?"

"Indentured too?"

"Have to look at the contracts. Nothing short of two years. Make it three to be safe."

Karl sucked on the stalk and looked at the harbor, the docks, and the town.

"Why can't I just sell 'em myself?"

"You could, but you'd be on the hook. You might make less than the hundred I'm offering. My guess is that some Hyraxian noble will walk in with a bucket and buy 'em all sight unseen."

"Really?"

"Maybe."

"I got a couple old 'uns that I've been meaning to get rid of."

"Men, not dead men," said Andre.

"What's the difference? That's what they'll all be once Brandon buys them."

Andre looked out at the black Hyraxian ships and recognized at last that the majority of them were not cargo vessels, but warships. "Yep, there is that."

"No deal on the hundred," Karl said. "But you got me thinking. I best go attend my business." He tipped his hat and hurried down the hill.

Andre sighed and went the other way into town to inspect the day's market.

Maaraw was neutral territory among the civilized worlds. A map of the planet was a complex six-color tapestry of vast black-and-white native lands and colored spot rashes for the claims of the five civilized worlds around the edges of the single great continent. Enskari, Lavland, Hyrax, Claremond, and Temple each claimed large coastal sections and there were recognized intermittent smaller enclaves scattered haphazardly, in between and far away. The largest claim didn't extend farther inland than a hundred kilometers; most were half that – just the fifty-kilometer control zone dictated by common law. The inland areas were left to the natives since no one had found good reason enough yet to bring the necessary resources to subdue the interior. The peoples there had not been a threat and they'd proven useful. The nearer tribes acted as intermediaries for the more inland ones for the raw materials the other worlds were eager to get: metals, timber, fur, and people. Maaraw was the system's primary source for slaves.

Andre knew that even on Old Earth at the time of the Unsettling, people had sold themselves. His own ancestors, he knew, had bartered their lives for a ride to Coronam. Indentured servitude was an established and not disrespected method of commerce, a necessity at times, a long contract for a great debt.

The tradition had remained the same during the centuries of isolation.

Then the 'civilized worlds' came to Maaraw and with them, ministers and true slavery.

The people all looked the same to Andre, the Hyraxian, the Templers, Maarawan and Lavlanders. They were all people. On a world where horses could climb trees and berry bushes ate insects, a man was a man. Sure there were regional tendencies, the red shades of the Enskari, the dark of the Hyraxian, but that was nothing. People within the same clan often had wider variations. On average perhaps there were minor discernible differences, but individually, it was impossible to tell a tanned and naked Claremondian merchant on a beach from a Maarawan hunter collecting clams. They were all from Old Earth. They were all Saved. Or rather they had all once been Saved.

That was the difference the ministers discovered. That was the difference that allowed them to segregate and condemn. To enslave.

Some of the Maarawans had deviated from the doctrine of the Saved, and because of this, they'd lost their human status. They could now be treated as different and damned, a clever philosophical distinction that allowed people to be chattel.

Andre knew that every planet had deviated. Some more than others. On the other worlds – planets with railguns and spaceships, the differences were dealt with humanely by the church. But not on Maaraw.

Strange how a few useful tribes were brought back into the fold while the interior people were just damned and dragged out of their homes to work sugar plantations or shipped off-world for who knew what. Convenient that.

Andre was a member of one of those lucky tribes. Early on by virtue of control of a trade route, the ministers had managed to reconvert his people in the nick of time, and they were all now Saved again. Never mind that not half of them went to services or believed in the infallibility of the prophet or even cared. It was business. It was survival.

Andre mused on these things as he often did when he walked the warehouses, looking at the terrified faces of the new captures.

"Lots and lots of 'em, eh, Bruin?"

Andre recognized Rooknee, a slave trader he'd dealt with before. Rooknee never called Andre by his first name. They were not friends.

"Never seen so many," said Andre. "The interior must be vacant."

Rooknee laughed. "Nay. Still plenty more."

There were hundreds of people in this one warehouse alone. There were at least five more like it and two more twice the size. Mostly they were men, all years from eight to eighty, but there were also whole families clustered in cages. All of them, men, women, and children young and old, stared at him silently as he walked by, their faces mud-streaked with tears and swollen with bruises, wild eyes filled with fear and begging. Hopelessness and terrible resignation.

"They know they're going off-world," said Andre. It was not a question, but Rooknee took it as one.

"Aye," he said. "I'd say mostly the men do. Hyrax needs meat shields."

"What's that?"

"You not hear that before?"

Andre shook his head and lifted his hand over his nose.

"It means they need men to take the shot and arrows from the Enskari."

"Soldiers?"

"Nay. They'll not be trained to fight, just to die. You not hear that Hyrax nearly lost a big war on one of them other worlds?"

"Which one?"

"I don't recall, but I know they lost lots of men. Hyraxian blood was spilled aplenty. They got a new plan now to fight wars. Have walls of slaves running into crossbows, coilguns, and fire. The Hyraxians then come in after, when the other side is tired of killing people."

"That's the stupidest thing I've ever heard."

"Nay, it's true. I heard it from a Hyraxer myself. At the kro. They lost many men on that other world. And ships and such," he added as if questioning the logic himself. "Plus, see, they're spread out. Hyrax has people here and Lavland and also holding down Silangan."

"Holding down?"

"Whatever they do there."

"Excluding all those ships in the harbor, there can't be more than a thousand of them here on the whole planet."

"You don't know how to count, Bruin. There are millions of them."

Andre wondered if Rooknee even knew what the word meant, but didn't correct him. Rooknee could be sensitive about his lack of education, his inability to read and cypher numbers. Andre remembered a knife coming out during a sums discussion a year before.

He didn't travel half as far as Andre did, trading to earn a living. Andre was known up and down the western coast and halfway around the northern. He'd seen the enclaves and the bases, the plantations and the mines. He'd seen more of the world than the space sailors he knew, much more. How much can you see in a spinning can? Andre had met nobles and beggars, traded in cotton and gold, hardwood, coffee, starch apple, men and children. He'd made enough to survive but never enough to settle down, never enough to keep him in any one place. He'd spent forty years wandering the markets, selling his skills as middleman and taking his cut first before losing it somehow. Barely ever having enough left in his pocket to move on to the next place. He was just over fifty years old now, rugged and sun-scraped, a bit rayburned. His hide was tough as a sea badger's for being out so much, a tawny ochre color that he'd noticed recently had a reflectiveness to it he'd only seen in farmers and desert tribesman, people who'd lived under a sky and not a roof. He was careful to cover up as much of his skin as he could when dealing with the pale upper classes and otherworlders. It bothered them.

Though they had the money and the power, standing militia with crossbows, coilguns, and flamers, Andre knew the otherworlders were really very few. He'd seen them, been among them in their cities and hamlets. In their houses bustling with native servants, some with skin as shiny as his, but fading from the shade. On the maps, otherworlders claimed large chunks of Maaraw, but he knew that the population, even in those chunks, was overwhelmingly Maarawan, fifty souls to one at least. If Maaraw ever got fed up, they could push these others all into the sea and not break a sweat. But the people didn't do that. They sold their inland neighbors and grew fat on the coasts. It was business.

"You selling or buying, Bruin?"

"I was here to broker for Karl Cabelson. He needed field hands, but I think he's going the other way now."

"Good idea."

"He'll go around me," said Bruin, watching the far doors slide open. "No commission for me this week."

"You got none of your own?"

"Not at present."

A Hyraxian officer accompanied by three soldiers and a Temple minister entered the warehouse. As if choreographed, all hands went to cover their noses at once, clutching cloth over their faces to fight the stench.

Rooknee said, "I gotta go." He joined the rush of other traders hurrying to bargain with the buyers.

With Rooknee gone, the people in the cages called to Andre.

"Help us, brother!"

"Save us!"

"What have we done?"

"My babies!"

They'd not been subdued. Not even a little. It was unbecoming. It would hurt sales.

Andre recognized his own callousness as he walked past the cages. His heart did not stir for these unfortunates. His mind understood the situation, recognized fate for what it was. He had his and they had theirs. Their cries were essentially the same as those of dolphins caught in a net, or a horse to be broken to pull a cart. A tragic turn in a single life, sad, but what of it? This was the world. Sorry, but not his problem.

Andre left the warehouse and went into town. He needed a beer, not because he was upset, but because he wasn't.

Coebler was swimming with people. He recognized the off-worlders by their clothes and strange accents, by the wobble in their walk from weakened spaced muscles compounded by redberry spirits which snuck up on you like a raptor ambush, took your tongue and legs and left you babbling in your own piss.

"I'll have a tankard of the redberry," Andre said to the barmaid.

He was at the Prongshell Kro, one of the many bars making bank today. It was too crowded to enter. He'd shouted his order through an open window at the back of the building the locals used when the tourists at the front spilled out into the street. Not very often.

"Five dollars," the barmaid said, handing him the clay cup.

"Five?"

The barmaid blushed. "Sorry, Andre. Supply and demand. Five Maarawan dollars or two Hyraxian."

He fished the coins out of his purse and put them on the sill. She paused before taking them.

He put another coin up.

She winked. "Thanks."

It was a cold drink on a hot morning. The afternoon would be stifling. The wind was falling to a breeze and soon would fade, making the air an oppressive blanket stirred only from cart and courier just enough to fill the courtyards with a mix of brine from the sea and stink from the warehouses. Already the smell of unwashed sailors – sea and space – overpowered the animal dung in the gutters.

Andre tipped the cup and swallowed a mouthful of sweet biting syrup. That was the trick of it. It was sweet. It lulled you with pleasure, made you drunk with it, and then, unless you took caution, left you wrecked and wanting. Too bad it didn't keep long enough for a space voyage. It would be fitting return export to the other worlds.

He took another deep draught and watched an Enskari soldier win an arm wrestle with a Hyraxian sailor and drink a toast together before going at it again. Farther distant, a diplomat – a Lavlander noble by his crest – looked on with contempt. The same expression was shared by a Hyraxian officer conspiring in the corner with some Claremondian gentleman who was a lather of sweat beneath his velvet cape. This was a Maarawan two-dollar bar – no, five-dollar bar now, he remembered, not the Hall of the Prophet. Such finery would either be ruined by the atmosphere or stolen at the end of a hand bow on the gentleman's way out.

Not Andre's problem.

He tipped his cup a last time and drained it. He tried to taste the alcohol on his tongue after he'd swallowed but couldn't. Good thing he didn't have more business today; his legs were softening up.

He left the busy streets and headed toward the docks, preferring the brine to the city sweat and desperation, regretting already the redberry.

He pulled himself on the back of a passing steam cart headed his way and lay down in the straw. The driver didn't notice or care. It could handle a ton of cargo even over these bad roads.

Andre stared up at the luminescent sky. He watched subtle auroras play across the blue of it in lighter blue waves, like ripples on a pond, until the black smoke of the engine settled over the cart like a miasma.

He looked over the side on a curve and saw the ships still arrayed in the bay.

The sea clouds had stopped their advance at the horizon, stopped by the heat and the false calm of the land. He listened over the chugging of the engine and tried to make out the calls of seabirds, bluebills and the widebeaks with the scaly feathers. He couldn't hear anything but the damn engine. He imagined all the birds doing the same as he, retreating and waiting. Fretting.

He realized then the liquor was not erasing the faces in the warehouse the way it usually did, but accenting them.

"Help us, brother!"

"What have we done?"

At the paupers' dock, he leapt off the cart. He watched it chug away up the broken road until it rounded the point toward the better marinas, and the air finally went silent save for a soft buzzing of insects.

A small tender steamed up to the dock in a cloud of woodsmoke and moored. Three men stepped off it and looked at Andre suspiciously. He ignored them and they quickly left.

Andre went around the pier to the beach and stood at the water's edge.

A gull stood upon a piling, watching him.

He knew he should have stayed in town, sidled up to some noble, sold his services for the slave market tomorrow. Made some coin. But here instead he found himself kicking his shoes off and wading into the ocean.

Was it the ships? Or maybe the untamed people in the warehouse. How had they not been conditioned yet? Why had no one explained to them how to slave? How had they not been broken of the whining? And then the ships. Those foreign ships in his bay. Always the foreigners stealing the best of his world, in crops and timber, fish, fruit, and people.

He'd not known a time without the foreigners. He had prospered as much as any Maarawan could under them, but somehow the mix today of ship and cries and redberry spirits sickened him.

They were all being taken off-world. That was it. That was the difference. They were being taken off-world to die. There was no question, no lingering ambition that if they truly hated their situation, they could escape and return somehow.

Andre had held a little fairy tale in his head that allowed him to cope with it before. Putting himself in their situation, he'd grasped the idea of escape one day, a promise to himself that if he couldn't hack the trouble, he'd flee and take his chances in the interior. But that was impossible for anyone taken off-planet. The civilized worlds had no place for them to run. They and their offspring would be forever excluded from the society and culture those places boasted of. The trivial distinction in evolved religion would forever condemn them to slavery and marked as chattel. He was witnessing murder in slow motion.

He'd believed Rooknee. Why else would Hyrax military be here? The Silangians were too wild to be transported, barely useful for the slave work on their conquered planet. Maarawans were better civilized, easier to control, more – much more – culturally related to the civilized worlds than that devolved place. They could be lied to and tricked and led along believing kinship, and be made to die instead of their masters.

The damn redberry fogged his mind and threw open memories and suspicions he'd forgotten and put away. Weren't we better than this?

A memory. A hope in the past. A child's vision of bees. Honey, sunlight shining like his skin. Visions of honey. Bees and honey. Honey. Bees.

Up to his waist in the water, his feet treading the broken bay-oysters, he saw the flash and shift of color – white, plasma orange, black cloud. He saw the shockwave come at him like charging clouds, spreading toward him at the speed of sound, a wall of burning mist and noise that hit him like hate and pushed him backward and under the water.

Honey. Bees.

He remained beneath the surface, watching the world boil above him, weightlessly below. When it had passed and his lungs ached for air, he lingered still, letting himself be engulfed by the depth of silence, the quiet, the peace beneath the sea of Maaraw, the great single sea of his world.

When he finally came up to breathe, he heard sirens and shouts behind him, sensed broken windows and fleeing birds. Death and ruin all around.

Off in the distance an arc of lightning skittered and jumped skyward. A static charge up the unseen sky thread. At the base of it, engulfed in a cloud of black oily smoke, smoldered a sinking Hyraxian warship.

CHAPTER NINE

ABSTRACT: The continuing ecological decline of Earth's ability to support human habitation and the ongoing wars for resources among the various houses and bands, leads Hildebrant researchers to recommend the abandonment of the planet. Using recently rediscovered technology, it should be possible to send ships from Earth to the distant Coronam system for colonization under the following conditions:

1 - The project must begin immediately and be completed within fifty years. (See Hildebrant Paper 33-2610: 'Inevitable Overthrow of the Congress of Houses'.)

2 - Expected cost for development and implementation of a new suitable Fusion Wormhole Engine is estimated to be $38 trillion. This will accommodate up to twelve colony ships (see below). Participating houses will evenly split the cost of the engine. If a house chooses not to participate or cannot, their space will be made available to other participating houses, who will also assume the costs.

3 - Preliminary plans for standardized colony ships are under development. These ships are designed to carry 750 tons of human cargo (approximately 10,000 people) and 2.5 million tons of general cargo and equipment (including livestock) at liftoff. Houses may adjust these ratios at their will and peril. It is felt that these ratios of people to cargo offer the safest transit, allowing for only ten to thirty per cent loss to cryo.

4 - Construction cost for each ship is estimated at $12 trillion. Ratio cargo estimated at $3 trillion. These totals are above and beyond the engine costs and will be borne by each house independently.

5 - Participating houses must provide full political assistance in their respective spheres of influence to this endeavor. Local laws are to be rescinded or altered upon request, and security forces activated when needed.

6 - It is understood there is enormous risk in this undertaking. The Leadership of the Congress of Houses and the Hildebrant Society assume no responsibility or make any guarantees as to the success of any aspect, whole or part, of this proposed undertaking.

Excerpt from Executive Summary, Paper 34-2610: 'Earth Evacuation Proposal'

The Hildebrant Research Society,
Presented at the biannual meeting of the Congress of Houses
March 1, 2610, Juneau, Alaska – Old Earth

26, Seventh-Month, 937 NE – Hall of the Prophet, Temple

Prophet Eren VIII strode slowly down the gray ivory halls of his palace only half listening to his morning reports. Jessop, his new First Advisor, had met him at the door of his chambers after breakfast. Jessop was a perky young man, barely five and forty, two and twenty years younger than the prophet, thirty years younger than the Second Advisor, Hansen, who was away this week celebrating a birthday somewhere on Havilah with his family. Eren couldn't remember where. He wouldn't see him again until summer conclave when the Twelve Apostles would assemble with him. Several of them were around the palace now, but they didn't bother him daily the way eager Jessop did.

"The arc traveled up thread and damaged the orbiting *Gauntlet*."

"The what?"

"The *Gauntlet*. That's the name of the Hyraxian warship over Maaraw. It was damaged."

"Oh aye," said Eren.

The prophet's attention wandered through the windows, to the courtyard orchard. It was still in bloom. The beauty and simplicity of the scene outside was far preferable to the complex concerns of this briefing.

"They're blaming Enskari of course," Jessop said.

"More retaliation for the *Pempkin*?"

"That's what they claim, but it's too early to tell. It might have been an attack or an accident. If an attack it might not have been Enskari. Maaraw has rebels."

"Damnable planet," said the prophet.

Eren's silk slippers slid across the floor with a soft scratching step lighter than the shoes of his advisor, and a world apart from the boots of his trailing guards.

"The boat was a warship," Jessop explained. "It had a plasma cannon."

"I thought those didn't work on the ground?"

"Oh, they work. The problem is the radiation shielding. Housing the energy requires so much metal that few ships can handle the weight of it and stay afloat. If you don't have enough, the weapon is more dangerous to the crew than any enemy. The Hyrax are trying a balancing act between safety and buoyancy."

"And failing."

"Aye, the containment was breached. It was catastrophic to the ship of course. A hundred fifty Saved perished on the ship. Two other Hyraxian boats nearby sank as well. Another two hundred lost. The harbor was contaminated." He thumbed through his papers. "Estimates are three thousand dead in Coebler."

"Saved?"

Jessop wrinkled his brow but then said, "Maybe a hundred of the dead in Coebler were off-worlders. Of those, most of them were Saved. A few from Enskari. Some of the killed Maarawans were Saved, but the majority of the dead were slaves for the market. They were left behind during the evacuation, victims of the radiation cloud and resulting fire. Five and twenty hundred souls dead in cages."

"Souls, but not Saved," said the prophet. "May God be just to them."

"This may likely be the cause of the recent unrest on Maaraw."

"Slave revolts are nothing new. It'll quickly be put down."

"Some are calling it a religious uprising."

"Are they?"

"Aye, Your Holiness."

"I'll send a man to help." The prophet threw open a door leading to a balcony and stepped outside.

A guard hurriedly followed him through before Jessop could pass the threshold. The guard surveyed the porch and courtyard below before retreating to a far corner to wait. Another guard stood at the door behind them, armed crossbow hanging at the ready.

"Prince Brandon—" began Jessop but the prophet silenced him with a raised hand.

Eren breathed in the sweet odors of the orchard and smiled. He listened to the calls of birds and let the cool morning air ease over him like a prayer.

Opening his eyes, he saw clumps of white apple blossoms belying the season, a faux winter in early summer, a beautiful recollection of the turning of time. The pear trees with their pink blossoms sprang up among them like love. The cherry trees had been brighter, their time had come and gone, but if he looked really hard, he could discern new fruit sprouting on the branches.

A single gardener, a bondsman, drove a wheelbarrow down the grassy path. He pushed his tools beside a cherry tree and began to dig.

"Do you know what he's doing?" Eren pointed to the gardener.

Jessop leaned over and looked. "I think he's pulling a weed. Aye. It's a native grab vine. It's climbing the trunk of that tree."

"It's an apple tree," said Eren. "Jonathan apples, I believe. My favorite. Direct descendant from Old Earth."

They watched the gardener pull the vine from the roots and then cut it away from the tree. Jessop rocked on his heels, but Eren ignored him.

The gardener tossed the uprooted plant into his wheelbarrow and set out again. There was a sick tree among the pears, its yellow leaves a symbol of another season.

"What is it that troubles you, Jessop?" Eren said, watching the worker.

"It's troubling that Hyrax is playing with such dangerous weapons, Your Holiness. The explosion on Maaraw shows the viability of planetary bombardment with plasma bombs."

"Aye?"

"This lends credence to the rumors about the armada and new weapons Prince Brandon plans to use on Enskari. Weapons of mass destruction. Weapons of mass murder."

The gardener inspected the yellowing leaves. He crumpled one up between his fingers and smelled it. He was careful and studious. He took his time, time that Eren watched him in silence while Jessop fidgeted uncomfortably.

"Your Holiness," Jessop said.

"I'm here, brother."

"As the guardians of the species, shouldn't we intervene?"

The prophet sat down on a bench and gestured Jessop to join him. The advisor squirmed in his robe, still not used to the palace attire of his rank. He rearranged papers in his arms, dropped a pencil, and picked it up before sitting.

"Are you settled then?" asked Eren.

"Aye," said Jessop.

"War is coming," Eren said. "War is an ugly business."

The gardener inspected another tree, kicked at the ground, rubbed the bark, and looked into its branches.

Silence stretched on.

Jessop said, "Aye. War is terrible. I've been studying the archives. Reading about Old Earth."

"Are our libraries on Temple different from those on Claremond?"

Jessop said, "Aye, the archives are wonderful. I'm still amazed at the Unsettling. What a miracle that was. What a miracle this place is."

"Quite. God's gift for another try."

"Another try?"

"To get it right."

Jessop looked at him quizzically.

Eren kept his eyes on the gardener. He watched the man rummage through a sack and take out a flat stone.

"What has struck me," said Jessop, "is the great loss of life on Old Earth and the fragility of it. We were ten ships at the Unsettling, each with ten thousand people."

"There were twelve ships," said Eren. "Two were lost before we left."

"Aye, two house ships, twenty thousand souls left behind."

"They weren't lost. They were destroyed. The wormhole engine triggered prematurely. They were annihilated in the event, as was the Moon."

The gardener sat down on the dewy grass with his stone and began to sharpen an ax. The sound of the slow meticulous scraping strokes barely reached the balcony where the two clerics talked.

Jessop said, "So barely a hundred thousand of us arrived here. More were lost in the landings. Maybe seventy thousand Saved made planetfall. That is such a small number compared to the billions and billions that were lost."

The prophet laughed and again Jessop looked at him with a quizzical stare, this one a little hurt.

"I'm sorry, brother, but when I hear numbers that big, they mean nothing to me. My mind cannot imagine that. I'm told to imagine stars or sand, but I always think it's like counting beans in a jar."

"I see."

"I'm sorry," he said, patting Jessop's knee. "Go on. You need to speak your mind."

Jessop took a deep breath. "We're all that's left. When I read of the wars on Old Earth they frighten me. I too can't imagine numbers that big but they terrify me. So many people died in strife. The planet was destroyed. It took a miracle to save the few that got away."

"Aye," said Eren. The gardener turned his ax and went to work on the obverse side.

"How can we let it happen again? Should we not use all the church's power to stop it?"

"You need to look closer, brother. The lessons of Old Earth are more complicated than that."

"But life—"

"Is not all the same," said Eren, turning to his advisor. "There have always been wars. Even here. Every civilized world endured centuries of strife. City wars, and state wars, and then the final continent wars. Even holy Temple had these wars. Only after these wars did orthodoxy and unity prevail."

"There's talk about resource wars now," Jessop said.

"And that is related to the issue more than the others," said the prophet. Jessop shook his head, not understanding.

"The most terrible wars on Earth were also the holy wars. The great religions of Old Earth unified against each other and fought."

"United Christendom prevailed," said Jessop. "But at the cost of the planet."

"Aye. What if we could have won the war with the loss of only a single continent? Would that not have been better than the whole world?"

"Aye, of course."

"So it is how I see this war coming with Hyrax and Enskari."

"You'll sacrifice millions of people on Enskari for the sake of Hyrax?"

"For the sake of Coronam. For the entire system."

The gardener stood up and walked heavily to the sick tree, spit on his hands, rubbed them together, and swung his ax into the trunk.

"There is an order to our lives and our society, and the decline of that order is at the heart of all strife. It is this order which fosters unity. Holiness is obedience. Obedience is stability. Stability is peace."

The sound of chopping echoed off the walls of the courtyard in crisp clean thumps.

"On Old Earth the shards of religion reunited. Christians of all sects came together. It was God's will to reassemble his children, but the fractures were too deep. We came up short. The thousands of religions became four, then three. Those final three were all descendants of Abraham: Jew, Muslim, and Christian. It should have been easy to finish the work, to unite the world again, but we fell short and the wars continued. That is when God gave us the miracle of Coronam, his holy crown."

The chopping stopped. The gardener put down his ax and leaned against the tree. It fell over in a crack of splinters and a splash of leafy branches.

"We were separated a long time. God's test. Now that the worlds are connected again, we mustn't fail. There is an order, there is tradition. We must not fail to keep it."

"Your Holiness, I cannot in good conscience say that the Queen of Enskari is any less holy than the Prince of Hyrax. Brandon has done terrible things on Silangan – slavery. Genocide. Zabel is loved by her people like he is not. She is as strong if not stronger than her father. Brandon is cruel and greedy. He peoples his court with bastards and hoards treasure while his people starve. Zabel's reign, as near as we can tell—"

"People are starving everywhere," the prophet said. "And nay, Brandon is not the prince I would have him be, but he is the prince we need."

"Why?"

"Rebellion. The Millers, Mumblers, Bucklers, Tremblers. Reformationites."

"Aye, some of them are very radical, but the Enskaran church is nearly identical to the Orthodox Saved."

"Nay, it's not."

"It would only take a word from you and it would be. You don't even have to make it a law. Just a temporary dispensation for a single woman ruler."

"Do you know what's the matter with that tree down there?"

"What? Which one?"

"The one the gardener cut down? It has a disease, sour-rot. It's a disease. A nasty one. It won't kill the tree, but it'll change it into something else. The fruit will become bitter, nearly inedible. The rind hard as leather, the leaves will cut flesh. There's no mention of it on Old Earth. It's a local disease. A remnant of the original flora perhaps. Or a mutation. A mutation." He said the word again, tasting it as if it were as bitter as the fruit. "See how it's already spread to that other tree? The gardener will take those limbs down with the yellow leaves. He'll cut it at the trunk and pray it stops there. If it doesn't, he'll take the whole tree down and any others."

"I get it," said Jessop a little impatiently. "He's a purger, but—"

"Humanity was broken because of rot like that. We have only to look at Old Earth and see how mutations disrupted safety and peace. The institutions that built the greatest societies were eroded by compromises and dispensations."

"But the church of today is different than what it was at the time of the Unsettling. Much different. Things change."

"We must draw a line, brother Jessop. We must defend humanity against itself. It's a slippery slope. By God's mercy we have made it this far, but we must stop now. We must maintain our traditions. The way things are now is the way they should be. It is the only hope for humanity. This is what God has shown me. As certain as I draw breath and will eat of those healthy trees this summer, I know we must hold the line. We have order in this society. It is those malcontents who threaten it. Change is the enemy."

The gardener cut branches and piled them up.

Jessop said, "Millions may die. Saved who were just born in the wrong place."

"If we must lose half the orchard, to save the other half, so be it."

Eren glanced at the guard on the porch with them. A native Templer, stout and pale. The scar on his face a mark of his class, guild, and purpose. Sworn to the security of the church. Lowborn but noble in his vocation.

"Do not think that I am an aberration, Kendall," the prophet said, using Jessop's first name. "I'll tell you this because I see your soul is troubled. This has been the goal of every prophet since before the planets reestablished communication. This plan was passed down to me. We have never had the might before. Brandon allows us finally to achieve this. We no longer need to compromise. We now have the might to withstand and direct. And not a moment too soon. It is God's will that at this time when the people are resisting our guidance that we have the ability to truly correct them."

The gardener took a saw and cut a branch of a neighboring tree with yellowing leaves.

"You must see the miracle in this, brother Jessop," the prophet said, returning to formality. "We are called the Saved because God saved us from the ruins of Old Earth. Like he guided Moses through the Red Sea, he gave us an exodus across the stars. It was the miracle we needed when we needed it. Brandon is another one. He is our ax to cut out the rot and put the garden in order. The miracle we need when we need it. There are herds of golden calves upon the worlds, brother Jessop."

"And Zabel is Aaron? I don't see it. The queen is ignored outside of Enskari. Claremond couldn't care less. Lavland's under control."

"The pretender on Enskari is a symbol. In the hearts of dissenters, she is an ember that can ignite a holocaust. Her destruction will be a blow of obedience."

"And Hyrax will invade and occupy."

"Accompanied by the church."

"And the wealth of one world will be transferred to another."

"There is an order of status. This is the way. Rank earns resources. Hyrax has shown its supremacy over Enskari by remaining faithful. But don't worry. There are faithful on Enskari yet. It won't be razed. Only cleansed."

Jessop cleared his throat and kept his face turned away. The gardener piled the cut branches and wiped his head with a handkerchief.

Eren said, "When the work is over, we'll put away our tools. Brandon will be blunted or removed. Peace in the system. Order restored. Glory to God."

"Seems a little arbitrary," Jessop said.

"Explain."

"How is it we've chosen this moment to be enshrined and not another?"

"Have you seen the abominations from Jareth's World?"

"No."

"They are mutant monsters. Their skin is like scales. They are more lizard than man. They have inner eyelids. Their worship is as primitive as rain dances. Would we be that?"

"There's no connection—"

"There's only connection!"

Eren's raised voice drew the gardener's gaze. He saw the prophet then and threw himself to the ground prostrate.

"Arise, good and faithful servant," Eren called down to him. "Carry on your work."

The gardener got up slowly, bowed low several times, and then hurried off, pushing his wheelbarrow full of trimmings.

"I often envy the simplicity of men like that gardener," Eren said.

"He's a bondsman. Practically a slave."

"He is content. He knows his place. He is useful and is free from the weight carried by nobler beings. Noble is not a rank, but a responsibility. Noble above non-gentry, monarch above noble, prophet above monarch."

"Man above woman."

"Of course. And Saved above gentile, civilized above savage. This is the order we are to maintain. This is our charge."

"Rich above poor?"

"Aye," Eren said. "For that is God's mark of grace. Wealth allowed the Saved to be Saved."

Jessop sighed.

"Brother Jessop, how have you come so far in the church to still have these doubts?"

"On Claremond the church functioned differently."

"Used to," Eren corrected him.

"Aye," said Jessop. "Used to."

"Well now you know the truth of it. Can you continue?"

"Aye, of course," he said. "Enskari?"

"The worlds are facing population problems," said the prophet. "We've multiplied and our resources are limited. Wars are useful. They are the fire after a harvest. A culling would not be so bad."

Jessop bit his lip.

"We are the guardians of the species," Eren said, putting his hand on Jessop's shoulder. "The species. Not one man, not one house or even one world. All of humanity. We must safeguard them, cut out the disease and maintain the traditions. To do that sometimes we do things that are not pleasant. We must play politics. We ally with the avaricious Prince Brandon of Hyrax."

"And make a minister from Claremond First Assistant to the prophet."

Eren smiled. "Aye," he said. "Politics. But don't take it so hard. You're young and it's good for me to have a pupil again. Just never contradict or doubt me in public. Ever."

"Nay, Your Holiness," Jessop said.

Eren stood up and stretched. The guard stepped forward, ready to move.

"Besides, Kendall, the war may never come. We have purgers on Enskari who may kill the pretender before it comes to that."

CHAPTER TEN

Poachers Beware:
  All wild livestock is the property of the king.
  The penalty for killing one of the king's bears is death.
  The penalty for killing one of the king's boars is death.
  The penalty for killing one of the king's stags is death.
  The penalty for killing one of the king's fowl is death.
  The penalty for wood taking, root digging, mushroom gathering, or seed collecting is two and twenty lashes.
  The penalty for willful trespass upon the king's hunting acres is two and twenty years servitude.
Official Notice; Posted and Proper
Hyraxian High Game Warden

19, Seventh-Month, 937 NE – Venison Hall, Royal Hunting Lodge near Soria, Hyrax

He'd gone to bed drunk or he'd have recognized the danger from the creaking door. Instead of threat, Prince Brandon turned the sound into a fold of his dream, justified it, used it in his fantasy. It was the women coming to please him, the Baroness Devall and her sister, Pamela. They were slinking up to his bedside, clothes falling away like autumn leaves, their bare skin erupting in gooseflesh in anticipation. They would submit to him now. Now he was more than noble, more than monarch. In his dream he was more than prophet. He was ruler of the entire system. He was Emperor.

The baroness had rebuffed his not-so-subtle overture to become his mistress – his next mistress. She'd been as impolite as possible without causing scandal and demanding retribution from him. Brandon was not used to being rebuffed, but then again, he'd never approached someone as high as the baroness before for the task of entertaining his bed. By her house and rank, she could be his queen. They could marry and all Hyrax would rejoice that their bachelor prince had finally settled down with someone worthy. But he was not for settling down. Besides his playtime, he dangled the hope of marriage like bait among the houses of Coronam. A union with him, the head of the most powerful court in the system, was one of the most powerful weapons of persuasion Hyrax possessed, that and its vast military. Both must be used wisely if Brandon were to achieve his dream.

The prince nuzzled his pillow, imagining it to be flesh – subdued, scented, noble flesh. Worshiping flesh.

It was a stumble and grunt that roused him, the misstep on the raised platform obscured by night darkness. The tone suggested male company and not the baroness or her sister.

He awoke reluctantly, not wanting to part with his dream. With wine-bleared and tired eyes, he saw a silhouette over his bed. In the gleam of starlight shining through his window, he saw the ax. Confused, he watched it rise above the shadow's head, pause and then fall toward his head.

He rolled left as the heavy blade plunged through his pillow and into his bed beneath.

Wrapped in satin sheets, he was cocooned and bound in his own bedding but away from the attacker.

The shadow pulled the ax free in a cloud of feathers.

Another shape moved to the other side.

It was a big bed – four could sleep under its embroidered canopy – but it was not a fort.

The new shadow – a man, wiry and poorly clothed – carried a blade, not a sword or a dagger, a blade. A kitchen knife, a peasant tool, a shard of sharpened metal, raw and rusty.

"Guards!" yelled the prince, writhing and kicking to free himself from his sheets, his senses focusing and firing. "Guards!"

The ax fell again, grazed the prince's calf, sunk handle-deep into the soft mattress, and caught on a spring beneath. The axman pulled and tugged and finally stepped onto the bed to dislodge it.

Brandon squirmed and freed his arms. He pulled himself the other way where the rusty blade thrust at his chest.

He rolled back and caught the man's wrist with both hands.

"Guards!" he grunted.

The man slammed his free hand into the back of his knife-wielding fist like a hammer driving a nail.

Unable to hold it, Brandon could only interfere with the trajectory of the steel. He pushed it as best he might, forcing it away from his chest and into his arm.

The blade sunk into his flesh up to its leather-wrapped handle. It penetrated his arm and stuck into the bed frame below. The gnarled hands that drove it released it, leaving it there like a stake in the lawn.

Brandon gripped the handle, but could not pull the blade free.

Flashing in the starlight, another knife – this one shorter and dirtier than the first that impaled his bicep. The man with the gnarled hands flicked it open with a thumb, its blade locking fast with a rusty click. Brandon saw the tip of it had been broken off, been reshaped and resharpened.

The axman stood above him on the bed. He heaved his weapon to his shoulder, raising it above his head in both hands.

Brandon struggled to move, but two inches of knife pinned his arm to his bed. He rolled and plucked it out, hearing the tear of sheets, the flutter of feathers, the rip of flesh. He felt the pain then, the burn in his arm unlike anything he'd felt before, deep and through. A fire in his flesh. A fire.

The room erupted in fire.

Screams and flames. His canopy bed an orange light. The man with the ax, a conflagration of burning rags and glowing steel. His frame a picture of blazing cloth and melting flesh.

Horrible howls were sucked into the jellied fire and fed it brighter and hotter.

The man with the knife rushed to the window, the air behind him a wave of angry hisses – a swarm of crossbow bolts finding his back in needle-thump bites.

He staggered but moved forward, and crashed into the glass.

Amid the swarm of bolts, a lance found his neck, pierced it, slowed, and stopped half its length deep. He ceased then, his body on one side of the open window, his blood dripping from the point of the lance on the other.

It was surreal and distracted the prince for a moment until the smell of the cooking man and burning bedclothes stung his nose. He rolled off the bed and kicked the smoldering silks away.

Yelling men surrounded him. They rushed this way and that. They pulled the man from the window and sprayed the royal bed with chemical extinguishers, filling the room with white smoke to mingle with the fat, black, sooty cloud.

Raw napalm still burning on the man did not extinguish so easily. Guards pulled the smoldering remains from the bed and doused them deep and long with dry fire retardant. The dead man sizzled and spat, popped like water in cooking grease before the flames settled into a dying hiss.

Prince Brandon tried to stand, but hands held him down.

A stretcher appeared and was placed beside him. Gauntleted fingers lifted him onto it. Someone was kind enough to cover his privates with a coat.

Beyond the coat Brandon saw then his burned feet and winced.

Four men lifted the litter into the air and at a double march carried the prince out of his bedchamber to the resident doctor.

"I'm going to want some answers about this!" Brandon roared to the room. "Get them!"

★   ★   ★

The burns were superficial, the ax cut a nuisance, but the knife through Brandon's left arm was serious and threatened to leave the prince crippled for life. Surgeons worked on him through the morning and the day, through the evening and well into the night before they finally wrapped the arm and set their regent to rest under a heavy dose of painkillers and triple guard.

He roused at noontime the next day from blank dreams of dull aches. No baroness, no emperor's crown. Just the gnawing soreness in his arm.

"Your Majesty."

Medics circled him and crowded the bed. One tried to put a thermometer in his mouth; another studied him earnestly through thick spectacles. Everyone was talking at once.

"There was muscle damage."

"Possibility of infection."

"I don't think the blade was poisoned."

"Slight scarring on your right ankle."

"Leave me," the prince said but his throat was too dry and no one heard him.

"A sling for two months."

"Maybe more."

"Shouldn't be a limp."

He coughed to clear his throat.

"Don't strain yourself."

Fingers went toward his eyes followed by a small glow light pointed at his face.

"Slight nausea is to be expect—"

"Leave me!" he roared.

The room fell silent, all eyes big and frightened.

They retreated like receding ripples in a pond, bowing as they went.

Using his good arm, Brandon sat up in the bed. His head was groggy and his mouth was parched.

"Bring us water and our ministers. Now."

Pages appeared with water and food.

Brandon drank nearly a liter and ate a handful of grapes and some cheese. He looked around the room. It was not his royal chambers. It was some place in the deep bowels of the lodge. Underground. Windowless. It smelled of moist earth and old wood, heavy and still. Sound absorbed in meters of earth. It felt like a bomb shelter. It probably was a bomb shelter.

Minister Tobias, Admiral Mola, Captain Nicandus of the palace guard, and Sir Kolbert entered the room together. All looked dire and concerned except for Kolbert, who smirked like it was all a joke.

"What are you grinning at, Kolbert?" said Brandon.

"You are a tough bastard, Brandon," he said. "You can fight off two assassins in your sleep."

Brandon scowled at his friend, trying to hold him in a cold stare, but couldn't. He'd known Kolbert too long to intimidate him with a scowl. Brandon snorted, then laughed and grimaced when he shifted his arm. He lay back on a pile of pillows and looked over his men. "Where's D'Angelo?"

"The holy apostle from Temple is not well," Nicandus said.

"You mean he's drunk," said Brandon.

Tobias nodded.

"What about his minsters? What about that one man who seems to actually know what he's doing?"

"Minister Rendelle?" said Nicandus.

"Aye, that's the one."

"I've not invited him, sire," said Tobias.

"And that kept him away?"

"I've tried to keep this as intimate as possible."

Tobias glanced at Kolbert, who smiled and said, "He tried."

"Fine," said Brandon, waving his good hand as if dismissing the bother like a fly. "What happened?"

Captain Nicandus stepped forward. He was in full dress uniform, velvet cape and gold cap. With a salute and a snap, he removed his cap and clicked his heels before speaking. "It appears that three men breached the grounds. Two made it to your room. All are dead."

"Who were they?"

"We don't know yet."

"How'd they get in?"

"From the south. They killed two pickets, two house guards, and three servants."

"I saw what happened to two of the assassins. What of the other men?"

"The other was killed by a picket," Nicandus said.

Minister Tobias dragged a chair over and sat by the side of the bed. He ran his fingers wearily through his beard. "He was cornered outside the grounds waiting with a cart. He died trying to escape. As for the women—"

"Women?"

Tobias nodded. "Two women poisoned themselves after killing your door guards."

"A suicide attack?"

"We don't know. Could have been an accident."

"Where were they found?"

"You know that little closet across from the privy by your room?" said Kolbert. "You know the one. The one where those twins entertained us last spring? They were in there. Can't say they died with their boots on. Or bras." He winked.

This time Kolbert's levity irked Brandon. The man was the closest thing he had to a jester. He was three months older than the prince; they'd grown up together. Kolbert had spent his four and thirty years of life in the pursuit of entertainment. He was an infamous playboy who'd broken up more noble marriages than the pox. What he had in frivolity he lacked in discretion but then made up for in aim. He'd killed four men in duels that Brandon knew about. One of them over a gambling debt, the others, of course, over women.

"So the pickets and doors. What about the hundred other soldiers between the fence and my bed? Do breasts and bows explain how they got so close?"

Tobias shook his head. "They had to have had help. Inside. And they had money."

"They were organized," said Mola. "At least one of them was from off-world."

"Where?"

"Temple."

"Temple?" Brandon felt his ears grow hot.

Tobias nodded. "One of the women."

"So we have the prophet to thank for this?"

Tobias shook his head and stroked his beard back into a white cone. "Nay, nay. Eren wouldn't do this."

"Someone in his court?"

"I doubt it."

Admiral Mola said, "They were most likely mercenaries, Your Majesty. Some of them at any rate. The one with the ax showed signs of extended zero-grav exposure."

"How? He was a spent match."

"Bones," said Mola.

"And who fired a flamer into our bed?"

Nicandus straightened and stared straight ahead. "That was one of my men," he said. "He was the first there. It's all he had. He had to act fast. The killer was about to—"

"A for effort, F for making our bed into a barbecue."

Nicandus dropped his eyes. "He's under arrest," he said. "I'm hoping you'll forgive—"

"Aye, okay. If I don't execute him, I'll give him a medal."

Nicandus kept his gaze down.

A stream of dust fell from an upper support and landed on Kolbert's shoulder. "I'd say it was Lavland." He swept the dust away with the flick of a silk handkerchief. "Revenge for conquering their greedy little planet."

"I don't think so," said Tobias.

Kolbert produced a flask from under his tunic and unscrewed the lid. "Claremond? Enskari? The Silangan savages?" he said. "You have no shortage of enemies, Brandon. Homegrown and across the worlds. Great men make great enemies."

"I think the man who stabbed me was local," said Brandon.

"Why?" Tobias asked.

"Something familiar about him. His hands. His knife, maybe. Aye," he said. "The knife."

"You were stabbed with some sort of skinning thing," said Kolbert. "A butcher's tool. Probably had pig blood on it. Make sure you keep on your pills. Not just for the rash anymore, old friend." He winked.

"Not that knife," said Brandon. "The other one. The flip knife."

"I didn't see that," Nicandus said.

"I did," said Brandon.

"Bring us the weapons from the attack," said Nicandus and a guard left the room.

"It might have fallen out the window," said Brandon.

"See if it did," Nicandus said and another guard hurried away.

Kolbert offered Brandon his flask but the prince refused. He drank another glass of water and had another piece of cheese.

"It's good to see you have an appetite," said Tobias.

"Don't think I haven't noticed you sat down, Tobias," Brandon said. "That means there's a long discussion ahead."

"It can wait until you're better."

"If you thought that, you wouldn't be in that chair."

"Nay, I wouldn't be." He sounded tired.

Brandon recognized then that Tobias was wearing the same tunic he'd worn at the welcome dinner the night he'd been attacked.

"Have you not slept?"

"There's been much to do. Word of this incident mustn't get out."

"I think it would do wonders," said Kolbert. "Show what a fighter prince we have. Put the fear into his enemies."

Admiral Mola cleared his throat.

"What are you doing here?" said the prince.

"You invited me," Kolbert said. "Fun and games. Hunting quail in the morning, stag in the afternoon, and beaver at night. Don't you remember?"

"Not you," said Brandon. He was growing tired of his flippant friend. He was attacked in his bed. Nearly murdered. Kolbert wasn't helping. He was about to ask him if he didn't have something else to do, when Tobias spoke.

"Admiral Mola brings news," he said.

"Well?" said Brandon. "What is it?"

Tobias rubbed his eyes and Mola shifted on his heels. Captain Nicandus stayed at alert.

"Oh," Kolbert said. "Me. It's me, right? I can't hear this?"

"Oh for blazes, Tobias," said Brandon. "Just out with it."

No one spoke.

Kolbert finally said, "Perhaps I should—"

"For blazes!" said Brandon. "If Kolbert had wanted me dead he could have killed me a thousand times. He needs me alive more than anyone. I pay his bills."

"Ouch," Kolbert said. "But true."

Tobias gave a heavy sigh. "All right. First to the matter at hand. I suspect either your brother or Enskari is behind this attack. I lean toward Enskari. This has Nolan Brett's stink about it. That damned dirty devil. We should have sent the Templer purgers after him."

"You sent Templer purgers to Enskari? Hate to be them," said Kolbert, tipping his flask.

"May I continue?" Tobias asked with obvious irritation.

Kolbert winked and tipped his flask for another sip. Brandon took inventory of his injuries while he waited for Tobias to heal the one to his pride.

"The timing of this attack is too perfect," Tobias finally said. "Retaliation for the ministers. There's money and influence and deviousness in this."

"I think it's your brother," said Nicandus and then blanched.

"Why?"

Pulling himself back to attention, he said, "The purgers have done nothing on Enskari yet. If I remember, they have just arrived. This plot was planned before and we suspect it had help from within the court."

"Eric is on Terel. He's a continent away."

"The perfect place to be," said Nicandus. Sweat poured down his forehead, but he kept his eyes straight and his back straighter. The captain of the guard had been a constant presence, seldom if ever offering an opinion on anything. He had never been so outspoken before and the change did not go unnoticed by Brandon.

"True, we have many enemies," said Brandon. "We don't need to look off-world for those who would have us dead. There are millions of peasants who don't know their place here on Hyrax and blame me for their failings and lightning fires. There are gentry in my own court who don't appreciate their station and desire more. There may even be family who covet my throne. There are Saved and gentiles, savage and soothsayer who'd see the fall of the House of Drust."

"The house wars are over but not forgotten," said Kolbert.

Tobias threw him a look.

"Just gossip. Nothing treasonable."

"It stinks of Nolan Brett," Tobias said. "It stinks to high heaven of it."

"Why don't we just bribe the man?" said Brandon.

"He is ambitious and devious but there's nothing we can give him better than what he has, short of your throne."

"What? He's shunned by the system. He's cast out of the Saved. Excommunicated. He's been sentenced to death by the prophet. Whole worlds want his blood. He's doomed. Tell me we can't buy him with clemency."

"We can't."

"He's that loyal?"

Tobias rubbed his eyes. "He's no fool."

Brandon felt his blood pressure spike. It was easy to grow frustrated with Tobias. Even when he wasn't physically tired, his advisor always seemed spiritually so. His vigor was fading but he was too valuable to dismiss, even when he gave cryptic patronizing answers to direct questions. He was the oldest of his ministers. A man in his seventies Brandon had inherited from his father. A devoted man, twice widowed, all children grown and gone. Now he lived only for government. He could retire but would not, stating, "I'd rather be useful." He was a pragmatic peacemaker. Brandon knew he didn't relish the drive for conquest the way his new ministers did, but Tobias had gone along dutifully and offered his prudent advice to the best of his ability. He understood the nuances of diplomacy better than anyone in Brandon's court. He'd squared off with ministers from all the Saved worlds. He knew Nolan Brett from before his rise in Zabel's court.

Even as a noble courtier, Tobias had warned his monarch of that man's danger. He'd told Brandon many times to beware Sir Nolan's ambition; it rivaled his own.

Brandon took a deep breath to calm himself. "All right, Tobias, until we know differently, we'll assume it's Enskari behind this. What shall we do?"

Nicandus made to speak but did not.

Tobias said, "Mola brings news of lost ships."

"The Maaraw thing? You've been in space a long time. We know all about it."

"Nay, sire," said the admiral. "The *Astro* has returned. The *Silangan* and the *Bandima* were captured by Sommerled."

"What!"

"We lost over a thousand tons of cargo," said the admiral. "Mostly silver. Some gold. A good amount of sugar, lead, salt, timber, and grain. Mostly silver though."

"God blast them to hell!" Brandon threw his glass at the wall, where it shattered.

An alarmed medic came forward with a bottle of pills. He retreated quickly after seeing the look on Brandon's face.

"Details," Brandon said to Mola.

"The convoy was attacked by two ships. The new design. Fast. Well armed. I don't know how they found us, but they did and swept in. They outflanked the *Astro* and caused it to flee for its life down the well. The other ships were taken. The *Astro* crew saw surrender lights as it ran."

"A thousand tons, and they ran?"

"They were outmatched," said Mola.

"They were scared," put in Tobias. "Sommerled himself threatened them with the *Pempkin*."

Brandon flopped back in frustration. "Damn Captain Clelland. I don't know whether I'm angrier at him for spacing a hundred men or for letting two of them live to tell about it."

"It's become a rallying cry on Enskari," said Tobias.

"Actually to every mariner going against us," Mola said. "Some Claremond pirate mentioned it in an attack – before we burned them to cinders."

"Well, at least they weren't spaced," said Brandon. "God forbid they die by vacuum instead of fire."

"You're bleeding," said Kolbert, pointing to Brandon's arm with his flask.

Brandon ignored him. "Tobias, how much have we lost to Enskari pirates, this year?"

Mola said, "They weren't all Enskari—"

"How much!" Stitches snapped under his bandage.

Tobias said, "With this? Six thousand tons, give or take. Two dozen ships."

"Value?"

"It's difficult to measure," he said but added quickly, "Worth more than the entire combined economies of Claremond and Temple for the year."

"Lost in half a year...."

"Aye, sire."

"Those are shit planets," said Kolbert. "All they export from Claremond is moldy cheese. From Temple, moldy books." He grinned at his own wit.

Brandon said, "And they wonder why we space them."

"There's plenty more gold on Silangan," Kolbert said.

"It's not just that we're losing it. It's that we're giving it to our enemies, you fool," snapped Brandon. "Admiral, how goes the armada?"

"There we have good news," said Mola. "It's coming along nicely. It will be unstoppable."

"Even with the loss of the gold?"

Mola hesitated then said carefully, "Raids on our convoys have put us behind. But for every ship that gets taken five make it through."

"I remember when that number was ten. Twenty."

Mola nodded. "The pirates are more aggressive. We are stretched. The armada, however, will settle it all."

"Which brings me to my next bit of bad news," Tobias said.

"Worse than my treasure fleet being stolen?" Brandon felt the penetrating eyes of his advisor. They no longer frightened him as they once did, but they still commanded his attention. He realized his temper had gotten the better of him. In a calm, cool voice, he said, "What is it?"

"My spies tell me that Enskari has sent colony ships to Tirgwenin."

"Oh for blazes," growled Brandon through gritted teeth.

"They went west. We have little control over the western route," added Mola.

"Our guess is they're already there," Tobias said. "They needed to be there at least a month ago to take advantage of the growing season."

Brandon looked at Tobias, letting the serene, determined mood of his advisor seep into him like a cool drink of water. He was prince, soon to be emperor. There'd be setbacks. He had to expect them. Forcing his voice flat, he said, "Is there more?"

Tobias said, "Though we don't know much about Tirgwenin, we expect it to be at least as rich as Silangan. It is harder to get to, but the people there should be easier to conquer. The planet is protected by a ring that'll play havoc with ship-to-ground elevators. The remoteness of it will make it hard to attack and being on our far flank would offer a strategic base from which to raid our eastern trade routes across the Gap."

"You mean the routes already being raided?"

"Aye," said Mola. "More so. Much more so. From there they could hit Silangan."

Tobias said, "If they set up permanent settlements, it will be difficult to uproot them."

Brandon laughed, surprising himself. "Who cares?"

"What?"

"Who cares? It's a stupid little colony. They'll die. How many people are we talking about? A thousand?"

"More like two hundred."

Chuckling, Brandon said, "This isn't a crisis. It's interesting, but it's nothing. We lost thousands to settle Silangan. They'll never last on Jareth's World."

"Didn't the prophet give it to you anyway?" asked Kolbert. "I mean, by holy dictate the planet belongs to us – *you*. They have no claim."

"A landing is one thing," said Tobias, "a permanent base is another. A lasting occupation is a grave threat to us and the order we represent. Their culture will spread – their population, their power. Think of the treasure they can pull out of there."

"Two hundred people on a foreign planet is nothing to worry about, Tobias. As I understand it, Jareth's World is wild. Uncivilized. Like all the worlds that were found at the Unsettling. We had better tech then, and think of the thousands we lost. Turning Coronam's jewels into a place fit to live was the hardest thing we've ever done. Think of the thousands who died of plant poisonings, animal attacks, disease – starvation, before the crops took; lightning with no shielding. Those colonists will have all that *and* scaled savages."

"But—"

"They're doomed," said the prince and laughed. "Noble Tobias, you are a worrying one. You find threat in everything. We should celebrate this. Two hundred Enskarans are going to die. I take that as good news. I'm glad you thought to bring me some."

"There is worry, Your Majesty," Tobias said. "If Enskari gets a base—"

"It'll bankrupt them. What does it cost to get to Tirgwenin?"

Mola said, "Along the western route? Millions. It's the most costly, desolate, and dangerous journey I can imagine."

"Resupply would be equally expensive and dangerous?"

"Oh aye," said Mola.

"It took us ten years to subdue Silangan. Let's be stupidly generous and say they can do it in five, which is impossible," said Brandon. "That means it'll be four years too late. The armada sails in a year. Enskari will be purged. Problem solved. They can put a hundred thousand people on Tirgwenin – without a civilized world backing them, they're just a bunch of starving marooned apostates."

"Sire," said Tobias. "There is—"

"Fine." Brandon waved his hand again. "Mola, send some ships to check it out. Find this settlement and destroy it. Capture or kill them. They're trespassers."

"Finding them will be harder than a needle in a haystack," Mola said, his eyes wide and worried. "And the cost—" Another wave of the prince's hand cut him short. "Aye, of course. It'll be done, Your Majesty," he said.

"Thank you," said Tobias.

A soldier entered the room and presented himself to Nicandus with a snap salute. He presented Nicandus with a small knife before turning sharply on his heels and leaving again. The captain of the guard examined the weapon briefly and passed it to Brandon.

"Why did we want to see this piece of junk?" asked Kolbert.

"Aye," Brandon said. "I remember this knife. Look at this peasant blade. See how the tip was broken off but then reworked to save it?"

"Looks like junk to me," said Kolbert.

"Do you not remember it, Nicandus? Two years ago? The poacher? We found a blade tip in a bone of a slaughtered pig?"

"Aye," said the captain. "The warden found it. He searched Soria until they found the knife it matched. We hanged the owner."

Brandon said, "This is that knife."

"How can you be so sure?" said Kolbert.

"I remember it. I stabbed it into the poacher's son as an example."

"Did you kill him?"

"I thought I did."

"Bastards have brothers," Kolbert said.

"Aye," said Brandon. "There you see, Tobias?"

"What, Your Majesty?"

"It's not Eric or Brett or Enskari. It's just a vengeful peasant."

Tobias didn't look so certain.

To Nicandus, Brandon said, "Punish the peasants. Decimate the local population."

"It shall be done."

"Killing one in ten, isn't that what that means?" said Kolbert.

"Not right?" said Brandon, reaching for his friend's flask.

"You're the prince."

Soon to be emperor, he thought. He took a drink. "Nicandus. Make it one in six."

CHAPTER ELEVEN

The current economic stresses facing the kingdom – decreased tax revenue from a harried population facing now decades of declining harvests, old debts from the war of ascension and new demands for stronger defenses – are being exacerbated by a new and unforeseeable pressure: Silangan treasure.

The enormous increase in the silver supply from Silangan mines among the civilized worlds has created an inflationary cycle that is devaluing currency on all planets. The Hyraxian dollar, still the standard currency for interworld trade, is now figured to be worth about two thirds of what it was fifty years ago due to the nonstop minting of new silver coins. While prices in the marketplace have kept up due to necessity, tribute has not. This deficit will only increase.

Since Enskari does not have access to such off-world resources, adjustments must be made for the health of the Crown: taxes and tariffs need to be modified immediately and then indexed to account for inflation.

Enskari Ministry of Commerce Memo
4, First-Month, 933 NE

30, Seventh-Month, 937 – Vildeby, Enskari

The streets from the port elevator to Government House were lined with cheering people. Police with linked arms struggled to keep them away from Sir Ethan Sommerled's coach as it passed. He stood in it waving his hat in large gregarious motions so as to be seen by the farthest spectator.

He'd never seen the street as clean. It'd been swept and washed. He saw for the first time the cobblestones shining in the summer sun. Above him, strung between telegraph poles, were garlands of fragrant flowers. They rained soft petals down on the procession as it passed beneath. When it turned into the heart of town, the blossoms were joined by streamers of ticker tape.

The crowd's roaring applause echoed between houses into a deafening din and Ethan thought to plug his ears but did not, continuing to wave his hat and smile and be loved by his countrymen.

Behind him, every once in a while, he was sensible of the change in tumult from the throng. Cheers were replaced with boos and hisses, shouts and curses as the captured Hyraxians passed by. The threatening tones would then be put aside for louder cheers, shouts, and awestruck whispers as the trains of treasure were carted next up the street.

The carriage Ethan rode in was from the Royal Collection. It was white and red, and gilded with gold and jewels. Six purebred horses, tall and groomed, easily carried it along. The queen had never ridden in this carriage, he was sure. It was too high and too exposed for a monarch whose loveliness and strength quaked the worlds. Ethan knew the carriage. He'd seen it used by Zabel's father, Theodore the Thrice, before his death. Now, Ethan, lowborn but knighted, loyal and loved by the queen, stood where only a king had stood before.

He waved to the rich and poor alike, but mostly the poor. He knew he was a symbol. He knew the parade was as much for his queen as for him. They were both symbols of the new evolution, the glorious new society. He, low become high, loved by all Enskari. She, female become ruler, loved by all Enskari. Or at least all the Enskarans that mattered.

Past the commerce centers with their tall stone buildings with the long lightning aerials, they necessarily passed beside the Reedy River and through the burned district. A sudden storm and plasma leak had burned six city blocks to the ground ten years before and it had yet to be rebuilt. Where before there'd been smoke-billowing factories weaving textiles and making plastics, now there were hovels and shacks. It was a shanty town, the Enskari version of the Hyraxian favela he'd seen from Lavland to Silangan, a pocket of poverty in the greatest city on the planet. The faces of the desperate and destitute were the same on all the civilized worlds. If it weren't for the flags, he could imagine himself on Temple or Claremond.

The parade organizers had done their best to conceal the slum, if not from him atop the high carriage, then from the people who lined the streets. Also, too, he thought, from the captives who might yet be returned to their homes. Politics and image were important. The victory parade was proof of that. What good is filling your captives with fear if you show them your weakness as well?

Ethan understood it as a weakness. Most of the nobility were noble in name only. He knew bondsmen who'd sold the last half of their lives to a factory to pay for their children's education. That was noble. His own grandfather was one of those. Ethan Sommerled never knew him of course, but he was remembered in the family for his sacrifice.

Ethan had seen the in-name-only nobility. He'd fought in the revolution when some mighty houses rose against the House Genest after Theodore died without a male heir. They made terrible wars, killed count and commoner alike in a mad dash for his throne. Their greed cost the planet an eighth of its population by official record.

Ethan had been in space but came home to fight in that terrible war. A lowborn, he could never command, so acted as sergeant and navigator apprentice until the day over Southland when the captain of his cutter was sucked out a six-centimeter hull breach.

He'd seized his chance. He took command of the wounded ship and while it spewed air and plasma in low orbit, he ran rings around a rebel corvette and three tenders. He dropped them each into the sea. Four hundred Saved lost on their side.

He was knighted for it.

He'd never forget seeing the queen for the first time, kneeling before her. She held the heavy sword in both hands as she tapped his shoulders with it. Her eyes were scared but firm – the look of a soldier who knew their orders and accepted their fate, but had yet to be tested. The look of one who understood the sacrifice asked of them and would give it. He loved her the better for that. If he was loyal to the House Genest before that moment, he was a devoted zealot to Queen Zabel afterward.

Looking beyond the heads of the crowd, over the fabric walls erected between road and ruin, Ethan saw the faces of the poorest of the city. There were many of them. Many more than he remembered. They stared at him with dirty faces, balancing on rooftops that threatened to collapse beneath them, topple them into garbage and gutter. Some watched, others waved, drawn into the pageantry of an event they could only see the top of. Most, however, looked on with disconnected interest. They stared at him with a cold hatred that sent chills down his back. Ethan's heart sank as he understood. Nothing he'd done would affect them. This triumph was not theirs. They felt more kin to the captured than to the conquerors. The carts of gold and silver, sugar, oak, and cotton might as well have been painted billboards for all the good it would do them. Their miserable lot would not be improved. If anything, he represented a threat to them. This parade, meant to inspire Enskari, would enrage Hyrax. When they came – and they would come Ethan knew, these poor unfortunates would be the first grist tossed into the mill to stop them.

Ethan waved his hat wider, faster, more furiously. Some of the merchants on the street paused their cheers to wonder at him. He caught himself and stopped, realizing he looked manic, like a man signaling a distant ship on the horizon from a waterless island.

He turned back to the crowd of more fortunates, away from the hopeless starving poor to the middle classes, the merchants who might benefit from his catch. After the nobles had taken their cut, this cotton would go to their factories for cloth, this sugar to their bakeries for breads. He hoped that some of that might find its way to the poorest of the city. Stolen or cast off, they might get something to improve their lives from his efforts.

It was the best he could hope for and he had to be content in that.

Things were as they were. *God would raise and lower his Saved to their proper stations as he would.* It was a Buckler aphorism and the thought of it was heresy even on Enskari. It challenged the nobility, it challenged order. But so did he. So did his queen and her throne.

The carriage turned toward Government House, past blockades keeping the lower classes out, and up the long grassy courtyard road. He saw the coaches of the nobility waiting for him along the route. It comforted him to see opulence and wealth and he quickly forgot the dirty denizens of the slums. God had chosen him to be among the nobles. Though born of merchants, his house was noble now. He belonged here now. He forgot about the sugar to the poor and thought only of the jewels to his queen.

He slowed his waving, adopting more subtle, dignified gestures, less effusive. Reserved and confident, acting like he belonged here.

The nobles didn't cheer. It wasn't their way. They stood in clustered groups along the grass road, servants offering them wine and cakes, watching the procession through opera glasses and under wide veiled hats. Some nodded to him in greeting, most looked grim and grave, wearing their traditional mask used when facing an uncertain situation. Some however stared at him with the same loathsome disdain he'd seen from atop the shanties. No. Worse than he'd seen. These looks were of jealousy and hatred.

As if to reflect his changing mood, lightning struck to his left. In leaping sparks it ran down a column of inky black smoke. The thunder silenced the outside crowd only for a moment before it rose again louder as if the noise had been planned for his entrance.

In the sky Ethan saw no clouds but plenty of smog. Vildeby was not alone in this. Like the poor, it was a constant across the civilized world. He'd read it had been the same on Old Earth. He knew a little history, more than most. He'd studied it after being knighted, thinking that he needed a better education to mingle with the gentry. It took him only a single ball to realize that that wasn't the case. The past was nearly as meaningless to them as the future. They focused on the present, their current position and wants. It surprised him at first, threw him into a fit of depression actually, for a short time. He'd thought he'd find lofty minds in court. But like the poor who dared not think beyond their next meal, the gentry didn't think beyond their next party. He'd encountered a few high minds, a few great souls, the queen being paramount, but in the end he was disappointed to see that people were basically the same everywhere. He took it as a philosophical sign and used it to reinforce his beliefs and justify his rise and station.

The carriage halted before a red carpet. It stretched twenty meters into the building between a palisade of marble columns supporting nothing but sky. Between the columns stood the highest dignitaries, arranged in order of rank leading up to the marble steps beyond which Ethan saw the queen seated and waiting for him.

He climbed down from the carriage, bowed low with a flourish of his hat, stood up straight and marched up the carpet.

The carriage pulled away and curved around the loop, drawing the rest of the parade behind it.

At the bottom of the stairs, Ethan paused and bowed again before climbing them and bowing before his queen.

She extended her gloved and jeweled hand and he took it and kissed it. He breathed in the delicate perfume on the soft velvet garment before looking into her eyes. They were dazzlingly blue beneath her red hair. She was painted pale, as was her fashion. His own skin was a tawny bronze from sun and radiation and he felt a little ashamed of it as a mark of the laboring class.

If the queen minded or cared, she didn't show it. Instead she gestured for him to take a seat at her right.

"You are welcome, Sir Ethan," she said. "Let us see what you have done. Sit with us."

"Aye, Your Majesty."

Of course his chair was lower than hers, but it was the greatest honor he'd ever received. He saw looks of contempt ripple over the faces of the pale gentry when he sat.

The two highest members of the cabinet, the Ears of the queen, Sirs Edward and Nolan, stood on either side of them; Edward on the queen's left, Nolan on Ethan's right.

They all watched the parade pass without speaking. They might have been able to share a word, an aside spoken closely to overcome the noise, but no one did. The Ears stood and watched; the queen surveyed. The nobles finally took their eyes off the throne when the treasures came by, the bales of fiber, sacks of sugar, and stacks of silver and gold ingots. They applauded then, flapping their gloved hands together in muted appreciation.

When the last carts had passed, an hour after Ethan had sat down, the noble crowd moved closer.

Bugle sounds and military music struck up from some unseen band. A line of soldiers in parade marched in formation. In the midst of them, Ethan recognized Sir Gael Aderyn – Admiral Aderyn, he recalled.

The honor guard peeled off and Aderyn alone marched up the stairs. He had a confident step that went beyond his reputation as the most successful sailor of the planet. He was of a noble house, cousin to the queen, trained for leadership, gifted with courage. Ethan took note of his gait and mannerisms, thinking that while he had tried his best to act like he deserved to be there, Aderyn was born here.

At the top of the stair, the admiral clicked his heels and bowed his head. It was a small gesture, exact, refined, and practiced. It spoke volumes of their positions and Ethan regretted his earlier gushing, overdone bows.

"Admiral," said the queen in reply to his deference.

Aderyn's eyes shot from her to Nolan for an instant before landing on Ethan. There was something about that glance—

"Sir Ethan Sommerled," said Aderyn in his deep baritone voice. "Arise."

He did.

They stood face to face, a half meter apart. The same height within a centimeter, their eyes met, locked. Held.

Ethan's earlier giddiness evaporated under Aderyn's stare. The admiral had circumnavigated the system twice. He was a legend.

The admiral was three decades older than Ethan but his eyes were as sharp and vigorous as any man he'd ever met. They bored into his own like they were plumbing his soul. They made him want to turn away, to hide his face in shame, confess himself a pretender and beg for mercy, but he did not. He held, and after a long moment that felt like hours, felt his own eyes begin to peer into the admiral's and delve—

"You are awarded the Queen's Cross for valor," said the admiral, breaking into his thoughts.

A page with a red velvet pillow materialized beside them. The admiral removed the ribboned medal from atop it, lifted it over Ethan's head, and draped the award on his shoulders.

He caught Ethan's eye and winked at him. The effect on Ethan was like being shot, such was the surprise and wonder of it.

The bugle sounded and a cheer went up among the soldiers, loud and crisp. Beyond the barricades the crowds joined with shouts and whistles. The soldiers hurrahed. The gentry clapped politely.

Aderyn reached to shake the hand of Ethan, who gratefully took it. "Well done, sir," said the admiral.

Ethan's heart raced – terror turning to rapture. He mumbled, "Thank you, Sir— Admiral."

Aderyn leaned in and whispered in his ear, "You know, Ethan, your lot isn't half the cargo I brought in."

Ethan froze.

Aderyn broke out into a loud booming laugh. He slapped Ethan on the back so hard it made him stumble.

Ethan finally smiled.

"Aye, that's a spaceman," the admiral said. "Enjoy, my boy. We both know what else can be."

Ethan hadn't heard the phrase since his days as a merchant marine. It was a sailor's motto meant to say that things could be worse. The terrors of death in space, plasma fires and vacuum were beyond mention. It was the space sailor's version of the soldier's 'Eat, drink and be merry, for tomorrow we may die.' 'We both know what else can be.'

The phrase connected the two captains as nothing else could. A bond of calling and calamity. They were both sailor captains, their nerves and courage tested, their mettle confirmed. That was all that mattered. Everything else was trivia.

The queen stood and everyone bowed. Ethan matched his level to Aderyn's, a few degrees lower but not as low as it'd been before.

"We have called a ball in your honor, Ethan," said the queen.

He blushed when he heard her use his name.

The queen and her court led the others into the main hall, which was decorated with colored glowglobes and more flower garlands. An orchestra prepared and servants hurried with trays of wineglasses and plates of food, red grapes, sausage, and cheeses.

The queen took her throne and called the first dance.

"Sir Ethan," she said.

The room fell silent. The queen extended her hand.

Ethan bowed again and took it. The orchestra began. When Ethan didn't immediately move, the queen tugged his arm to wake him from his dream.

"What a day this is," he said and whisked Queen Zabel into a waltz.

The crowd applauded as was customary. Ethan barely heard them. He had ears only for the music, eyes only for his queen.

They danced and swept the floor for two rounds before the queen waved a silk kerchief to invite the rest of the party to join in.

The dance floor flooded with people. Ethan expected the queen to quit him then, to return to her throne, the gesture complete, but she didn't. She danced on with him, tugging his arm when he was timid and racing him to the tempo. She was light on her feet and Ethan could float on his.

He met her challenge and they spun and skipped amongst the other dancers like water down rapids. She laughed gaily and his grin was so wide he thought he'd dropped his ears.

Finally the music stopped and the dancers turned to applaud the orchestra and the queen.

Ethan bowed low to Zabel, thinking how he'd happily crawl across fire for her.

The queen flicked open her fan and cooled her neck before returning to her throne.

"Nay, Sir Ethan," she said to Ethan as he tried to follow her. "You stay and dance. Dance with all the maids. Be merry."

"Any dance now can be only a pale shadow to the one I've had," he said.

"Nonsense," she said. Her smile melted him. "Go and dance. Allow us to cool. This devilish makeup is like a blanket."

"Then we should have it off," he said before he could catch himself.

He looked at her in horror, but then she laughed. "Oh, you rogue," she said and went to her throne, where she was met with a tall glass of chilled wine.

Ethan looked around to see who else had heard him. He'd misspoke. He'd meant only that she should be comfortable, but even outside the innuendo minefield of the court, it could be misconstrued.

The orchestra began another dance, a formal one with lines and partners facing each other, one he wasn't prepared for. No one seemed to have heard what he'd said. He'd not spoken so loudly, and so with some relief, he left the dance floor in search of a cold drink.

"I can't believe you handed all this wealth over to the Crown." It was Captain Tir Hasin. Ethan knew him well. He'd headed the last expedition to Tirgwenin on his patent. The men he'd left there were scheduled to be removed and replaced with the new settlement, the one with Morgan and his Bucklers.

"I'm sure he took his share." They were joined by Sir Nolan Brett.

Ethan bowed to the Second Ear. "Sir Nolan," he said. "You honor me."

"What about it, Sir Ethan?" said Hasin. "Did you take a share?"

"The crew were paid," he said. "I left my share in the spoils for the Crown."

Hasin shook his head. "You're going to wish you had that money," he said. "Your planters will need things."

"It is a rich and bountiful country," Ethan said. "You said so yourself."

"If you get rid of the natives. They're all thieves and beggars. Cutthroat savages."

"At Rodawnoc perhaps," said Ethan. "But we're landing at Placid Bay. Hundreds of kilometers away."

"The natives—"

"Won't have history with us there," Ethan said, cutting him off. "They won't have complaint of our people."

Hasin bit his lip. Ethan knew his rebuke had hit home. The captain made to argue, but after glancing at the Queen's Cross around his neck, said merely, "They should be there by now. We're well into the season."

"Aye," said Ethan, taking some red grapes from a passing tray. "And your men on their way home."

Sir Nolan asked Hasin, "How many did you leave on Tirgwenin?"

"Six and twenty. At Rodawnoc. A hellish mosquito island on a terrible coast. Poor and plagued."

"It's on the equator," added Ethan. "Admiral Aderyn himself chose it as a location to spot Hyraxian incursion onto the planet. Because of the ring, it's one of the most likely landing zones. One day I'm sure there'll be a port there. Or nearby. But not now. It isn't the most pleasant place."

"It's to be abandoned?"

Ethan nodded. "Placid Bay is the best location for a new settlement. That's where they are. Ships can be inserted near Rodawnoc and then sail easily to that bay. It won't add more than a day or two to the journey."

"If the seas are calm," said Hasin with a growl. "Which they most often aren't."

Ethan threw him a look of his harshest disdain. It was difficult to muster, his mood so buoyed by the occasion, but he did it just the same. The terrible and tragic reports from Hasin's time occupying Rodawnoc were nothing but whining and blame-casting. Hasin had blamed everyone from his troops, to the captains that supplied him, to Ethan and even the Crown. How he still managed to be in good graces at court after so many vitriolic accusations and blamings was beyond Ethan's understanding. Obviously he had powerful friends.

"It's a rich and bountiful world," said Ethan. "It needs only the right people to cultivate it."

Captain Hasin, finally sensing the hint, excused himself as the music began a new round of dancing.

Ethan Sommerled craned his neck to see if the queen was available and wondered how he'd ask her for another dance. She was at her seat in conversation with two men Ethan didn't know.

Sir Nolan said, "You have but a year left to your patent, do you not, Sir Ethan?"

"Two. I'll lose it if I don't have permanent occupancy by 939."

He nodded. "That's right," he said. "Captain Hasin is right though. You need money. They'll need resupply. You mustn't be so optimistic."

"That remark was meant as comment on Captain Hasin's methods not my foolishness," said Ethan. "It's all arranged. More settlers will sail with supplies next year and join them at Placid Bay."

"If you don't mind me asking such a delicate question," said Sir Nolan, "how has this been paid for?"

"Not the treasury, Sir Nolan," said Ethan. "The queen offers me moral support only. The money comes from the planters themselves. They provided the funds for the journey and most for the next. The new settlers will make up the rest.

"Ah aye. Bucklers," said Nolan. "Of course. What use is Enskari money if they're never coming back?"

Ethan understood what he meant, but the phrasing irked him. "Loyal Enskaran," he said. "They'll make a new world for the glory of the queen, the throne, and the House Genest."

"Still, some of the money is yours, is it not? And your money comes from the queen?"

"I have an interest in the enterprise," he said. "It's an investment."

"Like you leaving your share of these spoils to the Crown," said Sir Nolan.

"No sir," said Ethan. "I left them because I am loyal to the queen and Enskari. The funds are from our enemies and will be used no doubt to defend us against them."

"A patriot?"

"Aye. Of course."

Sir Nolan turned and bowed to the queen, who was approaching with Sir Edward.

Ethan, caught off guard, turned and bowed foolishly low.

The queen giggled at him. "Arise, Sir Ethan," she said.

"Aye. Your Majesty. Blessed be to thee, Sir Edward." He nodded to the advisor.

"And to thee," he replied and fumbled with some papers in his hands.

The music stopped and the crowd of cavorting nobles paused their merriment to watch them.

The queen said, "Sir Ethan Sommerled, it was our pleasure before to bestow upon you a mark of our favor on behalf of the government. It is now our pleasure to bestow upon you a mark of our personal favor on behalf of the world."

Sir Edward handed a stack of documents to Ethan, who accepted them, blushing. What a day of days, what a triumph, what a moment. He wished his parents had seen this, his grandparents, his struggling ancestors as far back as the portage to Enskari from Old Earth, selling themselves for a chance to succeed in the stars. Today that promise was realized. He flashed on his own years of struggle, rising through luck, larceny, and labor. He remembered the poor along the road and found hope for them that rose with his own excitement and disbelief as he thumbed through the papers just presented him.

He felt Sir Nolan lean over his shoulder and read them as he tried to make sense of what they all meant.

"These are the estates in Southland," said Nolan.

"Aye," said Edward. "Sir Ethan. Here you have an estate with an income worthy of your rank and accomplishment." There was little happiness in his voice, but the queen's smile made up for it.

Ethan was speechless. He knew the estates. He'd visited them once. They belonged to – used to belong to – Lord Ellsworth.

Before Ethan could speak, bow, or thank anyone, Sir Nolan turned on his heels and walked straight out of the room.

CHAPTER TWELVE

34) Along with fluctuating magnetic fields, microcrystalline lattice barriers surrounding the planets orbiting Coronam shield the worlds from most of the effects from the star's frequent and violent solar storms. Passing through these barriers requires specific skill and patience. These barriers act like a semi-permeable membrane, and safe passage through them is only possible at certain speeds, otherwise, the lattice can severely damage, destroy or even rebuff entry.

What is the maximum safe speed for entry into an atmosphere?

A - 5,000 km/h
B - 1,000 km/h
C - 500 km/h
D - 100 km/h

Navigation/Pilot's Exam, Enskari
(Answer: C)

12, Eighth-Month, 937 NE – Tirgwenin

The landing ship slid down the elevator thread from the *Hopewell*. The ship that had carried the planters across the vast empty expanses of space could not land, could never land. It was connected to the planet beneath it by a long single thread it had spun itself, held taut by the planet's rotation and the ship's propulsion since the *Hopewell's* orbit was too low to effectively counterweight. Tirgwenin had rings. It was the only planet in the system that did. Some were mist, others dust, but some, notably where ships were wont to anchor, were full of rock and asteroid. This meant either low orbit beneath the rings or high orbit above them. Lower was safer, but both required greater expenditure of fuel than traditional geosynchronous plans. Low orbit was a temporary solution, but better than planetfall with parachutes and cushions, which allowed for no return.

Henry Dagney looked out his window at the micro-flashes of resistance and listened to atmospheric crystal scratch the sides of the ship like sandpaper on pitted glass. The light changed and darkened, lightened again, and then ran the prism from violet to red until finally settling on a white-yellow glow of morning clouds.

Breaking cloud cover, Dagney caught his first clear view of the surface of Tirgwenin.

He saw a vast ocean, blue as midnight carbuncle, stretching from a yellow-green shore to the horizon. Distant lightning strikes flicked and flashed; auroras skittered like children chasing chickens.

"There to the north," said Governor Morgan, tapping on the window. "You can't see it, but just over that horizon is Placid Bay."

"Is it much different from down there?" It was Nicholas Pratt, craning his neck around Dagney for a better look.

Governor Morgan had brought the assistants along for this trip as a morale booster: 'To get some land legs under ye and to behold the wonder of our new home.'

"It'll be similar," he said. "But more inland. Placid Bay is well named. It's beautiful."

Robert Aguirre was airsick and only nodded. Nicholas Pratt forced a smile and Dagney kept his face to the window, hiding fear in his reflection.

Though an official assistant, Captain Upor did not sit with the planters. He'd not spoken to any of them in weeks. He was on an upper deck of the lander now with a dozen sailors he'd brought along to help with the evacuation of the military garrison left on Rodawnoc. The station was to be abandoned; the men were to be collected and taken aboard the *Hopewell* and returned home. After that, Upor would see to the landing of the colonists, their bodies and cargo, to be taken far north of Rodawnoc to Placid Bay for permanent settlement.

It should have been a joyous time for the planters, celebration for the arrival at their new home, but aboard the ship and in the cabin with the assistants, it was all fear and worry. They'd missed the planting season.

Their hope, Morgan had told them, lay in Mathew, the other assistant. It was an honorary title. The native Tirgwenian had not been consulted on any aspect of the endeavor so far. He was, after all, a savage, and was always treated more like a pet than a man. He was a mascot who helped market the enterprise to Enskari separatists looking to escape Connor's Guard and the coming Hyraxian invasion. Now Morgan looked to him as his company's best chance for survival.

They were headed to Placid Bay. Mathew was captured near Rodawnoc, where they were about to land and rescue the men left there. Mathew's only encounter with Placid Bay had been from the deck of a landing ship before he was taken off-world. He didn't know the peoples who lived there except by reputation. They were not any more warlike than his own people, he'd told them, and he believed he'd be able to communicate with them. He was to act as a translator and goodwill ambassador, but now also, as a primary negotiator for winter food.

They'd left Freeport with nothing to show for it but wasted time. The crew had taken on fresh water, but the planters had not acquired anything they needed, not meal or corn or seed. Not winter plants which they bargained for, not medicine which they begged for, not butter, lard, or salt. Not the horses they'd paid for, nor the cattle they'd been promised.

Morale had sunk to a dangerous low. The planters saw they had no cattle. They could read a clock, calculate the month, realize they were well past planting.

Dagney, as an advisor to the governor, a member of the ruling council, knew the situation before Morgan addressed the colonists when they were again underway after Freeport.

Dagney had stood with daughter and son off to the side, a picture of a strong determined family as was required. Still sick from the pox, drained from what had happened to Millicent, and of course the death of his wife, it took every ounce of deceit Henry had and then some to pretend that he was confident in their future. He was grateful that it had been the governor and not he who'd made the speech.

"My friends," Morgan had said. "My brothers and sisters, blessed be."

"And to thee," came the return, weak and worried.

"What I'm about to tell ye is being told to our friends aboard the *Mallow*." He produced a prepared speech and adjusted his spectacles. "We knew we'd be tested. It is now begun. The supplies we were to gather at Freeport did not materialize."

Shrieks and worried murmurs rounded the deck ring. Dagney pulled Millicent closer to him. To her credit, she put on an assured stoic face that might not have been all false like his.

"There's no good pointing fingers or finding blame," said Morgan, responding to some question or comment Dagney had not heard. Perhaps one from the governor's own mind.

"We should go home!" someone yelled.

"Aye. Turn around!"

Morgan shook his head. "Nay. We cannot go home. We have no home."

The murmurs fell away into an eerie silence.

"We'll press ahead," Morgan said. "We can survive. We will prosper. The land is beautiful and bounteous."

"We'll starve!"

"Nay. We have seed corn," he said. "We will eat that this winter if we must. Our resupply ship will bring us new seed, more and better, in the early spring. We have only to endure a little time. It will not be as easy as we had hoped, but it won't be as bad as some of ye fear."

"I'm for throwing myself on the queen's mercy," yelled Mrs. Archard.

"You are criminals," said Captain Upor. "There is no going back."

The captain had every right to be there, but it surprised Dagney to actually see him below decks. Morgan too looked taken aback.

"We are pilgrims. The way is hard, but we have God," Morgan said, sliding into his pulpit voice.

"And there's no passage back," said Upor. "I've no place for any of ye. Best accept your fate."

Though unable to account for his motivation, Morgan had insinuated that Upor had mutinied, that he was the cause of their misfortunes. Henry Dagney had his daughter's account besides; Millie had reported what she'd overheard on that awful trip down deck. Still he hadn't believed it. Now, seeing the captain flanked by armed sailors, speaking with his back to the bulkhead, strong from close gravity, well fed and wine-warmed, cavalierly ignoring the panicked faces of eighty Saved before him, Dagney thought the impossible.

Along with the rest of the colonists, Morgan stared at Upor. What it was everyone expected to see, hear, or happen from their pilot, Dagney didn't know, but he watched the man with them. Perhaps they were hoping for an apology, a sign of jest, hope, a promise, or maybe everyone just wished him dead.

Upor stared back a moment then made a half bow, turned and exited the deck followed by his sailors.

Eyes turned to the governor.

Morgan looked at the written proclamation in his hand, then dropped it to his side. "It'll be hard," he said. "But we shall endure."

A week after that, Dagney was not surprised when Upor would not enter the Kanluran Cloud to search for salt as he'd promised. The pilot explained it was too dangerous to go in, which might have been true. He said he was pressing on to Tirgwenin so the colonists might still get their seeds in the ground, which was obviously false. It was then mid Seventh-Month, too late even then for the planting of seeds they had.

What had most surprised Dagney was that Morgan was surprised. The governor spent days trying to see the pilot, to convince him and explain that at this late date, salt was more important than time, their food source now being heavily reliant upon the fish in the bay. The pilot was always too busy to see him and finally sent a note explaining that it was his ship and he was responsible for its safety and his crew, but not so much 'the cargo'. Dagney understood the pilot's use of 'cargo' to mean the colonists, but Morgan, ever unimaginative, wrote back explaining that 'the cargo would need to be eaten since they were already too late to plant'.

The pilot had not responded to Morgan's letter. Communication between the crew and the colonists ceased beyond a brief daily written communiqué regarding ship operation, current position and ETA. The constitutional walks to the higher gravity decks Millicent and many of the colonists needed were only allowed after much letter writing, but it was limited to only as far as one deck below the crewmen's quarters. Many people blamed Millicent for this. Henry mourned for his daughter's reputation among his neighbors, but knew he could only wait and allow the crisis to pass. New troubles awaited them.

Two days before the landing, Mr. Hale, Upor's ill-mannered first mate, came below decks for an inspection, accompanied, everyone saw, by six armed sailors. He informed everyone that they had arrived and were at that moment spinning thread to the surface as part of their planned evacuation of the soldiers left by Captain Hasin the year before. Hale found the governor and told him to assemble the assistants and whatever other colonists he wanted first to see Tirgwenin. "To get a sense of the land they will now inhabit," he'd said.

Morgan called his assistants together and told them to prepare to land with the rescue contingent and see their new home. "Ye need to see this, to come back excited and warm for the place. It'll go far when we land in Placid Bay to soothe the others."

"What about Mathew?" Dagney said. "Do we bring him along?"

"He'll have to come eventually," said Pratt. "We might as well get used to him."

But Morgan understood. "Aye, I see, Henry," he said. "Maybe we shouldn't. Placid Bay is one thing – hundreds of kilometers from here. There he'll be an immigrant like us, but if he sees Rodawnoc, his home, he might escape."

Aguirre said, "What's to prevent him from escaping in Placid Bay?" There was fear in his voice, near panic. He'd been that way for weeks. He'd been so bad, so upsetting to the others with his rambling doomsaying madness that Morgan had finally told him to remain out of sight until they landed and arranged for the company's little supply of spirits to be used to settle him.

Morgan combed his hair out of his eyes with his fingers. "It's not an easy decision," he said. "We're going to need to trust him. He's important."

"Exactly. He's too important to lose."

"Pratt, what do you think?" asked Morgan.

"Leave him on the ship. Tell him there's not room. When we get to Placid Bay we keep a close eye on him. Chain him there if we must. Coercion works nearly as well as trust."

"Henry?"

Dagney looked from the near-hysterical visage of Aguirre to the somber defeated expression of Pratt and lastly the beaten and worn face of Morgan, governor and high minister of the Bucklers. "I'd like to think that we had a chance here to do things differently," he said.

"What does that mean?" said Aguirre.

"We're given a chance to start again on a planet, as a people. We don't want to make the same mistakes."

"What does that have to do with survival?" said Aguirre. "What is it with you pie-eyed Dagneys? As practical as a paper knife. No sense of reality."

Dagney thought to ask Aguirre to be more specific, to tell him to his face what was whispered about his daughter, but held his tongue. He said instead, "It sets a bad precedent, Alpin. Coercion and lies. Oppression of the weak. Isn't that why we left Enskari? To escape that? To not have that? Shouldn't we at least try to begin our adventure on a positive note?"

"Adventure? Listen to him," Aguirre said, or rather screamed. "You're a fool, Dagney!"

Dagney saw tears on Aguirre's cheeks. He was crying, but no sobs escaped him. It was his eyes watering down his face, streams of tears flowing out of his wild, unblinking eyes.

"We're well underway," said Morgan. "The beginning is long gone and the music is what it is. We'll leave him on the ship. Make ready. We'll land tomorrow."

Dagney was not as surprised as the others to find that Upor had personally invited Mathew to accompany them on the landing, doing so in a manner that gave the others no chance to stop it. The tall Tirgwenian was escorted in by armed crewmen at the last minute, and took a seat among the other assistants without a word. Dagney watched him closely, trying to read him, to gauge if he was planning to run, but he was as inscrutable as ever. His tattooed yellow skin, reflective even in the ship's low light, made him look unreal, while his long sable hair, bound up in a ribbon, was at once civilized and wild. A strange border creature in Enskari clothes and savage skin.

The landing ship decelerated down the micro-thread and gravity became a burden. Dagney found it hard to breathe and reached for an oxygen mask. His arm felt like it was tied down. With effort, he reached the mask and wrapped it around his face before turning the wheel to start the flow. The others followed suit except for Mathew, who noticed what they were doing, but turned his face back to his window as Jareth's World filled it.

The ship splashed down with a crash that made Aguirre shriek and chipped one of Dagney's teeth. The ship bounced and rocked on the sea, which was much angrier up close than it had seemed falling in to it. Meanwhile, light outside the window was the clearest and most beautiful Dagney had ever seen. He watched it in wonder and then in between swells, off in the distance, he saw the wooded shoreline of Rodawnoc. It was green and lush. He smiled to think of the untouched forests, ached to set his chisel into ancient wood, to make something useful and beautiful out of a wild tree. It was a treasure of timber, the like of which, like the light itself, he'd never seen on Enskari.

Sailors rushed about the craft without and within, freeing it from the thread and attaching the beacon buoy so they might find it again. The ship spun around and Dagney lost sight of the coast, seeing only the infinite expanse of blue-and-white water. Turning to see if he could find the land out another window, he caught Mathew's gaze. While Aguirre pinched his eyes shut and gnashed his teeth, and Pratt sucked at the oxygen mask, Mathew smiled. More, he smiled at him. Dagney was taken aback for an instant until he realized he too was smiling. His grin broadened and Mathew looked pleased to see it.

The Tirgwenian turned back to his window and Dagney pondered the change in the man. He'd never seen him any way but stolid. That smile was surprising, not just because it echoed his own excitement in the face of the unknown, but because he'd never seen such an expression on Mathew before. He had never seen any expression on his face before.

From somewhere beneath decks an engine came to life and rattled the hull with tremors. Loud and throaty, the voice of it carried up from some unseen deck along with the smell of grease and diesel exhaust.

The ship lurched, spun, turned, and straightened. It moved toward the shore, chased by the wind, pursued by sooty smoke exhaust.

The sea was rough and the ship, though fifty meters long and a third wide, heavy and half its hull below the waterline, was still buffeted by the swells. It staggered across the water.

Morgan, commenting perhaps on Aguirre's rising discomfort, said, "We're fine. The landing ship is designed so space sailors can't sink it."

"I've heard of plenty of landing ships sinking," said Aguirre. "They're notorious for—"

"Shut your mouth, Roger," said Dagney. "Try to enjoy the ride."

Aguirre's cheeks flushed and his red eyes flashed to the other assistants and finally to Morgan, who regarded him impassively. Aguirre tightened his seat belt, leaned back, and was quiet.

The noise from the motor was persistent and loud and curtailed more conversation.

★   ★   ★

An hour later, the ship slowed and stopped in the shoals, a hundred meters from shore. The motor was turned off, an anchor dropped, and the ship fell into an eerie silence.

It lasted only a few moments and then the compartment filled with men running through, sailors taking off their reflective radiation vests and donning orange water preservers over ballistic armor. Dagney figured that one counteracted the other if the men were to fall overboard.

The assistants stood and stretched, feeling the full gravity, holding themselves up against their seats, the rocking of the ship taxing their muscles so much the more. Even Mathew, strong, tall, and slim, who Dagney had assumed was immune to discomfort, staggered and swayed. Like his earlier smile, it surprised Dagney to read emotion on the Tirgwenian's face. He'd seen the man happy and now vexed. It was a revelation. He'd almost come to believe that his race was incapable of human emotion.

A sailor poked his head in, a petty officer by the insignia. Dagney didn't know the man's name and he didn't introduce himself. "Mr. Morgan," he said. "The captain said ye come ashore now with the other assistants to become familiar with the place."

Morgan, leaning heavily against his chair, panting with the exertion, said, "Is Upor taking all the men who've landed here before?"

"Aye, all he has left," the sailor said.

"What does that mean?"

"We lost one at Freeport. Dedikodu was put off there."

"What?" said Morgan, his eyes big and worried.

Dagney understood.

The sailor Dedikodu had been to Tirgwenin before. He knew the place. He knew where they were going. He could lead people to them. He could lead Hyraxian ships to them.

"Put off or fled?" said Morgan. "Was he not bonded for the voyage?"

The sailor rubbed the stubble on his face. "Aye, and for two years more if I remember."

"So he might have just run off on his debt?" Dagney asked.

"Aye," said the sailor. "But that's not where any sane sailor would choose. Freeport is a booger."

"We'll have to take your word for that," said Dagney. "We didn't get a chance to see it. We weren't allowed off the boat."

"Aye," said the man with a shrug. "Suit up, Governor. Captain said we're leaving straight away."

Morgan looked desperately at his assistants.

"We'll come along," said Dagney.

"Thank you, Henry."

Pratt stretched his neck. Aguirre looked ready to cry but stood up.

Mathew pulled on his coat and they all marched out to the landing deck.

Upor and a contingent of armed sailors were already assembled as the landing dinghy was brought out of its bay in the side of the ship.

It was a square-hulled plastic tub of a boat. The front section was hinged to open forward, providing a ramp for easy egress on a beach. It was powered by a heavy sputtering diesel engine that weighed the back end down and raised the bow a half meter above the water as it maneuvered to the gangway.

Upor marched on with his men. Dagney followed Morgan with the others, fighting their own fatigue from atrophied muscles. They settled on a bench and the boat was pushed away and turned toward shore.

Dagney saw the thread beacon glowing on the water between sweeps and swells and tried to make out the thread extending from it into space above-world, but of course couldn't see it. Maybe if it'd been as big as the one he knew in Vildeby, he might have been able to find the line from this distance. Maybe not.

Water splashed over the sides and leaked through the front, quickly filling the bottom of the boat with ankle-deep water. Aguirre watched it nervously. Dagney took confidence from the sailors, who ignored it and kept their eyes fixed on the shoreline.

The sky was cut by the orbiting rings, a bisection of crystal cream in a dome of a scintillating blue. Deep and clear heavens with flashing crystals like he remembered from his youth in the countryside of Enskari when he hunted wood for his father's shop. He'd not seen the day shimmers in years. He'd forgotten about them, the momentary prismatic sparkling of Coronam on a crystal sky. 'Day-twinkling' it was called. He couldn't wait until Millie and Dillon saw them.

The boat jarred to a stop, throwing men forward and down into the leaky, water-filled hull. They'd hit a sandbar.

"Get out and push us off," ordered Upor. Men leapt over the side and struggled to free the lightened craft. The pilot looked at the colonists as if he were about to chide them for not going over with his men, but refrained.

The water was halfway up Dagney's calf when the boat was finally freed and the sailors climbed back aboard.

"I can't swim," said Aguirre.

"Why am I not surprised?" said Dagney.

"No sailor knows how to swim," Upor said. "Such knowing only prolongs agony."

"Then why the preservers?" said Morgan.

Upor ignored the question.

Aguirre looked fit to be sick as the boat pushed past a system of low island dune breakwaters and sped toward the far wooded island which was their destination.

"Push us right up as far as it'll go," Upor said to the motorman.

"Aye, Captain."

The boat skidded up the sandy beach and stopped. The front panel fell forward, slapping the island with a heavy weight that sent a cloud of black flies into the sea-salted air and a wave of leaked water onto the beach.

Without ceremony or order, the sailors climbed onto the land followed by the assistants. Mathew, the last to exit, scanned the tree line with his usual expressionless face. Dagney caught Morgan stealing glances at the Tirgwenian as they walked.

"The colonnade is at the far end of the island," said Morgan. "An hour's march."

"Methinks two," said Upor, looking at the muscle-weakened colonists. "Fetch some crutches to aid ye. Try to keep up."

Upor left one man with the boat and then led the others up the beach. The colonists followed fifty meters behind the sailors, leaning heavily upon walking sticks and gasping for breath in the hot late summer air.

"Can we not walk in the shade at least?" said Pratt, gesturing to the trees.

"Nay," said Morgan. "Too thick to pass easily."

"Are there snakes?" Aguirre asked.

Mathew answered him. "Doa-andze. It's like a snake."

"I don't think I want to know about that," said Dagney. "Let's save our breath."

Black flies and buzzing gnats flew at them as they walked. The flies bit and the gnats were easily inhaled. With the heat and sand, the stinging smell of salt and seaweed, their aching bodies and foul moods, it was the hardest walk Dagney could remember. Even Mathew suffered and swatted, waved away pests with wide sweeps of his hat.

Ninety minutes later they turned from the beach and followed the sailors' tracks into the trees. Mathew paused and examined the area, squinting up and down the beach, staring into the trees and listening.

"What is it, Mathew?" asked Morgan.

Mathew shook his head. Dagney didn't know if that meant it was nothing or he wouldn't say what it was. Morgan let it pass and they all entered the woods.

The trees on the edge were bent and gnarled, windblown sculptures of wood and vine. A little farther in, behind the protection of their sacrificed kinsmen, the trees were taller and straighter, but still grotesque. They were twisted and tortured, root and trunk bent into knots around themselves more like petrified vines than timber. They looked ancient and rugged; their bark was harder than oak, which made Dagney smile. Above them in a perfect convex canopy, long fleshy green leaves spiraled around each other into a domed shade canopy. It made Dagney think of umbrellas and imagine some maniacal bonsai sculptor nurturing these alien plants into a picture of chaos and usefulness.

The path they followed was a narrow animal trail that the sailors had widened with swords. The slashing delayed them and the better path allowed the trailing colonists to catch up with Upor's company just as they entered a clearing.

"Hullo!" cried Upor. "Hullo? Friends and Saved. Come out. We're here to relieve ye. Hullo!"

His voice was sucked into the woods, blown inland with the steady breath of ocean wind. The company of armed sailors, colonists, and one native stood and listened. No voice came back to them.

"Don't look like anyone's been here for a while." It was the petty officer who'd roused the colonists for the trip.

"Nay," said Upor. "Morgan?" He spoke the governor's name without looking at him. "You were here longer than I."

"The palisade is in dire disrepair," Morgan said. "The soldiers must have quit it."

Dagney scanned the fallen timbers, which he recognized as having once been the walls of a fort. It hadn't been large, maybe fifty meters on a side, roughly starlike for defense. Two-meter-high walls with varying spaces between the warped posts. It was breached in several places but he couldn't tell if it was the work of men or weather.

"Separate and search," ordered Upor.

The soldiers, weapons at the ready, fanned out into the forest. Mathew went with them. Dagney and the other assistants watched him go with concerned expressions, but didn't follow. They couldn't manage the work of walking any more if they had to. Instead, they went in the palisade with the petty officer and Upor.

The shelters within the fort had fallen in, the thatched roofs rotting and wind-torn. Dagney recognized sawed wood and some rusting nails but otherwise no sign of civilized habitation. No metal or mark that any Saved had been there.

"Weren't there supposed to be soldiers here?" said Pratt, looking around.

"One and twenty," said Morgan. "Well equipped and able."

"Gone now," Aguirre said carefully, lowering himself to sit against the wall.

Dagney didn't think Morgan looked surprised to have found no one here. Upor looked interested but also not terribly surprised to find the camp deserted.

"I don't think much of your new home," said the petty officer to Dagney.

"Nay," said Dagney. "We're not to be here. We're going on to Placid Bay. A pleasant place."

The petty officer shrugged and kicked at a mound of overgrown soil.

"Captain," he said, "methinks I found one."

Upor and Morgan walked over. Aguirre craned his neck from a meter away. Pratt leaned against a post and watched from a distance. Dagney wiped sweat from his forehead with a soaked handkerchief, feeling the salt in the air stinging his pores.

The all looked down on fleshless bones.

"It's a leg," said Upor, pushing dirt away with his sword. He revealed a femur and a pant leg. The petty officer knelt down and inspected it.

"It's not native," he said. "Enskari weaved."

Dagney took the measure of the leg, then knelt and dug where the head might be.

"He's not buried properly," said Morgan. "Too shallow."

"He wasn't buried at all," said Dagney. "He was covered. Wind, I'd say. Animals took his flesh while he was above ground. See, the bones are bleached. He fell here and died."

"And was eaten," said the petty officer.

Dagney found matted brown hair and a broken skull under a few centimeters of soil.

"Caved in," said the petty officer. "By a club or ax."

"They're dead," said Upor. "All dead. We'll call the men back and set up a camp here for the night."

"Why not just go?" Morgan said.

"I sent the ship back to the *Hopewell* to fetch the others. This is as far as I take ye."

"What?" said Morgan. "Nay. We need to gather and go to Placid Bay."

"This'll do."

"Nay. Nay nay nay. Anywhere but here, not after what Hasin—"

"This'll do," said Upor. "Aye, it's too dangerous to go on. Haven't the time or men. This is where ye settle."

"You mutinous bastard!" Morgan shook with rage.

Upor calmly turned on his heels and marched out of the palisade.

The color drained from Morgan's face as if a stopper had been pulled. He stumbled against a falling wall.

Exhausted from the digging, Dagney slumped to the ground beside the dead man. He looked up at the petty officer, who regarded him with a piteous confirmation of the pilot's order. He shrugged his shoulders and then followed his captain out of the ruin.

PART TWO
HASIN'S COMMAND (TWO YEARS PRIOR: 935-936 NE)

'Insanity is doing the same thing over and over again
and expecting different results.'
Anonymous

CHAPTER THIRTEEN

This will be my last letter to you. The governor and his cronies sail back to Enskari today aboard the Panther. *I pray this letter and my others find you well. I have entrusted them all to a good man and have faith they will.*

Please refer to my previously dated missives for the particulars and sundry complaints against certain gentlemen of this service. There you will find a true and ample discourse of the whole voyage, the incompetence of the leadership of this enterprise, their intolerable pride and insatiable ambition, and the terrible missed opportunities they have neglected among the many mistakes they have provoked. Suffice me to summarize: the situation on Jareth's World is beyond the ridiculous. At every turn we have been plagued by incompetence and stupidity. Fools direct a disaster.

For some months now we have been ashore this new and bounteous place. The native savages of this world are weak and troublesome yet our command has made us into whimpering fools before them. We beg pardon to cut a tree, permission to cross a river, patience to abide on the ground! They trade away our best goods for grain instead of for gold and guides.

It is for this reason I have chosen to remain with a company of fit soldiers on Tirgwenin. Finally in command, I will endeavor to undo the damage and wasted time of my malicious, lying, backbiting, incompetent predecessors and gain this place for the glory of the Crown.
Letter to Sir Nolan Brett from Captain Tir Hasin
17, Eighth-Month, 935 NE

20, Tenth-Month, 935 NE – Rodawnoc, Tirgwenin

Enskari Church Minister Gayle walked the perimeter of the fort with Captain Hasin, inspecting it for weakness and rot. Hasin was proud of the palisade. Fortifications were his specialty. He'd fought on Enskari, in Austen, where he helped subdue the peasants after a famine uprising by wiping most of them out. As he was keen to mention, while there he'd overseen the construction of several 'permanent presences'. Gayle found the whole thing boring and a waste of time. There were much more pressing issues at hand.

"The wood is related to oak," said Hasin.

"Actually sir, I think it's more akin to pine."

"Nonsense. It's hard, not soft. Oak is hard. Pine is soft."

Gayle thought to explain how it was only the trees on the edge that were hard, and they only on one side. The bark facing the wind and sea was calloused and rough, but only a few meters from the edge in the forest, the trees were uniformly soft like pine. He'd made examination of the genus and had even measured the thickening bark on newly exposed trees. It was all in his notebooks, but he decided not to mention any of this to Hasin. "The food supplies are running low," he said instead.

"Nonsense."

Here Gayle felt he had to press. "We were under-provisioned to begin with, Governor. Some of it has gone bad and become infested with those blue flies. Then there's the men pilfering it. They're bored and restless."

"Talk to me not about the men, Minister. That is my affair."

"But you asked me to keep track of these things."

"The supplies, aye, but tell me not about the men. That's morale. That's soldiering, not scholaring. My job. Not yours."

Hasin tapped a post with the butt of his gun, listening to the thump as if it held secrets.

There were one hundred seven Enskari Saved on Rodawnoc in Hasin's fort. Ten officers and gentlemen, one civilian – Gayle – and the rest soldiers and sailors pressed into the enterprise. There were a handful of sergeants and corporals who showed some discipline or at least the ability to follow an order after a fashion, but the rank and file of the men acted like they'd been conscripted straight out of prison, which was indeed the case for some. They were a rowdy undisciplined rabble. They stole from the storehouse, fought with each other, lay around, were insubordinate to their betters, and were generally drunk. When Captain Stewart went on this last scouting mission up the coast, the twenty men he took with him had to be rounded up at the end of a Gauss rifle.

But this wasn't Gayle's concern. Captain Hasin – no, Governor and Admiral Hasin now, self appointed – was in charge of those affairs. Gayle was here to chronicle. He hadn't wanted to stay. He had no lust for adventure. He had no dreams of gold and conquest like Hasin, no fantasies of farming like Alpin Morgan. He was just a scholar and a naturalist tricked into making the most dangerous voyage his people had ever tried. But he was here now and he had to make the best of it. He'd leave with the resupply if he had to stow away on the ship, but he shouldn't have to. Hasin would make him his herald, a publicist. He'd return to Enskari to sell the admiral's triumphs to the court, so he'd get to go back. And if Hasin didn't have riches to show for his obstinance, Gayle knew he was the fallback. His notebooks of sketches and observations would describe a verdant garden and draw investors. Morgan might return with a shipful of refugees for Placid Bay, but Hasin had plans to turn Rodawnoc into a military stronghold from which he'd fight the hated Hyraxians and plunder the planet. It was a plan first laid out by Admiral Aderyn. This sickly fly-infested island was on the equator and so able to monitor planetfall. Of course Hyrax could land other places, but the planet's rings made it tricky. A permanent base would need equatorial access eventually and Rodawnoc was an obvious choice.

Hasin hadn't been ordered to make a fort. Hadn't been ordered to stay. He'd come along with the last survey with soldiers as a protective detail for Morgan, who, under Sommerled's orders, was there to scout locations for a permanent settlement under his royal patent. Hasin had taken it on himself to make Aderyn's fort as an excuse to remain behind, unhindered by the sensible governors he'd so clashed with.

It was a bold plan. Gayle admired him for it. The *Panther*, the *Hopewell* and the *Enskari Star* would return home with tales of Hasin's insubordination and petulance. He'd be infamous. But, if Hasin later returned with riches, all would be forgiven. Then, provided he got backing from the right people in court, he could return to Tirgwenin and continue his Cortez-like conquest, and worming his way onto Sommerled's patent as a military necessity.

Gayle had written these thoughts down in his private notebook but even as he sussed out Hasin's motivations he thought that he was giving the man too much credit. Gayle had logically deduced a method behind the madness, but he was not so sure Hasin was that bright. As the days waned on the weather grew worse, and the food disappeared, and the men talked of revolt, the governor/admiral could speak of nothing but glory. Gayle began to think that in fact Hasin was little more than a zealot. A dangerous zealot, half-mad with visions of conquest and an unhealthy obsession with Hyrax. He would talk about the Hyraxian conquerors of Silangan with a sort of awed contempt, jealously recounting the tales of the invasions, how a few hundred Hyraxian soldiers had toppled empires and returned with an entire world's treasure. They had to be stopped. They were the greatest threat to Enskari and he had to match their cruelty to succeed by handing Tirgwenin to the queen. If he got rich in the process, so much the better.

"Sir, the supplies," said Gayle. "We won't have enough. We'll run out of food in less than two months even with rationing."

Hasin pushed his coilgun through a gap in the posts and aimed down the barrel. Satisfied, he pulled it back and re-holstered it. "This is a land of plenty, Minister. God will provide."

"Governor—"

Hasin turned on him with a scowl. One hand rested on his sidearm, the other played with his mustache. "For a man of God you have surprisingly little faith."

It was not the first time Hasin had questioned Gayle's fidelity to the cloth. Usually it was about his order of monks who'd changed allegiance from the prophet to the queen. Although it was the law and Hasin and everyone had done the same, somehow it was a weakness with the clergy.

Gayle tried again, "Governor—"

"God will provide." Looking over the minister's shoulder, Hasin drew his gun.

Gayle turned to follow his aim.

He saw them before he heard them. Three Tirgwenians moving silently through the thick underbrush. It always surprised Gayle how stealthy they could be, how quiet and hidden in the underbrush. Their skin was near golden-yellow and reflective besides. They were tall, taller even than the Enskari, who were known for their height. Standing at an average of two meters, they had ten centimeters over the average Enskaran. Their tattoos, black and blue against their bright skin, might aid in their camouflage but to the civilized, they were always unsettling.

"Alert," said Hasin. Then louder called, "Alert!"

Behind the wall, Gayle heard men scramble and rush, pass the order, arm themselves with coilguns, crossbows, and swords.

Gayle recognized Onuieg, and his wife, Jessya. He didn't know the boy's name.

Jessya raised her hand in greeting. "Pax," she said.

Gayle raised his hand. "Pax," he said.

Onuieg carried a spear, a three-meter-long shaft tipped with a ten-centimeter blade fashioned from some sharpened purple shell. Its polish glistened in the light as if it were covered in oil. Gayle suspected a poison. A short recurved wooden bow was strung over his shoulder and a small quiver of half a dozen arrows hung at his waist. Those he knew were poisoned.

"Pax, Enskari," said Jessya. "Snag om food."

Hasin turned to Gayle for a translation. The naturalist had become the company's de facto translator.

"They want to talk about food," he told the governor.

"Tell them we'll trade for all they can spare."

"Uhm," began Gayle, but Jessya broke him off.

"Nay, Enskari. Vi have ingan."

"They say they don't have any," said Gayle.

Hasin rolled his eyes at the woman and addressed Onuieg. "Listen, we'll trade cloth and pots. We have necklaces and fine boots."

Gayle had tried to explain to Hasin that it had been long understood that the Tirgwenians were matriarchal, but he either forgot that or deliberately ignored it. It made for difficult negotiations.

Onuieg said in near common tongue, "No food. And also more withal, doa time."

"Doa?" said Hasin.

"I think that means danger," said Gayle. He remembered hearing the term used before to describe certain types of plants and reptiles.

Jessya nodded. "Aye. Doa, danger. Little skyvand, past anno. No food. Also and more withal, you take Mateya. Good hunter. No food now."

"I think they're talking about rain, about a drought," said Gayle. "Also about missing that man who left with Morgan. Mathew we called him."

"No rain past anno." She pointed up.

"Nonsense," said Hasin. "It rained yesterday."

"No food-vand," she said. "No food-wat-ater," she said, stumbling with the word.

"The damn heathens are stupid as all hell," said Hasin.

Gayle thought the opposite. He was impressed at how quickly this little family, their primary link to the island, had picked up their language. True, there were many similar words, their linguistic roots stretching back to Old Earth before the Unsettling like his own, but they adapted much quicker to the Enskari ways than the Enskari did to theirs.

"Vi and you promise," said Jessya. "You stay. No food."

She was referring to the deal Morgan had made. The previous expeditions to Rodawnoc had taken all the surplus food on the island. It had taxed the natives. The drought had made things worse and the pox had taken some of their best people. This was all explained to them when they first landed, back when Sommerled's governors were in charge. Then, Alpin Morgan had negotiated with Jessya to allow them to stay unmolested on the island under the strict stipulation that they'd be responsible for their own feeding. If the Tirgwenians had any surplus they might trade that, but the Enskari visitors were not to raid their villages or expect any help. Under Morgan and Sommerled's men, they'd kept to the deal. But now those people were halfway back to Enskari in the *Panther* and Hasin was in charge here.

"Bad Enskari take food. Aftens back."

"Va var it?" said Gayle to Jessya, trying a simple phrase.

"Five fighters," she said, holding up as many fingers. "Two aftens – nights ago. Corn silo and, uh...." She stammered then raised eight fingers. "So greeses. Robbers."

By cough and clank Gayle become aware of fort soldiers circling their little group. They spun up their coilguns and took aim. The Tirgwenians noticed them and Onuieg lowered his spear a little.

"What the devil are these heathens saying, Gayle?" said Hasin. His chest was puffed out and he waved his gun casually.

"Greeses?" Gayle said to Jessya.

She nodded.

To Hasin, Gayle said, "They say we robbed their grain silo. And something else. I don't understand." He shook his head to Jessya. "Greeses?"

The boy stepped forward and snorted. "Gayle oo forsto," he said to Jessya. Then he dropped on all fours and kicked the sand up with his hands like he was rooting around.

Gayle remembered seeing an animal like that in their camp.

"Pigs," he said. "Someone raided their food and stole eight pigs." Gayle raised eight fingers to Jessya and said, "Eight. Eight greeses – eight pigs."

"Pigs." She nodded. "Robbers."

Hasin didn't look surprised, which made Gayle feel the fool.

"Must be some misunderstanding," Hasin said. "Tell them I can't keep track of all my men. They're a lively bunch. Prone to get in trouble."

"I won't," said Gayle.

"What?"

"I can't," he said, hearing the threat in the governor's voice.

Hasin looked from Gayle to the tall natives and back at his men.

"Longmire," he called to one of his soldiers. "You know anything about this?"

Sergeant Longmire, one of Hasin's favorites, stepped forward, his charged single-shot rifle held in the crook of his arm.

"Aye, sir," he said, looking at Gayle. "Some of the men were out 'sploring and thought they were wild beasts. If they want to claim ownership, they should consider fencing them in. They'd be easier to catch then too."

"There you have it," said Hasin. "No breach of trust. Just a misunderstanding. Longmire, fetch a chest of trade for the sparklers here."

"Aye, sir."

Gayle remembered seeing the creatures in a pen. He waited to see if anyone would try to explain the grain silo with an equally unbelievable tale, but no one did.

Jessya turned to Gayle. "Va?" she said.

He couldn't meet her eyes. It was all a lie and he knew it. It was a pantomime for his benefit so Hasin wouldn't look like the lying backstabbing bastard he was. Gayle finally laughed out loud, struck by the irony of a soldier preferring to look like an undisciplined commander rather than a cheating politician. He was bucking for nobility.

"Gayle," said Jessya. "Va say stranger? Taly my."

"Sorry," said Gayle. "A mistake."

"Five mistake?" she said showing as many fingers.

"Aye," he said, still not able to look at her. Instead he looked at the boy and Onuieg. They'd lost weight since he'd last seen them. They were never in the peak of health, but they were worse now. He saw their ribs through their skin and imagined he was looking at his own flesh in a few months. The short-term gain of a few pigs would play out in the long-term starvation of the fort. He saw it plainly. They needed help to survive and yet they kept alienating the only people who could help them.

Longmire appeared with a small wooden chest and handed it to Hasin. The governor opened it and looked inside with feigned awe and wonder. He turned it around to show Onuieg. It was filled with glass bobbles and colored thread, several pairs of shoes, a couple of combs, a mirror.

"Tell them to take this with our apologies," he said to Gayle.

The minister couldn't find the words, so instead gestured to the chest and then to the natives.

Not surprisingly they scoffed.

"Damn ungrateful louts," said Hasin. "Do they know we could wipe them out if we wanted to?"

Onuieg's grip on his spear tightened and Jessya's hand fell to a knife on her belt.

Oblivious to having been understood, Hasin said, "Tell them to take it. Tell them to get us more pigs and we'll pay for them."

Without waiting for Gayle to translate or for their response, Hasin turned and marched back to the fort. The soldiers, smirking, followed him in.

Gayle finally looked at Jessya.

"I am so—" he began.

She stopped him with a raised hand.

"Gayle," she said. She dropped to one knee and then deliberately dropped a finger into the sand. "Rodawnoc," she said.

Gayle nodded. "Rodawnoc," he repeated. He knew the name of the place.

She pointed to herself and her people. "Rowdanae," she said.

"Rowdanae," he repeated.

"You Rowdanae also?" she said.

"Only for a while," he said. "We'll go back to Enskari soon."

She seemed to understand.

"We Rowdanae," she said. "No bees."

"What?"

"No bees."

"No bees?" he repeated.

"You no bees?"

He raised his hands showing he didn't understand.

"Rowdanae," she said again. "No bees." She gestured to the woods, toward the interior. She waved wider as if encompassing the distant lands, the mountains and places far beyond. "Outside. We ha not...no bees. No bees. No food in draught."

"Your crops failed," he said, thinking he understood. "The pollinators disappeared when there was no skyvand – no rain?" It made sense. She was saying that there was yet another reason why they were stressed.

She shook her head. She glanced at Onuieg, who shrugged.

The boy stepped up again.

He reached into the chest and took out a handful of glass marbles. At least someone liked Hasin's attempt at appeasement.

The boy dropped the lot in the sand and said, "Folk."

Gayle nodded. He knew the word or at least something that sounded the same.

The boy nodded back and smiled a wide bright grin. Beautiful teeth, thought Gayle. And to think they have no dentists.

The boy took a handful of marbles and dropped them in the sand. "Folk," he said. "Ha bees."

Jessya smiled. Onuieg looked on.

The boy picked up a couple of marbles and held them up. "No bees," he said. He dropped them in the sand a half meter from the others. "Rowdanae," he said. He gestured from the big pile to the little. "Rowdanae," he said. "Outside. No bees."

"Bees?" said Gayle. "Like in buzz?" He twitched his finger around as if tracing a flying bee.

"Aye," said Onuieg.

"What about it?" Gayle lifted his hands again, showing he didn't understand.

The boy said something to Jessya and then to Onuieg. They responded but it was all too fast for Gayle to understand. His stomach rumbled. He said, "Greeses? Vor more greeses?"

Jessya pinched her lips and blinked. Gayle saw her interior eyelid flash pale before her normal ones clenched.

"Greeses and game, inside." Jessya pointed inland.

"Far?"

"A might."

"Good. Thank you," he said.

She nodded. The boy stood up and went back to his father, leaving the marbles in the sand.

"The promises," said Jessya. "Rodawnoc. No bees. Doa. Winter will be hard."

"Aye."

"Pax," she said, turning to leave.

"Wait." Gayle picked up the marbles and dropped them back in the chest. He carried it over to them.

"Yours."

"Canno eat it," said Onuieg.

"Nay," said Gayle. "But it is something."

The two adults glanced at each other.

"Aye," said Jessya. "Bost, taya day."

The boy stepped forward and took the chest. That was the boy's name, Gayle remembered. Bost.

"Pax, Bost," said the minister.

The boy smiled. "And to thee," he said. "Pax, Gayle."

The small family collected themselves and walked away.

The minister stood outside the fort walls and watched them disappear into the forest. At their leaving, he couldn't help but feel like he'd just lost his only friends in the world.

CHAPTER FOURTEEN

Dear Roger,

I know you meant well, but I must inform you that your request has been categorically denied. You must keep to the fifty kilograms of personal belongings and no more. And these will be subject to approval.

Your argument that the ship can carry your cargo is not incorrect. Under the original plans, we envisioned thousands of tons of materials traveling with us, but as you know, we've changed our thinking on this. We have chosen to quadruple flight safety devices and open the journey to more people. These changes should grant us ninety-eight per cent survival rate for the trip of 12,000-plus people.

As we've stated for years, instead of material, we invest in minds. We will bring engineers and scientists, craftsmen, farmers and diplomats, but also and especially artists, poets, and philosophers. I know your United Christendom doesn't recognize saints anymore, but you understand the concept. Those are the kinds of people who we desire to have make up the bulk of the colonists – the brightest and most enlightened among all of humankind.

That's not to say there's no place for you. Our friendship and your early financial support have reserved you and your family place aboard the ark, but it is vital to us that you understand and support our philosophy. We are earnest in our stated goals: we are going to a new world to begin again. We are NOT going to remake the Earth. We will make a better world by not making the same terrible, selfish, world-killing mistakes our ancestors did. We will co-operate and not compete.

As such, we will not need your gold. We will not need your robots. We will not need your nuclear weapons. We will not need you if you continue in this kind of thinking.

With the recent support of the Hindu Federation, I am in a position to refund you your entire investment should that be your desire. Please let me know your wishes as soon as possible so that we may open the space to others if these terms are not agreeable to you.

Letter from Jareth to Unknown Investor
November 12, 2336

13, Second-Month, 936 NE – Rodawnoc, Tirgwenin

"Look alive!" said Hasin, surprising a sleeping sentry slumped against the wall. "Is your gun charged?"

"Nay, sir. It seeped away."

"Wind it on the hour," he said. "You might only have one shot with that, but it's a hell of shot. You'll be sorry if you don't have it."

"Are we expecting an attack, sir?"

Hasin wanted to strike the man for addressing him so casually. Unsoldierly. But he held back. The man, Dedikodu, he was called, was one of the healthier men. And he knew the area better than most. Hasin needed him.

"Mind your post," Hasin said and walked away.

He marched the perimeter of the fort, scanning the darkness through gun slits by lightning strikes. The storms here were terrible, wet and furious, but the lightning strikes were nothing to what was a daily event on Vildeby. His hut had been the only strike near them. The flagpole had been too high. He'd used conductive carbon thread. An obvious mistake.

He paused at the south wall and searched the darkness between the posts for his returning men and saw no one.

At the supply hut, he checked the lock and found it sound. In the gap around the door he could see the garrison's meager remaining provisions; a bit of salted native pig and a half-empty barrel of tack. The other boxes were empty and kept for show. But he didn't think he was fooling anyone; the men were starving and they knew it.

Gayle had warned him. He'd even anticipated that the natives would leave the island. After the raid on that little farm, the minister had told him not to expect any more help from them. He explained that their crops had been decimated by drought, their stores by Enskari raids and 'they had no bees', whatever the hell that meant.

Gayle had suggested the men fish in the shallows, but they were soldiers, not fishermen. They might take an animal on the hoof when on the march, but wallowing in the mud was beneath their honor. Hasin knew how to feed his men. The same way he'd fed his men on Austen, the same way all conquering armies survived: they took what they needed from the conquered. To this, he'd sent his men, armed and hungry, to the native village to bring back food.

He moved past the barracks and garbage pile.

The fort was windblown and bleak. Hasin had built it and he hated it. He'd wanted to press inland back in the fall but his scouts never brought back news of treasure or empire, no organization or riches. Then the storms came, and they were visited by the pox. The garrison hunkered down to await resupply in the spring, besieged by the weather.

"Ahoy!"

Hasin rushed to the gate and there met his lieutenant and his men, returned from the village. Gayle stepped up beside him. The gate was thrown open.

"They're gone, sir," said Longmire. "The entire island is abandoned."

"Nonsense! We're still here. Obviously the island is not abandoned."

"Begging ye pardon, Governor. What I meant is that there ain't no more natives about. They've all skedaddled. Left us high and dry, they have."

He knew what he'd meant, but he didn't like the news and so had humiliated his new officer. The man was of course too stupid to realize it.

Hasin could hear the 'I told you so' in Gayle's clearing throat, but to the man's credit and survival he kept it to himself.

"Ye men go get warm," said Hasin. "Lieutenant, stay."

The men staggered toward their barracks, Gayle, Hasin, and Longmire tarried before the gate.

Longmire had been promoted to acting lieutenant after Stevens and all the other officers had drowned in a river the month before in a tragic and unexpected turn.

His promotion had probably saved his life. Longmire had turned in five of his fellow soldiers for pilfering food and they'd been set under the lash. One had died. The other four knew well who they had to blame for it. Moving the man to the officers' quarters was only prudent. Longmire was no officer, but he was a soldier. He'd served under Hasin in Austen and had not died or deserted, so in Hasin's eyes, he was as good as his kind came. He also followed orders and knew who fed him, like an animal. But now there was no food and Hasin had to do something or lose not only Longmire but the entire garrison.

"Well, damn them to hell," said Hasin. "We'll make them pay for their treachery."

"What would ye have us do, sir?"

"Gather the company, all but a skeleton crew to remain here to wait for resupply, which is due any day now," he added, like he believed it. "We will do what it is we came here to do, goddammit! Get the men ready to move out in the morning."

"Aye sir," said Longmire and quickly walked to his hut.

"We'll leave the sick and infirm. Maybe five more," Hasin said to Gayle. "That ought to be plenty to guard against a deserted island."

"Aye, Governor," said the minister. He had his book with him and scribbled something in it by the light of the sentinel's torch.

"What are you writing there?"

"I'm making a record of Longmire's report."

"Wait,' he said. "Maybe we don't want to write that."

"Why not?"

Hasin paused, thinking how this would look to the nobility back in Vildeby. "Well, aye. It goes to explain the hardships we have here and the duplicity of the natives. They have no mercy for us, we shall have little for them."

Gayle sighed. The minister was weak and sentimental. No soldier, but he had his uses.

"You will of course accompany us on the excursion," said Hasin.

"Of course," he said. "How long will it be?"

"As long as it takes."

★ ★ ★

Three weeks later Hasin and his surviving company were far up a river he had yet to name. Behind them, two and twenty Saved had been left at the fort with the bulk of their provisions but still faced starvation rations.

Hasin's inland company had survived by scavenging. They'd raided crops and homes on the march, taking food and valuables as they came upon them. The boats they were in now were a product of those raids.

Their journey had begun badly. After leaving scouted territory, they were quickly lost and wandered in circles and down dead ends for many dark days. The terrain and weather confounded them and cost them time, provisions, and four men. Eventually however, the weather let up, the ground gave meaning, and they recovered their bearings.

They saw natives occasionally but always at a distance. If approached, they ran away and disappeared as if into secret tunnels or the aether.

The villages they sacked had been deserted. The first ones they came to, like Jessya's little hovel on the island, were long abandoned, but as they pressed inland, they found signs of recent evacuation, some possibly just moments before the Enskarans arrived. They'd found warm cooking fires, half-washed linen, and abandoned personal possessions – shell necklaces, ornate finger bowls, fine woven cloaks, children's toys. The natives had precious little to begin with so Hasin took the fact that they'd left anything as a good sign. He was scaring them. He was conquering. Most importantly though they found food: grain, small livestock, even bread loaves and spices. It was food enough to keep them going, moving ever toward the awaiting silver and gold. Toward glory.

The landscape had changed gradually but dramatically as they moved away from Rodawnoc. The wild forests on their little forted island, choked with briars and vines, had been so thick they could not move through them. These were left behind some fifty kilometers inland, and the forests became parklike and magnificent as if some divine agency had planted a garden. The trees were spaced and broad, reaching high above them for fifty or a hundred meters where their branches, even leafless as they were then in the winter, offered canopied shade and shelter to the meadow grass below.

Minister Gayle was at some wonder at this, commenting that "A man could drive a barge wagon at a gallop through the forest and have no worry of crashing." Hasin had liked the analogy and was surprised that the effeminate scholar knew what a barge wagon was.

The forest travel was easy enough but slow, and Hasin moved the company toward the rivers where, unlike the strange forests, there was sure sign of human activity.

Though Gayle insisted they were farms, Hasin saw little to recommend that title to the swatches they found. Gardens came more to mind. They were little cultivated patches of land among many other suitable untilled patches and some wild ones. They were placed haphazardly, without apparent order or logic. Gayle, usually one to be impressed by the natives' ingenuity, had even commented on the foolishness and inefficiency of having so little land planted. Hasin saw it as sure proof that the Jareth's people had devolved since coming to Coronam.

They'd seen many gardens in the last few days. They'd seen worn trails near along the river, smelled cooking smoke, and even heard voices from the banks. Not in dire need of supplies, Hasin left these places unmolested, knowing he'd need supplies on the way back.

"Look, Admiral," said Gayle, pointing upriver.

Hasin followed the scholar's finger and saw a group of natives standing in the shallows, their yellow skin bright and sparkling. They kept wary eyes on the company but didn't move.

"They don't look armed," said Hasin, fumbling with the strap of his field glasses. "What are they doing? Why haven't they run like the others?"

"They look like they're waiting for something."

As they watched, there came a turbulence in the water, a rush and a cascading splash, spreading from the middle of the river toward where the people stood near the bank.

In unison, the people – twelve or thirteen of them – took a step back. From beneath the surface each lifted a three-meter-long pole. These poles were connected to netting. As the splashing surged toward them, they braced themselves against their poles.

Hasin could see it was fish making the tumult. He recognized silver-sided black fish. Edible and delicious. As a mass they rushed and splashed out of the water in panic.

When the fish reached the shallows in a frothy bubbling body, the natives dropped their nets and snagged them.

"We should talk to them," said Gayle.

"Aye, get some of those fish, and find out what's upriver."

Hasin ordered Gayle be taken ashore on one of the smaller boats while the company kept a distance so as to not frighten them away.

In the meantime all were to be ready. They put down their oars and took up weapons. They had plenty of ammunition: crossbow bolts, arrows, and slugs for their coilguns. Many of their rifles had failed but were lugged anyway for parts and pantomime, as if the natives knew what they were and knew to be afraid of them. Hasin figured the bows were the most effective deterrent to the savages since they understood what those were. Militarily however, they were the least effective of his arsenal – not including the broken Gauss rifles, of course.

The rain had let up and the sun shone in a sparkling blue sky above them. Gayle spent an hour with the savages onshore, talking to them while they collected their catch and placed it in baskets. When he returned to Hasin, he carried such a basket with a goodly supply of fish.

"What'd ye have to give up for that?" said Hasin.

"Nothing. They offered it before I could even ask."

"Aye," said Hasin, looking at the shore. "They have more than they need."

They watched as several natives went back into the water with baskets of fish balanced on their heads. They waded until the water was neck-deep and they struggled against the current. They looked about them and then dumped the dead fish into the water and returned to shore.

A moment later another frothy tumult erupted where they had been and dolphins breached the surface and devoured the offering like dinner.

The company watched the spectacle to completion. Only when the water was still again, and the fishermen gone over the bank, did Hasin order the boats forward.

"There's a large village up ahead," said Gayle. "It's called Pemioc."

Hasin looked at his minister, drawing his eyes from the river and the strangeness he had seen. "Good," he said. "Good."

★　★　★

The next day they found the village of Pemioc. Set on the right side of the river among a series of low hills, the village was larger than anything they'd yet encountered. A tall palisade of ten-meter posts surrounded it, walling it against the outside. The river too was blocked by tree trunks, cut spikes, and sandbars that required careful and slow navigation to keep from being grounded.

They arrived at dusk and the natives were waiting for them. They stood on the shore armed with bow and spear and watched as Hasin with three of his boats snaked their way to the dock. The other four were left in the channel awaiting a signal.

"Do you see it?" Gayle asked.

"Warriors," said Hasin, looking at the painted designs on their skin. It was something he'd never seen before, blue and reds, ochres, white and black. Each man decorated with designs both abstract and terrible. Fangs and staring eyes around zigzags and crescents. Their eyes, to a man, painted in a black stripe like a burglar mask, their whites made to look bigger and burrowing because of it. There were fifty of them if there was one. The numbers made Hasin nervous. He'd not seen so many at once before and he'd never seen them fight.

Gayle stood on the bow. "Pax!" he called. "Pax!"

The men didn't move.

Their boats came closer.

Longmire's coil rifle charged with a hum at the stern. Hasin heard him slide the bolt open and insert the iron slug before snapping it shut.

"Keep it wound, Lieutenant," said Hasin.

"Aye, sir."

The foremost boat nosed into a wicker dock and Gayle leapt out to catch it. He uncoiled rope and tied the boat down. Hasin was impressed at how casually he did it, turning his back to the heathens even – a thing he would never do.

When the boat was tied, Gayle went directly to the assemblage. Hasin kept his men on their boats. He saw the glows of their charged rifles and turned to watch the shore.

"Vi strangers," said Gayle. "Far away in the sky." He pointed.

"Enskari," came a voice. Hasin couldn't tell which one had spoken. Neither apparently could Gayle.

"Vem?" he said.

"Here." A slender woman stepped out from behind the crowd. She was clad as the others, loincloth and paint. A glistening spear in her hand.

Hasin realized to his surprise that many of the warriors were women.

"I am Christiana," the woman said.

"I am Minister Eddie Gayle." He made a low royal bow to the savage then said, gesturing to the boats, "Yonder is our leader, Admiral Tir Hasin."

The woman nodded as if she already knew.

"Come ashore," called Christiana. "Welcome to Pemioc." She spoke in a clear unaccented voice that carried easily to Hasin.

Hasin considered for a moment then stepped out of the boat.

"Bring in the others," he said to Longmire.

Longmire signaled the boats behind, who alerted the boats in the channel. They all moved toward the dock.

Hasin strolled up to Christiana like he was a visiting king, which he would be soon.

"Admiral Governor Tir Hasin," he said with a half bow to Christiana. "At your service."

"I am called Christiana," she said. "I am sent from the, eh...." She stammered for the word. Then huffed once and started again. "The leader of Pemioc sent me. She has arranged a banquet for ye."

"You know us?" said Gayle.

"Some," she said.

"How have you come to speak our language so well?"

"I learned it."

"Who—" began Gayle.

"What's with the soldiers?" said Hasin, cutting him off.

"A sign of respect," said Christiana.

"Sign of strength?"

"Yes, that too. This is a trading village. Not all people are enlightened."

"Peace through power," said Hasin, nodding agreeably.

"Peace," said Christiana. "Settle your men in those huts there." She gestured to a row of buildings. "Rest, then we'll feast."

"Will your leader be there?"

"Yes."

"Splendid," said Hasin. "Lieutenant!"

Longmire appeared at his side. "Sir?"

"Form up the men. We'll settle in those huts."

"Guard on the boats?"

Hasin stole a glance at Christiana, who watched him coolly. His eyes fell to her small painted breasts. They distracted him for only a moment. "Two men," he said, remembering where he was. "As normal."

"Aye, sir," said Longmire.

"And, Lieutenant," he said. "Keep 'em hot."

Longmire winked. "Of course, sir."

The men formed in parade and in lockstep, their rifles changed and armed, marched to the huts.

"I'll see everything is ready," Christiana said. "See you in about an hour."

"Splendid," said Hasin.

The painted soldiers broke ranks and wandered away, oblivious to the danger they were in. Hasin had only to utter a single command and his men would have turned their weapons upon them. Coilgun and crossbow, sword and dagger would have cut them to pieces. Hasin scoffed. Fifty people – some of them women – to defend a city this size? What arrogance. They must be used to fighting cowards.

"How many people do you think are here?" said Gayle to Hasin. "It seems to me this place can hold thousands, many more than are here. Now, I'd say only a few hundred Saved are here, not including us."

"Souls maybe, but not Saved."

"Nay, of course," said Gayle. "But I can remedy that. Tomorrow's the Sabbath."

"That's right. You brought your kit."

"A missionary should never be without it."

"You think you can baptize the entire city?"

"I can try."

The huts were like long houses and barracks-like, which pleased Hasin. They were dug into the ground to about waist-high, then mortared bricks rose to two meters before beams and thatch bent inward to make the ceiling.

Beds ran along the sides of the space. Down the center under a high thatched roof was a path set with a series of small fires burning hot and nearly smokeless. These heated the space and provided some light. Oil lamps cut from blue wooden gourds were placed along support posts and gave off a sweet tropical scent. The light they provided could be regulated by adjusting a spongy wick at the top.

The soldiers all wanted to peel out of their damp clothes and sleep on the soft cots, but smells of roasted meat and sweet spices roused them. They were as cleaned up as they could be and ready to a man when Christiana reappeared in an hour to escort them.

Hasin was surprised they were allowed to bring weapons but was more surprised when he saw the savage soldiers had left theirs behind.

A big bonfire burned in a wide fire pit in the center of what Hasin thought of as the town square. He and his men were marched in front of the people in parade once around the fire. The natives bowed and greeted them with "Pax" and "Welcome."

Hasin and Gayle were given places at a table with local dignitaries.

"This is our leader, Lisa," said Christiana. "This is her husband, Peter."

"Glad to meet ye," Hasin said.

"Pax," said Gayle and bowed.

"Pax," they responded.

Hasin sat down and became aware of low drumming from the darkness. Another sound, a harp perhaps, joined the soft drums and together the music rose to a complex melody unlike anything he'd heard before. The low thrumming drum was chant-like, and the strings a call.

Hasin saw the Tirgwenians all bow their heads for a moment as if in prayer, but no one spoke. The drums rose in volume and speed, booming between the houses and off the palisades in approaching crescendo. The harp ascended in undulating pulses, birdlike and deep. It all ended suddenly and the natives together said, "Om."

"Are you seeing new and strange things on your travels?" asked Lisa, smiling at Hasin.

He realized his face must have betrayed some emotion he wasn't sure he wanted to convey. "Oh, aye," he said. "Tell me how ye know our language."

"We learned it when we heard ye were coming."

"How?"

"The Rowdanae told us," she said. "We don't need to speak of them."

"Ah," said Gayle. "Jessya and Onuieg?"

"Aye," said Lisa, dishing a lump of steamed grain into her bowl. "They came to us."

"Where are they?"

"You'd have them?" said Peter.

"Aye," said Gayle.

Lisa nodded to Christiana, who got up and left the table. "Christiana will bring them," she said.

"How do you eat this?" said Hasin.

"Cover it in honey." Lisa waved a dripping stick of it over her bowl like a wand. "Then take tambin petal like this." She peeled a leaf off a large red flower in the middle of the table. Hasin had thought it was a table decoration. "Scoop the root meal like this." Using the petal as a spoon, she put the leaf and honey-soaked grain into her mouth and smiled with satisfaction. "If you want it more salty, choose leaves nearer the heart."

Hasin did as directed. "It's delicious."

The second course was fried fish and figs, butter, and more honey. For dessert they had honey cakes. Throughout the meal they drank water and sweet honey mead that had intoxicating properties.

Tasting the mead, Hasin ordered his men be given only water. "They can be unruly when they drink," he said.

Lisa nodded as if understanding.

They ate in pleasant company, small talk among Hasin and Lisa. After a while dancers appeared and frolicked around the fire in whirling acrobatics to new music Hasin couldn't identify. Gayle spoke animatedly with Peter. He took out a book and showed him pictures he'd drawn and asked about them. Peter would tell him something and Gayle would scribble new notes. In between talking and writing, he drank more mead.

"You speak our language so well. It's a marvel. Did you glean all this from Jessya?" Gayle tipped his cup to his mouth and spilled much of it down his front. A servant refilled it the instant he put it back on the table.

"It is not so different from our language," Peter said. "Are there many languages among the civilized worlds?"

Hasin noted that he'd not answered Gayle's question. It was a skillful deflection, but a deceit all the same.

"A little regional deviance, but the same tongue. Yours is the first truly different language I've heard."

"It's not so different from yours. We all came from Old Earth, did we not?"

Christiana returned. "Your friends will join us soon," she said.

Gayle's glassy eyes lingered on her. Hasin thought it might be time to send him to bed, but then he'd have to carry on politeness with the savages alone, and he wasn't sure he was up to that.

"Is Lisa your real name?" asked Gayle, turning to their leader.

Her tawny skin sparkled in the firelight where her clothes were open.

"Nay," said Lisa. "We thought it would be easier for you."

"What is your name? If I may ask?"

"Lahgassi," she said. "Leader of the Pemiae tribe. My husband is Pytul. Christiana is called Krikhuia among us. She is our daughter."

"Krik," she said.

"You are very accommodating, Queen Lahgassi," said Gayle. "And Krik."

The younger girl smiled at the mention.

"I am no queen," Lisa said. "Only a leader. Pemioc is a crossroads. We are traders. Most of my folk are away now on the land. We'll assemble again for trading at rendezvous in the spring."

"What do you trade?" said Hasin.

"Everything."

"Do you know gold?" he said quickly. Perhaps too quickly. Then he added more casually, "And silver or other metals. That's what we trade for on Enskari. Show them your chalice, Gayle."

Gayle reached into his bag and came up with a small gold chalice, the centerpiece of his ministerial rites. "This is used in our most holy sacraments," he said. "We all drink from it and it unites us."

The Tirgwenians nodded.

"Aye," said Peter. "A good ceremony of friendship."

Gayle said, "It's not about friendship. It's about devotion to God."

"May I hold it?" asked Peter.

Gayle glanced at Hasin, who nodded assent. Gayle handed it over.

"It's heavy," Peter said. "And beautiful." He studied the etchings on the side and lifted it into the light.

"Do you have gold here?" said Hasin. "Like that chalice? Silver maybe?" He showed them a ring on his finger.

"That's nice," said Lisa. "Mostly we trade honeys and pollens, grains and fish. Inland there's more call for metals. It's mined there."

Jessya, Onuieg, and Bost appeared in the firelight, slowly trudging toward their table. Except for the boy's, their faces were all turned down.

"Pax, Gayle," said the boy.

"Pax, Bost," said Gayle thickly.

Jessya spoke in low but urgent tone to the leader. "Lahgassi, dem robber folk."

"Hush," Lisa said. "Manners."

"There was some confusion with pigs – grease," slurred Gayle. "It was an unfortunate thing. They didn't have them in pens. How were we to know?"

"Day knew," said Onuieg.

"Manners!"

"Perhaps they are not all friends?" said Peter.

"Nay," said Lisa.

"Perhaps we should let the Rowdanae return to their work?"

Lisa turned to Hasin. "Is that all right with you?"

"Of course," he said.

"Go," she said to the family.

They left quickly without another word, though Bost lingered a moment and waved at Gayle, who returned the gesture. When they were out of sight, the minister cast a dark glance at Hasin that under other circumstances would have gotten him a crisp slap across his chin. Hasin pretended not to notice it.

"Ye should make peace with your neighbors," said Lisa. "If ye plan to stay at Rodawnoc."

"What neighbors? Everyone's gone."

"They will return," she said. "Others will come. Thrive there. Learn the ways, seek the bees and ye will be welcome."

"Seek the bees?"

"Symbol of harmony," said Christiana.

"Oh," said Hasin. "Of course."

Gayle slumped but caught himself before falling off his chair.

"These mines ye speak of," Hasin said, sensing he had little time. "How far are they?"

"I don't know," Lisa said. "I've never gone that far up the river."

"So it's accessible by the water?"

"Aye."

"We'll head there then."

"You'll leave in the morning," said Peter.

"What?" said Hasin. "We were hoping to stay a couple of days to rest. Trade for supplies and such."

"We haven't the provisions for that," said Lisa. "It's been a hard year. Take this feast as a gift and continue your journey. I've heard that the mountain folk have surplus this year. Among them you may trade for what you need, but perhaps not for what you want. Get those things you need to survive, for it is hard living on Rodawnoc. In the spring, if you are still here, you are welcome back for rendezvous."

Gayle snored in his chair.

"Rest tonight," Lisa said. "Be gone by midday."

With that Lisa, Peter, and Christiana got up and left. They bowed politely but wouldn't linger.

The company dismissed to their beds. Longmire and two soldiers carried Gayle. Hasin tarried at the fire watching the Tirgwenians' faces in the light watching him, their expressions curious but cautious. It was quite the contrast. Lisa had not showed much interest in them, not asked them any questions at all beyond inane pleasantries. Nor had she told them anything useful, with the possible exception of the presence of mines inland. He'd need to talk to Gayle in the morning to see if the scholar had learned anything from Peter. Who taught them the language, for example. Surely not those dumb savages.

★ ★ ★

A steaming vat of root meal and honey was waiting for them outside their door when they woke the next morning. At early dawn, the courtyard was deserted but for a few painted warriors who kept their distance and watched on them.

They ate heartily. The food was heavy and good.

After breakfast, the Enskarans reluctantly collected their things and mustered to their boats.

The morning was cold, the sky filled with low gray clouds, which broke in places, allowing amber sunlight to seep through in puddles. This light moved in patches across the ground and when it would land upon a Tirgwenian, their skin would glitter like faceted gems. Upon one Tirgwenian guard, however, Hasin remarked that he didn't just glitter, but something about him flashed.

"Gayle," he said, pointing to the one who'd drawn his attention. "Is that gold?"

The minister squinted his bloodshot eyes and balanced himself on unsteady legs. "That breastplate?" he said. "I don't know. It could be copper."

"No. It's too bright," said Hasin. "Too yellow."

"Perhaps." He wiped beaded sweat from his forehead and stumbled toward the boats.

Hasin kept his eyes on the Tirgwenian. "And they said there was no metal here."

CHAPTER FIFTEEN

Man's place in nature is to subdue it to his will. This is God's commandment, this is man's purpose. Subdue nature and make it his own for he is master over nature as God is master over men.
United Christian Scripture

11, Third-Month, 936 – Half day inland from Pemioc, Tirgwenin

The evening, after leaving Pemioc, a clamor on the admiral's boat caused the entire party to go ashore. Dedikodu didn't mind. He'd been paddling against the current all day and his hands were open blisters. He was in the fourth canoe, third behind the lead, but as the river was quiet and the men silent in their labors, he could hear the argument between the admiral and his lackey, Minister Eddie Gayle.

The admiral's booming voice carried over the slow river, perhaps intentionally. "Of course they stole it!" he bellowed.

Hasin had been in a foul mood since they'd left the village, pensive and short-tempered. Dedikodu had assumed that he, like the rest of the men, was unhappy at having to leave Pemioc. The village was nice – the best place they'd seen since arriving on this godforsaken world. They'd been warm and dry and fed. The beds were comfortable, the food delicious and filling. The people, though unsaved savages, were friendly, even comely. That Christiana for example was a ripe young thing and had been the topic of conversation since the men first saw her.

"We don't know that," said Gayle. "I don't remember."

"They got you drunk and robbed you. It was intentional," said the admiral. "Or are you saying you're so inept that ye lost the most precious piece of your sacrament kit in the river?"

Their boat nosed up the bank and Hasin stormed off into the woods. Gayle followed with a beaten gait.

The rest of the boats pushed up and disgorged men in a sloppy, muddy landing. Longmire ordered two to stay with the boats and took the rest with him up a hill to shelter beneath a big tree. The rain had started at midday with an earnest effort and then settled into a lingering drizzle that showed no signs of abatement.

Longmire ordered Dedikodu and his mate Alex to gather wood for a fire.

"Ain't no lightning here," said Alex. "Only reason I'll go under that tree."

"Can't remember a storm on Enskari that didn't have lightning," said Dedikodu. "Which do you like better?"

Alex shrugged. He turned over a fallen log and dug at the rotting insides. "It's a reminder we ain't home, isn't it?" he said. "All wrong here. Cold, rain. Nothing here. Trees this big that ain't been cooked by God's fiery fingers. Women wearing paint like it's clothes. Yellow people that don't feel the cold. None of it natural."

Dedikodu thought about that for a moment. Everyone called the Tirgwenians yellow, but he saw them more gold. He'd seen similar tones on Enskari, some strippers he knew in a tavern in Moxly by the warm coasts of Austen had tans like Tirgwenian skin, but they didn't shimmer like the Tirgwenians did. He remembered hearing something about silicates in the air that protected the planets and a theory that the savages here had somehow adopted the same thing to protect themselves from Coronam's rays.

Not that he'd seen much of their sun these last few months. When it did shine, it cast ring-shadows dim as night. Winter on Rodawnoc was a wet, overcast, miserable, cold affair. They were equatorial and yet the nights were positively frigid. Back at the fort, he'd go to sleep with a warm tea beside his bed and every morning, he had to chip the ice out of his cup for coffee.

The insects were strange and worrisome too. The red flies bit like mosquitoes, silent and painless until they flew away with a piece of flesh in their gobs big as your little finger. There was a terrible reptile on the island as well, a six-legged crocodile that could climb trees. It could run faster than a man, swim like a fish, and swing like a monkey. They could come at a man from anywhere and men were rightly terrified of them.

The people they'd met were, up until Pemioc, a useless slovenly bunch. Dedikodu couldn't imagine them standing in the way of Hasin's grand plans of conquest until the day before. There he'd seen tall proud Tirgwenians, unafraid and strong – far different creatures than the starving people from the island.

"There ain't nothing we can burn without first drying it out," said Alex.

"Bring some anyway," said Dedikodu. "We'll make it Longmire's problem."

Alex smiled mischievously, exposing the gaps in his grin, three teeth missing in front, God knows how many in the back. He looked thin and weak, his color not what it should be. With a start Dedikodu thought that he looked like the poor beggars from Rodawnoc. They all did.

"Get back here with some wood, ye miserable sons of whores!" cried Longmire. "Be back in the count of twenty or I'll put ye both under the lash."

It was not an idle threat. Longmire liked the lash. He liked giving it, he liked watching it. He was a terrible man who had no business leading men, but Hasin liked him. For not the first time on Tirgwenin, Dedikodu actually pined for the time he'd spent enslaved under Captain Upor. That man was a bastard too – they all were – but at least he wasn't a sadist.

Alex loaded Dedikodu's arms with ground fall. There wasn't much. The area seemed to have been picked over for firewood. The only reason they'd found anything was that a tree had fallen recently. The root knot was still caked in mud, exposed like a nest of worms in a muck clod.

Longmire looked at the soaked kindling the two brought back and got that terrible vindictive grin he got before he did something cruel. Before he could do it, however, Hasin returned from the woods with Gayle five paces behind.

"Get the men in the boats," he ordered. "We're going back."

"To the island?" asked Longmire.

"Nay, to Pemioc. Those heathens stole from us."

"It was just a little thing," said Gayle.

"Minister, you are a fool." The admiral turned on him like he was about to strike him. Gayle obviously thought he was and recoiled, stumbling a step down the hill. "It was not a little thing. It was gold. Do you know the value of gold? Do you not know the sacrifice the Crown endured so you may have gold? Gold arms ships, Minister. Gold saves lives. Gold is the metal of God! You of all people should know that."

Gayle looked weak and beaten. Dedikodu felt sorry for him. None of them wanted to be there, but the minister in particular didn't have the skills to abide. He'd had a soft life and Tirgwenin was anything but soft.

"It's a precedent," said Hasin. "Longmire, damn you! Get the men to the boats."

"Aye, sir." The lieutenant began to physically pull men up from the ground. "Stand up or I'll lash the hide off ye!"

Dedikodu was happy he was already standing.

The admiral raved on. "It's a test, you see. They're testing us."

"I don't know about a test," said Gayle.

"It is to me. If they think they can steal from me – an Enskaran officer – they've got another think coming. We need to make it clear who runs this place now."

Longmire shoved Dedikodu down the hill as they reluctantly returned to the boats.

In short order everyone was aboard again. The command came to turn downriver. It made for easy travel; the current was strong, the water mud-flooded from upriver.

Dedikodu didn't like the tenor of Hasin's voice but he was happy to be returning to Pemioc. He was sure the minister's chalice, for that was what the whole thing was about, a little gold cup smaller than a coffee mug, would be returned in quick order and hopefully they'd be allowed another stay in the village. He didn't relish the idea of sleeping in the boats again or bivouacking in the muddy banks where the damn crocs could find you.

At dusk the admiral ordered the boats ashore. As near as Dedikodu could figure, they were yet a couple kilometers from Pemioc.

Longmire assembled the men on the bank into battle lines and Hasin made them march. They quitted the river and went through the forest where the mud didn't suck their boots from their legs. When the palisade was in sight, he stopped them

"Make 'em hot," Hasin ordered.

The standard-issue coilgun musket was a single-shot device. It fired a magnetic projectile down a barrel of oscillating magnets to velocities above the speed of sound. Such was it introduced to Dedikodu, but he didn't really understand it. All he knew was that he had to wind it for a charge, load the slug through a breach in the top, and aim down the barrel. He'd fired his gun once before but he'd been trained in reloading and charging until he had calluses on his hands, the same calluses which were now open blisters from all the rowing. He was an average reloader. He could reload his coilgun every other minute for ten minutes before he grew tired and it was closer to one every three. Then one every five. The coil was hard to wind and the weapon was exceedingly heavy. It would drown a man if he fell into the river with it over his shoulder. Everyone had cut their shoulder straps because of this fear.

Weapons charged, the men re-formed ranks and marched toward the wall in a picket. A hundred meters from the palisade they turned toward a narrow road meandering through the low wet grass toward a gate in the wall.

Dedikodu saw a tower to the side of the gate with a single figure watching them. The gate was not barred. The massive doors stood ajar, several meters wide.

"Stay alert," said Hasin. "Await the command. Keep 'em hot."

The musket weighed on Dedikodu's shoulder, bruising his collarbone. He tried to balance it in his palm like the others but he'd never learned the knack. He was a sailor not a soldier. He'd been captured aboard a Maarawan ship in a pirate raid and traded to three captains before finding his way aboard the *Hopewell* in the indentured service of Captain Upor. With the weight of his gun on his shoulder now, and the tense fear he sensed among the men, he longed for the weightlessness of that duty. He only had four more years to serve out and then he could return home to Maaraw.

The column marched toward the gate, approaching the settlement from a side they'd not seen.

A Tirgwenian moved out and met them fifteen meters from the wall. "Pax!" he said and raised his arm. "Enskari reback?"

"I want to see Lisa," said Hasin without slowing his step. He passed the Tirgwenian and behind him came the men.

The native paused for an instant then sprinted toward the gate. He wore a light jacket and leggings, leather sandals, and a small knife at his waist. His spear he'd left at the gate.

He overtook Hasin, who didn't even turn to acknowledge him, and dashed inside.

Hasin arrived at the gate and pushed it open wider without breaking stride and led the column inside.

Gayle was close behind him, but not walking in step with the soldiers. He alone was unarmed. Every man was steeled, sword, dagger, knife, or ax. Most had muskets, the others crossbows or longbows.

Inside the gate was a wide cobblestone path that snaked among the structures between plots of garden and grass. The road curved around a low hill upon which stood woven clusters of beehives. A few insects buzzed the area, hardly a fraction of what the hives promised. Dedikodu didn't know bees and assumed they at least had the good sense to stay out of the rain.

Deeper in the village, Dedikodu heard shouts and calls, some urgent, some soothing.

Along the road they marched. They were joined by curious villagers who gawked and marched with them, laughing and excited. There were wide-eyed children and small catlike dogs who mewed and snuffed at them, always staying close to the children's heels. Dedikodu saw an old man with a wad of dough in his hands kneading it as he followed them, flour up his arms dampening in the rain. Several women carried half-finished baskets and absentmindedly wove them as they walked, following the Enskarans into the heart of their city.

And then there were soldiers.

Dedikodu identified them by their weapons but not by their paint. They were not adorned as before. They looked far less dangerous without the decoration and Dedikodu felt a little relief at this. It was short-lived though, for as he passed one up close, he saw an oily poison sheen on the long blade atop a three-meter spear.

There were hundreds of people around them when they arrived at the square where they'd feasted the night before. A low fire burned and sizzled in the pit, a small thing compared to the grand blaze of the previous night. Here Hasin ordered them to stop.

"Battle line!" he barked. The men fanned out though they weren't sure which direction to face. They were surrounded. Longmire lined them up based on the direction Hasin faced.

Lisa and Peter emerged from the throng. She blinked at them as if she'd just been woken up, her inner eyelids closing an instant before her outer ones as if trying to shake the sleep out of both sets.

"What's the problem, Admiral?" she said.

"Who do you think you are?" Hasin demanded.

"I don't understand," she said.

Gayle stepped forward. "It's about my chalice. My cup?" he said. "I seem to have—"

Hasin cut him off. "You give us a little food and think you can get away with anything?" His voice was a menacing growl. Unhinged was the word that came to Dedikodu's mind.

"You think you can lie to us?" raved Hasin. "You think you're in charge?"

"Admiral—"

"Rotten thieving savages!" Hasin roared. "Burn 'em down! Men, burn 'em down!"

There was a moment's pause, a small silence where Dedikodu could hear raindrops in the puddles while he held his breath.

"Burn 'em down!" repeated Longmire. He brought his own musket to his shoulder and fired.

The shot was loud and horrible. It ripped through Peter's chest like it was paper and wounded a half dozen others behind him.

The shot pulled the men from their stupor, and acting as trained they filled the air with fire which filled the camp with screams.

"Kill 'em all!" screamed Hasin. "Bring me the gold!"

Dedikodu shook with terror and pulled his weapon down to recharge and reload. He'd shot with the others, a blind volley, but it hadn't mattered. He'd killed with it. The Tirgwenians were so thick he couldn't miss and the shot so powerful it killed in a line from him to the wall.

"Fire at will!" came the command. Dedikodu didn't know from whom.

Some of the men rewound their guns, crossbows and coil. Others drew knives and chased after the fleeing savages.

Hasin stood over the woman called Lisa. She was wounded and on her knees. He unholstered his sidearm and checked the safety. He fired the gun point-blank into her side and she collapsed to the ground, eyes wide in horror and surprise.

"There's gold here! I want it," Hasin hollered.

The men wound, reloaded and fired. If they couldn't see a man, they shot into huts. The bullets exploded through them and out in a wave of splinters.

Tirgwenian bodies lay dead and dying all around. Their blood was as red as theirs and colored the mud a dirty death.

Soon it was just Alex and Dedikodu in the square. The rest of the men had abandoned their slow weapons and gone at them with blades.

There was shouting from behind them and Alex set toward that. Not wanting to be left alone, Dedikodu followed him.

The Tirgwenians had formed a pocket of resistance around the beehives. The little rise in elevation gave them some advantage. From there they did not retreat but fought anyone who tried to close in. A dozen Saved lay dead on the ground, pierced with lance and arrow.

The bees were now awake. They swarmed the soldiers and spun around one figure in particular. It was Christiana. She sat in the midst of the hives – right in the middle. It was difficult to see her, so thick were the bees swarming her head. At first Dedikodu thought she was dying, killed by the stinging insects, but she was not. She stood unharmed and hummed a buzzing noise while swaying as if to soft unheard music. Her eyes were closed but she was alive.

"Stay your wrath, brothers!" Gayle ran toward the hives, trying to put himself between the soldiers and the defenders. "Let me—"

A Tirgwenian arrow struck him in the back of the leg and he stumbled and fell.

"Nay, I—" His speech was cut short as his jaws snapped shut. He spasmed, then shook and seized up solid as if cement had hardened in his veins.

Dedikodu ran forward and grabbed the minister by the collar and dragged him to cover.

Longmire appeared with a small company of soldiers with crossbows. From behind a low wall they volleyed bolts into the natives.

Gayle shook and chattered. The wound wasn't bad, not life-threatening on its own, but it was surely poisoned. Dedikodu could do nothing but cradle the man's head and slide a piece of leather into his mouth to keep him from destroying his teeth. He'd need them if he recovered.

Hiding with Gayle, Dedikodu watched as Longmire and his squad methodically killed each defending savage. When the last one fell, Longmire strolled up to the hives and waved the insects away.

"They have no sting!" he yelled.

Christiana alone sat amongst the bees, humming and serene. Longmire raised his evil whip and brought it down upon her head.

She fell over on her side, her head ripped open. Blood streamed down her face.

He grabbed her by the hair and pulled her down from the hill. She kicked and fought but only when she was at the bottom of the hill, when the hives behind her were toppled and set afire, did she scream.

★   ★   ★

Into the darkness went the mayhem. Shrieks subsided by and by, replaced with wounded moans and the crackling of burning houses. Hasin ordered every nook and cranny to be searched and all spoils collected for his inspection. What they could not take with them, they were to destroy.

Dedikodu did as directed. Part of him, the better part, recoiled at what he was doing, but another part, a darker older animal inside him, ran with the vicious hunt like a wild animal. He forgot himself and his humanity after a time, and struck down man, woman, and child with club and dagger, and ransacked tiny homes for tiny treasures of metal and curious things. It was a madness and it gripped him for hours. Then all at once for no particular reason, he stopped what he was doing and sat down on the ground and cried. Beneath the screams of raped women and dying men, he was sensible to the low droning of bees nearby. He focused on that and removed himself from the rest of the slaughter.

When dawn came they were slow to recognize it because of the light from the burning town.

"Where's Lisa?" cried Hasin. "Her body was right here. Where is she?"

Dedikodu was in the square sitting in the spot where'd he'd feasted with the dead just the day before. He looked over to where the leader's body had lain and saw only darkened mud where it had been.

"You there," cried Hasin to him. "Did you see what happened to her?"

"Nay, Captain – Gov – uhm Admiral," Dedikodu said, wiping his eyes. "Maybe someone dragged her body away."

"Or she wasn't dead," said Hasin.

"A goodly many heathens escaped into the woods," Longmire said, gesturing out the gate toward the hills. "A goodly many."

"How many dead here?"

"We count three hundred five and sixty bodies of savages," said Longmire.

"Our losses?"

"Seven dead, one and twenty wounded, including Minister Gayle."

"So we lost a third."

"Aye."

Dedikodu did the math in his head and figured it to be more than that. They'd started with seventy, lost four to weather, one to a crocodile, and now near thirty more, for to be called wounded here was to be grievously wounded. That seemed closer to half to him.

"How many savages escaped?"

"A good many."

"How many, goddammit!" yelled the admiral.

Longmire shrunk from Hasin. "Eh, a hundred at least. Maybe more."

"Too many. They'll return. Load up the boats. Leave the dead. Can any of the wounded walk?"

"Nay sir, not a one," said the lieutenant. "They're stricken as stone with muscle cramp."

Dedikodu watched as the admiral considered his options. No man wanted to be left behind, dead or alive. The idea of leaving their mates in the bloody sand of this terrible place would not sit well with the living. The idea of leaving live ones carried a real risk of mutiny.

"Bring down the boats. We're leaving."

Longmire drafted eight men to retrieve the boats, Dedikodu among them.

They took one of the Tirgwenian canoes and pushed it through the maze of obstacles into the channel and poled and paddled two kilometers to where they'd stored their stolen boats.

They moved quickly and quietly, stopping at every sound from the woods or river, Dedikodu expected at any moment to be pierced a dozen times with poisoned vengeful arrows.

But no arrows came. No threatening noise reached Dedikodu's ears beyond the sounds of distant slaughter still happening, and a low buzzing around his head. A bee had followed him up the river and now flew around him like an orbiting satellite. He swatted it away with his hat, forgetting that they wouldn't sting.

With the others, he untied a boat and aimed downriver. Silently in the morning glow of an alien and now bloodied world, they guided the boats back to the dock where they'd been welcomed before.

By happenstance, Dedikodu was in the admiral's boat. While he waited his turn to move into the canal, he accidentally rummaged though Hasin's personal chest. He found it under the mess kit, wrapped in a linen dinner napkin beside his socks: an iconic golden cup.

CHAPTER SIXTEEN

Jareth's World is primed for our conquest. I have left an indelible mark upon the place.
Excerpt from letter to the Court of Zabel Genest from Captain Tir Hasin
6, Eleventh-Month 936 NE

6, Fourth-Month, 936 – Rodawnoc, Tirgwenin

They left their boats on the shore of the island and trudged the sand and briar for several kilometers inland until they found the fort. They'd been seventy men when they'd left. They returned as nine and forty. The fort they returned to was in ruins – whole sections of wall had fallen in and only a single structure still wore a roof. Littered across the courtyard were dung and debris and unburied bodies. Of the two and twenty men who'd been left there, only fifteen still drew breath and that not well.

The men from the expedition fared better, but only a little. When they saw the condition of the fort, they despaired.

"What?" they cried. "Where's our resupply?"

"Must have been delayed," said Hasin. "Get the men to work, Longmire. We need a defensible fort."

"Aye, Admiral."

"Governor now," he said.

Gayle thought this was a good sign; perhaps the man was coming to his senses.

The minister had been little more than cargo for the return journey. The Tirgwenian poison had held his muscles in flex for two days, wracked him with palsy and pain throughout. Blessedly, he was unconscious for most of it. When it finally cleared, his muscles were spent, his tendons torn, and his body one big bruise. He rode in a rear boat with other recovering men and watched helplessly as Hasin unleashed madness across the countryside.

When he could write, Gayle recorded what he remembered of the massacre, trying to make it sound at least a little plausible that his commander had acted properly. It wasn't easy. In his private journal he poured out his horror and hatred in vitriolic phrases that would get him hanged by Hasin if he found them.

The booty from Pemioc was a joke. Pillaging soldiers had found a few metal fragments, mostly copper – the breastplate the admiral had seen that morning turned out to be copper. They found also brass bowls and some steel, which surprised them. They recovered a few small pieces of gold and silver jewelry among the dead, but not enough to fill even a coffee cup.

From a sailor called Dedikodu, Gayle learned of the hunt for Lisa's body. They'd not found it. Her husband's corpse lay where he'd been shot, but the leader's was gone.

Hasin killed everyone save for two hostages: Christiana and Bost, the child from Rowdawnoc.

They were transported in the middle boat, tightly bound and guarded, more from Gayle than the enemy. Christiana was horribly used. Her face was grotesquely bruised and swollen and a bloody stain between her legs was more than Gayle could contemplate. He put his attention to praying that the resupply ships had come and he could abandon this hell once and for all when they got back.

Gayle's influence over the admiral was now nonexistent. Hasin had learned that his minister had put himself between attacking soldiers and the natives, and to him that was treason. Gayle knew that it was only because he was a minister and not completely under his command that he hadn't already been hanged, that and his propaganda journals.

"You got what you deserved, man," Hasin told him. "May that arrow sore grow septic. May you lose the leg for it. Maybe then you'll remember whose side you're on."

Hasin no longer spoke; he raved. He was a madman, bloodlusted and vengeful. When Gayle tried to imagine what it was he was so angry about, what it was he needed to draw such terrible retribution for, he figured that it was because he'd not found the treasure he sought. He blamed the miserable starving Tirgwenians for their poverty in not making him rich.

Gayle many times tried to approach the prisoners. The men would not help him. Anyone seen talking to the minister was suspect and not two consecutive days went by that Longmire did not use his whip on someone in the company. Once he used it on Gayle. Gayle stopped trying to talk to prisoners after that.

Along the river, they had passed through new areas that had not been scouted or seen by off-worlders. Occasionally they encountered a yellow native who greeted them curiously with signs of welcome and calls of "Pax," only to be cut in half by a musket slug. But these were few and far between. Usually, as if word of their coming had spread faster than the river flowed, they found only emptied villages. These Hasin put to fire, explaining the military necessity of it – 'to make safe the fort and its position'. Though where their fort was in relation to where they were, no one could tell. Gayle saw only bloodlust, hate, and senseless waste.

They took what food they could carry and destroyed the rest, for the same reason, according to Hasin: 'To weaken the enemy'. They set fire to the huts and ripped up the plantings. Gayle marveled at how much work the men did to ruin gardens when they wouldn't plant one themselves. It took hours to cut the orchards down, rip up the seedlings and roots. It was heavy exertion to destroy when the fires would not take in the rain. And the men were not strong. The food they stole spoiled quickly in the damp of the water-soaked boats. A pink mold the men came to call 'Lisa's Revenge' spread like a shadow overnight. A small bite of molded meal caused vomiting and stomach pains, loose bowels and disorientation. In greater amounts, it killed outright.

When Hasin sent his troops inland chasing smoke to find villages to destroy, Gayle waited with the boats and mourned. He thought to call out to the guarded prisoners, apologize, give them hope – say something, but again and again, he didn't. Was it fear or shame, he no longer could tell.

Soon they found no more villages. No more fires. No more food.

They let the current take their boats to the sea and followed the coast the wrong way for a week before discovering the error.

In the end Hasin had killed hundreds, maybe thousands, of people and all he had to show for it were leaking boats of famished souls and a few kilos of metal.

*　　*　　*

Gayle buried the bodies in the fort and nursed the sick while able-bodied men repaired the walls. In a few days, the fort was back together, the men put at ease, the sick set in the shade, and the last of the plundered provisions secured out of the muck in a repaired storehouse.

Hasin returned to habit and walked the walls, thumping the posts with the butt of his sidearm, testing for who knows what. He found Gayle resting under the shade of the windward wall.

"Minister," Hasin said, calling him over.

"Aye, Tir?" Gayle used the man's first name deliberately, proffering no title to the beast. He didn't seem to notice.

"Talk to the prisoners. We need food. Find us some edibles quickly. I don't know how long we'll have the run of the island."

"What are you afraid of? Surely you killed every person between here and bloody Pemioc."

"Nay," he said. "They're out there. They're close. Very close." He looked at the inland wall as if expecting a sudden rush of cannibals.

Gayle looked too and saw only gnarled trees blowing in a warming wind. "It's spring," he said.

"Food, minister. Food. Do some good." Hasin went back to checking the walls and peering into the trees.

Gayle found the captives in a lean-to guarded by two men too sick to stand.

Bost greeted him when he came in. "Pax, Gayle," he said but there was no warmth behind it.

"Pax," he said.

"What kind of things are you?" said Christiana. "What kind of vile monstrous horrors are you people? Have you no souls?"

Gayle blushed. His mind went to the scriptures he'd studied and doctrines of the Saved but found nothing to say.

Her face had healed some from her first tortures but was still bruised and torn. There were scratches down her cheeks, suggesting Hasin's ringed fist, while the lines of blood down her shirt suggested Longmire's whip.

"How old are you?" Gayle said.

"I am eighteen," she said. "Bost is nine summers."

The boy looked up at hearing his name. Gayle couldn't face him.

Christiana said, "There is not a creature on all of Tirgwenin that is as cruel and evil as you and your kind. What madness has come over you?

Are you not our siblings from the old world?"

"It is an old ailment," Gayle said to the floor. "Greed."

"Damn you for it."

"I need your help," he said.

She laughed.

Gayle nodded but said, "We're all going to starve to death if we don't find some food."

"Good."

"Good? You want to die?"

"Of course not, but you? You are diseased. For the sake of nobler creatures than you I will die."

"Us dying is only a temporary cure," he said. "There'll be more. It's inevitable. If not from Enskari then from Hyrax. They're worse."

"I'm sure you think so," she said.

"Krik," he said. "Please, we're hungry. Bost is hungry."

She glanced at the boy and Gayle looked too. He was as bruised as she was. Gayle cringed to think that he'd been put through the same unspeakable horrors as she.

"There're some roots I know, and some insects you can eat, but it's hardly enough for all of you."

"Better than nothing."

"Have you tried fishing?" she said.

Gayle smiled.

"Der som gumbnut tree," said Bost.

"What does he mean?" said Gayle.

"It's a hardy plant. Most folk plant a few of them in their gardens for hunger. Bost said there are some still on the island. There might even be some roots called hortmal."

"Can he describe them?" Gayle said.

"Vis them you," said Bost. "Gumbnut."

"He says he can show them to you."

"He understands well," said Gayle.

Christiana said, "He's very smart."

"You speak like you were born to my language."

"The tree is not very nourishing and requires a lot of preparation. It's hard to cut and chewy."

"What's chewy?" said Hasin. The governor had slipped in undetected.

"An edible tree hereabout," said Gayle.

"How do we know she's not lying? It could be poison. She could be trying to kill us."

Gayle couldn't answer and wondered how much of his interview the governor had overheard.

Hasin said, "We'll torture her to be sure."

"What?" said Gayle. "Are you joking?"

"In the name of the queen."

"I can't allow this," said Gayle.

He looked at the girl with her battered face and found her smiling. He followed her gaze and saw her watching a little yellow bee crawling over her arm.

Hasin laughed. "Damn it, man, do you not know what Connor does for God in the name of the queen?"

"The same as the purgers do in the name of the prophet."

"And he's not starving."

"No."

"God be praised!" Hasin said. "I'll send in Longmire. You stay and interpret."

Gayle shrieked, "You are a swine!"

"Alert! Alert!" It was a call from outside.

Hasin drew his gun and charged the chamber as he rushed out. Gayle followed.

Men were gathered at the inland wall. Some were frantically charging their muskets. Others ran to other sides under orders from Longmire.

Gayle moved to look between the poles.

Outside he saw a party of Tirgwenians. There were only a few of them, maybe twenty, but they were painted for battle. They held their long lances in their hands and had their short bows slung over their shoulders. The thought of arrows made Gayle groan. They were just at the tree line, twenty or so meters from the walls. They stood there, looking at the fort.

"Clear," someone called.

"Clear here," answered another voice from another quadrant.

"Clear to seaward," came a third.

Then the fort fell silent.

The whole island seemed to fall silent. No voices, no clang of sword or shuffle of boot, just the wind in the trees.

Then someone fired a musket into the line of yellow people.

The shot went wide but the hypersonic boom split branches and drove the natives back into the forest.

They were chased by a dozen more shots. If any hit, Gayle couldn't tell. Gauss muskets, for all their power and impressive technology, weren't particularly accurate at range. Their terrible strength always lay in their reputation and their effectiveness in massed fire. He remembered an adage he once heard among the soldiers of this very fort: if a man wanted accuracy, he went with a crossbow. If he wanted power, he used a railgun. If he wanted consistency, he went with his sword.

"Movement here."

"And here!" came another voice.

"Seaward. Two of the bastards!"

"Fire! Fire! Fire!" screamed Hasin. More than the whir of the magnetic guns, the sonic booms of the shot, or the splintering of trees a kilometer away, the sound of Hasin's voice unnerved Gayle most. No, more than unnerve. Terrify. He'd never heard the man this way before. He was panicked. He was afraid.

Sporadic shooting continued for the rest of the day, though after the first volleys no one reported actually seeing any of the savages. They shot at bushes and likely hiding places. They shot for effect. They shot to remind themselves that they were in charge.

That day they did not leave the fort to search for food. They did not hunt for Bost's gumbnut trees, or the hortmal Christiana had mentioned. They ate the last of their stolen meal and reboiled ancient coffee grounds to make a bitter cup.

Sentries walked the fence all night, called out reports, and fired into shadows. No one slept.

Come morning the world was as it was when they'd gone to sleep except for a single arrow lodged in the door of the governor's hut.

"How close were they to shoot that?" someone asked.

"Close," said Dedikodu. "It didn't come over the fence. It came through it."

Gayle looked down the shaft toward the wall and calculated that the missile had indeed not come from a long arching path over the wall, but from a narrow slit through it. The very slit he'd looked through the day before.

Gayle glanced at the governor, who'd recovered his demeanor of calm. "Keep 'em hot," he said. "Spare your ammunition for actual targets."

★　　★　　★

For three days the fort was so besieged. For three days they ate the last of their food and then had none. For three days they saw no one, but knew they were there. New arrows appeared each night in new locations.

On the fourth day, Hasin found Gayle writing in his journal in his hut.

"Go get that Pemioc princess," he ordered the minister. "Clean her up. Make her look presentable. Bring her under guard to the inland gate."

Gayle didn't argue and did as he was told.

The prisoners had been given nothing but water since the siege began and were both weak and delirious.

"Krik," said Gayle, waking up the young woman.

She blinked incoherently, her double eyelids surprising him and reminding him of the weirdness of the world and his desire to be off it.

He heated some water and cleaned her up as best he could. He dressed her in his own work clothes. They hung on her like a shroud but it was better than the torn blood-stained rags she'd been left with.

Gayle had a suspicion of what Hasin was up to.

Bost watched Gayle from his bed of rotting straw but didn't move.

When he'd done all he could with Christiana he lifted her up and with the help of a guard, marched her to the wall.

Hasin and a company of ten armed men waited for them.

Longmire bound Christiana's hands behind her back and hobbled her with a short leather tie around her ankles so she could walk but not run. Finally, he took a foul handkerchief from his pocket and blindfolded her with it.

"Open the gate," said the governor when it was done.

The gate opened.

"Minister. Take her, march out ten meters, and stop." Hasin handed him a stick with a white handkerchief on it.

"Me?"

"You," he said with a finality that made Gayle remember Hasin's rage at him after Pemioc. "Go out and get their attention. You can do that, can't you?"

Gayle felt lost between worlds, an outsider in all places.

He knew not to argue with Hasin. The man was off the edge, a tempest of madness and fear, and a touch of Lisa's Revenge thrown in from the last of the rations. He stared with wildly blinking eyes, doomed and deserving.

Meanwhile Longmire watched him, rubbing the handle of his whip like it was sex.

Gayle said a prayer under his breath and wondered if his God could hear him so far from home.

Leading the bound and beaten girl, he walked through the gate.

Ten meters out he stopped and glanced behind him. A row of kneeling musket men were framed in the gate, their weapons charged and aimed at him and his captive.

He turned toward the woods. "Hullo!" he called, waving the flag. "Pax. Minister. Pax. Snag!"

As if the trees morphed to people, a half dozen Tirgwenians appeared. Some were painted soldiers. Three however, he recognized: Jessya, Onuieg, and Lisa.

The Tirgwenian leader had been terribly wounded. Her left arm was a stump ten centimeters from the shoulder and her breast on that side was gone too. She had black bandages around her torso. She was pale and gaunt, but her eyes were as sharp and clear as ever and filled Gayle with an inexplicable hope.

"Pax!" he yelled to her and waved as if meeting old friends, relieved to see familiar faces. "Pax! Pax!" She did not smile back, nor speak or wave. Gayle remembered where he was and what he was doing, and hope fled him like breath under a boot.

"We have your whore daughter!" called Hasin. "We'll trade her."

Gayle flinched at the governor's insult. The Tirgwenians readied their bows.

Fear gripped the minister. He turned to run back to the fort, but stopped seeing muskets there.

"Bring us food – pigs and meal – enough for a hundred men for a hundred days!" Hasin yelled.

The faces of the savages were hard and unmoved, even Lisa's.

"You have a boy too," she said. "Bost, a Rowdanae. What of him?"

Onuieg and Jessya fidgeted at the mention of their son.

"Sure," said Hasin. "I'll throw in the little brat as a sign of good faith."

"Krik," said Lisa. "Hold feeday!"

"Damn ye savages!" hollered Hasin. "Speak so I understand ye or by God, I'll cut you all in half and eat your livers, starting with this one."

Lisa wiped a tear from her cheek.

"Aye, Tir Hasin," said Lisa. "You'll have your ransom. Keep her safe."

Christiana said suddenly, "Nay, Mor."

"Food can regrow faster than an ailing heart, my daughter."

Jessya whispered something to Lisa; Onuieg nodded in urgent agreement.

"Bring out the boy so we may see he too lives," Lisa said.

"Nay," said Hasin. "Ye have one week, then we'll start eating children."

His words hung in the air like a stink that even the wind wouldn't touch. It was broken only by Hasin when he ordered Gayle back to the fort. "Come back now, Minister."

Before returning, Gayle said, "Bost is alive. Understand? Bost is alive. I'll do all I can."

"Don't make us come out there and get you, Minister," said Hasin.

Gayle led his captive back to the dying fort.

★   ★   ★

Food began appearing the next morning and continued arriving each day thereafter for a week. At first it was gumbnut tree, then sacks of meal and grain, then pigs and fish. Then there were caged birds Gayle had never seen before, which were eaten before he could even sketch them. There came many different beans and meats he couldn't identify. All these were left on the road during the night to be collected come dawn.

The men's spirits rose with each new shipment. Hasin's talk turned from fortifications, retreat, and survival to treasure again, to glory, and a spring offensive.

Gayle listened and nodded but inside his guts twisted like he had Lisa's Revenge.

★   ★   ★

Ten days after the 'parley', as Hasin referred to it, 'the ransom demand' as Gayle thought of it, the minister was shaken out of an evening nap by a loud boom.

At first he thought it was musket fire, the start of the final battle, but then realized it was too loud and only a single report.

Outside his little hut, he followed men to the seaward gate and out upon the beach. With captives under their knives within the fort, the men were confident of not being harassed when venturing out a little ways.

The sun cast long shadows. The sky was a darkening blue-black, day shimmering but sliding into night. Gayle was momentarily struck by the beauty of the moment. A bee buzzed happily nearby and his heart was at peace for a moment.

"There it is!" cried a man. "Two points to port of straight out!"

Gayle followed the gazes of the other soldiers. In the far distance he saw a plume of steam vapor stretching from the sea into the infinite blue above.

The anchor line. Resupply.

Men ran back to report. Help had arrived.

★   ★   ★

Back in his hut, Gayle immediately set to packing. He was leaving this planet if he had to steal a boat, climb the line by hand, and storm the ship above.

As night descended, fiery auroras snaked like battle standards across the alien sky and the sailors took heart. The lights, rare on Tirgwenin, were a reminder of home. The lightning strikes were a chorus of nostalgia, the ozone air a perfume of civilization.

That next morning Gayle awoke to the sound of cheers. A boat had been sighted and would soon make landfall.

The world was not in accord. It was awash in lightning and storm. Squalls burst in all directions – violent gusts of wind that bent the trees and tested the walls. Waterspouts and sudden waves chased across the seas. By noon, black clouds materialized out of blue sky, like islands above them. Lightning-fed and fast, they poured rain and electricity down with equal measure. Between them, the higher atmosphere turned from sapphire to pale milk as a massing solar storm buffeted the planet.

Even so, Gayle wandered the fort with a feeling of elation, like a prisoner about to be paroled.

He stopped by the inland gate and peeked out to look at the woods. He wanted to see if the food had been left and stared at the spot for a long time trying to understand what he saw.

It was incomprehensible. He traced the outline with his eyes and turned it in his mind. Still not understanding, he opened the gate and went out.

No one stopped him.

Ten meters from the gate, at the place he'd stood with Christiana in the path in the clearing, was the body of the Tirgwenian hostage. Or rather, what was left of her body.

She was bound to a cross of wood upside down. Her limbs had each been cut from her torso. The pieces dangled from the wood by bloody leather straps. Her head had been severed and lay at the foot of the inverted nightmare like an offering.

Gayle circled the thing like a listing drunk. Around and around. It was as if it had a terrible gravity of its own. He tried to move away, but found himself pulled back. He trampled rings in the grass before his legs gave out and he fell to his knees.

His breath came in short gasps when it came at all and his eyes filled with blinding tears as he tried to make sense of it.

Hasin had done this as some kind of statement, some kind of terror tactic to continue his conquest. With resupply, he no longer needed to parley. Fresh provisions, fresh troops, fresh weapons.

Gayle wanted to die and for a moment wished it. What kind of people did this? What kind of people did he come from?

He stopped breathing and fell over in a faint.

★   ★   ★

He awoke within the walls, slumped against the gate. Someone must have carried him inside, but he was alone now. He stood up, seeing the thing still outside. It dug at his mind and pulled him. He fought the gravity of it and turned the other way. He wandered through the deserted fort, out along the path, past the wind-blown briar and to the beach beyond.

The resupply landing craft had arrived.

Hasin, in full dress uniform, shook the hands of the men coming from the sky.

The sky pulsated and throbbed in Coronam's distant fury and Gayle knew then that God had indeed noticed Tirgwenin.

Gayle ran back to the fort.

He found Bost still bound in the corner of the lean-to, unguarded and starving.

The boy looked at the minister with cold distant eyes.

"Bost," said Gayle. "You've got to get out of here."

Bost didn't move. Gayle pushed the boy over and dug at the bindings around his wrists. When they were untied, he went at the ones at his ankles.

When Bost was unbound, Gayle lifted him to his feet.

He wanted to explain, to apologize – to say something, but words were not what was needed.

He dragged Bost, weak and broken, by the arm out of the lean-to, nearly pulling him off his feet. He led him to the gate and beyond the walls toward the forest.

"Go," he said. "Go."

Bost stared disbelievingly at the thing in the clearing.

"Run, Bost!" said Gayle. "For my soul if not for yours. Run!"

The Tirgwenian boy then understood. He moved, stumbling forward over the muddy road, past the horror that had been a princess, and finally into the forest.

When he was out of sight, Gayle collapsed and wept. Behind him came flashes of lightning. He heard distant thunderclaps and the sound of men arguing, but nearer and closer, just out of reach, came the soft and pleasant droning of bees.

PART THREE
MAROONED

'The old world is dying, and the new world struggles
to be born: now is the time of monsters.'
Antonio Gramsci

CHAPTER SEVENTEEN

Placid Bay is reached from the sea up a lazy, meandering, but deep and navigable river to a plain of cut trees and waiting fields. There are ample forests for timber, rich wildlife to hunt, fish-thick waters, and rich nourishing soil for planting. The climate is temperate and welcoming....

    The local inhabitants have been diminished by the pox, to which our people are mostly resistant. What few locals remain inform us that they are quitting the place to move inland. When settlers arrive, there will be constructed dwellings waiting for them. It is a paradise. Placid Bay is so perfect it is as if God himself readied the place for us.

Letter to Ethan Sommerled from Alpin Morgan
Account of Second Tirgwenian Expedition
7, Ninth-Month, 935 NE

13, Eighth-Month, 937 NE – Rodawnoc, Tirgwenin

"Gayle reported this to me when he got back to Enskari," said Morgan. "He'd served me as a naturalist on Sommerled's earlier expedition."

Morgan glanced at his assistants, Pratt, Aguirre, and Dagney. They huddled together around a fire in the palisade some distance from the riotous soldiers and their mutinous pilot. Their faces were wan and downcast, the story he'd just told them the final note of calamity. He regretted telling them but they had to know what they were facing

"The solar storm was severe, the worst ever seen on Tirgwenin, not that there was much to compare it to," said Morgan. "The orbiting ships were exposed and in danger. They didn't have the provisions Hasin wanted in any event. Nor the men to spare. The resupply was an evacuation, but at Hasin's insistence, they left a score of soldiers here to maintain some kind of claim and guard against Hyraxian landing. Six and twenty. As you can see, not a Saved soul survived. They're all dead now."

"As we will be," said Pratt.

No one spoke to contradict the assistant.

They stared into their little fire as if it would speak to them. It did not warm them. Their cold was not of that kind. An alien wind blew the embers hot and carried the smoke away.

The search parties returned without success, no sign of the soldiers or anyone. When Mathew's party returned, Morgan signaled him over, but Upor intercepted him first.

Morgan struggled to his feet, his muscles angry at his weight, his joints at the soft sand. Sweating and grinding his teeth, he hurried to the pilot and his native assistant but arrived just in time to see Mathew walk back into the forest.

"Where's Mathew going?" Morgan said.

"I sent him out."

"He's under my authority, not yours. You forget yourself."

Upor looked at Morgan. His eyes traced the beads of sweat running down his face, his crooked walking stick, his gray hair. "Aye, of course," he said. "Sorry, Governor. I forgot he wasn't part of my crew."

"Where did you send him?" Morgan shook with exertion and rage.

"I sent him to seek the natives. To discover the fate of Aderyn's men."

"You sent him out of the fort at dusk?"

"Why wait? We're in a hurry, sir. I must get off-world right away. The storms here are awful."

"You sent him dressed in Enskaran costume into a forest crawling with enemies?"

"He's one of them," he said. "Have you no faith in your man?"

"Are you trying to get him killed? Are you trying to kill us all? You damn murdering bastard!" Morgan raised his stick to strike the pilot, but one of the sailors grabbed his arm.

Upor looked not at all concerned.

"Get some rest, Governor," he said. "You'll need your energy. The rest of your company will arrive soon." Upor turned his back to him and strolled out amongst his men.

Morgan stood with the soldier a long while. The soldier smirked at him.

"Do you know what—"

"I do as I'm told, sir. I know my place," said the soldier. "Maybe you can pray to your disloyal God. Now that ye are off Enskari, maybe he'll listen to Bucklers."

★　　★　　★

For supper they had bowls of stew made from some native animal and Morgan and his assistants drank it hungrily from the pot, passing it between themselves wrapped in a shirt to keep from burning themselves, a gulp to a man then the next until it was gone.

"We were never meant to be here," explained Morgan. "Sommerled was adamant on the subject. This was not the place for us. This is a bad place, even before Hasin, this is not a good place to start a colony. Placid Bay was selected. That's where we should be."

"Maybe the natives are gone," said Pratt. "We just need to endure here like we planned. Eat the corn and wait for resupply."

"The resupply is not coming here," Morgan said. "The resupply is going to Placid Bay. They'll have no reason to stop here."

"They will when they find out we're here and not at our planned destination."

"And who will tell them?" said Aguirre. "The pilot?"

"He's been working against us from the start," said Morgan. "From the moment we lost the *Sebastian* to now. Delays, Freeport, now marooned. He's been against us at every step."

"Oh God, how have we fallen so deeply into the clutches of our enemies?" Aguirre said it as a prayer.

"We mustn't give up hope, men," said Morgan, wishing he'd said it with more enthusiasm.

"What of the fort?" said Dagney. "Am I wrong in thinking that Sommerled's patent is affected by it?"

"It's now in question. It's the queen's land here. Aderyn claimed the fort."

"And fifty kilometers inland," said Dagney. "By law."

"Aye," said Morgan. "We were to have Placid Bay, outside of Enskaran control. Our own colony. Our own land. Our own kingdom. Sommerled's patent gave him all the land to control – if he could colonize it. He has to have a permanent settlement here within two years or he forfeits. As for this place, it was an afterthought, a nod to Aderyn and the Hyraxian threat."

Pratt said, "So not only are we marooned, but we're marooned on the only piece of rock on the entire planet we cannot legally control?"

"Aye."

"Quite the coincidence," said Pratt.

"Aye."

Dagney said, "Can we reach Placid Bay without Upor?"

"Nay. It's hundreds of kilometers afar. Never by land. But it is but a few days by sea."

"You must convince Upor to take us," said Aguirre, his voice rising in panic. "You must, Governor. You are a gentleman. He must respect you. It's not far. He's Saved. We're his people. You must bargain with him. Beg if you must."

"Why is he doing this?" said Dagney. "Who are we to him? What offense have we done him?"

"I know not."

"Ask him, Governor. Placid Bay will be hard enough, but anywhere but here. After that story, after what Hasin…. Plead with him, Governor. Plead with him to take us the few more days. After so many months, what is a few more days?"

"I will try."

"In the morning," said Dagney. "Let us all sleep on this. A night's rest might soften the man."

"Of course." Morgan managed to say it with some confidence that seemed to settle the men.

They stoked the fire and rolled up in their coats for a bed.

Morgan stayed watchful, unable to sleep. He thought he was alone in his vigil when Dagney spoke. "Morgan. If he won't take us to Placid Bay, can you do me a favor? Can you ask the pilot if he'd take my children back with him to Enskari?"

"You'd entrust them to that man?"

"What chance do they have here, Alpin? Here – without Mathew?"

Morgan thought about it for a long time. "All right, Henry. I'll ask him."

★   ★   ★

Over the next days the planters from the *Hopewell* and the *Mallow* were conveyed to Rodawnoc. The landings were hard, each one. The sandbars and shoals shifted by the hour, the tides turned sudden and askew, tipping boats and making liars of the best steersmen they had. Two landing crafts upturned dumping cargo into the sea, food and provisions, personal things, private and loved, all lost to the water. Morgan did not know if it were God's grace or some other less merciful agent that delivered them, but not a single Buckler was lost in the landing. Some were dumped and had to be drawn from the sea, others swam to the shore, several had injuries, but none died.

Upor made a point of noting this to Morgan when he finally granted him an audience a week after they'd landed.

"Take us to Placid Bay. You have your orders. You must obey them."

Morgan sensed some softening in the pilot, but his answer was the same. "This is as far as I'll take ye. As pilot of the enterprise, and admiral of the ships, I may dictate the landing place if I see fit."

"Steer the landing boats north and take us the rest of the way. You don't need to pull the anchor, just point the ships north."

"Nay. Too dangerous."

"What danger? We are only in danger if you leave us here."

"I see it differently. I see the danger of losing some of Her Majesty's navy if we press on. We'll need these ships, these craft to defend against Hyrax and the purgers. I'll not risk them. You are here, Minister. I have delivered you as I am required. You may have no thought for your home planet, but I do."

"Nay nay, Upor," said Morgan. "This is not so. We speak of the sea vessels, not the spaceships."

"I know of what I speak, Morgan. I'll not risk them either. They are a part of my charge as much as the spinner and sail silk. I won't risk them. You are here. Be happy."

"Upor—"

"Dammit, Minister. I dragged you and your sorry criminals across all known space and you quibble about a few kilometers. This is Jareth's World. You're here. I got you here. I did this. Be grateful."

"Aye, I quibble," he said. "Hasin—"

"Besides," said Upor, cutting him off. "I haven't time to take ye. The year is late. We must be off. I must set off back to Enskari before the storms come. This is the danger of sailing across the night."

Morgan's lip quivered; he gripped his hands together in prayer.

A loud crack from seaward broke the day before he could speak.

Upor rushed out of his tent to the beach. Morgan followed.

The day was bright, the morning had been cold with a bit of fog, a hint of autumnal chills yet to come, but it had all burned off in bright spiraling auroras that danced the blue-black sky in greens and oranges east to west as Coronam kissed the wild planet good morning.

Morgan followed Upor out of the trees onto the beach to see the last of the towering waterspout falling back into the ocean.

A message light flashed in the distance, a pinprick of color floating above the sea, a signal light connected to a thread above the planet to the *Hopewell*.

Upor ran to his lookout and demanded answers. "What is it, man? Hyrax? Are we lost?"

Everyone held silent as the man read the light through a telescope.

"It's not Hyrax," he said. "At least I don't think so."

"Dammit, tell me what it is, not what it isn't."

A group of sailors had collected around them.

"It is an anchor thread," the sailor said.

"Aye, I can see that, you idiot," said the captain.

"It's ours," he said. "Aye. It's the missing one. It's the *Sebastian*, sir. It's the *Sebastian*. She caught up, sir. She's here!"

★   ★   ★

News spread to the planters quickly. It was the first bit of good news they'd had in a very long while. Their complement was whole. The *Sebastian* had not been lost the first week as they'd all supposed. She had followed them, delayed, but diligent.

Morgan told his congregation that their prayers had been answered. "Our friends and family have returned to us. We are a whole community again. God be praised." Privately, though, he wondered if it was a good thing or not, if it was God who'd brought them or another more cruel master delivering more sacrifices to this doomed place.

The *Sebastian* unloaded its cargo of planters and supplies over the next few days. The Bucklers sang songs of deliverance for their reunited comrades and cheered and cried and threw their arms around each other. The gleefulness was quickly tainted, though, as the *Sebastian*'s contingent learned of their plight, the gravity of their late arrival, their lack of supplies, and the terrible marooning. Morgan had not meant for Hasin's story to get out amongst his people – he'd told only his assistants, but it had found its way to the masses nonetheless. Someone had talked. He suspected it was Aguirre. He wanted to confront him, but he didn't know if he should chastise him for frightening the company or thank him for telling them something he'd not had the courage to. He left it alone.

★   ★   ★

Upor watched them from his tent on the beach surrounded by his men who had shore leave to work their muscles. They collected drinking water but otherwise didn't leave the narrow shore. Upor forbade any of them to have any contact with Morgan or his company.

Morgan daily went to the pilot's camp to beseech his help. Upor's excuse of not having the time to take them on was proven a bald-faced lie as the sailors remained there for weeks, playing sports on the beach and getting drunk. For all this time, Upor would not see him.

Morgan waited in the forest for a chance to talk to Lieutenant Bradshaw, the commander of the *Sebastian*. He'd received good report of the man from the planters, and believed him outside Upor's direct control and not a willing participant in the crimes being committed.

Morgan accosted him in the forest one day and told him their grievances. The young lieutenant listened earnestly and Morgan used all his skill as orator and minister to impart upon his speech the gravity of their situation.

"Do you not see what's happened here?" he said to him. "We are undone. We are betrayed. We are doomed. Will you not help us?"

"Aye, it appears ye have been wronged," the lieutenant said, "but I cannot go against Upor. I'd be flogged. Hanged, perchance. I am sorry. I cannot sail you to Placid Bay. It is out of the question."

"Nay. We are Saved and civilized. Is there no pity in you? He will not see me. Can ye not, for the sake of your own soul, ask the pilot a favor? Least let some of us return with ye. Our resupply will not find us here, even if we're still here when it comes."

"Nay, he'd not misreport where he landed ye."

"He may not lie, but he's under no obligation to do anything. Ours is a private venture. Our backers are not within his circles. We are God-fearing people who invested our lives and fortunes here. We are exiles and alone. He is under no legal obligation to help us beyond what he has done, and done cruelly. I am not so foolish to think he would raise a hand to save us after ruining us so completely."

Bradshaw kicked at the leaves in the sand and moved upwind of the latrines. Morgan followed him.

"See where I must find you just to take for a conference?" Morgan pointed to the toilet. "I am governor of this place by law and yet I must hide like a thief to speak to a nobleman like myself."

"Aye, ye are misused," said Bradshaw. "I will do it. I will have a word with him if such I may."

"Blessed be. Thank you."

Bradshaw returned to the beach. Morgan skulked back into the forest along briarous paths like a fugitive to his people.

He broke into the fort clearing at an odd place and had to walk around to the gate. He pretended to inspect the work as he went, trying to appreciate the pointed poles and firing slits but truly unable to focus his mind.

He noted only that the reconstruction of the palisade was nearly complete. Henry Dagney had overseen the cutting of new timber and the reassembly of the fallen walls. With the eager help of worried planters, it was again a defensible structure.

Morgan passed through the gateway. He waved to a man at the wall holding one of their few coilguns. He held it awkwardly in both arms, and kept his eyes to the forest just to the place Morgan thought the princess's body had been left. The guard didn't wave back to him.

They'd left Enskari with one hundred, five and twenty Saved. With the *Sebastian* now arrived, they had one hundred eighteen. It was a goodly number, much more than he'd expect after everything they'd been through. The fort had housed about the same number before and it would hold them now the same.

The barracks were standing again, their posts strong, new-cut and trimmed. Another testament to the carpenter, Dagney. Men laid thatch across the women's house and paused to watch the governor as he walked, measuring their plight he thought by his gait. He kept his chin up and nodded appreciatively at their work.

"Blessed be, Minister Morgan. I'd speak to you." It was Mrs. Archard.

"Aye, of course. Blessed be."

"Who is it that is in charge when ye are not here, I'd like to know," she said.

He removed his hat and wiped his face with a handkerchief. The walls cut the wind but the late summer sun shone down unshaded from a twinkling azure heaven.

"That would be my assistants, Wife Archard."

"Aye, but which one?"

"Are they not in accord? Is there a problem?" He almost laughed asking the question.

"It's the Dagney children," she said. "The girl mostly. She's impudent and rude."

"What has she done now?"

"Look up there and see." She pointed to the women's hut.

He squinted and saw Millicent Dagney weaving thatch on the far side, swinging the scythe to cut it.

"That's man's work," said Archard. "I think she's deviant."

"She's a carpenter's daughter. If she can help, we should let her."

"She drank with the men."

"Drink?"

"Coffee. She helped herself and sat with the men."

"Wife Archard—"

"And there's more. She wouldn't pray with us at breakfast. She took her food and walked away – right out the gate while Master Aguirre spoke prayer. *While he spoke prayer.* Disrespectful. I told Master Pratt and he sent me to Master Dagney, who of course stuck up for his little brat."

"I'll have a word with her."

"Is this not to be a God-fearing place, Minister? Would we make a start with—"

"I said I'd speak with her, Wife Archard. Good day."

He left her and went to his hut to be alone. He sat on his grass bunk sweating in the hot still air for a long while. He finally turned to his trunk and opened it. He dug out his pictures and looked at them. In the seeping light of an unfinished roof, he studied his paintings and sketches, the mountains and forests, rivers and seas he'd painted on his last visit to Tirgwenin. He could see how his own hand showed them in their best light. He'd painted them for the Crown, to advertise and entice. He remembered adding the warm colors and clear skies when they'd not been there at the time. He remembered adding them, but for the life of him, he could not remember what those places really looked like. His lying paintings had supplanted his own memory, propaganda for reality.

Of course if he wanted reality he had only to look outside, at the beach filled with evil men, at the forests dark with lurking dangers. There was truth. But not in his pictures, his hopeful pictures. He hadn't brought with him any pictures of Rodawnoc from before, not Hasin or his fort or any part of this accursed place. He'd left those on Enskari and brought only his copies of Placid Bay to cheer them on their journey and help when they arrived.

He had a painter's hand and a naturalist's eye. Eddie Gayle was better with the lines than he, but could not approach Morgan's knowledge of color and light. Gayle's work would make better etchings, but his, Morgan's, were in books in the queen's library. Outcast and heretic though he was, his art was of royal caliber.

Voices called him awake. He rolled over on his cot and looked around, half dreaming he was not here. He'd fallen asleep among his pictures. He straightened up and collected them from the floor.

"Governor," came a voice. "Your daughter, Governor. Daria. She's having her baby."

The news seeped into him slowly like a balm over a burn, finally taking hold and shaking him awake.

"I'm coming, I'm coming," he said.

He was out the door and three steps toward the hut where his daughter was giving birth when he heard the commotion and saw Mathew walk through the gate.

His Enskaran clothes were gone. He wore the beaded leatherwork of the natives. He waved when he saw Morgan and the governor stopped. He waved back and signaled him to follow.

He called to Pratt and Aguirre. "Where's Dagney?"

"In his hut."

"We'll meet there," he said.

Mathew was of that strange indecipherable race of tall yellow-skin glow-people, as Daria had called them once, but Morgan thought he looked even more dour than usual and it filled his stomach with butterflies and worry.

Millie Dagney opened the door to them holding a half-finished fish trap.

"Get your father," Morgan told her.

"He's sleeping."

"Wake him."

"He's sleeping. He's very tired."

Morgan gritted his teeth and stared at the girl.

"It's all right, Millie," said Dagney from inside. "Let them in."

The governor didn't like Millie, but he had to admire Henry Dagney. He was an expert carpenter and though he still rasped from the pox, his work was exceptional. His hut was the best structure in the compound by far.

"We'll speak alone," Morgan said to Dagney's children, Millie and the boy. He couldn't remember his name.

"Go along," said Henry.

"I'd hear it," said Millie. "I suspect this concerns Dillon and me as much as anyone."

Morgan felt his ears go red and thought of his daughter a few meters away.

Henry looked at Morgan and seemed to read his near collapse on his face. He turned to his daughter. "You will mind, Millie." The edge in his voice left no room for debate.

She took the little boy by the hand and led him outside.

When they were gone, Mathew wasted no time. "There is no food upon the island," he said. "And none inland. The people suffer. They have nothing to share. They would not have you here. They beg you leave. They say you are a blight upon them. You are not worthy of even Rodawnoc. You must go. You are not welcome."

"Did you not speak on our behalf?" said Morgan.

"The first expedition took all there was to share. The second took all that was left. There was bad weather and sickness. The crops were not sown this year. The Rowdanae are starving. Many have fled and sought help inland. But they are Rowdanae and may not be welcomed. Others remain here and struggle, seeking honey through hardship."

"We are not like those other expeditions," said Morgan. "Did you not tell them that? Can you not plead our case?"

"What is there to say?"

Morgan did not like that Mathew had returned to his native garb and knew the others felt the same. They looked Mathew up and down as if seeing him for the first time, wary and betrayed. Morgan was acutely aware that his assistant's speech placed him outside their company. His heart pounded in fear, his mind wheeled in horror. He swallowed and kept control as best he might. His hands shook. Panic would not serve his people and his people were all he could think of now.

"We are not visitors. We're neighbors," said Morgan. "We wish to be friends with the people here. We want to live in harmony."

"They do not believe that."

"I know that things – terrible things – have been done by our people, but give us another chance."

"Would you do things differently?"

"Of course. It's why we're here. We fled from that, from that evil that touched this place. It touched us too. We understand. We are different."

Mathew sat in a silence that filled the hut.

Morgan could hear murmurs and hoped his voice had not carried outside. His pleading tones and panicked worry could only frighten the congregation.

Mathew said, "They have nothing to share."

"We ask for nothing," said Morgan. "Only peace. Please, Mathew, have peace with us."

"Governor, I am not your enemy. I am your ambassador. I speak between the two as each would have me. I returned to you to do my duty, to show good faith and honor."

"It is noble," said Morgan. "You are a noble sa—"

Mathew smiled and said, "I must be true to all sides, Governor. If for my soul, I will have wisdom and peace. I will have honey to know my path and perhaps be brought back."

"You'd go back to Enskari?" said Dagney.

"Nay. Back to my tribe. If I am worthy."

"Aren't you from here?"

"Nay. I was marked Rowdanae when I failed."

"Failed what?" said Pratt.

"My passing. I was not worthy to remain. I was sent away. Rowdanae to Rodawnoc."

"What is this place?" said Dagney. "A prison?"

Mathew thought for a moment. "I have seen your prisons. There is nothing so cruel here on all Tirgwenin. But there are places here where the unworthy go when they're unwanted."

"Exile," said Dagney.

Mathew thought for a moment. "I wish I had bees," he said with a bitter smile. "I could tell you true then."

"Do you know the word? Exile?" pressed Pratt.

"Aye. It is a close word. This is a place of exiles. It is place for the unwanted."

"We are home, Governor!" screamed Aguirre. "You led us true!"

"Shut up," said Dagney. "Or by God I'll knock your teeth in."

"Can you tell them we mean them no harm?" Morgan said. "We'll move on as soon as we're able. In the meantime, take them gifts. We'll give them gifts. To make up for what was taken before."

"They lost people."

Morgan's mouth opened to speak, but nothing came out. He felt his lip quiver.

"I will convey your words and gifts," said Mathew.

★   ★   ★

Morgan called together all the planters he could and directed them to bring him wares to 'trade for peace'. In a distant hut, he could hear the muffled screams of his daughter in her labor pains. He'd yet to find a moment to visit her.

The planters collected things for Mathew to take to the natives: pots and knives, pillows and cloth, fruit seeds and lard. Things they could not easily part with, but each family in turn gave something as a ransom for their very lives.

Morgan and Mathew, together with the other assistants, chose what things would be best received and wrapped them in a parcel. They fed the Tirgwenian well, giving him Dagney's own hut to sleep in, and the next morning at dawn, they sent Mathew back into the forest burdened with their gifts and fading hope.

That same afternoon, after a day of labor, Daria, Morgan's daughter, gave birth to a baby girl. She was christened Diane by Morgan himself the following Sabbath. The new baby was the favorite of the colony and each planter in turn came to see her, to bless, and have their hearts warmed by the new little life.

"The first Buckler born free," some said.

"A beautiful child," all agreed.

"God's promise of new life here," said others.

"A damn pity," murmured the few.

For two days the camp had new vigor as Baby Diane infused them with a vision of hope and endurance. They set about surviving the winter, until come spring they would relocate to their promised destination in Placid Bay.

Morgan preached, "Keep hope, everyone. This is but an unexpected waypoint, not the end. We have only to keep together, keep peace and keep our faith and we will be delivered one and all."

On the third day after Diane's christening, Henry Dagney left the fort to check on some fish traps. His dead body was found arrow-pierced and floating in the shoals that evening.

CHAPTER EIGHTEEN

Their immediate profit becomes our longterm problem – pollution. As usual, our 'leader' class is tragically shortsighted, for poison and pestilence have no favorites and can't be forever contained. What then of our masters when they destroy us and this world? Where can they flee?
Anarchist Pamphlet, 2215 London, England,
Reprinted 935 NE, Enskari

15, Ninth-Month 937 NE – Vildeby, Enskari

Sir Nolan Brett pulled his collar up more to protect his clothes from the staining rain than himself from the cold autumn storm. He worked his way through the morning crowds of Vildeby's bustling streets, taking his time on his way to Government House. He wore a coat far beneath his station that allowed him to blend with the commoners doing business. He could pass for a well-to-do tradesman or maybe a revered manservant. His clothes spoke of a commoner with status instead of a noble in the slums.

Vildeby was in storm. Soot-summoned lightning flashed the sky and blew black muddy raindrops down like fleeing insects. He worked his way casually past the storefronts, pushing through crowds of hagglers and shoppers, sure to keep his step purposeful to defy eager shopsmen vying for his attention.

He was without bodyguard. His contingent of trusted men were elsewhere. They were not as good as he at blending in for all their lowborn grace, and he didn't like the attention they always brought him despite themselves. He might not be recognized for who he was, but the pickpockets and cutthroats of the city gutters would sense a man of standing when they realized he was trailed by armed protectors.

"Where's the sharing?" A man pushed a handbill into Nolan's hands and then one into the woman's behind him.

Nolan looked at the paper.

It proclaimed in four block headlines along each of its four sides, *The rich are richer and the poor are poorer. How's this different from slavery? What good are these people doing? This is how Old Earth was ruined.*

In the middle of the page was a cartoon. It showed a rickety staircase balancing on a sagging planet. On the topmost step was a wild drunken orgy of bejeweled gentry. To their patriotic credit, Zabel was pictured with a stern disapproving scowl, but was doing nothing to stop the others, who threw riches into a fire, soiled their clothes, took their neighbors' wives and spilled poison in buckets on the steps below.

Holding the noble tier aloft over their heads were a pack of caricatured merchants, fat and greedy, stealing money from one another in a ring of comical pickpocketing. Many of them were trying to climb the stairs to the upper step, but as part of a dance, the nobles above stepped on their fingers in turns.

Holding up the merchants were glorified peasants and factory workers, coughing and struggling with wise eyes and weak bodies, their bones visible under their skin. They shoveled and toiled and their wealth was sucked away by a vacuum that pulled not a few of them into it as well and showered gold and blood upon the upper steps. They too tried to climb to the higher levels, but like their betters, the merchants trampled the fingers of all who tried.

The peasants stood not on a step, but on Enskari itself, a planet caving beneath the weight of the structure, depressed like a deflating ball sucked of its air. It was black and sooted, stained with ink, and as Nolan examined the paper, wet with the Vildeby rain that tasted of copper and acid. The edifice upon the planet was doomed to fall, the supports sinking in the muck of the planet. It would collapse and kill everyone, a boiling vat of poison collected from the offerings of the upper classes waiting to catch and drown them all when it did.

Nolan admired the artistry of the piece if not its rebelliousness. He should have its artist on his payroll, so skillful were they in turning an abstract idea into an image accessible to the ignorant and illiterate. The makers knew not to identify themselves of course, not even an engraver's mark. Connor's Guard was surely already looking for them. God help them if Connor found them.

Nolan made to crumple the paper and toss it in the street, his breeding moving him to do so, but he stopped and instead carefully folded it and put it away in his pocket.

He crossed the square to where he could see a clock tower and quickened his step. The queen would be passing into Government House precisely at eleven thirty. She'd make a grand unpublicized entrance in the center of town as a show of strength and confidence. Her arrival was a secret, but a poorly kept one. A certain and specific few were sure to know it was happening. They'd be there now, waiting. Nolan was sure of it. He counted on it.

All a balancing act.

At twenty past, a line of rope was in place to keep traffic and gawkers off the road. Everyone now would know that something was happening.

Nolan moved closer for a better vantage point. He found a place revealing most of the lane approaching the seat of government and the gate itself. Here he stood atop a barrel gripping a gas lamp and waited. The lamp was lit at midday, so dark was the soot and storm.

Distant trumpets blared and were picked up in accord along the path until the queen's march was taken up inside the courtyard. Soldiers and police took positions as the public pressed the ropes. The rain came in gusts between the narrow streets, carried on sudden confused winds with smells of cooking oil and sweat, smoke, grease, and animals.

Nolan scanned the buildings overlooking the street and tried to find the window. He guessed at it but couldn't be sure. Time would tell. All a balancing act.

The court guard came first on horseback decked in red and blue, their white feathers gray wet streaks down their tall cylindrical hats thanks to the rain. Then came the musketeers, four columns of ten, their glistening coilguns on their shoulders, their steel helmets reflecting the gaslights as they passed.

Thunder joined the cheers of the crowd as the queen's carriage turned into the lane amid a gauntlet of lancers atop high-stepping horses. They were always a crowd favorite.

The royal carriage moved slowly forward at the pace of the quick-marching musketeers. Behind it Nolan could see a long line of other carriages containing the courtiers and hangers-on who'd followed Her Majesty down from Upaven. The ones needing to be seen, the vain gentry. They were the superfluous partygoers, poster children for the working class's dissatisfaction as shown in the cartoon he carried in his pocket. The important people at court, the useful ones, were already here waiting for Sir Edward's panicked meeting in an hour.

He couldn't see the end of the carriages and marveled at the audacity. Some of them were over-ornamented in gold and silver, jewels, feathers, and silks that rivaled if not surpassed the opulence of the queen's carriage.

As if in deference to their sovereign, the rain abated as the procession passed his place. Nolan could see Queen Zabel there alone in her carriage waving her gloved hand and tilting her head at her subjects, a trained noble serene smile on her lips.

Nolan waited for it to happen.

The shot was a thunderclap to his right. The bullet ripped into the carriage wall. It missed the window, sheered off the hind end of the golden lion ornament before passing through a lancer's horse at the neck, a washerwoman in the chest, a fisherman in the side and a char boy in the leg, killing all but the fisherman.

Before the screams, a hush settled over the crowd as they sensed the difference between a musket railshot and thunder. It was a localized pause as the people processed the information. Farther on, not knowing an attack for the weather, people cheered merrily as before.

Nearest the carriage, the veteran guards were first to act. Before the echo was gone, before the washerwoman's body was on the ground, or the boy bled out, the guards sprang to action.

Musketeers fanned out, winding their guns, clearing the road and taking up defensive positions. The lancers kicked their steeds and led the royal carriage forward at a gallop. The queen was thus whisked away.

The trailing carriages followed in panic as understanding spread like disease through the throngs of people and nobles. Cries rose like waves in a disturbed pond.

The queen's carriage disappeared through the gates. The next carriage faltered. Its wheels slipped on the wet pavestones and the horses tripped and stumbled. Before it could right itself, it was struck by a trailing carriage and then another. Four carriages crashed in total just ten meters from the gate, fouling the entrance for all.

Nolan looked up at the building and pointed. Others in the crowd had done the same.

"He's there! The assassin is there!" he yelled.

Everyone turned to see the open window.

"For the prophet! And the glory of Hyrax!" came a call from within. Then a man came flying out the third-story window.

He screamed drunkenly and swung his arms and kicked his legs as if to fly, but he only plummeted to the ground. Onlookers screamed in reply and fled the place where the man landed headfirst into the stones.

Before these new shrieks had finished, two men with drawn pistols appeared and bent over the body.

Above them in the window, two more peered out. "Just the one," called a man from the window.

The two on the ground turned the body over. The dead man's broken skull leaked gore into the inky rain like the juice from a split melon.

They tore open his vest and the crowd gasped when they saw the vestments of an Orthodox Saved minister.

"He used a Hyraxian weapon," called a man from the window.

"And that is why he missed!" said a plant in the mass of onlookers.

"Hurrah!" came the scripted answer. "Hurrah!"

The crowd picked it up and it spread up the streets of the city beyond where Nolan could see, beyond where any witness knew what they were cheering.

Nice touch, thought Nolan. Not only get the weapon's origin out of the way, but spin it all at once. No need to wait for the official report in the papers. The crowd would carry the outrage faster and better.

The plainclothesmen, never identifying themselves, called for a cart to remove the body.

Lightning flashed and the winds picked up. The crashed carts were drenched but attended to. A small petroleum fire among them looked to be under control.

A roll of thunder startled the people but they remained in place, used to it. They murmured amongst themselves about the audacity of the assassin, the story spreading out into the populations in low voiced echoes.

A dozen uniformed policemen arrived and loaded the body into an oxcart and set off toward Gray Keep.

Nolan retreated down an alley and then across another courtyard before ducking into a small dark cafe. He ordered a cup of strong coffee and sat down. He'd not finished a third of it before he was joined by one of the plainclothesmen from the street.

Nolan said, "That shot was pretty close."

Jim Vandusen, Sir Nolan's confidential secretary, shook the rain off his coat and sat down across from him. In low tones, he said, "You said to make it look real."

"Aye, that it did. Was that you I heard in the window?"

"You recognized me? I thought I put a nice Hyraxian accent to it."

"Where did you get a Hyraxian musket?"

"We didn't actually. The swine only had knives. Like he was going to get that close to the queen."

"Maybe he was supposed to buy one," said Nolan, looking out the dingy window.

"Maybe. After he arrived, he met once with the other priests and then went to Austen, to Blankenship and fished. There's nothing in Blankenship. I think he was a deserter."

"He'll be a hero now on Hyrax."

"Redemption is our business." Vandusen smiled.

Nolan envied his secretary's enthusiasm. It was all still a game to him. The stakes hadn't weathered his secretary the way they'd weathered him.

"Did you bring those papers?"

"Aye." Vandusen reached into a leather satchel hanging at his side. He rearranged a pistol and withdrew a packet of documents.

Sir Nolan Brett unlaced the seal and poured the papers out on the table. The waitress refilled his cup with thick black coffee and brought one for Vandusen, who asked if they had cream and sugar. The waitress said she'd see what she could do. She returned with a cup of thick cream and a spoon of honey.

Nolan read the papers while his secretary watched the window and stirred his cup.

They were in order and he'd read them twice already. He knew he was delaying the signature. Vandusen, he was sure, knew that too.

"How long will this give me?" he asked.

"If we spend it all?"

"Aye."

"After our due debts are paid, maybe two years, depending on changing expenses."

"Then I lose the estate?"

"Unless we've made other terms by then, aye."

It didn't pass Nolan's perception that his secretary spoke in the plural. Doubtless he thought this was some kind of loyal camaraderie, but it irked the Second Ear nonetheless. It was his land on the line, his fortune, his title and name, not Vandusen's. He'd mortgaged his inherited estate, the very land given his ancestors by Genest at the landing. The scandal that would come if he lost it in any manner would be unbearable. Losing it to these bourgeois bankers who'd subdivide it and claim his title would be beyond repair.

Vandusen took his eyes from the window and cast a sympathetic gaze at his master.

Nolan wanted to spit.

"If a word of this leaks out," said Sir Nolan, "I will see everyone involved tortured and executed." He said it in a bland straightforward way that reflected his complete confidence that he could see it done.

"I will rightly inform the lenders of this, and highlight the pages concerning it. There is a pain of death clause as you stipulated. They daren't breathe a word until the land is theirs."

"Unless," corrected Sir Nolan.

Vandusen blushed. "Aye. Sorry. So it will never be known."

Nolan scratched his name on the last page and tossed them at Vandusen.

His secretary quickly placed them back in the laced envelope and deposited them out of sight in his satchel.

Sir Nolan Brett sipped his thick bitter drink. "I heard Ethan spent a week on his new estate," he said.

"I heard that too. Took some time off his publicity tour."

Nolan had wanted that estate to pay his bills. He'd needed it, counted on it. Borrowed against it. Before he was on the edge, now he was in trouble. It was worse than even that. His creditors had believed his sure claim that the queen would give him Lord Ellsworth's estate after he was executed. Such had not happened. His word was now suspect as much as his purse. He'd been in damage control since Ethan's party.

"I've two years then," Nolan said. "Two years to ransom my own estate."

"It's a good bargain, sir," said Vandusen.

"Why would you say that?"

"If we win the war, we'll be rich. If we lose, we'll be dead. Do you think Brandon will spare us?"

"Brandon's Hyraxian murderers and those damned Temple swine won't set foot upon this planet except in chains."

Vandusen paused for a knowing second before bowing his head. "Aye, of course. I shall deliver these papers for you. One less worry—"

"Wait." Nolan shook his head at his own bombast. "Who said that?"

"That great patriotic speech? Why, you did, sir. You were quoted saying just that in yesterday's paper."

"I thought I'd seen it somewhere. No plagiarism then?"

"Nay. But had you said Temple would rue the day they sent their dogs after our beloved queen, I'd have to warn you that you were quoting Sir Edward. That'll appear tomorrow."

"How many men do we have on the propaganda campaign?"

"On the payroll? Eight writers and six and fifty rumorers. All the major newspapers are in line."

"And the minor ones?"

"In line or on fire."

"The underground ones?"

"Connor's after them."

Nolan took the flyer out of his pocket and handed it to his secretary. "See if you can find this man before Connor does. He's got talent. We could use him."

Vandusen looked at the page and turned it to read the four border headlines. "You think such a man who made this would ever work for us?"

"If we give him the choice," said Nolan.

"Aye." He put the pamphlet in his satchel. "I have an appointment and you should hasten to the queen."

Nolan nodded. "Please tell whoever wrote that line of mine to keep it up."

"Shall I offer him a raise?"

Nolan shot his secretary a look.

Vandusen smirked. "I will tell him, sir."

Nolan watched his secretary leave in high spirits on his way to the lenders and wondered how long it had been since he thought all this was fun. When was the last time he'd found humor in what he was doing, in the oppressive affairs of state? Surely there was a time when he liked doing this, when he could take his setbacks with grace. When had that been? Not for a long time, he realized. Not since the old man died and the wars for the queen's ascension killed thousands of nobles and a hundred times that many little people. That's what little people were for, but the thousands of nobles, that had sapped the energy right out of him, sure as hell. The costs of progress were high indeed.

The clock outside struck twelve and he pulled on his coat. The attack would upset the day's scheduling, but he had to be there, to comfort and connect. Eventually he'd see Sir Edward and have yet another panicked meeting with the First Ear. A wave of strikes to the east and a factory walkout in Southland. Taxes up, revenue down. Most of the gentry grumbling at the cost of saving their lives, for make no mistake about it, it was their lives they were saving. Brandon would burn them all and sleep in the ashes of this planet untroubled for the rest of his damned life if he got the chance. The Crown needed every penny for defense. Every penny.

It was a balancing act. Fear and hope. You could not let people give up, but neither could you let them relax. Edward was too temperamental to see the line. For safety's sake, the First Ear had planted himself snugly in the camp of fear. A bombastic Chicken Little who sent courtiers away in tears to buy suicide drops for the day the Temple purgers landed on their doorstep. Though privately, it could be said that Connor and his Guards, every bit as ruthless as the Temple purgers, were the symbol of fear on Enskari, publicly Sir Nolan had cast Sir Edward for the role. He was the man to sell war bonds, the old grizzled soldier, with a face fatherly and stern, who knew what was best for you.

The Second Ear would have been an obvious choice for the face of hope among the people. But not Sir Nolan Brett. Not him. Not the spymaster. No. Not nearly likable enough. He was the ugly, but necessary, unmentioned and unfazed force that moved behind the scenes, and that is how he liked it. How it needed to be.

Hope was represented by Sir Ethan Sommerled, the queen's newest favorite. Young and dapper, a daring swashbuckler and hero of all the planet, his was the cultivated face of the bright future.

It had been Sir Nolan's idea and he'd carried forth the campaign with effectiveness and diligence. Vandusen watched it happen with disbelief, knowing how the man had supplanted his master's goals by getting

Ellsworth's lands, but Nolan saw no problem in what he did. It was politics. He had no personal hatred toward the man. He was a perfect symbol and a likable person. Devout and loyal, handsome and optimistic – good traits to have for an icon. It had all been a perfect campaign. Nolan sent him on a publicity tour. A whistle-stop reenactment of his triumphal parade, complete with lifelike replicas of the treasure he'd brought back from his privateering. It had been successful on several levels. Part of the fear/hope balancing act, but also a good way to get him away from the queen who often lacked the discretion her office required.

Ethan led the confident drive that Enskari could not only fight the Hyraxian threat, but was certain to win against it. Enskari was a planet of heroes. He was proof. His campaign had filled the people with new energy and expectations of a bright future.

Thus the strikes and walkouts and social unrest among the peons.

Hope was a good thing, except when people stopped fearing properly. Optimism was no replacement for a well-armed army or fleets of ships patrolling space ways. A thousand feel-good coddling speeches wouldn't stop a plasma barrage or railgun assault.

To temper Ethan's overly successful campaign, a note of fear needed to be sounded.

He heard the echoes of that sound in the murmurs and gossips as he walked to Government House through the rainy streets of Vildeby. Edward would be beside himself. The queen would be rattled. He'd be the face of calm. His people would have a speech ready for Edward by nightfall, the very one that would be quoted in tomorrow's paper. Vandusen probably had it with him just now. The court would be in turmoil. With any luck several courtiers had died in the carriage crash. That would be a plus. In any event, the planet would be horrified and afraid. Connor's Guards would topple another house or two, Hyraxian sympathizers, secret Temple Orthodox Saved. Beheadings and fires. Patriotism rising above sympathy for laborers. Taxes would be paid, conscription quotas filled, the factories reopened with workers sent back to toil so Enskari would have a fighting chance.

He thought again of the flyer. It had showed poison as an abstract black ichor, but Nolan knew the chemical names, the ancient names of carcinogenic petrochemical pollutants, the unavoidable side effects of their modern lifestyle. Every planet suffered them. What else would they have? No trains or lights? No factories or commerce? Who'd weave the cloth in such needed volume if not the machines? The lower class lacked understanding, lacked knowledge of the nuance.

Of all the planets circling Coronam, Enskari was the most progressive, and yet there was dangerous unrest here that threatened to undermine those advances and expose their very planet to destruction by the old order. What an irony, he thought.

He corrected himself. There was one planet freer than this. One planet still a blank slate. The richest prize remaining around Coronam: Tirgwenin.

The ropes were down on the Royal Lane when Nolan turned onto it. The crashed carriages had been cleared.

He followed the sidewalk past his barrel and post and plodded toward the capitol.

This road where the attack had taken place was the same road Ethan had taken in his triumphal parade. Not an accident there.

A balancing act. Tiers of power and manipulation, weakening supports on a sagging foundation. Useful playing pieces that would eventually need to be sacrificed if the game were to be won.

Nolan remembered the parade and his thoughts fell on the flamboyant pirate, Sir Ethan Sommerled. He dissected the connections between the two of them. The queen's wants in Ethan versus her needs in him. Boisterous and loud, an actor one, silent and shadowy, a director the other. The estate in Southland that should have been his was now Sir Ethan's. Because of that, Sir Nolan Brett had two years to put his affairs in order. It sounded like a death sentence, advice to make a will. But Nolan was confident. Two years was all the time left for Ethan to plant a thriving permanent colony on distant savage Tirgwenin. If he didn't, his patent would move to someone else.

CHAPTER NINETEEN

First and foremost, it must be stated that the most notable difference among the people of Maaraw from the Saved of our world is a general lack of adherence and participation in religious activity. Heavenly matters do not carry the same import among these people as they do us. Maarawans claim to be believers but do little to act on it. They maintain a secular morality enforced by laws and custom while ignoring or giving but lip service to the more potent commands of God's scripture and the voice of his prophet. There are churches and barbaric ministers, but these are utilized infrequently – baptisms, confirmation, deaths, and holy days. Seekers of religion and truth are advised to go inland to seek the monasteries of 'bees and honey'. I do not know to what this refers. Perhaps it is a broken reference to Zion – the 'land of milk and honey'?

Journal of Missionary Minister Joseph Peters, First Maarawan Mission President

23, Second-Month, 814 NE

15, Ninth-Month, 937 NE – Broerens Province, Maaraw

Andre Bruin took the first group up the middle. Maylo had his right and Luft the left. Around the back was Asay, a former policeman with the newest joiners. His job, to keep anyone from getting away.

The plantation was spread out over a thousand hectares north-west of Iquiani, twenty kilometers from the coast. It was actually more of a collection of smaller plantations and ranches all feeding into the main one owned by Tomas Verkerd.

The raids they'd done before had all targeted otherworlders., The slaves they'd freed, the houses they'd burned, and the things they'd stolen gave their attacks an air of political resistance, an independent movement that Andre thought missed the point. Tonight he'd correct the misconception. Tomas Verkerd was homegrown Maarawan. One of them, and one of the biggest slaveowners in the district.

Andre's contingent came to the first outbuilding on the Verkerd property. It was clustered beneath a stand of black trees, olive, birch, and sand fir. The moons were in crescent, their light bright and warm enough for the work. He looked out up the fields of cut barley and rye, blue and amber stalks in the moonlight. Far ahead were the orange lights of the big house. Far to his right and equal distance to his left, he could see the lights of smaller stations.

At this station, there were five walled structures and twice as many lean-tos, corrals, and bins. Pigs snorted in some, horses watched from others. Chickens and goats shared space. Cattle in the distance. The walled buildings contained closed stables and hay storage, equipment and machines. It was a rich plantation with imported steam tractors from Lavland and industrial conveyers from Claremond. The livestock was Old Earth, but his manpower was all local third-generation slave.

Andre moved his group of twelve men into the trees and halted in their shadow.

"Do we figure the others are in place?" he whispered, looking at a distant station. He asked Charlie, his second in command tonight. But before Charlie could answer, Andre turned to his third. "Sam, get to cuttin'," he said.

Charlie held a crossbow in the crook of his right arm and wiped the sweat from his face with his left sleeve. "Aye," he said. "I reckon we're at time."

Sam ran out of the shadows to the wire pole.

Sam had joined just last month, but Charlie had been with him from the start. Andre had found Charlie stumbling dumb from a burning warehouse that day in Coebler, his rags on fire, dazed and lost. Andre had taken him and all the others he could away from that place that day. Charlie had stayed with him; most of the others had fled inland or been killed.

Andre watched Sam run up the telegraph pole like it was a knotted rope, hand over hand, until he reached the top. He saw the clippers gleam in the moonlight before hearing the satisfying clip, twang, and slither of a cut telegraph wire. They'd cut a lot of telegraph wires in the last few months.

With equal dexterity and more speed, Sam slid down the pole and rejoined them in the trees.

"Right," said Andre. "This is just the first stop. The prize is that house. Keep 'em quiet. No telling how bad it is. Third generation. No telling."

"Aye," answered the men.

"Let's go."

Andre swung his bow from his back and cocked it, setting the string and feeding a bolt from the receiver into place. He carried also a side arm coilgun in a holster. It was charged and ready but too noisy for now. He'd use his sword if he needed more than the five bolts his crossbow held.

Third generation or more was the favored age of slaves on Maaraw. First-generation slaves had people to run back to. Second and they could still imagine another life. Third, they were born and bred to it. Of course off-worlders would take anything, but third was the earliest generation local slaver buyers would take. Third generation was a warning to his people to be careful. Third generation was dangerous. They were unpredictable. As often as not, they'd fight for their masters rather than join their crusade.

Andre signaled his men to move out. Under moonlights and stars, like low shadows of hunched ghouls, they surrounded the barracks house in four groups of three.

Andre took Charlie and Sam with him to the front entrance.

There was a moment of stillness when all were ready, a communal held breath as they waited the command to act. Andre felt it in his chest and not for the first time, he wondered how he'd come to this, marveled at what his life was now, admiring his own defiance, knowing the inevitable outcome. Doing it all the same.

He gave the signal.

Like a closing hand around a river stone, he and his men swarmed the station house from all sides.

Andre moved to the front door, turned the knob, found it locked, and busted it in with his shoulder all in one motion. He heard similar sounds throughout the building, breaking doors and windows allowing his men inside.

Charlie found a glowglobe and wound it for light.

A Maarawan man, an overseer in white breeches, woke from a straw cot beside a table cluttered with dirty dinner dishes. The floor was strewn with work clothes and dirty boots as if it had just sloughed off a molting insect.

"How was the stew?" Andre asked the man.

"Who the devil are you?" he asked and then, probably recognizing Andre Bruin from the wanted posters, widened his eyes and stared.

Sam moved to the right door and Charlie the left, leaving Andre alone with him.

"How many souls in this station?" Andre said.

"This station? We got six and thirty slaves, five whippers – *overseers*," he corrected himself. "We had three and fifty, plus eight *overseers* before, but we cut them out after the harvest."

There was a crash and a struggle the way Charlie had gone. Andre saw the man on the cot glance at his boots just under his bed.

"You don't want to reach for that," Andre said. "And the wires are cut so that alarm won't do nothing." He pointed to a telegraph keypad on the desk.

"I can't run the thing," the man said. "Never learned." There was more sound of struggles deeper in. Andre couldn't tell if it was the same fight or another one.

The man glanced again.

"Don't," said Andre, raising his bow.

The distinct and sibilant hiss of crossbows firing filtered in, followed by a scream quickly muffled and silence after that.

"Mighty loyal, ye lot," said Andre. "Or scared."

The man settled back and waited.

"Aye," said Andre. "It'll all be over quick. Hopefully ye have been a good taskmaster and your wards will have no cause to harm ye."

To that, the man's eyes went large.

"I'm just doing my job," he said.

"Shhh," said Andre, listening.

The fighting was over. He heard low voices and some weeping, a chorus of gasps and prayers.

"Each station got about the same number of folks?" Andre said.

The man lunged for his boots.

"Damn ye!" Andre loosed a bolt into the man's neck.

He twitched and sputtered, but kept moving and reached inside his boot.

Andre cocked the next one into place and shot a second bolt through the man's wrist, pinning his arm to the side of his chest.

The boot fell to the floor; a flame pistol spilled out of it.

The man gurgled and twitched, fell back on the cot, then off it to the floor where he just gurgled.

Charlie came in with two Maarawan slaves, their faces scarred with the same chattel brand Charlie wore on his forehead, theirs older by decades.

"We going to get into trouble?" Andre said to the slaves.

The slaves stared at the shot overseer with open-mouthed disbelief.

"Did ye hear me?" Andre insisted.

Charlie said, "He's talking to you."

"What?" said one.

"Are there any of ye folk that are going to get in our way? I need to know."

"Nay, sir. Nay. You're the blessing we prayed for. You're the angel. You're the deliverer God has sent."

"Hallelujah."

"Don't know about that," he said.

"Hallelujah!"

"Now hush," Andre said. "Any of the overseers alive?"

"All but one and maybe your man there," said Charlie.

Andre pointed to the flamer. Charlie picked it up.

Men from each of the other sides crowded in the small receiving room.

Andre repeated his orders, not that he needed to, but as a custom to place their progress in the overall plan. "Leave five men here to talk to them, hold them for an hour then send them off. Oh, and of course burn this forsaken place to the ground."

"Aye, sir."

"I'd like to join ye," said one slave.

"Me as well."

"Most of us will, I'll bargain."

Charlie smiled.

"Then ye'll meet us at the big house after an hour. While ye wait do with these keepers as ye will. I won't stand in the way of vengeance."

The man he'd shot looked like he didn't like his chances.

Andre left five of his twelve with the newly freed slaves for a quick one-hour crash course on stolen freedom on Maaraw. They'd be given the choice to flee, join them, or stay put and wait the flames to clear. After an hour, every building would be set alight and the five would rejoin the others.

It was almost half his contingent but Andre had learned not to leave an open flank. The five would make sure the third-generations wouldn't come after them. Talk was cheap.

Maylo and Luft would do the same at the other stations and they'd all meet up in front of the big house and repeat the process with the one and twenty men remaining. Asay and his group would kill anyone trying to escape along the road before the house was full ablaze.

He'd met Maylo and Luft officially a week after the disaster at Coebler, though of course he'd seen them before fleeing the docks after planting the mine on the Hyraxian cruiser.

Andre had been leading a group of ten burned and ragged refugees through the most terrible terrain he could imagine, seeking the interior fifty kilometers inland, when he stumbled on their camp.

"We're the resistance," Maylo had told him. "I saw you on the dock."

"What are you resisting exactly?"

"The rape of Maaraw from outworlders."

"You burned up a city."

"Nay, we sunk a ship that was really a bomb."

"Aye," said Andre. "What was a plasma store doing below the barrier?"

"Exactly," he said. "You ever been inland?"

"Nay, can't say as I have," said Andre. "But if ye have, I'd be obliged if ye could help these souls get there and be safe."

The resistance fighters looked over the burned and ragged people, inspected their new brands, and fed them from their stores. The resistance was only a dozen men and woman, none over the age of five and twenty. Andre at twice that loomed over them with an aged authority that drew them like gravity. It was at this time his mind filled with amber visions of co-operating people, a rise of humanity, honey-soothed burns, bees and plenty, and clear skies.

"I saw light," Andre told them that night. "Your bomb was fire. It blew me down. That was air. In the bay – the sea. Water. Now I found ye talking of the planet. That be the earth, four of the five elements, so said the mystics. I'd say we complete it."

They stared at him like he spoke prophesy, the air a crackle of woodsmoke, the jungle around them holding its breath.

"I say we should not tarry now with this 'extractive economy' ye talk about. I say we look to honey," he told them, not wholly knowing his meaning then, but believing it wholeheartedly nonetheless. "I say we aim for the spirit. The fifth of the five elements. I say we free the souls. I say we stop this accursed slavery."

He'd not meant to speak so metaphysically, but that's how it had come out. Somehow it had made sense to him to put it that way to those eager-faced middle-class activists. Just kids really, looking for a cause and finding one. Finding him. They were none of them religious, but he hooked them with the sacred elements and then he rose to lead them.

★ ★ ★

They made the three kilometers to the big house in good time. They kept to the hedgerows and cottonwood wind blinds. Sam cut another three poles bare as they went, scampering up and down as fast as a squirrel. "I just like them wires better when they're slack and on the ground," he said with a grin.

"Aye," agreed Andre.

Half a kilometer out, they stopped and watched. The house was wide awake, filled with light and movement.

"Could the others have started?" said Charlie.

"Nay. We're the first. They had longer to go. What we're looking at here is them knowing we're coming."

"Help ain't comin'," said Sam. "They ain't got no wires."

"Must have been some farmhand out for a walk," said someone.

"Bet it was Luft's group. They're a noisy bunch. Give 'em trumpets, they'll be quieter."

"We turning back?"

"What do we do?"

"What we came for," said Andre. "We're not leaving 'til that house is a cinder."

"Aye."

He waved all his men together and ordered them out again into a picket.

"Nothing comes down this way, no man gets by. They have a long way to go for help, but for all we know they have a railgun bunker yonder. Don't want none of that."

"Aye."

The men spread out in a line across the road and between the hedges. Twenty meters between them, they marched forward and stopped at the gate.

In a few minutes they were joined by Maylo and Luft.

"My men are yonder there by that outbuilding," said Maylo.

"Mine are in the stalls," said Luft. He pointed to the barn.

"That outbuilding looks to be house-slave quarters," said Andre. "Clear it out first."

"It is slave quarters," said Maylo. "But it's empty. We checked."

"Damn," said Andre. "How many beds?"

"Fifteen, maybe twenty. Looks like some children amongst them."

"We gotta figure a dozen men armed and fanatic."

"Like us," said Luft, grinning.

"Aye," said Andre. "Take your positions."

Maylo and Luft returned to their men. Andre gauged the time and looked back across the fields. Behind him the three stations were now all alight, plumes of orange flame kicking skyward in limbs of fire.

Behind the house on the other side came the sound of coilgun and the glow of a flamethrower. Screams filled the air. That was Asay's there.

Lights dimmed but didn't go out inside the house and the night erupted in rifle shot.

"Was that one us?"

"Nay, Sam. That's the house, asking us to leave."

"What are we going to say?"

"Sounds like they got a lot of guns."

"Aye," said Andre. "But I doubt Tomas Verkerd trains his slaves to shoot them much."

"Nay."

"Come on." Andre looked back at the burning buildings and wished he could wait for those men to return, but he couldn't. He moved through the gate to an inner hedge adorned with animal-shaped bushes that stood black against the starlight.

A ripple of aurora skittered across the sky, the first hint of morning still hours away. It was orange and snakelike and spread out as if playing with the burning structures behind them.

More coilshot from Asay. Answers from the house.

"Take any shot ye get," Andre ordered his men. "Soften 'em up."

A shadow passed a house window and drew a fusillade of crossbow shot. The shadow fell still and didn't move again.

"Maybe we should save ammo."

"Aye, sir."

"Ahoy the house!" called Andre. "Ahoy the house!"

He was answered by rifle fire but none of it as much as stirred a leaf on the foliage near them.

"How far's that door?" said Andre.

"Five and twenty meters, I'd think."

"Think I can hit it?"

"Nay."

"Flask of redberry if I do."

"How many shots?" said Charlie.

"One," he said. "You think I'd cheat?"

"Aye," said Sam with a grin.

Andre waited for the firing to stop, for the air to be still and quiet. Drawing his pistol, he turned, quarter facing the house, and extended his arm full length. He took aim and fired.

The supersonic slug rung their ears and disintegrated the door.

"Tough door," said Andre. "If it'd been cheap wood, the shot would have just passed through it. Lucky us."

"What?" said Charlie, holding his hands over his ears.

"What?" said Sam.

Andre made a drinking gesture and they nodded.

"Ahoy the house!" Andrew shouted. "Ahoy the house! We'll burn you out in thirty seconds if ye don't answer."

There was a pause. Andre gave it a full minute before shouting, not trusting the ring in his ears. "All right, house. See ye in hell!"

Charlie passed him the hand-flamer taken from the first station. It was a nice one. Silver inlaid and engraved. The tank was full.

"What do you want?" came a call from inside.

"I'll be seeking a word with the master, Tomas Verkerd, if ye please."

"He's gone to market. He's not here."

"Nay. We know better," shouted Andre. "Here's my terms. All ye come out unarmed and we'll not burn ye alive. How's that?"

"I'd like to see you try!"

"That you, Tomas?"

"Who's out there?"

"Andre Bruin."

There was a weighty pause then, "What happened to you, Mr. Bruin? I knew you. You were all right. What in God's name happened to you to join up with these ruffians?"

"It's like this, Tomas, I'm a people person."

"What's that supposed to mean?"

"It means they joined up with me, you blackguard! It means slavery ain't a right condition. It means I'm fixing to free the lot of yours, burn your place to the ground, and kill ye and ye entire family, if ye don't show yourselves now."

An explosion roared across the field as some chemical or machine succumbed to the fire in the leftmost station. It sent a fireball into the sky that curled in upon itself before joining the auroras.

"I know ye have kids in there, Tomas. Come out now."

There was commotion in the house, shouts and weeping. Wails. Always wails among the house slaves. It was like it was taught to them.

"I can ransom us," said Verkerd. "I have money."

"Bring it out with ye."

"I don't have much here. But I can get it."

"Bring out what you have."

"Does that mean we can bargain?"

"Nay, but it couldn't hurt."

More wailing.

"I'm coming out."

Andre wound his gun and set another charge. He glanced to his right and left and saw the others were ready.

A man in fine clothes came out of the door carrying a small box.

"You gotta be kidding me," Andre said. "Cut him down."

"What?" said Charlie.

"That's not Tomas. That man's dressed for a ball not for a bed. Fifth-generation I bet. Lost cause. Kill him."

Charlie hesitated then took aim and fired a crossbow bolt into the man's chest.

Screams from within the house, female and shrill. Murmurs.

"Window," said Sam.

Three more crossbows let loose; at least one hit home and dropped the shadow in an upper room.

"They should keep the lights off," said Charlie.

Andre turned to his lieutenant. "Shhh," he said.

Luft's side shattered glass and Maylo let go a coil round. Andre couldn't see what they were shooting at but was certain that whatever it was wasn't there now.

"Wasting ammo out here, Tomas. I got grenades and this nice engraved hand-flamer you gave to…." He held it out in the light and tried to read the name engraved on it. "To… uhm, *to Mr. Fountain for loyalty and trust.* He'll be late for work tomorrow, by the way."

"You bastard!"

"Thirty seconds and I'm lighting fires."

"This house won't burn," said a different voice.

That explained the door.

"You want to bet lives on that?" said Andre.

"Why me, Bruin? I'm Maarawan. I'm one of you. I'm not one of those filthy off-worlders you're after."

"Twenty seconds."

"Let us send out the women."

"That's fine. But if ye don't follow, we'll burn them alive in the barn after ye all be dead."

Charlie glanced over at him.

Andre shook his head. Charlie returned to his bow.

"You're a collaborator," Andre said. "This isn't about our world and theirs. This is about justice, about cruelty. This is about the species." He almost added *bees.*

"I don't understand."

"Aye, you do," said Andre. "That's why ye live in a fortress. That's why ye haven't come out. That's why you're not going to come out."

"Wait."

"I'm going to destroy you, Tomas Verkerd. Whether that's financially or physically, is up to you."

"What's the difference?"

Andre smiled. Of course he'd think that way. "Bombs!" he called to his men.

Sam lit two petrol bombs and handed one to the man beside him. They were simple glass bottles filled with honey syrup and diesel with siphoning rags for fuses. An ancient design but effective. The fuses were lit. They burned warm orange, like the houses behind them, like the smiling sky above them.

The lighted bombs revealed their positions but showed they were serious. They were lit and burning, the fuses allowing but a minute or so before the bomb had to be thrown. Once lit, like the fire they made, there was no way to put it out short of a lake.

Talk in the house, cries. Wails.

Silence.

"Burn 'em out!" called Andre.

His man moved out of cover and ran at the house. Andre saw similar fighters at the sides, bearing their own burning flasks in their fists like participants in a hellish relay.

Musket fire from the house. One of his men went down. It wasn't Sam. It was another man, Jonez, his leg shot from under him in a ricochet. He tumbled forward, propelled by momentum. His bottle leapt out his hand across the yard and burst in a splash of fire that illuminated the front of the house like a malevolent sun.

Crossbows snicked in return fire. Andre aimed his pistol. Charlie covered his ears. Andre fired through the shattered door into the shadows within. It was the noise he was after, but he heard a cry after the shot. Not a cry of one wounded, but a cry of one seeing a friend destroyed.

The surviving men arrived at the house and flung their bombs through shattered windows and ran back to cover.

The house fired at them as they fled, but too late, the slow-coming volley bespeaking inexperience with their weapons.

Wails. Screams.

Silence but for the fire.

"Think they're coming out?"

"They can't stay in."

"That Lavlander did."

"He was insane."

"And Verkerd isn't?"

Andre considered the question. "He's not alone. Some will come out.

The fire will drive them. They'll chance the guns to quit the flames when it's at their ankles."

"Fifth-generations?"

"I'd think the earlier ones first, but aye, them too. The lost ones might value their lives in the end, at least for the moment before we kill them."

Charlie leveled his crossbow at the door.

A cry from within the house was an obvious signal. Andre pulled up his pistol and only then realized he hadn't recharged it. He scanned the dark shadows behind the bush for his crossbow, his night vision destroyed by the light of the burning house.

He heard shots from behind. Asay, cutting them down as they fled in the most obvious direction.

Then the sides and the front spewed people like ants out of a hill.

"Here they come!"

Before them was a cluster of people, some armed, some with their hands up, all running out of the house screaming. They tumbled ahead and then paused for half a beat while women and children were put around them, outermost of the cluster, like a wall. Then as a group they ran for the darkness.

Andre recognized Tomas in the middle. He wore dirty misfitting clothes and clutched pockets that bulged with heavy items. People slowed their steps to keep around him, acting as human shields for their master. Meat shields, thought Andre. Their obvious deference to the man exposed his poor camouflage.

His wife was with him, dressed in a satin nightgown and clutching a baby.

The house burned.

Andre stood up and showed himself in the light of the fire.

"Where do ye think you're going?"

One of the men stopped and raised his musket at Andre. Three crossbow bolts knocked him down: two in the chest, one in his eye.

Wails. Screams.

There were probably twenty souls in Tomas's cluster. Too many to subdue by hand with his few men. "Peel 'em back!" Andre ordered.

His men knew to spare the women and children if possible, but darkness and the callous cowardice of their quarry meant that they failed to spare them all. Or many.

Crossbows, coilgun, and napalm shot into the mass.

They fell like mowed cane, this cluster and those like it fleeing the other doors.

It didn't take long. A minute, maybe two, and all was still.

Andre took his men with swords into the mass, peeling the live from the dead.

The living were led to the carriage house and the animals were let out.

With the hand-flamer, Andre ignited the blacksmith's fire. He pumped the bellows.

Soon the mansion house collapsed. The fireproof walls were useless without the inner support and the walls fell like dominoes, spewing columns of bright orange embers into the sky.

All told they had but fifteen souls after the assault. They'd lost two: Jonez and one in Maylo's station who'd been killed by the foreman, who'd gotten away to warn the house.

The men from the stations arrived with a small contingent of freed enlisted slaves who'd just that evening been the property of Verkerd. These people stared wide-eyed at the happenings, anxious and excited, terrified and sad in turns. Andre had seen it before.

Among the plantation survivors were Tomas Verkerd, a baby daughter, and two children. His wife lay dead among the slaves in front of the house. Tomas had a bolt five centimeters into his thigh. To a person, the surviving house slaves begged for their master to be let go, volunteering their own lives for his and his beautiful family.

Luft told them all to shut up.

Andre pumped the bellows.

Maylo and Asay set fire to the plantation. Anything that would burn was to burn. Anything that could be broken was to be broken. Anything that wanted freedom was to be made free. Except the masters.

Verkerd held the children; the baby cried.

"Bruin," he said. "I didn't do this. I didn't ask for this. This just happened."

"Aye, I know," said Andre. "You inherited it."

"Aye, exactly," he said. "It's just the way it is."

"Uh-huh." Bellows up, bellows down.

Verkerd moved to anger. "This isn't going to work. You can't drive them off the planet. You can't free all the slaves. You can't. You're just making things worse. You're just a murderer."

"Uh-huh."

"What are you going to do?"

He found the brand among the others. Among those used to mark Verkerd's animals was the one he used to brand new slaves. Andre tossed it on the coals.

"It doesn't have to be any way," Andre said. "It's this way because we let it be this way. I say there's another way."

"What are you talking about?" Verkerd asked.

"I'm saying as a species, what's happening here on Maaraw and among the civilized worlds, is just a repetition of past mistakes. It's repugnant."

"What?"

"You don't need to understand." Andre's mind filled with a peaceful calm, a low droning hum, an echo of bees he could not explain to himself, so would not even try to explain to the slaver. He summed it up as best as he could. "I'm thinking of the big picture," he said.

"You would want to be governor?"

"Nay," he laughed. "Let me put it this way. Greed causes pain."

"What?"

Andre took the iron out the fire and buried the hot end in Verkerd's forehead.

CHAPTER TWENTY

Though Old Earth scientists had known about radiation and electromagnetic pulses for centuries, and thought they had hardened the ships of the Unsettling sufficiently against any solar interference, the fury encountered at Coronam was at once more unusual and more devastating than anything they'd imagined. Ships were lost outright in the storms during the fifty days from wormhole to landings. The ships that remained crashed to their worlds, their cargos of technology robbed and destroyed by fused circuits and wiped computer banks. Though scientists remained to record knowledge, theories, and practices, the inability to shield sensitive equipment even beneath the shrouding atmospheres of the planets, meant that it was for all intents and purposes lost to legend, and civilization rose up on more meager technical footings.

Fear the Sun: A Survey of Technology among the Civilized Worlds
Abraham Turringson
Hyrax, 901 NE

13, Tenth-Month 937 NE – Aboard the Fortuna *in the shadow lee of Hyrax*

Lady Vanessa Possad was dressed as elegantly as low gravity and her sensibilities would allow. The loose long flowing dresses she was partial to and had worn almost exclusively while on Enskari wouldn't do for space. She wore bangs and slippers, a tight blouse, and a fastened bonnet that contained her hair and made her look like a soap maker's wife. She envied men, who could bounce around in tailored uniforms, useful boots, and cropped hair, but for her fairer sex, even someone of her noble class, the fashion choices were hideous.

It didn't help that Brandon's court was spread out over six decks, each one with a different gravitation pull from zero to more than anyone was used to. Mostly, though, she was on the main court deck, spun to exactly one home gravity, but she had to be ready to move anywhere when summoned, exploring, or spying.

She'd fled Enskari after the attempt on the queen's life. She had been at the embassy waiting for Sir Temsil to arrive and tell her how to dress for the evening to best portray Hyraxian might in Queen Zabel's presence. He never showed up. Instead a letter arrived.

The missive said simply: *Lady Vanessa. There's been a failed assassination attempt on the queen by Hyraxian agents. Take the secret corridor behind Temsil's desk to the waiting steam launch and flee.*

It wasn't signed, but she knew Sir Nolan's handwriting even if she didn't know there was a secret corridor out of the embassy.

She'd hiked up her dress, kicked off her heels, and charged through the embassy offices. She rushed past alarmed officials, soldiers, secretaries, and unspecified functionaries who knew who she was but had never seen her or anyone of her class and gender move faster than the 'courtier float' – that magical trained gait that gives the illusion that a woman's dress is some kind of hovercraft.

She burst into the ambassador's office, past assistants and guards who hesitated to stop her because of her noble rank.

She ran straight to the bookcase and searched for the lever. She heard voices behind her, rising voices, discordant sounds of breached etiquette. Someone called for Captain Jasso.

"What is it?" he barked.

She didn't want to see Jasso just then. She never wanted to see Jasso, but now was particularly bad. He was a scarred and surly man, a killer by trade and preference, who did the ambassador's dirty work. A sexist lout; unless she had a noble man standing next to her nodding in agreement, Jasso would not listen to a word she said.

She pulled books down and kicked them. She reread the note seeking a clue as to how to open the damn door.

Falling to her hands and knees, she searched undersurfaces for buttons or latches and saw a switch under the ambassador's desk. She pulled it. The bookcase swung open a half meter before catching on the pile of books she'd tossed on the floor. She swept them away with her arms.

"What do you think you're doing, Lady Vanessa?" Captain Jasso stood above her, guards at his sides. He wore the condescending look he used on noble women to show that though they were socially higher in rank, he didn't think so.

She didn't have time for this. She stood up and handed him the letter.

He took it from her like it was the bill to a brothel. She watched as he read it, his lips moving, his expression faltering and failing.

She grabbed the bookcase and yanked it open.

There were shouts from the front of the embassy.

A coilgun report.

Captain Jasso turned toward the sound as crows fly toward gunfire.

Vanessa plucked the letter out of his hand.

Scream and shouts. The hiss of a flamer.

Jasso drew his sword and ran out of the office as a group of secretaries ran in. One barred the door while another threw papers into a pile on the ambassador's carpet. Someone doused them with oil.

Lady Vanessa wiggled out of her petticoats and pushed through the secret door. Beyond were stairs leading down. She took them in half dark as the ambassador's office filled with smoke and fire.

A flight down, she found a glowglobe, pulled it from the wall and wound it for light. Down another flight of stone stairs past two more doors, she smelled water and found an underground dock with a waiting steam skiff. She didn't know the man steering it, but he was kind and winked at her and told her to call him Jim.

The underground canal connected with the Reedy River. At full steam, Jim took her to the water docks of the Vildeby space elevator and introduced her to a Lavland pilot who'd get her back to Hyrax.

It was all a blur from note to elevator, a single motion of flight in her mind. Jim left her before she could thank him.

The Lavlandian pilot had a change of clothes for her and in ten minutes, two minutes before the news of the assassination attempt closed the elevator, she was riding the thread to his ship.

New papers said she was an heiress from New Harlem on her way home. She didn't know much about Lavland geography. She'd be hard put to find the continent of Lithu on a globe, let alone the city of New Harlem. When any of the other passengers tried to talk to her, she told them she had a headache in as few words as possible, unable to mimic a Lavlandian accent and afraid her Hyraxian one would betray her.

At the top of the elevator, Enskari guards searched for Hyraxian spies. She claimed noble rank and was treated accordingly. She was allowed to board the ship while half the hands were kept for questioning. The pilot set sail with a skeleton crew and made good time to Hyrax.

It had been she who'd first told King Brandon Drust and the court about the failed assassination attempt on Enskari.

He didn't act surprised.

"Can you offer more information, Lady Vanessa?" Brandon said to her, his eyes falling naturally down her neckline between her breasts. He was at his lunch table. There was enough food to feed a garrison, but he was eating alone and didn't offer her any. Guards stood by with weapons, advisors with papers; all looked hungry and bored.

She smiled coquettishly and fanned herself to hide her face until she was sure she could hide her revulsion. It took all she had. She thought of her dead family and remembered her goal: the complete destruction to a chromosome of the hated House Drust.

"Nay, Your Highness," she said. "I ran for my life. I suspect they arrested Temsil."

"Why would you say that?"

"Because Sir Nolan doesn't like him," she said with complete honesty. "He was looking for an excuse."

Brandon nodded. "You could have suffered the same fate."

"Aye."

"I'm glad you didn't," he said. Then, to an aid, "Arrest the Enskari ambassador."

"But, sire, that's an act of war," said the advisor. "We're not sure the queen really has arrested Sir Temsil."

"Are we not at war?" he said. "Have we not been at war with that accursed planet since that damned bitch stole the throne? Has not all of God's faithful been at war with that soon-to-be-cinder?"

"Sire." The advisor looked at his fellows for support. "Just because Zabel goes against custom and law doesn't mean the noble houses of Hyrax should do the same."

Brandon broke a wing off a fowl and sucked at it.

"Very well," he said. "Have him watched."

"We already—" began the advisor, but shut up when Brandon glanced at him. "Aye, Your Highness."

The king looked at Vanessa. "Lady, you have been through a terrible ordeal."

"It was nothing, Your Highness. It was my honor and privilege to serve Hyrax."

"You are a patriot?"

"Hyrax is my heart."

"We are Hyrax," he said. "And we appreciate it."

She ground her teeth behind her fan.

"Lady Vanessa, would you care to accompany us on my yacht? You have no pressing engagements, have you?" The advisors squirmed. Brandon cast a weary glance at them. "With all the honor your rank entitles you," he added.

But of course her rank was a fraction of what it should have been, would have been before the House Drust destroyed her family. "I'd be honored," she said and curtsied. "I enjoy the sea."

"Nay, my other yacht."

"The *Fortuna*?"

"You know it?"

"Only by reputation. Isn't it a man-of-war?"

"It is large, I admit."

And armed, she was sure. It was the ship he intended to ride to Enskari. "Then it is good that I haven't found my land legs yet."

He smiled and looked her up and down, his eyes finding her décolletage. Her fan went to her face.

The next day she found herself again in an elevator being dragged into space with the other cargo. The king of course had been shuttled. She'd be a couple of days behind, left to her own devices, which didn't bother her. She preferred that to the king's company.

After arriving at the top of the elevator, she boarded a military shuttle and was brought around the lee side of the planet to where the armada was assembling and the prince's flagship, the *Fortuna*, waited.

In the darkness behind the planet she saw only star fields. She couldn't make out the ships gathered there hiding from the sun's storms. After an hour of trying, however, she discerned lights that weren't stars, flickers and flashes of messages conveyed across the expanses of open space. Occasionally a silver hull would reflect light from Hyrax, a creeping mirror of a green aurora snaking across her world below. When one ship unfurled its wings and fired its plasma boosters, it shone like a comet. She followed it around the planet until light filled its sails in glowing golden petals.

She knew the *Fortuna* was huge, a converted man-of-war, a new special breed of ship, a flying planet, more armor than an asteroid, more weapons than an army, designed and built for no other purpose than war. Brandon's, she assumed, would be more comfortable than that made it sound. When she saw it, it looked like any other ship to her. She couldn't give it scale in the darkness, couldn't marvel at the massed weaponry, the forward guns, or the plasma cannons. She saw only another spinning silver bullet with a long trailing stem and folded petal sails. It was like every other ship that dared travel between the worlds under the eye of Coronam, their temperamental and unpredictable sun.

She boarded Brandon's ship and was taken to opulent quarters of full gravity and left to her own devices. Brandon was not yet on board she discovered. For two days she explored the massive craft and reconnected with the king's courtiers and nobles, fighting with dress and gravity in equal measure until she heard the king was aboard.

★　　★　　★

She adjusted herself in the mirror, cursing her limited wardrobe, but refusing to wear anything that would turn against her in different gravities. Taking gowned women to lower decks for a cheap peek was not beyond most of the king's court.

She made her way to King's Hall, where court was in session. She reflected on the expense of bringing the entire court into space. She'd heard counselors to Queen Zabel complain about the cost of moving from Vildeby to Upaven and could only assume that this meant that Hyrax was wealthy beyond sense.

"Vanessa," came a voice behind her. "Is that you?"

She turned to see Shannon Coles, a friend from finishing school. A year behind her. That put her at eighteen.

"Blessed be," said Vanessa.

"And to thee."

"Have you been presented?"

"Oh, aye." Shannon had gone with the full sweeping gown, hover walk, and hanging jewelry. She looked over Vanessa's tight clothes with some amusement. "It was just last month or was it two? Where has the time gone? It was wonderful. The king himself danced with me. One can't say that for all the girls presented that day."

"I'm sure it was wonderful." Vanessa thought back on her own presentation. She'd brought a dagger and had intended to kill the king with it that day. She would have had Nolan's man not approached her first.

"You should have been there," Shannon said with a pout. "Where were you?"

"The king sent me to Enskari."

Shannon looked at her with pity, fluttering her eyelashes and turning her mouth down in a compassionate frown. "Well, we all have our stations, don't we?"

Vanessa felt her ears warm, but cooled them quick enough. She had practice. "Well," she said. "Some of us need to be useful."

Shannon nodded, still taking in Vanessa's wardrobe. "Is this what they're wearing on Enskari?" she said. "I heard they were backward, but that outfit looks more like an exercise suit than something one would wear before the king."

"First time in space?" Vanessa said.

"What? Oh, aye. I was personally invited."

Vanessa noticed she hadn't said by whom. "You should get one of the men to show you the observation deck," she said.

"And where's that?"

"Up. Zero deck."

"Oh," she said.

Vanessa pushed by the silly girl and went down the stairs to court, noticing the drag on her legs increase with each step.

She slipped in a side door and took her place in the gallery with the other courtiers who cared enough about statecraft to actually watch the practice of it. Shannon, she was sure, was off to some distraction somewhere else in the ship, probably looking for someone to take her to zero deck who'd look up her skirt as she fought with her necklace. There were few women in attendance, a handful, six maybe. She was glad to see that she wasn't the only one dressed for the environment, but she was the only one unaccompanied by a male.

Brandon heard appeals for an hour, all from nobles who had the means to approach the king while he was in space. The king found for them in every case, however dubious.

Toward the end, his eyes panned over the gallery and he saw Vanessa and smiled at her. Her skin crawled. He whispered something to a page, who exited the room. She swallowed and braced herself. A few minutes later the page appeared and whispered in her ear that she was summoned to the king.

She glanced down at him and he smiled up at her. An advisor whispered something in his ear and the royal visage was disturbed. Brandon's expression became all business then.

He listened to the appeal before him, a land grab on Terel, a freeman standing in the way of an expanded hunting lodge, and he quickly found for the noble and left it to judges to figure the details. That settled, he stood. Trumpets blared to raise the room. Vanessa bowed with the rest of them as the king exited.

She left with the page who'd carried the summons. He was a young man, agile and strong, and she had to hurry to keep up with him. She was led through a maze of narrow and guarded corridors she'd not been allowed to explore before, to the king's private rooms on a lower gravity deck.

The page knocked once and then gestured Vanessa to enter.

The prince was seated before a window, his back to her, the stars rotating slowly beyond the meters of glass. Five other men were in attendance and watched her enter. One she recognized as Captain Nicandus, head of the king's house guard, three were clergy and the third was Minister Tobias, First Counselor to the king.

"Blessed be," she said. Since the king was looking away, she curtsied to Tobias. "Your Eminence."

"Blessed be to thee and welcome, Lady Vanessa," he said. "I heard you had quite the adventure on Enskari."

"Aye, Your Eminence."

"I suspect the king summoned you for another reason, but while you are here, I might impose a few questions on you, if I may. I seek advice."

"Advice? From a woman?" It was one of the clergymen.

Vanessa studied the clerical insignia but didn't recognize it.

"Where are my manners?" said Tobias. "Lady Vanessa, may I introduce Apostle D'Angelo."

Vanessa's eyes went wide. She stood in the presence of one of the Twelve and had bowed to Tobias. She felt awkward and confused, trying to remember the protocol for such things.

She curtsied to the man. "Your Holiness," she said.

She'd heard of D'Angelo, the drunk apostle sent by the prophet to advise the king, a figurehead behind which Minister Rendelle, the prophet's real man, worked.

"And this is Minister Rendelle," said Tobias as if on cue.

"Minister." Another curtsy. He bowed. She was taken by his sharp eyes. D'Angelo's had been glazed and unfocused, but Rendelle looked at her as though he were searching for soft tissue in which to plunge a knife.

"I've never been in such great company before," Vanessa said.

Tobias grinned. "May I introduce lastly, the First Advisor to the prophet, His High Holiness, Kendall Jessop."

The man was younger than she imagined anyone could ever be and hold such a high office. He looked at her with a calm expression she always thought a man of God should wear but had never seen before.

Again she curtsied. "Your High Holiness," she said.

"I'm surprised King Brandon sent you off-world," said Jessop. "Your loveliness would have enriched his court greatly."

"To speak to D'Angelo's comment," said Tobias, "Lady Vanessa is something of a rarity at court. A smart, useful aristocrat. I sent her to infiltrate Zabel's court."

"I was most certainly under the impression I was exiled," she said.

"She is a pretty spy," said Rendelle.

"And they let her go?" said D'Angelo.

"I fled. After the attack on the queen. I knew I was not safe."

"Hogwash," said Rendelle. "You had diplomatic immunity. They'd not have touched you."

"They arrested our ambassador for a time," said Tobias.

"What word?" said Vanessa.

Tobias said, "He's free now, but the embassy was overrun by angry townsfolk who all had military issue weapons and army boots. There were several deaths."

"I was there," said Vanessa.

"The building burned down."

"I suspect we started that fire," she said. "The secretaries were burning papers during the attack."

"That's interesting but must not leave this room," said Rendelle. "The masses know that it was the Enskaran heretics that torched that building and burned our countrymen alive as they defended their soil."

"Aye, Minister," she said. "As you wish."

Tobias went on. "Connor is doing another purge of the noble houses. Seems he's accused half the country of treason. He's seizing assets and burning gentry at the stake with copies of the Pretender Bull as tinder."

"Oh my God."

"Quite," said Jessop.

"Destroyed are the houses O'Shea, Boyce, and Kehoe, among others."

Vanessa gasped. "Boyce? They were such good people."

"So they were loyal to the prophet?" said Rendelle.

She hesitated. "I don't know that. I knew their daughter, Emily. She was nice. The family was on hard times. They'd been unable to pay the war tax and hesitant to liquidate their lands to meet it."

"I suspect commerce more than God is at the cause for most of this," said Tobias.

Rendelle threw him a glance. "Then their motives are doubly damned," he said.

Tobias shrugged. "Can I get you a drink, my dear?"

D'Angelo shuffled around a bar and poured himself a drink. Vanessa watched the amber liquid move out of the bottle into his glass. Retarded by the low gravity, it splashed in slow motion and fought the glass like a lethargic ooze.

"Nay, but thanks, sir," she said, but then realizing she really wanted some, "Well, perhaps a little one."

"Wine or whisky?" Tobias asked.

"Whisky," she said. "With a little water."

Tobias found a bottle under the bar and poured Vanessa a drink from it. D'Angelo scowled at the bottle and threw her another dirty look.

"It's old and well tamed," said Tobias, handing her the drink.

"You are kind," she said.

"No need to be so formal, my dear," he said. "We're all friends here."

This comment drew glances from everyone in the room save Brandon, who watched the stars as if in a dream.

It was excellent whisky, smooth and cool with clear ice cubes. For effect, she gave a little cough so the men wouldn't think she was accustomed to such drink. "Kehoe was loyal to the prophet," she said. "He hid priests in his basement and held sacrament every Sunday."

"I will pray for him," said Jessop.

"So we're done talking about money?" said Brandon from his chair. "No more lectures about wasteful spending? No more lectures about limited resources and imminent collapses?"

"We're still talking about that, sire," said Tobias.

"Sounded like we were talking about martyrs and the bitch who made them."

"Aye," said Rendelle. "I cannot believe no one has done away with that heretic yet."

"She's popular," said Vanessa before she could stop herself.

"Aye? Go on," said Tobias.

She was too well trained to squirm, so she extended her neck and spoke clearly. "There's something in the air. The Enskarans know what they're doing is different."

"Sin," said D'Angelo.

"Perhaps," she said, "but there's a camaraderie in it among the people, high and low, most especially the womenfolk. They're feeling a new empowerment."

"That explains a lot," said D'Angelo. "How long were *you* there?"

She blushed.

Tobias said, "Have there been other assassination attempts?"

She said, "There were always rumors. Connor's Guards terrify noble and commoner alike. There are public executions, some say of the traitors, some say for traitors to see and be afraid."

"Most likely both," said Rendelle.

"You used to be a purger, didn't you, Minister?" said Tobias.

"Aye," he said.

"And that's how you would do it?"

"Aye."

"Is Queen Zabel, the heretic usurper, plagued by advisors telling her that her planet is running out of resources?" Brandon spoke, but didn't turn from the window. Vanessa watched his reflection in the glass.

"I believe so, sire. They suffer also from pollution and civil unrest. There are strikes."

Everyone nodded as if this news confirmed some obvious fact she was not privy to.

"What does she intend to do about it?" said Brandon.

"Nothing's been proposed to my knowledge. Problems are being put aside for now in preparation for war with Your Majesty."

Brandon stared into space. "We have greater resources by far, do we not? With a chunk of Maaraw and all of Silangan?"

"We also have expenses greater by far as well," said Tobias. "Our troops on Lavland—"

"Haven't been paid. Aye, we know that."

Tobias bowed.

"Once we get Enskari, all this will be moot," said Brandon. "The universe united under a single emperor. It's destiny. We have only to reach out and take it."

Nicandus smiled. Tobias watched Vanessa. Jessop, who'd been listening with a subtle intensity that alerted Vanessa to danger, sighed softly at the king's remark.

Jessop noticed she was looking at him. "The system under a single church would be a blessed thing," he said. "Uniformity of belief is the strength of the species. For there to be peace, there must be agreement. For there to be agreement, there must be one head."

"The prophet," said D'Angelo and toasted another glass.

"Is there more you need of me?" she said.

"We're almost there," mumbled Brandon, still staring out the window, still distracted.

"Aye," said Tobias. "What of Tirgwenin?"

"What about Tirgwenin?" she said.

"We've received word from our outpost on Freeport – that's on Dajjal."

"I know where it is," she said.

Tobias smiled. "You do your sex credit."

D'Angelo scoffed again. "If the prophet could see this...."

"He does," said Jessop. D'Angelo shut up.

"Our outpost on Freeport captured a man set off there by an Enskari expedition to Tirgwenin. A man called Dedikodu. A miserable man, set off on Dajjal like so much rubbish but we suspect on purpose."

"Sir Ethan has a patent—"

"That bastard! I'll have his head on a stick," said Brandon.

Tobias kept his eyes on Vanessa.

She went on. "The patent was to set up a colony on the planet. He's had years to do it, but each attempt has failed. Tirgwenin is so distant and the way is treacherous."

"That it is," said Tobias. "And the patent?"

"He's trying again now. His agents set off with three ships. I suspect your man is from one of those. If they made it as far as Dajjal, they're doing better than the last attempt, which had to turn back."

"They'll reach it," Tobias said. "And the man set ashore knew exactly where the colony would be planted."

"It's a place called Placid Bay," she said. "I've heard it spoken of."

"Nay, it's a place called Rodawnoc."

She shook her head. "That's not—"

"Someone wanted us to know about the expedition and its changed landing location. Who in the court, would you say, would do this? Who involved in this unlawful excursion could be trying to help us find that colony?"

"Unlawful?"

"Aye, my dear," said Rendelle. "The prophet has given that world exclusively to Hyrax and the House Drust."

"But what of the laws of conquest and colony?"

"Laws are for those who don't have the prophet's love," said Rendelle.

"Love doesn't secure planets," said Tobias.

"The prophet's word is law," Jessop said.

"A debate for another time," said Tobias. "Think, Lady Vanessa, who involved with this expedition sent us this intelligence?"

"Perhaps the captain," she said. "He was trained on Hyrax I believe. Are you sure about Rodawnoc? That was not the place Ethan intends."

"We are sure indeed."

"The planet is ripe – unplucked," said D'Angelo. "It mustn't fall to Zabel. Beyond the resources – the metals, the gold and lead and platinum, there are foods and people. An entire race for us to use as God wills."

"Nay, not the folk." Tobias got himself another drink. "We've tried to subdue Tirgwenians and they're unfit for slaves."

"A little more whip is all they need," said Rendelle.

"Nay," said Tobias. "Lady Vanessa, may I pour you another? Yours is empty."

"Aye. Thanks," she said.

Tobias said, "We tried. They're different. They'd not be made slaves. Their will is too strong. An expedition a decade ago took some of them back here. One was a noble or the closest thing they had. A man of some standing. A man who had bees. He'd not be made to work, not be made to bow, not be made to do anything. He wouldn't even scream when tortured."

"What do you mean a man who had bees?" said Jessop.

"I mean he had bees. Two of them. I saw them. They orbited his head like planets around a star, just buzzing around. He didn't mind them. He liked them."

"Pets?"

"We think it's a mark of standing in their culture."

"Like our crowns?" said Vanessa.

"Aye. Possibly." Tobias took her glass and handed her a fresh one. He drank his straight, she saw. "We tried with one of their non-nobles and got a little further. He'd not fight for us, would never make a soldier, but we got him to work for a while. He'd work until he was tired then he stopped and would not be moved to work again until he had rested. He bowed when he saw it pleased us, but would bow also to commoner and livestock. It was a farce. Oh, but he screamed under torture."

"We can break them," said Rendelle. "It just might take a generation or two."

"They're the oldest of us and the most primitive," mused Jessop. "Is it of major import that Enskari is there first?"

"It's not a just a matter of a rich planet. They can raid Silangan from there across the Gap. Guarding that flank would strain our resources."

"Again with resources!" yelled Brandon. "I'll show you resources. There, see." He stood up and pointed.

The group, including Vanessa, moved to the window.

The armada had moved out into the light from behind the planet's shadow. The *Fortuna* was placed between them and the light.

There, out the window, Vanessa saw a cloud of gleaming ships of all sizes. Scores of them, no – hundreds of them, glistening against the night sky, thicker than the stars behind them.

"That is my resources. Who in God's heaven can stand against that?" Brandon said. "Resources? I'll take resources where I want them. Money? I'll mint it from Zabel's own fillings."

"The unification of all of God's children," said Jessop. "The planets united under the one true church and emperor."

"Emperor and church," corrected Brandon. "Not one and the same unless I'm to be prophet as well."

Jessop averted his eyes, the serenity in them waning.

"This isn't even all yet," said Brandon. "Look, Jessop, see how mighty Hyrax is? We'll have half this again and all full of soldiers." He spoke into the air as if his words were not meant for those present but for the universe and for all time. "With this force and the weapon we saw on Maaraw we'll take Enskari in a matter of a day. We'll purge the unfaithful and put the worlds right again. There is an order to things and that order is absolute. We'll teach whole worlds to know their places. Man before woman; noble before commoner. Forever. The way of things."

Everyone stared out the glass, watching ships lustrous in Coronam's radiance. Slowly turning as the *Fortuna* spun its gravity. It was hypnotic. It was a display of power unlike anything Vanessa had ever imagined before. She saw that even Tobias, who surely knew all the details of all that was coming, stood in awe at the mighty armada shining in the sky.

"When is it to be?" she whispered. "When do they sail?"

"A year still," said Brandon bitterly. "Such is the magnitude of our mission."

She thought of Queen Zabel, the beloved monarch, the icon of her gender, the hope of a people. She looked out the window at the ships, at the armada made to destroy her and them. She closed her eyes for fear of tears. "Such is the magnitude," she repeated.

CHAPTER TWENTY-ONE

The common pollinator of Tirgwenin is of the same native variety of bee originally found on all the planets around Coronam, Apis Coronaman. *Though nearly extinct on all the civilized worlds, this stingless species is found in abundance on Tirgwenin.*

Alpin Morgan Notebook
15, Fourth-Month, 935 NE (First Tirgwenin Expedition)

7, Eleventh-Month, 937 – Rodawnoc, Tirgwenin

Millie stared at Mr. Browne in the stocks and wondered if he were still alive and how she'd find out without catching the wrath of the assistants.

She glanced at him between blows on the root. Her club was splayed like a mushroom, the stone underneath already cracked and failing. The tuber in between was stringy and tough but better to eat than nothing, which is what she'd have if she didn't spend hours each day pounding the pulp from the manna-root.

It wasn't the real name for the plant. Mathew had called it hortmal, which Millie found fitting and proper. He explained that it was planted throughout the region as an emergency crop for times of starvation. Unlike a similarly intended plant, gumbnut, hortmal was difficult to find and prepare. It grew slowly but was hard to kill. Most of the island had been cleared of it, which he said was a very bad sign. Gumbnut was extinct on the island.

The native name didn't last more than a day. Hortmal became 'manna-root' by common usage. No explanation was given for the change, no author identified, and to Millie's experience no one had questioned why. She often thought about the name change when she pounded the roots into food in front of her little hut on the island fort, trying not to die.

It'd been two and a half months since her father's death. He'd been only the first, but his had been the worst of their losses. It had begun the fall from a happy to a terrible time, the plummeting of spirit that had only grown worse with each subsequent death and setback.

She'd never forget that day. She remembered how she'd imagined they were carrying a giant cocklebur, a lump of seed with sticky burrs poking out to catch a giant's sock and be carried away. But they were not burrs. The dozen protrusions were arrows and the seed was her father.

When her mother died, the colony offered them their hearts. There was sympathy and sadness. Quarantined and odd as they were, the colony had tried to help. However, when her father had been killed there was no sympathy to spare. There was only overflowing fear, panic, and despair. Millie and Dillon were left to themselves. There'd been no room, no time, no thought, heart, or energy in the colonists for anyone but themselves. They left his body in the little church and called an immediate meeting of the highest ranked among them.

Millie walked to the beach and found her brother building a castle with geometric shells and soft sand. The distant seas were stormy but far away. Above her the sky twinkled and glowed and the rings were bright and golden like a wedding band. It was warm on the beach.

She sat down and played with her brother for hours, not telling him about their father. Past horrors and future terrors were put aside for a while for her brother's castle of sand and shell. It was only when darkness and hunger made Dillon rise to return to their hut did Millie tell him that they were all that was left of their family.

Dillon had cried himself to sleep and would not be moved from his father's bed, where he had finally crawled in the small hours of that night. Millie had watched over him the entire time, watched him sleep, stared open-eyed and blank at the boy until the dawn light came. With the light came a bee into her hut. It was a small pearlescent thing, a distraction, the first thing she recognized outside herself and her brother in the long stretching hours of desperate darkness. She watched it in the gray morning light as it buzzed here to there and around. It circled her like a satellite in a gravity field being pulled nearer and nearer her hair with each orbit. She reached up for it and it landed in her palm. She studied it and saw the colors hidden on its back, the pollen on its legs, the feathery antennae, the two sets of wings, and the big deep eyes. It had no stinger.

It crawled up her arm and shoulder before taking wing to buzz around her head again. At another time, in another place, or maybe to another girl, it all would have been strange, but it was not to her then. She was numb and empty. She felt herself as a drained jar, drying and cracked. She marked her brother's breaths, thinking that each one was counted, that their count would be short because they were doomed. In this new world just then it did not strike her as strange when the bee entered her mind and sang to her. It buzzed and hummed and soothed her in sound unheard and soft. A single syllable, a single note, a single word and sign. Single but with everything inside it. A metaphor and a song.

A tear rolled down her cheek.

Her hand upheld, the bee landed and danced on her palm. It walked fingers to wrist, circles and steps, halting and turning. Its wings a flightless fluttering of motion and real sound. A ballet, smaller than the one in her mind, but related and kin.

Outside her hut came discordant voices calling all to assembly.

Looking out a window, she was shocked to see full light. The sun was well up. Dawn was past. It was past midday.

The bee rose from her hand and disappeared under the door, but left in her mind the humming as a distant background lullaby that stayed with her.

She tried once to rouse her brother, thinking he should take part now, but he refused and she let him.

She wiped her tears and took a breath and found she could stand and face the door and what it threatened beyond.

Morgan and the assistants stood in the town center atop crates so all could see and hear them. Morgan raised his hands. "Everyone," he said. "Blessed be! Blessed be. Everyone be quiet and listen."

They hushed, all but Daria Morgan's baby, Diana, who cried for them all.

Morgan said, "We know where we are. We know what we face. We know also that God is with us."

Millie nearly left then – not sure she could stomach a Buckler prayer meeting just then.

"This is Lieutenant Bradshaw, commander of the *Sebastian*." Morgan stepped back, allowing the spacefarer to step up on the makeshift platform.

"It is a bad fate ye face here," he said. "Unfortunate and surely to be trying. Many of ye have asked to return to Enskari, or anywhere but here, and I am sorry to say that this is not to be. The captain is firm."

"Murderer!" cried someone.

"Where is Upor?" asked another.

"The captain has returned to the *Hopewell*. The ships sail tomorrow. The last ship will take the thread tonight and then ye will be alone until resupply."

"They'll not find us here," said Aguirre.

"Aye," Bradshaw said. "The captain has agreed to let one of ye travel back with us to tell your people what has happened here. Where to find ye. They can so arrange for resupply or rescue if that's what ye will. Ye have one hour to decide who it shall be. It is to be one Saved only. One person. One soul with one chest luggage."

With that Bradshaw jumped down and walked straight out the fort to the beach.

The colonists watched him go in silence, shocked and terrified.

"Who will it be?" said Morgan. "Who shall we send back?"

"Now you're asking us?" said someone.

"Now I'm asking you." Morgan's voice was so soft and broken that Millie wanted to go console him. Strange that, she thought even then, that she should want to go to him, when it was she who was lately orphaned.

The debate was furious but quick. Millie saw that the assistants had one idea and Morgan another.

"We must send Governor Morgan back," said Assistant Pratt.

"I will not go," he said. "I will not abandon you. I will not abandon my granddaughter."

"You must."

"Nay."

"It is this way," said Pratt. "Whoever has done this to us has done it completely. We are undone. We cannot recover from below the level of influence. We must send someone who can argue the case and the crime to the highest echelons. Though here we be equal, brother and sister, Saved and minister all, in Zabel's court we are terrorists and outcasts. And yet it is there we must petition for relief. We must send a gentleman and a noble, a man who can rise above the slander and succeed where evil has had its way. It must be the highest of us. It must be you, Morgan."

The argument was sound even to Millie, which was unusual because she had never before really understood the politics that had led them there. She still didn't, and yet, when the vote came to elect Morgan, she raised her hand confidently, knowing it was not only the best choice, but the only one.

"Nay, I will not go," Morgan persisted.

"The people have spoken."

"I will be branded a coward. I will not leave. I have led us here. I will not leave."

"You are our only hope, Alpin. No one else can do what you can. You have the connections to Sommerled, who speaks in the ear of the queen."

"Could it not be she who has done this to us?"

"Nay, there are easier and cheaper ways to execute heretics," said Pratt. "You are again our only hope. Sommerled to Zabel. If not for justice, then for our survival, Governor. We are not where we should be. The ships must be told."

"Aye," said Morgan, his voice breaking. "Aye, but send another."

"No one knows where we are as you do, Alpin," said Pratt, the crowd behind him. "It is not an easy thing we ask you, but it is what must be done."

Aguirre spoke. "Wait. How do we know anyone will arrive home alive? Upor is not to be trusted."

"It will be aboard the *Sebastian* with Bradshaw," said Morgan. "I trust him. I would not trust Upor again to tell me the weather."

"We have only minutes. You must go, Morgan. There is no more debate. You must go now."

He looked out at the crowd and Millie again mourned for the man, the sadness in his eyes.

"Aye," he said into a silence broken only by the crying babe.

Then all was action and talk.

Morgan took promises that his things would be kept and his family watched over.

He took letters and kisses and was led to the beach. There, he bade them, "Flee fifty kilometers inland when ye can. Make you free of the Enskari claim on the coast. Free of Hyraxian influence – away from their war. Leave me some token to find the way and I shall return in the next year with all the help I can gather."

He boarded the little skiff that would take him around the shoals to the boat that would climb the thread to the orbiting ship.

Long after his skiff was out of sight, the forlorn colony stood on the beach watching the sea where it had been. Millie blended the sound of the waves to the music the bee had left in her.

★   ★   ★

That was months past and still she had the music.

Her father was buried in a burlap shroud five paces from the gate. He'd been but the first. Three more bodies were recovered arrow-pierced and dead in the first week. Five more people disappeared into the forest and never returned that month. Twelve others perished from pox or injury or poison. Three drowned. Nineteen total dead if the missing five weren't counted. Two dozen – four and twenty – if they were. Over a fifth of their number already gone and hunger hadn't entered the equation yet. But it would. It was coming. It was coming soon.

Millie pounded the hortmal – manna-root, savior food of the colony – with a rhythmic thunk, slide, thunk, and slur, turning it every fourth blow, pushing the mush into a bowl where with enough salt and bitter leaf, a touch of home spice, it would make a meal for her and her brother.

She looked at Mr. Browne in the stocks. He was accused of stealing from the general supply – a biscuit, as if there were any of those left. Aguirre had ordered him into the stocks for three days. Nicholas Pratt, fighting the pox, hadn't been strong enough to intervene, but Millie doubted he would have. Lately he'd been careful to choose his fights with Mr. Aguirre.

"You were not at church this morning, young Millicent Dagney," Aguirre said to her.

She looked up from her root and saw the assistant above her, his face gaunt. He had skeletal cheekbones that stuck out like shelves in a morgue, his sunken eyes cadaverous and dark, but wild within. Fearful and unpredictable.

"I thought we might be contagious," she said. "Relapse. We're pox carriers, remember."

"Ah," he said. "Aye. All right then. Perhaps tomorrow."

It was a lie, they were fine or as fine as they could be under the circumstances, but it had excused her and Dillon from another of the now-daily church services where Millie saw a steady and drastic alteration in the Buckler doctrine. Before her eyes, the All Community Congregation of Ministers and Friends, affectionately called the Bucklers, turned slowly from a communal egalitarian subsect of Enskari Saved to a rising oligarchy of favorites led by Aguirre from the pulpit. It started as an allocation of necessary work but soon degenerated into another class system where certain important people dictated the lives of others. Women were excluded from all decision making and 'proper attitude' became a measure of food distribution. The hated maxim of 'Keep Sweet', which had enraged Zabel's loyalists, had been reintroduced into the vocabularies of the colony leadership. The idea went beyond the womenfolk, of course. Mr. Browne's attitude had been bad. Most of the livestock brought from Enskari had been his and it'd all been taken. He'd complained about that. Now he was in the stocks for stealing an imaginary biscuit.

Aguirre looked down at Millie's small pile of tubers she had yet to pound. "How is it you find so many more roots than the others?" he said.

"The others look where are there are none," she said.

He laughed as if it were a great joke, but it was the truth. She realized that the forests and the fields were not haphazard and wild. One field was in fallow while another was used and a third was never cultivated outright, but planted with hardier plants – famine foods; hortmal, gumbnut, bitter berries and herbs. These were gardens and not forest. Once she recognized the gardens for what they were, she stopped hunting and started finding what was left. It wasn't much. The berries were mostly gone along with all the summer herbs, harvested by natives in the night away from the eyes of the colonists, but she found some roots digging with sticks in the old way, though she'd never done it before and how she knew to call it *the old way* was another one of the mysteries that she accepted in her new life like the bee on her hand and the stupidity of the others who'd not listened to her advice on where to hunt for the pulpy roots.

"I haven't seen Mr. Browne move for a while, Assistant," said Millie. "Maybe you should see to him."

"Did you not hear my order that no one should aid him?"

"I thought only—"

"Are you saying that I should be above the law?"

"Nay, only—"

"Laws are the province of men, young lass. I don't expect you to understand. Mr. Browne must be made to. That is his chore. Yours is to pound the manna-root. Mine is to lead. We all do our duties and none of us will do what we shall not. No one will see to Mr. Browne until his time in the stocks is over. It is his sentence."

"Aye," said Mille when he took a breath.

"Law is how we will survive these trials. Law and order are how we shall survive and create a new kingdom."

He spoke like that now, every sentence a speech, every encounter a sermon as if someone were recording what he said for posterity.

Millie said, "I only thought—"

"I did not ask you a question, Millicent Dagney. Keep sweet. Be seen and not heard. It is the women's way." Aguirre smiled at her and she wanted to break his teeth in, the ones that were left anyway, since he'd lost several.

He knelt down and brushed her hair with his hand like he was stroking a dog. She ground her teeth.

"Your father was a good man," he said. "When he died I thought I'd die. I thought I did. I remember wanting to die, running on the beach, praying for it."

He'd not been on the beach. But she'd heard about his manic rant the day her father died, a terrible exhibition of cowardice and despair that sickened the souls who witnessed it.

"But God saved me," he said. "God made me to understand that I am the savior of this place."

"You and Mr. Pratt," she said.

A shadow crossed his face but was quickly gone. "Aye," he said. "What I wanted to say –" he brushed her hair again, "– is that perhaps it is too much a burden for you to keep house alone. Perhaps you should join my house and I will care for you and your brother."

"It would not be proper," she said.

"Unless you are my wife."

"I am but—"

"You have no one to speak for you," he said.

"I can speak for myself," she said. "It is my right as by our doctrine."

"You do not understand," he said, patting her head. "Necessity makes—"

"It's Mathew!" came a cry from the gate. "Mathew!"

Aguirre looked around him as if he'd forgotten something important. Without another word, he stood and headed across the courtyard past the pilloried Mr. Browne and to the gate.

Millie stepped into the rain without her bonnet, wanting it to wash her hair clean of where Aguirre had touched her.

People came off their porches and out of their huts to see what the clamor was about. The narrow streets between the huts filled with frail colonists fearfully surveying the walls. Millie thought to check on Mr. Browne but saw Mrs. Archard keeping an eye on her and instead called for her brother.

"What's the matter, sister?" Dillon came from the widow Harvie's house. He'd been ordered to help her after her husband drowned. The widow Harvie was five years older than Millie and just as able and strong as she, but being one of the favorites and prone to complaining, she was assigned Dillon to help her all day. Millie, who didn't complain, did her own work.

"Mathew is back," she said. "Let's hear what he has to say."

"I'm sure they only want the menfolk," said the widow, following Dillon outside.

"Angie," said Millie. "Have you so easily lost your voice?"

"What do you mean?"

"We're Bucklers," she said. "We're supposed to vote with the men, be involved in our own fates. It's in our laws."

"Necessity has changed things."

"Why?"

"Necessity," she said. It was the refrain Aguirre used from the pulpit daily. Millie had understood the necessity of rationing, the necessity of armed guards and shared endeavor, but she hadn't been as understanding of the women needing now to be second place, or of certain families getting greater portions, or her brother, Dillon, having to work for the widow when Millie needed his help more.

"I'll go just the same," Millie said, taking Dillon's hand.

The widow tied her bonnet around her chin and followed but only after Millie and Dillon were a good ways ahead.

Assistant Pratt hobbled on a crutch with the help of two men and joined the rest at the entrance of the fort. Mathew was speaking when

Millie arrived. In one arm was a bundle of manna-root and in his hand a basket of fish.

"The people will not help," he said to everyone. "The closest ones can not. The farther ones will not."

"Will they leave us alone at least?" called someone from the crowd.

Aguirre stepped into the middle and raised his hands as if to quiet everyone, though no one was speaking. "We will have an assistant meeting, find out all this and then report," he said.

"It concerns us all," said Millie. "We'll know it now."

Aguirre shot her a look. "We'll tell you what you need to know."

"We'll know it now," she said again.

The rain pattered on their clothes and ran in and out under the wood walls in rivulets of mud. It was cold and their breaths puffed before them. No one spoke.

Mathew, dressed in native leather costume, looked out at the faces and then at Aguirre and Pratt. He put his basket on the ground and the roots beside it. He rocked his neck around his shoulders, working out a knot.

There was something different about him, Millie thought. She didn't know the Tirgwenian well enough to say what exactly had changed; she'd seen him only briefly in the halls of the *Hopewell* in passing, and during the brief moments within the fort before he was sent out to make peace with the natives and beg for help, but yet there was an aura about him that hadn't been there before. It might have been his clothing; it could have been his skin, reflective even in the rainy overcast day, like a light glowed within him, illusionary but distinct. No, it was something else, something in his eyes, in his demeanor, in the way he carried himself and spoke to everyone and not just Aguirre which the assistant obviously wanted him to do.

"Knowing a thing and understanding a thing are different," said Aguirre. "I see Assistant Pratt is up and about. God be praised. We'll meet together and report."

"We'll know it now," said someone across the way, echoing Millie's sensible request.

The crowd fell into murmurs, discussions of the way it used to be before 'necessity' had limited their information in a blatant and surprisingly welcome attempt to keep the people from despair.

The widow Harvie sidled up beside Millie and clicked her tongue. "Disgusting," she said. "Just look at that heathen."

"I'm sure the leather is warmer than it looks," said Millie. "It keeps him dry enough and I'm sure the mud is unavoidable."

"He's crawling with bugs," she said.

Millie wiped rainwater from her face and forehead, rubbed her eyes, and looked. There was something on Mathew's head, a movement. Not an infestation, but something. She stepped closer to see, but already suspected what it was.

Mathew looked up and saw her. There was a flash of recognition in his face, like a reunion of old friends. He smiled and she smiled back. Aguirre grabbed Mathew's arm and tried to lead him away. He pulled his arm back.

"I will tell you," Mathew said. "There are Rowdanae hunters who will slay you – families are all dead, their souls ache for revenge. But this is not everyone. Others say there can be place for you among the people, as the bees allow."

That was it. It was a bee on his head. It crawled across his scalp and then flitted into the air and circled him and landed again when the rain forced it down. He accepted it without concern, letting it crawl over his face or buzz in front of his eyes.

"What does that mean?" said Pratt, coughing. "Be plain, Mathew."

"Do you know the history of Earth?" Mathew asked.

"What?" said Aguirre. "We're talking food and shelter, life and death – not history."

"We are all of Earth," said Mathew, ignoring Aguirre. "My ancestors arrived at Coronam first on Tirgwenin. They would make a world in peace and balance."

"We would do the same," said Pratt.

Mathew shook his head. "Nay, brother Pratt. Ye would not. Ye would conquer. That is plain."

"That was the other expedition," said Pratt. "We are not like them."

"Not the same, but like," Mathew said. "Ye brought the pox—"

"We cannot be blamed for the will of God."

"Ye brought Master Dagney to spread disease," he said. "Ye would have it clear the place to take it for your own."

"Nay…." said Aguirre, but even Millie could see through his lie.

"This is the thinking that keeps the people from helping you."

"So they would kill us?" said Pratt.

"Some would, but they are apart. They are not many, but they are angry and lost and uncontrollable. The others will not slay you, but neither will they help. They offer you only the chance to prove yourselves worthy."

The bee flew from his ear and buzzed around him.

"Worthy?" said Aguirre as if it were a curse to God. "You call us unworthy, you stupid ignorant heathen. What do you know about Earth? Who filled your stupid head with this manure?"

The bee spun away through the crowd in widening circles. Millie watched it, wondering how it avoided the raindrops.

Mathew went on. "Tirgwenin offered the people a chance to begin again, as ye seek. We chose to do things differently than before. The old ways being unsustainable, unjust, and cruel."

"Someone gave you a diction class along with a false history primer," said Aguirre. "Who have you been talking to?" He glanced toward Millie, who watched the bee circle and dart.

"I am redeemed,"Mathew said with a grin. "Ye have given me that chance, I am here to offer it to you."

"Blasphemy!"

"Nay," he said.

"You expect to just walk out of here? Join your friends in the forest and starve us out?" Aguirre picked up a thick manna-root and brandished it like a club.

"I have brought you food."

"It's not enough," said Aguirre. "You traitorous swine."

Pratt coughed and began to speak. The crowd hushed to hear him. "Mathew," he said. "How do you know this about Earth and Dagney, and the pox, and all this? You did not know it before."

The bee flitted around and landed on Millie's head. She jumped and made to swat it, but caught herself and calmed. Mathew saw it on her head and smiled wide. Aguirre followed his stare and scowled at Millie. The bee settled behind her ear.

"Assistant Pratt," said Mathew. "I would tell you, but I doubt you would understand."

"Try me." The assistant coughed and swayed; the pox was getting the better of him by the day.

Mathew smiled sympathetically, sadly, a doctor over a dying patient. "The bees," he said. "I found peace and purpose and they found me."

"Bees?"

"It's their religion," said Aguirre to the crowd with undisguised disgust in voice. "They worship insects."

"Nay," said Mathew. "Not worship. Connection. Reverence perhaps, but not religion. It is awareness. It is planetwide – system-wide. Nay, wider. Wider than that, but few outside Tirgwenin have found it. You are all too caught up in your own hubris to hear the bees."

"Pagan. Godless heathen!" Mrs. Archard's voice carried far.

"Put aside your preconceptions," said Mathew. "Open yourselves to possibility. I know ye can be welcome here. Your souls are good but your ideas are bad. I can help you."

Voices from the crowd.

"We need food not prayer to a bug!"

"He'd be our king!"

"I've heard enough."

"Convert or die?" said Aguirre. "That's your ultimatum? You lying treacherous bastard!"

Millie wondered if what Mathew said was true, that her family had been brought here deliberately as a weapon to kill the natives. No sooner had she framed the thought than she knew instantly and certainly that it was so. She saw the images and heard the whispers in a dark room back on Enskari as if she'd been there. She knew also that Old Earth had failed under the mismanagement of men and some had fled in ships to start again. She'd heard the stories, but now she knew it as certainly as if she'd spent her whole life researching it, no – more than that, as if she herself had been there.

"It's not conversion," Mathew said. "I know what I'm saying is strange to you."

"Blasphemy and threats more like," said Aguirre.

Pratt spoke up. "What if we don't? How do we survive?"

The bee left Millie and joined the falling rain.

"There is famine on the island. The previous visits exhausted the place. Now even the hortmal is all but gone."

"So we must move inland?"

"Nay," said Mathew. "Ye will not be allowed far off the island. Ye are Rowdanae."

"What?"

"Exiles," he said. "You must prove yourself worthy to join the people."

"Circles," said Aguirre. "He's talking in circles."

Millie didn't think so.

"Must everyone be worthy?" said Pratt.

"Nay, not all the people have bees, but none repel," he said.

"What is he talking about?" said Mrs. Archard.

Mathew put on a pained expression. "Let me try to explain in a way ye will understand," he said. A second bee circled his head a half meter above him. "The history of your people repels the bees – it is repugnant to the place. It is tales of death and murder. Theft and cruelty. Ye know of Captain Hasin? This place still suffers from his cruelty and war."

"We are not—"

"That is why the people will wait and see."

"Wait and see what?" said Mrs. Archard.

"If ye will, uhm…repent," he said, lighting on the word with a smile. "Yes. Like that. Repent."

"Blasphemy!"

"Who does he think he is?"

The bee landed on Mathew's ear.

Aguirre brought his root down upon it crushing the insect against his skull, dropping the Tirgwenian scout to the ground, unconscious and bleeding.

"Chain him up," he said.

Millie knew then that Mr. Browne was dead.

CHAPTER TWENTY-TWO

One gentleman trained to the sword is worth a thousand peasants who brawl.
Noble proverb

13, Eleventh-Month, 937 – The Court of the Queen, Upaven, Enskari

The waltz was slow and touchy, one of the queen's favorites. She watched it from her chair on the ivory dais, tapping her fingers on the armrest as courtiers circled and swayed before her. She'd had the first dance with Sir Ethan Sommerled and then retired to her throne. Ethan followed her and would be beside her still had she not insisted he go dance with the other women.

Vandusen wasn't dancing. He wanted to, but felt that Sir Nolan would disapprove. Nolan worked in the background and dancing was not background. It was the center of attention, the day's event.

Ethan was dancing.

Queen Zabel had moved the court back to Upaven. Vildeby palace had thrice caught fire during the lightning blizzards that had killed hundreds of animals and scores of people when the city's rod grid had become overloaded. Coronam was having a particularly angry autumn and the atmosphere above urban centers, according to Sir Aldo, the Nature Minister, was disrupting the planet's ability to disperse the radiation. The soot altered, conducted, stored, and then released pent-up energy. It had sparked and arced between rods, melting them and frying buildings beneath. A dozen structures in the city had been set alight, the palace among them. Thrice.

New rods and forests of orbital fiber tendrils to tap the clouds had been installed to safeguard the palace and Government House in Vildeby. It was safe but the weather was still miserable; smog, electricity, and sooty gray snow. And the queen made the decision in a meeting to leave shortly after the last fire.

"It is miserable here," she'd said. "We didn't want to come back in the first place, but Sir Nolan advised us so. We're moving back to Upaven."

"The people need you here," advised Sir Edward, the First Ear. "Our enemies will see this as running away. The people need to see you strong and defiant."

"Your time back in the capital was necessary," Sir Nolan said. "But little is gained by remaining now. Moving back to Upaven could be spun as a return to normalcy, as it is the usual custom of the court to winter there."

"We are tired of the gossips here," said the queen. "We are tired of the weather. We are tired of the city. We will move back immediately."

"Aye, Your Highness."

"Sir Ralph Connor, our archbishop, we would know of the purges?"

"They are continuing," he said.

"Are there more houses to discuss?"

"None of such rank as to trouble you," he said. "But sympathizers abound. The prophet has allies and spies and we continue to root them out."

"What of separatists?"

"The Bucklers are gone, exiled," he said. "The Gibbers are in hiding, the Sisterhood of God's Own are new and in ascension but we have a line on them. There are some nature cults springing up as well, in the wilder places. Interesting, but not threatening."

"This is new," said the queen. "Who is this sisterhood?"

"Born in a nunnery. I don't know their doctrine beyond their claim that only women should speak for God because they, like God, give birth. It's heresy. It's mostly in Austen, but we've seen some pamphlets in the capital."

"Are they dangerous?"

"They threaten our priesthood," said Connor.

"Perhaps our priesthood should consider letting women join."

"They are not so dangerous as to make us do that," said Connor with a chuckle that made Vandusen wince in the corner.

"Nay, Sir Connor. It is not for them that I make this suggestion, but for us."

Connor's face blanched. He cleared his throat but didn't speak. He glanced around at the others.

"A noble gesture," said Sir Edward. "And doubtless such may happen in the future, but it is too soon and too fast, Your Highness, for such acts as those now. The people will not stand for it. They've had enough change for a while."

"Who knows anything of the people?" she said. "Who amongst you deals with commoners regularly? We nobles are outnumbered a thousand to one – nay, greater than that, and yet we think that our sluggishness is reflected there. The old are slow to change. The old in years, and the old in bloodlines. I'd like to know what the people really think." Her eyes fell on Vandusen in the corner. "You. You are Nolan's man. We are sure he sends you to the street. What is the sound from there?"

Vandusen was the lowest-ranking person in the room. He was there because he'd not been ordered to leave when the others came in. The queen and Connor, the Two Ears, three ministers, guards, and he.

Vandusen looked at Nolan for help. His master nodded assent. He stepped forward and bowed.

"Your Majesty. Reality changes fast in the lower classes," Vandusen said. "They have suffered the worse from our wars, the taxes, the hunger. Scarcity and trouble they would do without. Whoever and whatever gives them peace and security is what they will follow. Still there is a novelty with Your Highness. It is a cherished quirk in the people that they love you."

"What?" she said. "A quirk?"

"Aye, Your Majesty. I cannot account for it otherwise. It is a love of the underdog and a promise that things do not need to be always so. This is of course my interpretation, but in you is a symbol of positive change – an advancement that the worlds have not seen since the Unsettling. There is a yearning for change and progress, even if it's painful. A need to move forward."

"And would they accept female clergy?"

"If it was so," he said.

Connor coughed. Nolan raised an eyebrow.

"You are not in the majority," she said.

"Your Majesty, to me, it seems natural that women be allowed to be in the clergy. It reinforces your own position, which is based on the idea that women can be as great, if not greater than men. To deny them rank after the war denies your ascendancy and keeps the planet backward."

Nolan turned on him full then, but did not glare at him. It was more surprise. Whether for his belief or his audacity to speak it to the queen, Vandusen didn't know.

"What do the people think of all the new separatist sects popping up?"

"They are a curiosity."

"They are a threat to unity," said Connor.

"And not to God?" said the queen.

Connor stole another glance at Edward.

"It is a symptom of being under Temple's yoke for so long," Vandusen said out of place. He'd not been asked directly. It was a breach of protocol, but in so far, he went on. "It is that once freed they wish to explore." He was quoting Nolan now. He didn't know if he believed it, but it seemed appropriate and would, if nothing else, show he'd been listening to his master.

"We have thrown off the yoke and made our own church," said Connor.

"Aye, but it is much the same. It touches upon class," said Vandusen when Nolan didn't stop him.

"Class?"

"Excuse me," he said, his cheeks flushing, sweat dripping down his back.

"Nay," said the queen, "We would hear you."

Another glance at Nolan. Another nod.

"Noble, clergy, peon," said Vandusen. "As the queen has raised womanhood, so other downcasts seek—"

"A class war?" interrupted Connor. "This feeds into the nobles' fears."

Nolan signaled Vandusen to shut up now. He bowed and stepped back.

"We cannot be divided," said Sir Edward. "Hyrax is at the gate, the prophet sends his priests to kill. We can't allow another civil war."

"Sir Nolan," said the queen, "you've been silent too long. Speak."

"I don't know the subject," he said. "Do we speak of women in the clergy, or an emancipation of slaves, serfs, and indentured? Would we make a classless society? Or is it on civil war we speak again?"

She scowled at him.

"It is not my place to shape society," Nolan said. "But I will say that should change be wanted, the timing of it is as important as the shape it will be. Perhaps more so. Let us first fight off the wolf at the door and in the celebration, do all our deeds at once. Good, bad, or indifferent, that will be the time."

"So Connor should stop the purges?"

"Nay. We need the threat. For unity."

Connor didn't like that. His face flushed. Vandusen knew that the queen's purger saw himself as a holy instrument, not a tool for statecraft, which was what Nolan blatantly considered him to be.

"And we need the money," said Nolan. "From the forfeitures."

"The prophet's allies must be rounded up and contained," said Edward. "They came too close in Vildeby. That cannot be allowed."

Nolan had been harangued in front of the nobles at Government House for the near assassination of the queen. Vandusen had watched it with some excitement as his master turned it around and onto the prophet and Hyrax and the disloyal nobles of Enskari. Three houses had fallen that afternoon, Sir Nolan Brett's not among them.

"These are dangerous times," Nolan said. "For whatever reason, the court should move back to Upaven. The queen is wise."

"Some nobles will not be happy with the move," said Edward. "They will see this as withdrawing from their company."

"And influence," she added.

"Aye."

"I'd speak about Sir Ethan," said Connor. "Before this little meeting breaks up."

"What about him?" said the queen with that steel in her voice that Vandusen so admired.

"We spoke of class warfare," he said. "A movement of dissatisfaction with one's station. I feel that Sir Ethan may be the symbol for that."

The queen blushed.

Sir Nolan spoke. "As is the intent," he said. "I do not speak for the queen's mind, or for the future direction of our world, but Sir Ethan is a symbol of a unity between the classes and a suggestion, if not a promise, of mobility that has been going on for decades. We have merchants wealthier than first nobles and noble houses selling their crests for bread. It is merely a reflection of reality."

"It upsets the loyal houses," he said. "Reality and recognition are not the same. We would be better off with him gone."

Had Connor been looking at the queen that moment, Vandusen had no doubt that he would have fled for his life. Instead he and Nolan faced off.

Sir Nolan said, "Symbols are important."

"And there's the issue of his association with the Buckler heretics and also untoward rumors—"

"We'll hear no more of this," said the queen. "Move our court to Upaven. We would be there in the week." She stood, turned, and swept out the room.

The steel, the grit. Vandusen smiled.

Within the week, they were back at Upaven.

★   ★   ★

Jim Vandusen saw his master across the hall in a darkened corner watching the proceedings, watching Ethan jig and prance, center stage, bedecked in jewels. Sir Nolan Brett was not hiding, but neither was he was forefront. Those who knew the queen's spymaster knew that to find him you looked in the shadows. There he was.

He caught Vandusen's eye and the secretary came half to attention ready to move at a distant command. None was forthcoming, just an acknowledgement that he was doing his job. He might have been invited to court to fill out the ranks of courtiers for the queen's impromptu dance, but Vandusen knew he was now and forever Sir Nolan Brett's employee.

The dancing continued. A minuet, old and lively. Waiters brought fresh champagne flutes and offered him cheese. He'd rather have had a coffee. He'd overeaten at dinner, unaccustomed to so much variety. He'd thought to be in bed by now but the dance was just getting started.

Vandusen knew he was a placeholder at the party, a body to fill out the ranks of chairs until the wealthy could follow the queen upcountry. He could pass as a noble courtier as easily as he could a beggar, commoner, or merchant class. He'd been trained.

He'd not been the only non-gentry at the table. A naval man, captain by rank and newly arrived, by stance and musculature, was seated next to Admiral Aderyn.

The admiral knew Vandusen on sight, having had many dealings with the Second Ear. They shook hands across the table. "Hello, Jim, do you know Captain Upor? Recently returned from Tirgwenin."

"How do you do?" Vandusen offered his hand, not letting on that he had met the captain before when Sir Nolan had summoned him for a private meeting.

They shook hands.

"You dropped off Sommerled's colony?"

"Aye," said Upor.

"How do they fare?"

"When I left them they were fit and well, but I worry."

"Why so, sir?"

"Their leader," said Upor, sitting down heavily. Gravity weary. "A Minister Morgan. He's prone to making up stories, spreading lies and dissension. I fear for the colony. It is his way to accuse rather than lead."

"That is a pity."

"Aye."

"And a coward," said Aderyn. "He abandoned his colony."

"He did what?"

Upor nodded and drank and when he spoke, he spoke loudly so his voice carried up the table. "I landed them safe and sound, at a known location, but he was so unsettled at not being placed precisely where he wished that he left his friends and family to return even now to Enskari to complain."

"He left friends and family on a dangerous alien world?"

"Aye," said Upor.

Aderyn shook his head. "A coward and a liar."

"And a heretic," said Upor. "A Buckler. Exiled, they were."

"And they were left in peril?"

"Nay," said Upor. "Though you could not convince him of that. He saw danger in every tree, conspiracy in every leaf. Cursed the wind that the new world they wanted was not ready built."

"What did he expect?"

"A mountain of gold? Plowed and planted fields, servants to wait on them?" said Aderyn. The drink was getting to him. "The man was afraid of work."

"You say he's returned to Enskari?"

"Morgan would not board my ship," said Upor. "He said he didn't trust me. He took one of the lesser ships back, the *Sebastian*. Not a lucky ship. It's overdue. Likely lost."

"Bad storms this year," said Aderyn. "Coronam is lively."

The next course arrived and the admiral talked solar storms with Upor, sails and thread spinners, two spacefarers sharing tales as at a tavern.

"Are you a spy?" The voice came from a man sitting on Vandusen's right.

It took him a moment to recognize the Second Duke of Dexit. Vandusen shouldn't know him at all except for his work with Nolan. He'd been listed as a potential problem, an intemperate courtier who could be bought. His family's money, not great to begin with, was failing fast, mostly because of the out-of-control spending of the Second Duke of Dexit. There were also rumors of apostasy.

"He's too pretty to be a spy," said a girl at his side. Vandusen didn't recognize her. Sir Nolan hadn't dossiers on all the women in court like all the men. It either meant that she was harmless, new, or Sir Nolan had succumbed to gender prejudice. Knowing his boss, recognizing her comfort at court, Vandusen knew she was harmless.

"Nay," he said.

"Maybe you are the queen's new lover," said the girl.

"Nay, she has what she wants," said Dexit.

Vandusen cloaked his emotions behind a mask of calm he'd learned from his master. "What do you mean?" he said.

The duke tipped a flask into his cup of wine. Vandusen smelled the sweet perfume of a narcotic herb waft over the scent of veal and almond mint. Dexit raised his cup and drained it. He gritted his teeth and pinched his eyes. When he opened them, Vandusen watched his pupils dilate and sputter.

"She's the queen. She takes what she likes," said the girl.

"And *whom* she likes." The duke spoke with a thick tongue, smiling like he'd just made the cleverest jest imaginable.

"And who does she like?" said Vandusen.

"For the queen some are chosen, for the queen some are led, but why not have it all? She sleeps with Sommerled!"

The girl laughed like the joke was the height of culture. The Second Duke snorted into a handkerchief to hide his laughter.

Vandusen smiled and took a forkful of food, prepared to deflect the conversation as need be, but he needn't have worried. The Second Duke had a sudden urge to take the woman 'away' for a few minutes and exited the table unceremoniously when she didn't say no.

Sommerled was far enough up the table, on the queen's right no less, that he didn't hear the Second Duke's inane pun, but others nearer him had. If someone felt the urge to turn him in, Lord Dexit and his woman could be dragged to Gray Keep and tortured to death. Hell, failure to turn them in might bring the same penalty.

But this was court. Such would be the fate for commoners; the rules were different for the rich.

It was a common rumor that the queen had lovers, but officially she was a virgin. Vandusen understood that the premise was a diplomatic chit. The queen, as a virgin, could be wed and Enskari have a king. Prince Brandon on Hyrax had been the obvious choice and had tried to woo her in his own way before and after her ascension. This had angered peoples on three planets; on Enskari there were those who thought Zabel had no right to the throne at all, even to marry it away. On Hyrax there were those who thought Zabel was beneath their prince, and of course on Temple the clergy saw the queen as a symbol of rebellion. Time had not improved things. The only insult worse than the queen taking the throne after her father died, was keeping it when she could marry and give it to a man. She had not married, and so Hyrax and the Temple prepared war against her. Nevertheless, the chit was still in play. The queen must be a virgin. It was the official government position. To speak otherwise was treason.

But people talk. Rumors were rampant even if they weren't true. Vandusen knew through his master of half a dozen lovers the queen had entertained over the years. Each had been carefully picked and controlled. Each had been harmless to the state, each had been like Nolan himself, in the background, in the shadows. That was until Sommerled.

There were many on Enskari who thought the match would be well made. Noble queen and risen hero. Patriotic and enduring. Vandusen himself thought them a handsome couple and never begrudged the queen a lover and never thought her any less great for desiring intimacy. Under orders, Vandusen had fed letters to newspapers posing as the common man suggesting just such a union in the cause of planetary and class unity. The masses ate it up. There were even some nobles, forward-thinking and rare as they were, who thought the queen and Ethan Sommerled were meant to be together. But these were not the ones who mattered.

Change is always slowest at the top. The old and the old blood. Even the loyal noble houses still hadn't fully come to terms with a mere woman leading their world. The idea that she'd marry someone born of a lower class who would then rule above them was an idea beyond most of them and indeed threatened another civil war, as Archbishop Connor had implied.

Sommerled had earned his knighthood in service to the world. He was a stark contrast to the rich and needy useless people at the dance who'd inherited their titles from ancestors who'd been rich during the Unsettling. He showed them up.

It was only a matter of time.

"What did you say?" Sommerled stood in the middle of the dance floor, facing the Second Duke of Dexit.

The duke had been dancing with a different woman than the one he'd sat next to at dinner. This one was five years younger, a girl who'd just been presented to the queen the day before. Sommerled's partner had been one of the queen's ladies-in-waiting, an orphaned girl of twenty from a ruined house. A charity case, but lovely and sweet for all her parents' unwise choices during the civil war of her ascension. She hovered a few steps behind Sommerled, fumbling with her fan to hide her horrified expression, trying to steal glances at the queen.

The Second Duke stared Sommerled in the eye. He was a few centimeters taller than the captain and at least five years younger. For all his buffoonery, the Second Duke of Dexit was a fit and able man, well known among the court for his physique and also for his love of dueling, where he was considered one of the best in court, if not the planet.

"I don't know what *you* think *you* heard," said the Second Duke of Dexit. "But I'll not repeat myself to the likes of *you*." There was no hint of inebriation in his voice. He made a show of looking the hero of Enskari up and down with a derisive giggle. "Your parents cleaned my parents' toilets, probably mine too."

The music stopped.

The crowd stepped away.

The lady-in-waiting disappeared.

The duke smirked at Sommerled and raised his chin in challenge. It was met. Sommerled offered the traditional gesture, a slap across the face. His was more than a slap however, and the Second Duke spun and stumbled a few steps, nearly falling to the floor before he was caught by his retainers.

"Swords," said the duke, his eyes watering for pain and insult.

"Pistols," said Sommerled.

"You don't know anything, gutter-born," the duke said. "I was challenged. I choose."

"Dawn," said Sommerled.

"Nay. At once," said the duke.

"What is this noise at our ball?" said the queen.

"A personal matter," said Archbishop Connor, heading off the regent a few steps from her throne.

Vandusen threw a glance at Nolan, who was watching the scene with keen attention.

"A challenge?"

"A personal matter," he said again with that gravity that carried a final unarguable logic.

The queen looked at Connor, then found her Second Ear in the shadows. He raised his hands in a gesture of powerlessness. She turned to Sommerled and Dexit. The latter two bowed.

"We are not pleased," she said.

"The challenge must be met immediately," said Sir Edward. He'd stepped out of a group of old blood nobles who'd doubtlessly just told him what had happened. He had the look about him of a man who'd just been woken up. "Custom and law, Your Majesty. Sir Ethan made the challenge."

"Our party is ruined," she said. "Fine. Take your games outside in the rain." She turned quickly away and swept out of the room, her face behind a fan.

Nolan walked up to Sommerled and Dexit. They bowed to him while the First Ear and the archbishop nodded a greeting. "Blessed be."

"And to thee."

"It must happen," said Edward. Connor nodded.

"Aye," said Nolan, looking Sommerled in the face. The captain's calm was becoming. Dexit's giddy enthusiasm, less so. "Aye."

Without another word, and with Sir Edward a step behind him, Nolan left and followed the queen out of the room.

Most of the courtiers left the hall to reassemble in the courtyard, vying for the best vantage points to watch the coming duel.

Dexit was swarmed by friends who made bets as to how long Sommerled might actually survive a duel with him. The odds were long it would go five minutes.

Vandusen felt someone move behind him and turned to see Sir Temsil, the Hyraxian ambassador, rocking on his heels.

"I'd speak with your master," he said. "But he keeps putting me off."

"He's a busy man," said Vandusen, watching Dexit tip a cup and march away. "Is there no official channel you could use?"

"Nay, this is not official."

Sommerled caught Vandusen's eye and took a step toward him, before he found himself swarmed by more well-wishers.

Sir Temsil said, "There are certain neutrals on this world who are suffering from your Connor who have done nothing."

"Perhaps they should have done something then," said Vandusen.

"The prophet himself has spoken against this man for his many murders."

"The prophet has no voice here," said Vandusen.

"That's why I can't make this official, you oaf." The insult rolled off his tongue as natural as good morning. "It must stop," the ambassador said. "Sir Nolan must rein in his dog or—"

"Or what?"

Sommerled broke free and headed their way.

"Or all Enskari will suffer for Connor's sins when Hyrax arrives."

"I'll not communicate your threat, Ambassador," said Vandusen. "I'll keep my head. Good night." He stepped away and met Sommerled four paces onto the floor. The ambassador huffed and walked briskly away.

"Did you do this?" Sommerled said.

Vandusen was taken aback. "What?"

"Did you or your master sick that beast on me? To insult the queen in my ear so he might kill me?"

"Nay, Sir Sommerled. We have nothing but love for you, why would you think such a thing?"

Sommerled looked hard in Vandusen's eyes for the lie. He had a presence and Vandusen felt himself shrink a little under his stare.

"We love you," he said. "*Enskari* loves you and we love Enskari."

"Not all Enskari," he said.

"Well…. Nay, Captain. Not everyone."

"You'll be my second."

"Surely, there's—"

"If you truly love me, you'll be there."

"Why would you have me?"

"You and your master are not the only ones who know to use symbols."

"I'll need to ask—"

"What must you ask?" said Nolan. Vandusen did not like how easy he was to sneak up on that night.

"The captain has asked me to second him," said Vandusen.

A hint of a smile tugged the corner of the spymaster's lips. "If you wish."

"Aye then," said Sommerled.

"The queen would speak with you," Nolan said to Sommerled.

"Nolan," said the captain. "I cannot back out. You know it."

"Aye, but the queen is not happy."

"Can you not explain it to her? Tell Her Majesty that I'll see her in the morning. It'll be over by then."

"Ethan…." said Nolan.

"You couldn't find me," he said to the Ear.

Their eyes met in some communication Vandusen could only guess at. After a moment, Nolan nodded.

Sommerled clicked his heels and took his leave.

Vandusen and his master watched him go.

"Did you arrange—" Vandusen's question was cut off by a harsh glare. "Good night, Second Ear," he said.

"You know he'll insult the nobles again by having you as a second," said Nolan. "You're not noble."

"Perhaps, but he'll also scare the hell out of them," said Vandusen. "They know I'm your man."

They followed the crowd to the courtyard. It was lit round with gas lamps, a garden of Old Earth roses, cut and bare for the season but intermixed with native sadmarys for a winter blooming of delicate blue petals poking out of the snow. In the center was a frozen fountain, granite fishes and bird statues still as the water was then. A light snow fell, prickly ice, a cold fog that diffused the gaslight into a uniform yellow glow.

Vandusen saw Sir Ethan at one side surrounded with officers and military. Across from him were Dexit and his gang of young courtiers, drunk and loud.

A shadow crossed the window of the queen's bedchamber.

It could be random happenstance, a bit of bad luck among drunken partygoers, but Vandusen knew it was not out the realm of possibility that his master had arranged it to get rid of a problem.

There was no good result for this and that was why he thought his master had not orchestrated this. If Sommerled won, the nobility would be incensed more than ever, right of revenge for a noble on a commoner would be evoked and Sommerled's new rank questioned and tested. If Sommerled lost, who knew what the lower classes would do? He was their man, their hope, their symbol in the court. There could be uprising.

But uprisings could be handled even now on the brink of war – particularly now. Spin, propaganda, and military force were all at Nolan's disposal. Uprisings were unprofitable and troublesome, but controllable. Riots would be easier to control than another noble rebellion. It was not something trivial, but if the prize was right, it could be a justifiable cost.

And the queen could do nothing. She could not intervene one way or the other. For her heart and for the state she had to be silent. She ruled the planet but could not stop a drunken duel because tradition said it was personal.

Vandusen approached Sommerled.

"Good, my second is here," said the captain.

The other officers looked up in surprise at Vandusen's arrival. They shared a few glances but said nothing.

"What do we know about this knave?" said Sommerled, handing his coat to Vandusen and looking across the icy expanse at Dexit.

"He'll attack your legs first," said one officer. "An overhand feint and an ankle sweep to hobble you. It's how he killed Sir Thomas last year."

"He'll give no quarter," said another. "When you're down, expect the killing blow to follow. Regardless of begging."

"I don't plan on being down," said Sommerled. "Nor to beg."

"Nay, nay. Of course not," said the embarrassed officer. "I was just remembering Sir Thomas last year."

Vandusen spoke. "He's been trained by the best swordsmen on Enskari. He knows all the forms. All the rules. That's how he'll fight."

A grin spread over Sommerled's face and he nodded. "Aye, there's some advice."

The officers shrugged.

Sommerled and Vandusen approached the center of the courtyard.

A sergeant of arms with halberd, cutlass, and railgun waited for the two pairs of men to meet. Sommerled and Vandusen arrived first.

"Captain," said the sergeant.

"Bill," said Sommerled with a wink.

"Good luck, sir," whispered the sergeant under his breath. "Kill the bastard."

Vandusen stomped his feet to keep them warm.

Dexit was accompanied by the Baron of Yarrow. He was the leader of one of the most powerful houses on the planet, neutral during the war of ascension and yet to be punished for it. He was a symbol of aristocratic honor like few other living men could be. He was over eighty years old and should the seconds be called to finish the fight, Vandusen didn't relish the idea of killing the old man. In fact, it occurred to him, for political reasons, he should allow himself to be killed. Such was his thinking after working for Sir Nolan Brett so long.

"This is a personal matter," said the sergeant of arms. "Swords have been chosen."

A man walked up with two rapiers and offered them first to Dexit. He pulled one, whipped it, and stabbed the air to check its balance. Satisfied, he nodded.

"I'll take the cutlass," said Sommerled.

"What cutlass?"

He gestured to the sergeant's sword. "Is it not a sword? Is it not presented in the middle from a neutral source?" Sommerled, too, knew the rules.

"That unwieldy thing?" said Dexit. "Your funeral."

The sergeant drew his weapon and offered it to Sir Ethan.

"Good steel. Working man's steel," Sommerled said, feeling the weight. "And well kept. Oft used?"

"Nay, but it was my father's."

"It'll do."

Dexit laughed and then called out, "Let it be known that he chose to die with that sword in his hand. A real sword was offered him."

His crowd cheered and applauded.

"Let it be known," said Sommerled.

"Seconds retreat," called the sergeant of arms, who also withdrew. "Ye may commence," he said when all were back.

Vandusen watched the men face each other in the yellow ice light. Dexit raised his sword to his chin in the noble fashion. Sommerled limbered his wrist with circles of the heavy sword.

"En garde!" said Dexit and lunged.

"Rot in hell!" said Sommerled, grabbing Dexit's blade in his free hand and pulling. In the same single motion, he swiveled forward in a turn. It was a graceful muscular twist and brought the cutlass up and around his back and then over his head and down into the duke's shoulder, lopping off his arm from collarbone to third rib in a clean single bone-splitting cut.

The sound was muffled by the weather but carried fine the silence of surprise. There was a momentary stillness, a gasp of disbelief as Dexit wobbled and bled and then toppled to the ground in a splash of bloody slush. In an instant, the duel was over – thrust and countermove, stab and slash, and the Second Duke of Dexit was so much butchered meat in the royal garden.

Vandusen glanced to the queen's bedchamber and thought he saw Zabel Genest, ruler of all Enskari, beloved queen and revolutionary monarch, hopping for joy.

In another window lower the ground, he saw a figure he knew well: his master, Sir Nolan Brett. The figure stood unmoving. His eyes fixed past Vandusen.

Then a woman shrieked and men rushed forward. And all was chaos.

Sommerled gave the sergeant back his sword and examined his wounded hand where he'd grasped Dexit's sword. It bled freely.

Vandusen tried to aid him as was his duty as a second, but was brushed away.

"It's nothing," said Sommerled, wrapping a silk handkerchief around his palm. He deftly tied it as a field dressing, tightened it with his teeth like he'd done it a thousand times before.

When Vandusen looked back at the window, Sir Nolan was gone. When he looked behind him to where the spymaster had been staring, he saw the back of Archbishop Connor leaving the courtyard.

CHAPTER TWENTY-THREE

It is not that the knowledge of Old Earth is lost. It is not. It is only that we choose not to teach it lest the children get wrong ideas.
Memo from Royal Historian to Superintendent of Schools Lavland, 588 NE

30, Eleventh-Month, 947 NE – Maaraw

The steam cart carried High Purger Thomas Tarquin away from the elevator terminal through the city of Coebler toward the Zion Mission fifty kilometers inland. His driver, Minister Parkerm, was chatty and tiresome. As if thinking he was selling the place to a tourist, he pointed out landmarks and recited local history like there'd be a test on it later. "Hyrax landed in 882, Lavland in 887, Enskari and Claremond in 890. Saved ministry arrived with each expedition."

"Uh-huh."

"This is the first cotton mill. That was the first sugar mill there. Now it's a warehouse. That way is the red-light district. That way the governor's mansion. He's expecting to meet you, by the way. When may I say you will be available?"

"I'll let him know," said Tarquin.

"Those bananas are not actually bananas, they're a local plant mistaken for bananas. They're more like watermelons than anything. Do you know watermelons?"

"I have reading to do before we arrive." Tarquin closed the barrier between the passenger compartment and driver unceremoniously and sat back.

The purger had never been to Maaraw before and was sure he wouldn't like it. It was a wild place in every sense of the word. Nature encroached on every structure and human endeavor. Vines assaulted buildings, leaves littered the road, rust-colored dirt blew in the air covering the smell of progress. Under the wild odors of jungle forest, it stank of rotting compost and desperation of the poor. Every city had a poverty line, but the one he'd seen in Coebler was immediate and drastic. The natives wore rags, light cotton garb, and few had shoes. The dirt covered their feet and crawled up their legs like a mold attacking a tree.

The landscape was lush to a fault. Green forests checkered with red fields of earth, the wild plants ever trying to regain their lost land. Husbandry was done here by fire and steam shovel. Some worlds called for prayers from the prophet to get a plant to grow; on Maaraw they had to be fought back with blades.

At least for now.

He remembered some report about the planet's topsoil being depleted rapidly due to over farming, deforestation, or whatever. It was a footnote of a report he'd glanced at during his flight from Lavland after receiving his instructions.

He'd wanted to get away from Lavland but he never thought it'd be to Maaraw. He wondered who he might have angered, who among the prophet's circle could have done this to him. He put the thought away as quickly as he could, remembering and reciting his oath of obedience.

Maaraw was one of the hotter planets, second only to Silangan in average temperature. Though it was late fall or early winter, the heat made him think of summer on Temple. He hated summer on Temple. Moist and muggy. Sticky fog and suffocating humidity.

He rolled down his window and let the dusty hot air from outside replace the stifling hot air of the cabin. Sweat beaded on his neck and ran down his back. He smelled the diesel fumes of the conveyance engine and saw the steam puffs mix with the smoke and found comfort in it.

Loosening his collar, he turned to the papers he'd been given at the terminal.

The man's name was Andre Bruin. He was a native Maarawan, an ex-slave trader and smuggler. He had been one of the loyal Saved, but now he was a rebel.

He read the report, shaking his head, wondering why Temple was interested in this. He felt himself grow angry, becoming more and more sure that he was being punished for something, that one of the apostles had it in for him. This was obviously a civil matter. It was concluded the moment the man was captured. The threat was over. It was only a formality now to—

He read something that made him stop. He read it again. Then again. Then he finished the report and stared at the final instruction: *We leave it to you to answer this question: do we martyr this man?*

★   ★   ★

The monastery was once a distant outreach post, an old attempt to bring the natives back into the Saved Orthodox Church before the entire planet, except a select few clans, was declared apostate, thus beginning the slave trade.

The outreach now was minimal, the post a distant secretive place, a walled fortress on a hill overlooking vast jungles and a single weaving road to the coast.

The man had been brought here to hide him. His followers were still active, still raiding plantations and slave markets, attacking the trade of human flesh wherever they could before disappearing into the very jungle the monastery looked out upon. Tarquin could appreciate the irony of hiding the man here but thought it smacked of hubris and the kind of over-trickiness that so often turns to catastrophe. Perhaps he wasn't the only one to think that. His orders were to ascertain the situation and pronounce judgment on the prisoner within a single week of arrival, 'Three days being preferable'.

His rooms were modest, spartan, and clean. The monks who attended him were polite and didn't show the fearful deference he was used to. He found it a welcome change. They were true followers here, humble seekers and not political zealots he knew too many of in the upper ranks of the church.

He washed the road dust from his face and changed into clean robes. After a brief visit from the abbot, he sat with the monks and ate supper in silence with them as a lector read scripture from a pulpit. Tarquin was happy for the droning quiet that let his mind mull over the question Temple had sent him to decide.

★   ★   ★

He was up with the monks before dawn and after a breakfast of salted gruel, went to the stable to see his prisoner.

He was met by three guards, hardened mercenaries by the looks of them, who weren't allowed to enter the monastery proper. They seemed perfectly fine with that. They'd do as they were ordered, had already been well paid and would receive more when the job was done. What that job would be, was up to Tarquin.

The room he was to use had been a tack room. It smelled of horsehair, alfalfa, and dust. Tarquin could discern also the honest scents of worked leather and sweat. The floor was packed ground except for a space of new concrete in the middle of the room where a single iron ring protruded. There were no windows but the walls leaked light between the slats and showed in the dust like buttresses, or in the knotholes like spears of light. A coal oil lantern hung on a chain above a single wooden table. A stool sat on one side, a carved dining chair on the other. Tarquin was familiar with the arrangement.

There was a hard knock on the door.

"Come," said Tarquin.

A mercenary, Hyraxian, poked his head in. "He'll be here forthwith, High Minister," he said. "I've set up contingencies in the blacksmith's hut, just yonder across the way."

"Very good," said Tarquin. "Bring him straight in and chain him down and leave. Don't go far."

"Aye."

Tarquin turned to look at the wall and the man left. The boards were so old and brittle he thought he could push them down with a single shove.

He heard the prisoner approach and then enter the room with the guards. He kept his back to them and listened to the grunts and clatter as the prisoner was placed on the stool and attached to the ring in the floor. He waited for the guards to leave and then for his prisoner to test the ring, which he did a moment after the door was closed.

Tarquin turned and looked at him.

He wasn't sure what he expected to see, but he was disappointed nonetheless. He saw there just a small strongly built man with brown curly hair. His rags were suitably squalid, torn and dirty. Then there were the eyes, of course. The eyes were where Tarquin was taken aback. He'd not expected to see fear in them – this man was not that kind. He'd expected defiance, perhaps, or condescension, but not the curiosity that met his gaze.

"Do you know who I am?" Tarquin said.

Andre Bruin, the most dangerous man in the solar system if the Temple reports were to be believed, said only, "I do."

The short answer hung in the air like the falling dust, suspended in light, rife with meaning, double meanings, triple. Two words and an abyss of significance, that threatened to draw Tarquin into its depths.

"You're different," Tarquin said under his breath, sensing then Temple's perception of this little man.

"Nay," said Andre Bruin. "I'm not."

"Aye, you are," said Tarquin. "I wouldn't be here if you weren't. You wouldn't be here if you weren't."

Bruin put his hands on the table. His wrists were manacled together, five centimeters of cable between them and a chain connecting that to the floor. "I feel like Marley," he said.

"Who's Marley?" said Tarquin.

"Jacob Marley. An Old Earth story," he said, adjusting himself on his stool. "By a man called Charles Dickens." He rattled his wrists. "The chains of my sins."

"I don't know it."

"'Tis long forgotten."

"But you know it?"

"Aye. I do."

The words hung again, weighty and thick. Something in the way he said them, an inflection, a certainty.

Tarquin looked at the man and the man looked at him. "You haven't been tortured," Tarquin said.

"Nay," said Bruin.

"How's that?"

"I must have talked them out of it."

"I understand." Tarquin realized that the civilized worlds' control over Maaraw was not so great as to invite the direct wrath of Bruin's supporters. The strength of the rebellion was unknown, but its effectiveness was not. It had scared the powerful and brought him, a high purger, to the red-soiled planet. Moving Bruin out of the enclaves, into the law of the church, would insulate the invaders from retaliation, or so it was hoped.

So afraid were they, that they'd forgone their pound of flesh from the captured enemy leader. He had not a bruise on him, not a scratch put there in punishment, not a brand or a burn, not a twisted bone or missing finger. Except for the rags and the chains about him, he could be anyone, Maarawan, Lavlander, Silangian, Templer. A rational businessman, neighbor, brother – not the man accused of freeing thousands, killing hundreds, and challenging the very order of society

Bruin said, "I would suppose they brought you here to do their work. They'll reap unfair benefit from another's labor. Appropriate irony, is it not?"

"It's a little more complicated than that," said Tarquin. He met the man's eyes and tried to see his game. Did he think he could do such crimes and not be punished? Did he think if he was clever, society would be merciful? "Guard!" he called.

The door swung open behind Bruin.

"Contingency."

The guard smiled.

The high purger turned his back and faced the wall leaking light.

The sound of the truncheon striking Bruin's head made Tarquin wince but he didn't turn. He waited until the sounds of the dragged man and his trailing chains faded into the distant courtyard before he left and went on a tour of the abbey's struggling vineyard.

★　　★　　★

The next day he had the prisoner brought to the interrogation room ahead of him. Same as before, he'd be sat on the stool, chained to the floor at the table. This time Tarquin would make him wait. Bruin was in place before dawn. Tarquin went to him after supper.

The guard held the door open for the high purger as he stepped in. The room smelled of urine and blood. Bruin raised his head from the table but didn't turn around.

"You've messed yourself," said Tarquin.

"As you intended," said Bruin, his voice loud though his consonants slurred.

Tarquin came around the table and saw Bruin's swollen face and understood the thickness, but not the strength in his speech.

Bruin leaned his head back to see the purger through swollen eyelids. The last of the evening light faded in the cracks of the outward walls. Tarquin lit the lamp and sat down.

Bruin's rags were now filthy, stained with piss and blood. His skin, more scab than not, his face beaten, his feet burned, fingers bent and splayed. Crushed bones misaligned. He'd be crippled no matter the outcome of the visit.

A pound of flesh.

From beneath his robes Tarquin took out a bundle of folded papers and spread them out on the table. "You are accused of being a terrorist, of attacking peaceful folk up and down Maaraw, inciting rebellion and revolt," he said. "Do you deny your crimes?"

"I deny none of it," he said. "I had hoped for a trial though. Perhaps. But I guess you'll do."

"Me?"

"You."

"How's that?"

"I want to make a record."

"For what purpose?"

"So others near my place can understand, hear me, and get a head start."

Tarquin wrinkled his forehead. "I'm a purger, not a reporter. What you say to me will most likely be blasphemous and it is my calling to wipe such things out. Do you think you can change me?"

"Nay, not at all," said Bruin.

Tarquin wondered if the guards had rattled his senses too much for an interview. He should have overseen the work personally. He had not the time to wait for him to heal – one week, three days optimal, but he'd been assured that the guards were well heeled. Temple had used them before.

"You were captured at the Barlow ranch," Tarquin said. "Your own people turned you in."

"Fourth-generations," he said.

"What is that?"

"Slaves who've forgotten what it is to be free. Believers of lies, traumatized and injured. Brainwashed. I can't blame them. They were slow to learn and didn't know better."

"Could they not have just disagreed with you? Could they not have been happy before, and didn't like your malevolent actions – murder and mayhem? Must they have been brainwashed to want something different than what you offered?"

"They were taught an obvious false philosophy," he said. "They held it even after being shown its falseness."

"You are playing word games, Andre Bruin."

"Would you consent to be a slave?"

"Nay. I'm a minister."

"You had a choice of occupations."

"A calling."

"Aye, of course ya did." Bruin smiled. His teeth were broken and bloody. "Slaves don't get choices. Sorry – *callings*."

"We all have our role in society, Mr. Bruin. It's the way of things. It's as simple as that. It's the way it is, the way it's always been. The way it always will be."

Bruin said, "We all should participate in society, but we don't, do we? That's because society's goals are wrong. Our society – your society, the wrong society – is built upon the ideas of false scarcity and necessary greed. It's unjust and wrong. It's something we should have outgrown centuries ago."

"Is this what you told your followers?"

"Not at first," he said. "Didn't know it then. I said only Maaraw should be free. People should be free. It wasn't an elaborate credo. Slavery is wrong. The forces making us slaves should be fought. Slaves should be freed. Maaraw should be allowed to evolve without interference. It was political, not religious." He coughed. The long speech was taking something out of him. He went to wipe pink spittle from his lips but his hands wouldn't reach. He bent down and rubbed his mouth against the back of his manacled hand.

"And now?"

"Now I understand things better."

"Since when?"

"It's been an evolving process," he said, slurring his *s*'s. "I got my first bee shortly after I started. Two bees since I have been captured. Three bees last night."

"Bees?"

"They focus the mind."

Tarquin became aware then of a buzzing in the room. It might have been bees, but more likely flies coming to feast on the broken man's wounds.

"Looking back from this room, would you have done things differently?"

"Not a thing."

"Your wisdom didn't increase, then."

"My knowledge did."

"You kill people."

"So do you."

"You're saying we're not different. You see me as a criminal?"

"Of course you are." Bruin looked up at Tarquin under his swollen lids. "But we work for different goals – you to keep the status quo, me to advance us."

"Just a rebel, then." Tarquin felt disappointment. "Just another uppity nobody who didn't know his place and killed his betters hoping to rise."

"Not rebel. Revolutionary."

"You know the difference?"

"Aye."

"What's the difference?"

"I want to remove the entire system, not just change places with those on top."

"Because bees told you so?"

"I knew it before the bees, but they confirmed it. Ya see, I dared to dream."

"Uh-huh. Dared to dream, did you? Dreamed of what?"

"A just society."

"A society without slaves?"

"Aye, that'd be a good start."

"A dream?"

"An idea really. I was awake."

"And that's what started your reign of terror?"

"It's what led me to act."

"Just that?"

"Aye."

"What about indentured servants? Your own people arrived on Maaraw that way. Were they wrong?"

"In desperate times, people do desperate things. The scarcity was real by that time."

"It wasn't before?"

"Nay. It was manufactured but became real as the planet collapsed because of it."

"So slavery was good then but not now?"

"It was different. An imperfect solution. We can do better."

"Evolving truths," Tarquin said, naming the sin.

"Slavery is institutionalized," Bruin said. "The scarcity is man-made. It's extractive, unjust, demeaning, and cruel. It is holding back our species."

"Robbing people of potential?"

"Aye."

"And killing people doesn't?"

Bruin sighed. "Not my first choice."

Tarquin found the list of casualties among his papers. There was buzzing around the lamp.

"Six hundred five and twenty casualties in your rebellion so far. Two hundred six and thirty tortured or maimed. You are a cruel man, Andre Bruin."

"Removing the obstacles. When reeducation won't suffice, removal is required. It is a culling."

"A culling? Now you sound like a zealot. You sound insane."

Bruin shrugged, or rather tried to. His left shoulder was dislocated.

Tarquin wondered how the man was carrying on this conversation. He should be screaming in pain. Had they given him something?

Bruin said, "Insanity is doing the same thing over and over again and expecting a different result."

"What does that mean?"

"It means that humanity got another chance and we're blowing it."

"You're talking about Old Earth again?"

"Aye."

"Imagined legends and fancies. No one knows Old Earth. Those records were lost."

"Nay. For some they were buried, for others they're just not talked about. Temple has extensive archives. You've seen them."

It was a lucky guess, but still Tarquin felt uneasy with Bruin's certainty. "A typical appeal to the good ol' days."

"You are not listening, High Purger. I never said they were good. I said the opposite. I said they were being repeated."

"Explain."

"Extraction economy, ya blind git. Theft of labor, theft of assets. Misallocation of resources. Hoarding and selfishness to the favor of the few to detriment of all."

"That's all human nature. It's how God made us. We've made the best society we can under these conditions."

"Nay. It's not God. It's humanity. It's about choices we make."

"You talk of history, history shows ours is the only viable society."

"Nay. It doesn't. It shows only that personal greed when backed by overwhelming resources crushes evolution and ethical behavior. A trait that served us in one situation is holding us back in another. We need to think bigger. We need to think of the species. How big is your family?"

"I had a brother. My parents are dead. And of course, I'm celibate.

Bruin shook his head, obviously displeased by the answer.

Tarquin turned to his papers. "You're middle-class, though born of peasants. You rose to some success as a trader. Curiously enough, you yourself traded slaves among other things."

Bruin didn't react.

Tarquin shook his head. "Your education was rudimentary. You can barely read. Who filled your mind with these ideas?"

"They're obvious concepts."

"Nay. Nay, they're not."

Bruin shrugged again.

Tarquin found his lists. "Where is your base camp?" he said.

No answer.

"Who is giving you aid?"

No answer.

"Where are you getting weapons?"

No answer.

"How strong is your army? How many men?"

Nothing.

"Make me a list of all the members of your rebellion you can remember."

Bruin coughed. "You don't really expect me to tell you these things do you?"

"Not today," he said. "Tomorrow I'll learn some of it. The day after, some more. In three days, I'll have it all."

Bruin smiled, the edge of his mouth breaking the scab on his cheek. "You know better than that, High Purger."

Tarquin sighed. He'd dealt with people like this before, mad people who went to their graves screaming in anguish but without saying a name.

"You're a misguided zealot and a fool," said Tarquin. "And yet you've managed to start something here on Maaraw that has the worlds worried. Do you know why?"

"I do."

Those words again. Like a catchphrase, a motto. A cantrip.

Tarquin said, "What does this future world you would have look like?"

"I don't know. Honestly, I don't. It's a new chance. We have new tools."

"What?"

"I don't know what shape it will take. I've not seen that far. I know only to begin. I could not stand by and see my fellows so mistreated. I snapped and I acted. I did. But where it goes…. I dunno. It's evolving. No one can see the future, I only know that the future must be different from the past or we've squandered our chance."

"What do you know of either? You're an ignorant peasant."

Bruin coughed, thick and dry. "Imagine a just world, High Purger. See it in your mind and the bees may come to you."

"Bees? Symbol of industry, right? I've seen the symbol in cathedrals. Is that your socialist icon?"

Bruin laughed.

"Mr. Bruin – Andre," said Tarquin, steepling his fingers. "I am here to determine your level of threat. I think I was chosen – though of course no one says these things to me – because I understand how politics and faith need to work together. I understand, though don't always agree, with compromises to further the cause."

"Compromise is good."

"Not always."

"Aye, that is true. Not always."

"You threaten the worlds of Coronam, the great houses. Hyrax, Lavland, Claremond, even Enskari. All of them, even your native Maarawans."

"Sharing the love."

"Not one of them wants to face you directly, and they don't want to team up."

"Oops."

"They don't want the blame for killing you, so they called me in."

"You've made up your mind then?"

Tarquin paused. The man spoke with such certainty, like he knew Tarquin's orders, like he'd read them. "Temple, the prophet and the apostles, are curious about you. We all recognize an apostate, but there's more here."

"My philosophy is sound. It is yours that is flawed. Yours is an anchor that once secured the people but now is only a drag. I don't blame you. It's just time to cut the rope and sail on."

"Your metaphors are getting tiresome."

Another shrug.

The buzzing grew louder. The flies getting hungry. The sun was long down. The room had cooled. The oil lamp flickered and cast orange-tinged shadows on the red ground.

"I don't see the danger the presidency sees in you. You're just a mad zealot, rebel idealist in a dream world."

"You know who else spoke in metaphors?"

Tarquin shook his head. "You don't understand the seriousness of the situation."

"Don't I?"

"Nay." Tarquin shook his head and then shouted, "Guard!"

The door swung open and two men entered dragging a third between them.

"Do you know this man?"

Bruin stared at the new prisoner. He'd been tortured and beaten but Tarquin knew he recognized him. "His name is Asay. This is your lieutenant, Asay. Do you recognize him?"

Silence from Bruin.

Tarquin nodded.

One guard pulled Asay's head up by the hair while the other drew a knife from his belt and drew it across the man's neck in a single slicing motion.

Blood poured out of the slit throat like a wave, then a spigot, then slowed, pulsed, and stopped.

The guards dropped the dead man to the floor in the pool of his own muddy blood.

Bruin shook.

Tarquin smiled. "We'll talk more tomorrow," he said and gathered his papers. He glanced at the dead man and his prisoner and then left like he was late for a train. The guards followed him out. As they locked the door, an unnecessary precaution, Tarquin could hear the angry buzzing inside. He imagined a cloud of flies gathering to feast on the dead.

*　　*　　*

The third day Tarquin waited for the prisoner to be brought to him after the midday meal. He kicked at the bloody mud pool and thought of the prophet on Temple, his glorious connection to God, divine word and will. He traced that force from God's spokesman through the hierarchy of the church, to the apostles and the quorums, to the bodies and ranks, and then unto himself and saw it stretching downward through his subordinates to the people, noble and peasants, to the criminals, and finally to the blood pool under his shoe.

Bruin was in the same rags as before. He stank as before. He looked worse for his wounds. Old wounds were always uglier than new. None had been added to him but the healing had hardly begun.

He might have been able to walk, but the guards didn't let him. They dragged him inside in leg irons, deposited him on the little stool and chained him to the ring as before then retreated out the door with a lazy salute and a sneer.

The door latched closed and Tarquin stood in the corner measuring his man. The light shone across him in parallel slits and the lamp added its ochre glow from above. It was already warm from the midday sun. Maaraw had but two seasons, 'hot' and 'hotter' he was told, and shade was a commodity more prized than silver. They had shade, but the air was still and fetid with oily smokes and human stinks. Unless a breeze found its way through the cracks in the wall it would only get worse.

And the flies were already gathering. Tarquin listened to the buzz in the rafters and watched Bruin.

"There was something about you," said Tarquin. "When I first saw you, I thought there was something, but it was all my tired mind."

"Nay," said Bruin, his voice thick and dry. He coughed. "Nay. I'm nothing. I'm one man."

"A killer," said Tarquin. "You may add Asay to your list of victims. You killed him as surely as if you drew the blade yourself."

Bruin coughed some more.

Tarquin sat down. "I think deep down you might be a good man. You mean well, but you're misguided. You don't understand. You've been led astray and become a menace to the order the holy prophet and his servants have blessed the worlds with. You are a threat to the continued peace of the worlds. Your removal is required. It's a culling."

Bruin cracked a smile across his blood-caked cheeks. "What peace?" he said. "Last I heard, your prophet and Brandon were about to plasma-purge Enskari."

"Another threat."

"A challenge to vacant ideas and dried-up men."

Tarquin wondered if he'd be able to get on a transport that night or whether he'd have to stay longer in Coebler. This was over.

He said, "You were Saved. You were among the elect. Your ancestors were chosen from the dying of Old Earth to live. You talk history but you have no gratitude, no loyalty, no sense of it."

"Slave ships and tyrants."

"You'd rather be dead?"

"I'd rather be among Jareth's people."

Tarquin laughed out loud. "What fanciful notions you do hold," he said. "You are a fool, Andre Bruin. You'd live on Tirgwenin? Among the primitives, starving and sad? You pine for the noble savage? It's a myth. I've seen them. They are a stupid race, weak and wretched. Living out of mud huts, poor as the worst Maarawan beggar – all of them. You talk of evolution and admire a devolved society. Savages, savages all."

"Don't be so sure."

"Oh, you've been there? I didn't know you traveled off-planet? How were the hotels?"

"I've never been there."

"You continue to disappoint me, Mr. Bruin. So much trouble for such a stupid man." He pulled his papers from his robes and found the page he was looking for. From his sleeve, he found a pencil. "You are a base criminal," he said. "You are condemned."

"There can be a just society," Bruin said. "You just have to imagine it. When enough of us do, it'll happen. I did. I do."

Tarquin looked up from his writing and said, "Who are you talking to?"

"The record."

Tarquin shook his head. "That's not what I'm writing. This document is a different thing entirely."

"I've made the record," he said. "The record will be there, with the other records. And you will be damned. Others may pick up the path where I have left off. I hope they do. It's that or we're done. You see, it's all about progress. I don't know where it goes, but I've taken it to this ending. I have walked as far as I'm able. There are wilds to claim beyond what I have seen, places I can't reach. I may have reclaimed some ancient paths, but from where I was, it is progress. Others will walk these roads again and they will come this far as I have taken them and then onward to the thickets and they'll cut through those and go beyond. To the future – guided by people like me."

"Nice speech," said Tarquin, "But you're wasting your breath. I'm not recording any of this and you won't get a chance to do it again."

"I'm speaking for the record and for the future. For the hope of inevitable change."

"Contradictory," said Tarquin. "Hope is uncertain. Inevitable is not."

"Hope that the inevitable change happens sooner than later." Bruin, broken and shackled, talking through shattered teeth with a torn tongue, still argued with him as if he could change the outcome, as if the seriousness of the situation was no more than a parlor game, a friendly debate, a newspaper interview.

"Andre Bruin," said High Purger Tarquin. "You killed peaceful people, robbed them of their goods, and fomented rebellion."

"I took action against injustice," said Bruin. "I freed human beings who were slaves."

The purger put down his pencil and looked at his prisoner. If there was fear in the man, he did not sense it. He saw resignation in his swollen face, a keenness in his eye, but heard disquieting confidence in his voice. Tarquin already decided, had started to make his pronouncement, but decided to play along a little longer. He'd never get out before dinner and it was mutton tonight. He'd stay for that. "You expected to free them all?" he said.

"Of course not," said Bruin.

"What did you hope for?"

"Critical mass," Bruin said. "I wanted to remind humanity of our better nature before it was too late. Before we ruin another world, another dozen. I don't know if we'll get another chance."

"You're talking of Old Earth again?"

"Aye."

"Insanity will not save you."

"I'm not insane."

"Do you see why it's so hard to take you seriously? You act like you were there, like you know all about what happened on Old Earth."

"I do."

That certainty again. That damn phrase. Flies buzzing in the room. The morning past noon, the noon beating down. The room getting hot.

"How?" said Tarquin. "Maaraw isn't famous for its history classes."

"I know about Earth the same way I came to know the truth. It was a moment of breakthrough, a memory of forgotten justice. I dreamed of a different way, a different order and I was rewarded."

Tarquin relaxed, recognizing familiar patterns. "You would not be the first false prophet I've executed."

"Nay," said Bruin. "I'd be your fifth. You murdered those two brothers on Lavland, the farmer on Claremond, and that witch on Temple. The farmer was insane, a parasite was in his skull. The others though…aye, I know about them. Like me, they each had a revelation."

It took a moment before Tarquin could speak. No one outside of the Court of Apostles could know so much about this.

"Tell me about your revelation," said Tarquin finally, his voice suddenly hoarse.

"It was like a psychic shout. A scream that resonated with vibrations that were always there, but I'd been deaf to. You know how your brain shuts out the view of your nose?"

"What?"

"You see your nose. Your eyes see your nose. It's right there on your face, how can you miss it? It's in the way of your vision. But it's distracting, so your brain conceals it. The vibrations are like that. We ignore them. They seem to be in the way of other things that seem more important at the time, but they're always there. Not knowing what to do with them, we shut them out, but they're always there. Once you start looking, you can sense them, like seeing your nose, but only if you look in the right place with the right eyes."

Tarquin swallowed, remembering the witch on Temple saying something similar to this. "You were a trader, a contract businessman."

"Mankind was my business," said Bruin, laughing.

"Aye, you were a slave trader?"

"Nay," said Bruin behind a wide grin. "Dickens again."

"The Old Earth author."

He nodded. "Slavery is wrong," he said. "It is unnecessary and cruel. We should have long outgrown it. We did once. Returning to it is like not seeing your nose. Nay, it's worse. It's putting on blinders, ignoring the truth, deliberately forgetting lessons we already learned. It's retrograde. It's willful selfish ignorance and dooms the species to extinction."

Tarquin said, "How did you know about those others?"

Bruin smiled, a bemused little smirk that would have received a heavy blow on any of Tarquin's previous interviews.

"High Purger Tarquin," he said, "cruel hand of a backward faith, you think I'm speaking in psychological or spiritual terms. I am not. What I know and what I see is as real as the light in this room. I have plugged into truth, like a telegraph line – a network that leads me to a library. A communication stream that connects all of enlightened humanity. The jewels of Coronam might be the worlds, but the luster is much humbler."

Tarquin's attention had been directed solely at his prisoner and this malicious web of lies, so he'd not noticed the infestation in the room. He became aware of it then, as if Bruin had increased its volume. The buzzing of insects was a din, and it rose and fell with Bruin's breathing. Tarquin turned around expecting to see a black cloud of flies upon some carrion in the corner, the blood spot in the mud perhaps, but he saw nothing.

"Above you, High Purger," said Andre Bruin.

He looked up.

And saw a ring of bees.

"Mankind killed itself on Old Earth," said Bruin. "We had paradise and we destroyed it. Nay, that is wrong. We did not. A few greedy selfish monsters did it and the rest of us were too weak and enslaved to stop it. The killers poisoned the air, polluted the seas, savaged man and beast alike."

Not a fly. Not a one. They were all bees. They circled above the table, a hundred of them flying counterclockwise, horizontal and true as if orbiting the hanging lamp as a star. "Why are they doing that?" he whispered.

"I'll say it again for you and for the record. We got another chance," said Bruin. "I don't know why. I don't see that far. I'm sure there are some who do, but I don't. You understand I can only access what it is I'm equipped for and enlightened to. I've barely scratched the surface. These bees are not mine. Three is the most I've ever mustered. These others are sent to me for strength."

"Sent?" said Tarquin. "By God?"

"Nay, purger. By my brothers and sisters. By your brothers and sisters."

"Mine?"

"How big is your family?"

"What?" Tarquin's head spun. The buzzing interfered with his thinking.

"Celibate you may be, but you would not let a child of yours suffer if you could stop it," said Bruin. "You would feed your brother if you could. Maybe your cousin, his wife. Their family. That's the key, brother Tarquin. We're all related. My family. Our family. Our species. Our universe."

Tarquin cowered beneath the bugs. He crossed himself and fell off his chair.

The buzzing was loud, louder than it had been, louder than it should be. Then he realized the sound was not sound at all. It was in his mind. It droned without him and within him. The bees were in his mind. The sound, the vibration, the noise of it.

The bees descended from the lamp and swarmed to Bruin. They orbited his head in a uniform band, a droning crown, a living halo.

Tarquin screamed. "My God!"

The door flew open and two guards rushed in. They stared at them wide-eyed and worried.

Tarquin raised his hand and pointed a shaking finger at Bruin. Bruin smiled back at him, a calm smile, forgiving. Beatific.

"Kill him!" Tarquin roared over the droning in his mind.

And the guards drew their knives.

CHAPTER TWENTY-FOUR

There is a decisive new urgency in preparations for the coming war. Timetables have been pushed up drastically. I do not know the reason for the sudden change, but I do know it's costly and desperate. This new pressure comes partly from Brandon's ministers, but also from Temple, from the prophet himself.
Decoded Missive from Lady Vanessa Possad of Hyrax to Sir Nolan Brett
20, First-Month, 938 NE

11, Fourth-Month, 938 NE – Vildeby, Enskari

Alpin Morgan sat in the anteroom of Kent Castle watching his hands shake, waiting to be called by the Second Ear of the queen. They shook a lot now, so much so that he'd begun to suspect that it was more than an emotional reaction, possibly a physical one. It was possible though. He might have had a stroke and not noticed. He didn't need to have had a stroke for this. His frustrations were enough to account for the spasms, enough and more. He felt the shaking rise up his arms to his shoulders, into his neck and jaw where he ground his teeth in helplessness.

He'd been waiting for an audience with the Second Ear all morning, enduring contemptuous stares from bodyguards in the wings and the condescending glances of nobles who were shown straight in. Beggars and peasants were led past him, some looking terrified while others like they'd just escaped a madhouse or a prison. He'd been granted an appointment but only after he'd mentioned Sommerled. He hated doing it, but had had no choice.

His appointment time had come and gone and many hours more. When asked if he wanted to reschedule, no excuse being offered for the delay, Morgan declined and said he'd wait for Sir Nolan, his business was pressing.

His trip from Tirgwenin back to Enskari had been a nightmare. The

Sebastian, slower than the *Hopewell*, had been caught by a storm before they'd reached the Kanluran Cloud. It'd set them back a week as they fought the solar storms hiding behind asteroids that melted before them. It had damaged the ship. They'd stopped at Freeport for a month's repair where much of the crew mutinied and joined privateers recruiting at the outpost to hunt Hyraxian silver ships.

Mutiny was heavy on Morgan's mind during the trip. He fretted and paced his small quarters until the carpet was bare. He wrote frantic missives to his supporters, wondering all the time how far the betrayal went. Most of his letters were to Sommerled. At Freeport Morgan learned the news that his patron had been given the Queen's Cross. This gave him new hope. Sir Ethan Sommerled was the hero of his people, the darling of the court. Once Sommerled learned of the terrible mutiny the Bucklers had suffered on their pilgrimage to Tirgwenin, he'd surely take action and see that things were righted quickly. Of course that bastard Upor would be called to account, but mostly and more importantly, ships would be sent to relieve his people – provisions and transportation to their proper destination.

These were the thoughts that eroded his health and troubled his mind to near insanity during the months the *Sebastian* traversed the endless expanses of space. Damaged sails and half crew, setback, storm, and malefaction each a plague that at every turn, delayed Morgan's arrival. Morgan felt each slow moment in his heart, remembering his family abandoned at Rodawnoc. Thoughts of his newborn granddaughter, Diane, born in the shade of the derelict palisade, drove him to near madness. He filled his journals with prayers and betrayals and had tomes of letters to send when he finally arrived at Enskari.

And of course, the ship could not dock at Vildeby. That port was overrun with warships and the lowly transport *Sebastian*, limping on half sail and broken batteries, made port in Patterson on Austen. It was not the city Morgan needed. Not even the right continent.

After traveling four months in space he endured another month on rail, and then had to wait again before he could meet with his benefactor. Fully five months after leaving all he loved on a hostile alien beach, Morgan met with Sir Ethan at an Enskari tavern to tell him what had happened.

Sir Ethan listened to the tale of tragedy, bad luck, and mutiny from beginning to end. Morgan told it in a rush, overeager to recite a part he'd over rehearsed for months. The story, nonetheless, took an hour and when he was done, Morgan took wine from Sommerled and drank it deep on an empty stomach.

"He put ye right where Hasin was?"

"Aye. In the very fort," said Morgan. "What was left of it anyway. The very place. The worst place."

The table fell silent. Morgan was spent. Sommerled weighed the terrible news.

"You are too late," said Sommerled after Morgan had drunk the glass dry and the effects were already in his head. "Upor beat you by a month. He's been to court and gossiped. He's painted you a fool and a coward. He's cozied up to Gael Aderyn. Aye, Admiral Aderyn. You will not go attacking his word."

A new coldness found its way into Morgan's mind. A strange thing because he could not imagine events turning worse than they already were, but here it was. "You doubt me?" he said.

"Nay, friend Alpin. I believe every syllable you have said. Our endeavor was undone. You and your people are gravely wronged. I just don't know what to do about it. The destruction of the colony is well and truly done."

He'd not weep, but Morgan was sorely tempted to do so. "Will you not speak with the queen?" he said.

"It is a tricky affair," said Sommerled. "My position is not as secure as I would have it. The court is fickle. No position is safe. Not mine, not the Ears'. Not even the queen herself."

"Nay?"

"And it is worse. You are a Buckler."

"As are you," said Morgan.

The captain gave him a stern look. "That kind of talk can do neither of us good. Connor and his Guard are more powerful than ever. There is no more expedient way to disappear than to go against him and his charge to maintain the Enskari Church."

"I'm sorry," said Morgan, his voice breaking.

"It's all right, friend. But know that things are not as they were when ye embarked. The Hyraxian threat grows worse by the day. I have been charged with defending the planet from invasion. This is where I must spend my efforts."

"You are not at court?"

"Nay, I have made enemies there," he said. "I am safer in space. And I am better in space. We're building ships. We'll defend this world."

Morgan sensed the patriotism that had made Sir Ethan the symbol of Enskari. His mind however, his heart, his hope, was not on Enskari but a savage world at the farthest expanse of reachable space.

"My family is marooned," he said. "In hostile territory. Without provision or hope of resupply."

"The resupply will find no one at Placid Bay?"

"Not a chance," said Morgan. "And they were underway before I landed."

"Pity."

"Aye."

A silence enshrouded the two. The walls of the tavern closed in a little tighter around Morgan and his mind. He watched his hands shake and felt his jaw tense. He dropped fingers below the table when Sommerled saw them.

"Can you aid me financially?" Morgan said.

"What do you need?"

"I need to outfit another ship. Make a resupply."

"I can get you some," he said. "But not from me."

"Oh?" he said.

"In fact," said Sommerled, "it would be best if our association came to an end now. Publicly at least."

"But it is your patent we're are striving to perfect."

"Aye," he said. "And that is noble and I know you will succeed, but times are what they are. I am not as fixed as I would be."

"But the patent—"

"Is not necessarily more important than our lives," he said. "Would not you send your Bucklers fifty kilometers inland to be free of Enskari?"

Morgan pursed his lips, looked down at his lap and nodded.

"As is right," said Sommerled. "Enskari is not perfect. I am working to help here, but I cannot sacrifice myself or my position for your colony. The court was happy to see us populate a distant planet with peoples they did not want. The feelings have not changed. Bucklers are heretics; the colony is an exile. They are outcasts. Criminals. Forbidden to return. You yourself are subject to arrest if found out. There'll be little sympathy for any this, particularly now when the very ground we would need to seed for sympathy has been so thoroughly salted by Upor and his accusations."

"You are the hero of Enskari and this is your colony."

"Associating the two will do no good."

"But the association is there. Could not the attack on the expedition be really an attack on you?"

"Of course it is," said Sommerled. "That is what I'm trying to say. There are forces arrayed against me – against us. They are formidable and subtle. I myself was nearly murdered in a duel but a month back. These are dangerous times. My enemies are many. I know some by name. Most are on Hyrax and Temple but there are some here too and I cannot let them beat me."

Morgan had visited this conversation so many times in the preceding months. His mind now reeled at the disjointedness of the reality of the moment versus his imaginings of it. Instead of justice and relief, hope and salvation, he was once again facing defeat and ruin. The shaking went up his back as if chill water ran down his shirt. In a hoarse half whisper, he said, "I will try to save my family."

"As you should, brother Morgan. I will give you what assistance I can, but you'll get nowhere going to court accusing Upor of mutiny. Wait, what of Bradshaw? Will he testify as to the mutiny?"

"Would that help?"

"Not in public at this point, but in private, maybe. With the queen, perhaps. But only if we know who is really responsible."

"Bradshaw took the *Sebastian* away. I don't know where he went. Perhaps for a routine cargo run. Perhaps to privateer. There was some talk of that."

"So he's likely a year gone, if he survives whatever he's doing. Neither journey is particularly safe at this point," said Sommerled. "We cannot assail Upor. He has cut you too low. As long as Upor is high, your reputation cannot rise."

"I don't care about Upor," he said. "Damn Enskari justice. I just need to save my family."

"Good," said Sommerled. "That is an achievable goal. And who knows, if you succeed there, we may still see justice for the other."

"Hope springs eternal."

"Listen, Morgan, what you have told me fills me with fear. It tells me that my enemies are more powerful and clever and ruthless than I could ever imagine. It tells me that they're willing to murder hundreds of people just to make me look bad."

"Surely it can't be just that?"

"What else is there?"

"Tirgwenin. The patent."

"Who wants it? Savage and far away. Worthless for all but exiles."

Morgan's brain was spinning. He knew all this, but felt like he'd forgotten it, as if all this knowledge had been knocked out of their cubby holes in his fear and panic. Putting the pieces back in place was a trial.

Sommerled said, "The patent is meaningless if we lose the war. If we win it, if I win it, I'll have patents aplenty, I'll be in a position here perhaps to see Bucklers safe here on Enskari."

"And if not?"

"If not, you'll take your people fifty kilometers into the interior and try your best."

"This is harsh."

"It is," said Sommerled. "I never like losing people – sailors, soldiers, friends. It is terrible thing, but it is a reality. I am sorry for the loss of your people."

"They are not lost yet."

Sommerled nodded. "Nay. Of course not."

"I need a ship and provisions."

"Aye." Sommerled sighed. "I can give you neither. My position will not allow it."

"But your patent—"

"Minister, you are confused. You must listen better. I am charged with the defense of Enskari. I cannot give you ships, for the effort needs them. I cannot give you provisions for the same reason. I cannot use my station to aid you at all."

"Nay—"

"But, as a private citizen, I can lend you money. I have some income from new estates. I can see to it that some are transferred to you. Then you may find a ship, provision it, sail to Tirgwenin and be with your family."

"You have so much?"

"Not so much," said Sommerled, "But you still have friends here too, do you not?"

"Aye, some."

"Then your path is clear," said the captain. "Good luck. Write to my office and keep me informed. We'll persevere."

Morgan looked into Sommerled's face, seeking mercy and help, but saw only determination. Calculation. He was a man used to sacrificing other men. Morgan was not that kind of man. Sommerled could cut losses and carry on. Strong leaders could do that. Morgan, for the first time in his life was happy he was not such a leader. He would have no soul.

The men stood and shook hands. Sommerled turned with a sharp click of his heels and left Morgan to his own devices.

★　　★　　★

Morgan could not let himself give in to despair, though it was hard. He was an old man. His best years were far behind him. He'd never thought to see this place again, never imagined he'd again be upon Enskari or in Vildeby or have need of money again. To underwrite this trip, he'd sold all he possessed, ancestral home and title, furniture, clothes, livestock – everything but what he carried aboard ships and was now marooned with his imperiled family on another planet. His physical resources were nonexistent. He was a pauper. The one thing he'd thought to trade on, his good name, was now also taken from him. Even his champion, Sir Ethan Sommerled, hero of the planet, the queen's own newly named Master of Defense, could not help him.

And yet he had to try.

His people waited for his help. His daughter, his granddaughter. Everyone.

He contacted his old acquaintances, sympathetic backers of the first expedition, Bucklers who were even then preparing to leave for Tirgwenin when he brought news of catastrophe.

Upon their charity he threw himself for food and shelter. They took him in as good Saved believers. Morgan told them of the mishaps, walking a careful line of optimism and despair, afraid of scaring them away while needing them to give up even more than they already had to save the planters.

"The colony is not lost," he told them. "It is only delayed. We need now a ship with provisions and a way to move everyone to their proper place in Placid Bay. See? It is but a slight delay." Morgan spoke with a feigned confidence, a lie he was confident God would forgive him for because he knew that by the month, by the day and hour, the planters at Rodawnoc were dying. He tried to tell himself they'd found food or made alliances with the natives, but then he'd remember Hasin and Upor and tears would tumble unbidden from his eyes. He sniffed them away and put on a smile, a confident lying grin, and he'd beg the funds for rescue, claiming all was well enough.

"We have barely enough food ourselves, Morgan. We are hounded and hunted and tormented for our beliefs."

"So much the more reason to emigrate," he said. "So much the more reason."

Things began to brighten. Though each moment was a struggle, every thought a dread of what was happening literally worlds away, Morgan found himself saying prayers of thankfulness. He was keenly aware of the irony when he mentioned among other blessings, the accursed Archbishop Connor, the queen's own purger, for without him, he was sure he'd not been able to raise a penny more for the endeavor.

By Second-Month Morgan had a ship, the *Oracle*, commanded by a gentleman captain, Sir John Kebra, who'd lost an arm in a fight with pirates off Lavland's reaches. And then the *Pitt*, an older ship, but strong and stout. Together they were about three quarters of the tonnage of the first expedition and Morgan set about filling them with provision and hope.

New settlers stepped forward to colonize with them. Some were bright-eyed eager youth looking for adventure and riches, while others were being driven off the planet by Connor's harassment and arrests. Several had pleaded in court for amnesty on the grounds that they were leaving the planet anyway. To save jail costs, the judge had ordered them exiled. Another ironic lucky strike: the court wanted the ship filled and gone as fast as Morgan did. Morgan wondered if there'd be any Bucklers left on Enskari at all when he left, any not in jail or dead that is.

Provisions were hard to come by and expensive. The whole of the planet was gripped in the fear of war and invasion. Morgan thought surely it would have abated after so much time, but the tensions had only ratcheted up. New stories of a great Hyraxian armada circulated like a miasma in every corner of the world. People began hoarding. Meanwhile, the military bought up all metals and supplies for a grand defense fleet commanded by Sir Ethan Sommerled, Master of Defense.

Even though Morgan kept himself furiously busy, traveling across the world meeting with distant associates, Bucklers and Saved alike begging for charity, the time limped by. Not a moment passed that he did not recall the marooned people on Tirgwenin and feared that when he finally reached them, there'd be nothing to save.

The gamble he and the colonists had taken to send him back alone had of course been countered, and countered most effectively. Every interview Morgan had on his quest for help was hampered by the rumors of his cowardice begun by Upor and spread through society like scandal. Morgan told again and again the careful tale explaining the situation. Careful to blame 'providence' and 'bad luck', he explained how he'd been chosen to return alone as the most able to arrange for relief. He left Upor out of it as much as possible. He left Sommerled out of it too. He put on his confident smile and pretended that his ruined reputation was a misunderstanding and not another assassination attempt.

After the longest winter of Alpin Morgan's life, the ships were ready to go. Captain Kebra declared a departure date of 12, Fourth-Month, 938, which was but a day shy of the anniversary of the previous expedition's departure and seven and half months after Morgan had left Rodawnoc.

On the tenth, however, two days before departure, the ships were seized by the Crown.

★　　★　　★

Morgan looked around Sir Nolan Brett's waiting room again and clenched his fists to still the trembling. He compared the anteroom to the many others like it he'd visited these last months, each time swallowing his unjust disgrace and begging for help. He told himself this was like all the rest. No, this was easier. He needed not money or supplies, but only a simple signature allowing Kebra's fleet to embark on the rescue mission. A telegraph note to the port authority and all would be well. He could be in an elevator en route to the *Oracle* within the hour.

He shifted in his chair and folded his hands to hide them. Outside he heard a clock chime but lost track of the count before it had finished. He knew all he needed to know. It was afternoon. It was late. It was getting later.

"Mr. Morgan?" said a young man to him.

"Aye?"

"I'm Jim Vandusen, Sir Nolan's assistant. He asked me if you—"

"I'm staying here until I see him," said Morgan with more force than he intended.

Vandusen tilted his head slightly in surprise.

Morgan said. "Sorry. I mean, I will wait. I can wait. I must see him. I have come so far. I am so close."

"My master asked me if you would come in now."

"Oh. Oh, aye. I am so embarrassed."

Vandusen gave him a tight little smile that was the best Morgan could hope for.

He offered the assistant his hand to shake, but Vandusen didn't take it, didn't notice. Morgan buried the trembling hands in his coat pockets.

"Follow me," Vandusen said as if Morgan didn't know where the door was by now. He'd only been watching people go through it all day.

"Sir Nolan, Second Ear of the queen, may I present Mr. Alpin Morgan, late of Tirgwenin, here to petition you."

Sir Nolan stood at his window overlooking the city of Vildeby. Alpin saw in the distance past the Reedy River, a car rising up the elevator thread, the very one he had hoped to be on this day. "Sit down," said the Ear.

Morgan stepped into the room behind a chair but didn't sit. He'd been sitting all day. Then he thought that it might not have been a politeness, but an order, and moved around the chair and sat.

"What can I do for you, Mr. Morgan?"

Morgan cleared his throat. "Sir, I thank you greatly and in humility for the opportunity to speak with you thus. I know how busy you must be and for me to—"

"I am busy, Mr. Morgan," Nolan said, turning to face him. "Pray, be to the point."

With the window light behind him, Morgan couldn't read the man's face but there was no confusion as to the temperament in his voice.

"I would have you grant a writ of release from service for the ships

Oracle and *Pitt*, the ships I have commissioned to relieve the colony on Tirgwenin."

The Ear paused and looked at Alpin for a long moment.

Not being able to see his face was unnerving but Morgan kept his chin up, facing the man, looking surely to where his eyes would be in the silhouetted figure, putting all the confidence in his demeanor he could. His hands were fixed in his lap.

"I'm confused," Nolan said after a moment. "You are Sir Ethan's man, are you not? Why not have him act for you? He could release your ships."

"It is true that he is our patron – meaning the colony, sir."

"Your colony of Bucklers."

Morgan had come to this interview in the hopes of saving his rescue mission, fearing the worst that he could be denied his petition, now he sensed that there was a terrible third possibility for the interview – his arrest and torture as a separatist from the Queen's Church of the Enskari Saved. His hands shook the more and he buried them deep in his pockets before raising his chin again, finding that it had fallen.

"The All Community Congregation of Ministers is the official title," said Morgan, "But you may call us Bucklers. But call us also Enskaran, patriots who'd journey so far to extend the realm."

"Outcasts," said the Ear. "Undesirables."

"Rightly suited thereby for the task at hand."

Morgan perceived the Ear nodding and when he turned to look at his assistant standing by the door, Morgan thought he saw a sliver of an appreciative smile.

"To answer your question, sir," continued Morgan, feeling a spark of hope at last. "Sir Ethan does not even know I am here."

"What? But you mentioned him in your request to see me."

"For past association," said Morgan. "He is still our patron, but you will understand that the Master of Defense has other things on his mind right now. He commands a new fleet, does he not?"

"Aye," said Nolan. "Ships of his own design. Do you know the *Merry*? They're like that."

"I don't, sir."

He grunted and shrugged. "Nay, of course not. Nevertheless, I think also that Sir Ethan would rather not be associated with you."

"We Bucklers were suited to the chore of the colony."

"Aye," said Nolan. "But I meant your reputation, Mr. Morgan. You are not well liked."

"I'll not deny that I am a Buckler," said Morgan. "But I will deny that I am a coward. The events on the journey to Tirgwenin and my – our people's – subsequent marooning are terrible. I was chosen to return to seek redress."

A thunderclap exploded out the window, startling Morgan and turning Nolan to look. Lighting strikes needled the horizon as far as they could see. Nets caught it and glowed with energy while auroras danced green over the smog layer.

"It can be beautiful at times, can't it?" mused the Ear.

"Aye," said Morgan. "To return to the matter, Sir Nolan. You must know the people on Tirgwenin are without provision, set alone in hostile lands, not where their relief is to find them."

"Upor—"

"Upor lies," said Morgan.

The Ear turned back to Morgan and his face fell again into shadow. He slid around his desk and sat down. "That is not my concern," said Nolan. "Upor might well be lying, though why he would do such a thing is beyond me."

"I doubt that," said Morgan and instantly regretted it.

The Ear cast another glance at his assistant in the back. What his reaction was, was of course unknown to Alpin Morgan. He knew not to turn around.

Morgan raised a trembling hand and wiped sweat from his forehead. "You are in a position to release the ships," he said. "You, or Sir Edward or Sir Gael."

"Or Sommerled."

"Nay, sir. He cannot."

"Cannot?"

"You knowest he cannot," said Morgan.

The Ear nodded. "Because if he did, he'd be helping separatists at the expense of the planet."

"That's how he must see it."

"And you expect me to see it otherwise?"

Morgan felt his jaw quiver. "Sir, my family is there. My daughter. My granddaughter. They are in terrible ways. I have moved heaven and earth to arrange relief for them. We were set to leave tomorrow, but my legally commissioned ships were seized yesterday. They are but two ships – unarmed, and the journey is a mission of mercy. Two hundred Saved abandoned and forlorn, as far from home as can be imagined. I can save them. I was going to save them. I would be saving them had we left but a few hours earlier. I need only one act of kindness from you and all is not lost. A tiny writ. We will remember you as our savior. I pray you sir, I pray you."

By the time he'd finished his plea, Alpin Morgan wept openly. Desperate tears rolled down his cheeks and off his chin. He didn't wipe them off, but kept his eyes on the man who could, with a flick of a pen, allow him to have a chance to save the colony and his family.

The Ear's face betrayed nothing.

"I pray you, sir," said Morgan, "As Enskaran, as Saved souls, children of the Unsettling, brother and friend, I pray you."

"You beg well," said Nolan.

"Lives are in the balance."

Sir Nolan rolled his neck on his shoulders. He said, "There is a war coming. Make no mistake about it. Prince Brandon has a mighty armada and it's destined to come here. It will come."

"These rumors have been circulating for years."

"It is no rumor, Mr. Morgan. Hyrax is coming to Enskari. Temple purgers gather for invasion. They come soon." Nolan paused and looked into some middle distance through the floor. "They're coming soon. They're in a hurry. Brandon is greedy, but the prophet is spooked."

"I don't understand."

Nolan looked at Morgan as if just remembering he was there. "Nay, of course not," he said. "All you need to know is that a mighty armada sails to destroy us. We are fighting for our lives."

"These are but two ships," said Morgan, not liking the sound of this. "It seems unfair to choose these two. There are hundreds of ships around Enskari that have not been seized. Traders arrive by the hour."

"I know the ships you speak of," he said. "The order to seize them crossed this very desk."

"Then it was you?"

"The *Oracle* and the *Pitt* are big ships, long-distance vessels, traders meant to stay out and weather Coronam's wrath. In short, Mr. Morgan, they are armored ships. It's much easier to arm an armored ship than to armor an armed one. We haven't the metal. They are needed. They will stay with the defense fleet."

"They are but two ships, fully stocked and ready to travel." The tears poured down his cheeks again. "Surely they cannot be of that much help."

"You think me unfair?"

"I'd not say so, sir."

Nolan smiled. "A diplomat at heart."

"Two ships...."

"I seek to save millions on this world, our culture, our queen. You seek to save a few score people who knew what dangers they were walking into and who by your own suspicions might well be dead already."

"Nay—" moaned Morgan, telling himself it wasn't true.

"If we survive, you can petition the courts for redress of your supplies, but I will not release the ships until the threat is past."

"It is as if the universe itself would destroy the colony," cried Morgan, raising his shaking hands to heaven. It was a terrible display, a complete failure of etiquette and manners, but he couldn't stop himself.

However, when Morgan turned his gaze back to Nolan, he saw something. There was something in the Ear's eye, something in the way he'd glanced to the unseen servant in the back of the room that suggested a horrible truth to Morgan.

He lowered his trembling hands and got up out of his chair. He bowed quickly to Nolan and then Vandusen, and walked swiftly out of the room.

In the hallway outside his office, Morgan caught his breath and rubbed his temples with shaking fingers. It was not the universe that had undone them. It was Nolan.

CHAPTER TWENTY-FIVE

It is not a question of leadership or hierarchy. Government is necessary. Some will lead, others will follow. That is instinctive and good. That is not the issue. The problem is greed, theft, and injustice perpetrated across generations of victims. It is the continuation of cruel dynasties built with stolen fortunes upon bloody foundations whose sole purpose becomes not the betterment of the species, but the protection of a privileged class. This class hoards resources beyond their use, and power beyond their wisdom.

I do not wish to create new dynasties. It's not about replacing them with us. It is about paradigms. It is about potential. It is about resource management and surplus. It's as simple as this: we naturally nurture our families. We need only recognize how big our family truly is.

Excerpt from Jareth's speech 'On Empathy' to the New World Envisionist Conference

New Cornell University, February 5, 2330

18, Fifth-Month, 938 – Rodawnoc, Tirgwenin

Dillon Dagney lay on his belly, looking under the wall into the forest, fearing for his sister.

He'd told her he wasn't hungry, that she didn't need to sneak out of the compound and hunt for food again. She didn't need to risk so much just for a few berries and mice. He'd be all right. But she wouldn't stay. Even when he begged her to stay, crying on her shoulder that it was too dangerous for her. The forest was dangerous, there were sparklers out there who would kill her if the beasts and the disease and the plants didn't. And what if she was discovered out of the compound without permission? Aguirre would beat her because he'd warned her once already and put her in the stocks the time after that. If he caught her again, she'd be whipped, left behind when the others left, or maybe even hanged. It was too dangerous.

"You'll be fine," she'd said.

"It's not me I'm worried about." He tried to think of words he could use to tell her, to remind her that they were all they had left. Mother dead on the ship over, father the first of the colony to die here, him by savage sparkler arrows, in the water, in the mud. Did she not remember? He tried to find words that he'd not tried before, words that would work this time when no others had ever worked before, but he didn't know where to look for those words.

"I'll be fine. I know the forest."

"The sparklers will kill you if they see you."

"Some might," she said before she caught herself. "No, silly. I'm okay. I know how things are. And don't call them that."

"But they do sparkle."

"Well…." She put her broken hand spade in her sack and tied it.

"Aguirre will hang you," he said. "Like he did Mr. Rusmus. He'll leave you hanging and no one will even be here to bury you."

"He won't catch me."

"He might!"

"Shhh," she said.

Dillon thought about yelling, of betraying his sister to save her, but he didn't dare.

"If Aguirre grabs me, I'll tell him I'm just doing the job we were brought here for. I was looking for natives – *sparklers*, to infect with disease."

"That's terrible," he said, wiping tears off his dirty face.

"Aye," she said and kissed him.

"Can we do that?"

"Infect them?"

"Uh-huh."

"Nay, not anymore. They've grown resistant, but Aguirre doesn't know that."

"How do you?"

She'd peeked out the door. It was as dark as the deepest part of the night. Only the rings cast pale reflected light over the island. Morning was still far away.

She said, "You stay in the hut until after everyone is up then you can go about your things." She kissed his forehead again, lingering a moment longer than usual. "I'll be back tomorrow morning. If anyone asks about me, you know what to do."

"Lie," he said.

"Aye."

"We might leave tomorrow."

"I'll be back in time."

"They might eat you."

That stopped her.

Since Morgan left, she'd turned sixteen; he'd turned nine. Neither marked their birthdays when they passed but happened upon them in the darkness of late-night conversation when, afraid and hungry, they huddled against the snow-blown winds with empty stomachs. He remembered that night months ago when they wished each other happy birthdays. It had been the only bright moment on an otherwise terrible day.

Mathew, the onetime assistant and Tirgwenian guide, had been kept under guard since he'd been attacked by Aguirre. He'd been tortured and starved. Everyone was starving, but he was made to suffer so much the more, as if it had been his fault the colony struggled. Pratt had argued for his release, to use the native to better their situation, but Aguirre, even then, had his supporters and made him stay bound.

For months they'd lived on beetles and bitter grass, the gum-scratching stalks from the marsh, the slugs they found under logs. Sometimes a bird would happen in, sometimes a shore party would find a fish, but mostly the months of winter and spring were a starving time.

The pox rose among them and slew many. Dillon recalled the day Diana, the newborn baby, died. It was terrible. The day after that, Daria, the baby's mother, died as well. Whether from the pox, starvation, or a broken heart, it didn't matter. Dead was dead and it was the way of things on Tirgwenin. Natives outside the walls shot arrows in at random, and anyone who dared go out was more likely to never return than come back with food. Except Millie, who moved in secret and never came back empty-handed.

As the colony disintegrated, a new horror arose. Aguirre seized control and claimed an edict from God. He claimed he spoke for the Almighty and claimed their trials were brought upon them by their own wickedness. "God has favorites," he told them. "God loves the righteous best."

And Aguirre selected who among the survivors were righteous and demanded that they be treated better than the others. A hierarchy began in complete opposition to the tenets of the Buckler faith. Dillon asked Millie about it, for even he knew what was happening was wrong and different from what the colony was supposed to be about.

"They're resorting to old forms," she said. "Old habits. Old errors." She was surprisingly calm about it.

"You should say something to them," said Dillon. "Remind them. We are all brothers and friends."

"Nay," said his sister. "We must be silent. There is danger in disagreement."

"Even when they're wrong?"

"Especially when they're wrong."

Millie had changed since coming to this planet. Dillon's sister's new caution and strange calm was more terrifying to him than anything else.

Aguirre and his select became nobles and the rest of the colony served them. When someone spoke against the new order, which grew increasingly unfair, that man was punished. Sometimes the punishment was severe. Sometimes he died from it – 'God's will'.

The food failed them and 'select' or not, all starved. Everyone suffered. Millie kept Dillon and herself fed better than most by sneaking into the forest and finding hortmal in the abandoned gardens. They were hungry, but thanks to her, they did not starve.

Aguirre many times picked on Millie at church services for her silent defiance. She kept her tongue but her eye was sharp and condemning, a thing she couldn't turn off, Dillon thought. Another frequent target was Pratt, who, though chosen as select, still tried to remain a Buckler and work for the survival of the entire colony. The most common prey of the venomous sermons, however, was the wild planet itself, its plague of natives who 'sparkled with the light of hell' and would need to be eradicated. The personification of this was Mathew, their hostage, their prisoner, their onetime support. After each sermon the erstwhile guide suffered new humiliation and torture – stones, burnings, insults, and of course starvation.

Millie visited him. She snuck into the hut and stayed long hours. Once she took Dillon. He was horrified by the man's condition and amazed at his demeanor. He'd not say the sparkler was happy, but neither was he the broken crying wreck he'd thought he'd see. Everyone had seen the public beatings, the torture, heard the whippings, and smelled the fires. Dillon wanted to die just knowing about it and yet Mathew was strangely content with his lot. Even that day he visited him, his little hut filled with bees, swirling around the space like dust devils, their droning at once soothing and terrible, Mathew was serene.

Millie had a bee too. Sometimes she had a couple. Sometimes more. Dillon wanted a bee, and had asked Millie for one, but she said she couldn't give them. They had to come themselves.

The day they'd remembered their birthdays was the day Mathew died. After church, Minister Aguirre took his friends to the hut for their daily routine of pain on the man and found him gone. Instead of bees, flies hovered over him.

"Should we bury him?" someone asked.

"Nay. He was not human. He was an animal. Butcher him. We'll have a feast."

"What?"

"You heard me," Aguirre said.

"Brother Aguirre," said Pratt. "You go too far."

"He's an animal. Men eat animals. He's beneath us. Cook him."

That was the first. That night the fort was filled with the sweet smell of cooking flesh. Millie would not partake of any but to Dillon's surprise she did not order him to stay away.

"It's just meat now," she told him, her voice breaking, a tear rolling down her cheek. "It's all right if you want some."

"I'm not hungry," he said.

She hugged him and they hid in their hut during the feast and talked about birthdays.

The next week Aguirre proclaimed that God had chosen some of them to feed the others. Aguirre allowed cannibalism was the new law. The decision of who would feed whom was left to God, but when Pratt stood up and publicly accused Aguirre of madness, he was arrested, tried, and executed. After hanging the three days of his sentence, he was cut from the gallows and the colony fed upon him.

Millie and Dillon didn't leave the hut.

The weather broke into springtime. Deaths from exposure diminished while executions increased.

When suspicion fell on the Dagneys for their insolence, Millie began to attend the feasts and took plates of food and disappeared with them. Dillon watched her bury her portions in the ground. Dillon, to his shame, ate sometimes. The manna-root was so terrible and he was so hungry. Millie never chided him for it.

The colony was down to seven and forty Saved. One hundred five and twenty had set out. Diane had added one, only to die later. They were a third of what they could have been and so Aguirre declared that it was time to move into the interior.

Fifty kilometers as planned. God had told him that it was safe, that the unclean had been purged and it was now time to make the city of God on Tirgwenin. In the coming days they would venture out of the fort. On their way they'd hunt for food, surviving on sparkler meat until God told them to stop.

Shambling dirty people – starving, scurvy-ridden and weak – milled around the camp collecting what few belongings they dared carry away. Many buried their things in the ground, making little graves of the precious things that they had brought with them from Enskari. Alpin Morgan's gear was all buried, his paintings and chests along with Daria's things. Diane's cradle. Everything they couldn't carry was to be burned or buried. Dillon didn't know why, but Aguirre had said it must be so. Therefore, weak as they were, they dug holes or burned the last of their lives in a central fire, standing around, watching it burn.

That's when Millie decided she'd make one last trip out of the fort.

It was for food. She'd gone for food. She'd slipped out the hut door in the darkness and disappeared. Dillon retreated to his bed and wrapped his blankets around himself. He shook the rest of the night, not from the cold but for fear.

When the sun came up and she wasn't back, he went to the wall behind their hut and lay down in the little hole she'd dug under it and waited for his sister.

He tried not to be sad. Being sad didn't help. But he was worried. Millie was gone and time was short. She could get lost in the forest or be killed like so many of the others. It was daylight now and Aguirre could catch her and kill her when she came back. Then Dillon would be alone with no one to help him make the trek inland.

Aguirre had told them it would take a week to reach their destination, maybe longer. The distance was nothing. Healthy people could walk it in a day on roads, but of course there were no roads and they were not healthy. They were in hostile territory and had no stated destination. They'd move as a group for safety, cross the water at low tide and be on the mainland. They'd travel at the pace of the slowest of them.

All the food the colony had left was packed up to be doled out by the select. All the food the colony had, was, of course, human meat and Millie had gone to fetch them something else.

"What are you doing, little Master Dagney?"

Aguirre stood behind Dillon with two of his select, Johnson and Mylton. The selects were easy to identify; they were healthier than the non-selects. Millie said they also smelled of rot, but Dillon had never sensed that, only seen their muscles beneath their rags compared to the bones of the others. Johnson and Mylton were Aguirre's favorites. They were the ones who arrested dissenters and punished them most often.

"I'm looking for sparklers," said Dillon. "Keeping watch."

"And where is your fair sister?" Aguirre's broken-toothed smile sent a chill down Dillon's back.

"She's collecting what we shall take."

"She is not in the hut."

"She may have gone to the privy. She is not well."

"Oh," said Aguirre, a positive brightness in his face.

He stepped to the wall and peered out between posts. Johnson and Mylton stayed back watching Dillon with cold menacing eyes.

"She'd not be outside in the forest, would she?"

"I think she's in the privy," said Dillon.

Looking through the wall, Aguirre said, "I liked your father, little Master Dagney. I feel somewhat obliged to see your family through this hardship."

"I'd think you'd want everyone to make it."

It was Millie.

She stood a few steps behind them near their hut. Johnson and Mylton jumped when she spoke. Aguirre turned around slowly as if he'd expected her to appear thus. Dillon swallowed a dry throat and noticed fresh mud on her knees.

Aguirre smiled his broken smile for her. "Where have you been?"

"Preparing for the evacuation, Minister Aguirre." Though not in her voice, there was defiance in her eyes, a challenge in her chin. Her color was as good as the selects', perhaps better. All of these things were dangerous. Dillon swallowed again and coughed.

"Your knees are muddied."

"I've been burying treasures," she said. Sharp eyes.

Aguirre's smile curled a little. "We leave at the tide," he said.

"Tomorrow then?"

"Aye. We'll not wait on you."

"Nay."

Aguirre and his men strolled away.

Dillon got up from his hole and watched them go. "How'd you get back in?"

"The hole by the privy."

"I almost sent them there looking for you."

"I'd have been all right." She stared after Aguirre and his men.

"What is it?" said Dillon. She had that look on her face, that resolved expression that would get her into trouble. This one however was tinged with worry and fear.

"It's nothing," she said unconvincingly. "Get your things together."

"I'm ready. Most everyone is."

"Fine." Her expression the same.

"Did you get us anything to eat?"

"Aye, but I left it in the forest. I'll fetch it later. Leave room in your sack for it."

"How much room?" He thought of his books and his father's boots he was nearly big enough to wear.

"Not much," she said.

Most of the colony went to bed early that night, but Millie stayed out late. Dillon knew she had to collect her forest findings, but she was gone much too long for just that. From between the slats of his hut he could see the central fire. It was being tended all night. The guards were on late alert and he assumed some people were like him, too worried to sleep. Several times Dillon thought he saw his sister's shadow cross in front of that fire moving between the huts like a cat hunting prey. He tried to stay up to ask her what she'd been doing, but fell asleep before she returned.

When he woke up, she was already dressed, or maybe still dressed from the night before. She offered him a bowl of berries with a bright smile that was as good as sunshine.

He took the cup, reached inside and gasped. "Honey?" he said.

"Aye."

He scooped the red berries and honey into his mouth with two fingers, pausing between bites to suck the sweetness clean from his hands. Millie watched him in the early gray light.

"Aren't you having any?"

"I've eaten."

The thick sweet honey and tart berries was the best meal he'd had since arriving on the planet and Dillon was dizzy with excitement for it. Millie watched him eat as if taking nourishment from the sight. When he was done licking the bowl, he said. "Have you slept?"

"A little. Enough," she said. "Now finish up. We have a big day today."

Outside the sounds of the rousing camp were clear and cluttered. Mylton poked his head in their hut after a while to make sure they were awake. He didn't knock.

"Come or be left," he said.

"Aye," said Millie.

He looked at her hard before leaving.

"Aguirre said he liked Father. What do they have against you exactly? Against us?"

"Nothing new, I hope." She put wrapped bundles of roots and berries in her sack and a jar of tawny honey in Dillon's. "They sense we're different," she said. "But I've been quiet since Dad died so they couldn't do anything about it."

"They put you in the stocks."

"That was nothing," she said. "If I had spoken my mind more often, I'm sure they'd have found reason to do something really terrible to me. Some blame me for the marooning. Some think I did something with a crew member that led to all this."

"They said that?"

"Nay. Not to me, but they do. I overhear things."

"They killed Mr. Lawrence for less."

"I'm lucky," she said. "I'm a girl. Not many of us left. I suspect that has much to do with it."

"You're scaring me."

"Sorry," she said. "It'll soon be over."

"How?"

She smiled. "Come on."

They joined the rest of the colony in the middle of the palisade. Aguirre and his selects were standing by the gate watching everyone assemble.

When they were all together and accounted for, Aguirre spoke. "God has chosen us to defeat this world," he said, "to conquer it. Soon these hard days will be behind us and we'll live in the light of the Lord in eternal wealth and comfort."

"Why are we leaving this place?" said Dillon. He meant to say it to Millie only, but in the silence after the announcement it carried.

Aguirre put on his smile. "Why are we leaving? Because we must," he said.

Dillon shook his head, not understanding. He looked up at his sister, who kept her eyes on Aguirre.

The de facto governor looked out at his people. "Ye are weak, I know. Ye have forgotten the necessity. We spoke of this. Morgan has failed. It is apparent. We have no relief coming from off-planet. The only thing that'll come from the sea will be enemies – Hyraxian pirates and Enskari killers. The prophet's own purgers. We are the chosen of God. We. Why else would God test us so?"

"Amen," said a few of the others, selects mostly.

"It was always the plan to move inland," said Millie to Dillon, but loud enough for all to hear. "We just haven't been able to go before now for the weather."

"But shouldn't we stay here where we know it's safe?"

"There's no food," she said. "We have to go."

"It was the devil who told us to stay here, Master Dagney, through a sparkler heathen. It was a trick, a trap to starve us. We have endured the trials, now it is time to go."

"I'm afraid." Dillon spoke quietly this time so only his sister could hear.

"It'll be okay," said Millie. "We really have to. There is no more food here."

A bee circled her head, weaving figure eights and hovering over her bonnet, its soft droning a calming purr.

After a hymn and a prayer, Aguirre led the people out of the fort.

Just a hundred meters away, Dillon paused to look back at the fort. It was so small and vulnerable. A strange assemblage of rotting wood, windblown and bent, taking up space in a thicket of gnarled trees. On one of the posts someone had carved a word. Dillon read but couldn't make sense of it.

"What's Pemioc?" he said quietly.

Millie answered. "The place Aguirre thinks he's going."

"What is it?"

"A native village. The biggest around here."

The bee swooped and landed above her ear in her bonnet. She didn't react.

"It's fifty kilometers away?"

"More than that. Days and days by river." She thought for a moment and then said, "Straight from here, I'd say it's about one hundred, two and twenty kilometers."

He was about to ask her how she knew this when several selects turned and glared at them. They'd been speaking in hushed whispers, unintelligible to anyone but themselves, but still louder than the silence the others needed.

They lowered their eyes and fell in line.

The colonists shuffled forward like silent sheep, their eyes darting to the trees and dunes as if the landscape itself would rise up and strike them. The crossed the channel to the mainland and walked along the trails that had not been trod for over half a year for fear of being murdered on them.

They walked for hours, slowly, methodically, as quietly as they could. They stopped for water and a short rest and then went on again, slower but quiet as before. At nightfall, they stopped to rest.

They could have been a hundred kilometers from the fort or five. There was no telling. Dillon thought to ask Millie, but she'd already retreated under a tree to make a nest for them.

The selects distributed food to the people, portions appropriate for their class and station. Dillon and his sister didn't even approach, knowing there'd be none for them.

They made no fires, not little ones to warm the meat and themselves, not a big one to frighten away the animals. Protection that night was by select guards who picketed the place with small arms, coil muskets, and crossbows. They looked inward at the colonists as much as outward at the land to make sure all was quiet.

Millie and Dillon secretly ate their own provisions, pounded hortmal, dried grubs, berries, and dollops of honey in water. They ate in silence, watching the pale faces of the other dirty terrified planters shine in the ringlight like phantom heads above their dark clothes, the glint of metal in their hands, jumping at crickets and breezes.

Dillon fell asleep before Millie, who, like the guards, watched equally without the camp and within. When he woke up the next morning, cold and dewy wet, Millie was already up or perhaps hadn't slept at all.

While the sky was still but gray and no amber rays from Coronam had yet touched the place, Aguirre and his selects stood them all and marched them deeper inland.

For days it was like that. March, eat, sleep, march. The going was slow – so slow. They stopped frequently to rest, to refill their canteens from puddles and streams, to halt and listen to the forest about them, wide-eyed and jumpy, and then with a wave of Aguirre's hand and a spread of his stained and broken smile to start off again.

As they moved inland, the trees became much taller and sparser than they'd been on the coast. Taught to know something of trees from his father, Dillon was surprised to find few saplings. In fact, the ground was surprisingly bare of undergrowth. It was mostly grasses and ferns but also a few flowery vines and prickly shrubs with thick knobby branches that were easy to avoid. It made for easy walking. A horse would have no problem running through the forest, nor a steam cart at full speed between the trunks. The trees were spaced, enormous, and tall, their branches high above them, forming a leafy canopy. Wind would ruffle the leaves and make light fall between them like splashing pools of gold in the shade. The forest had a look of a columned cathedral more than any forest Dillon remembered from Enskari.

Amongst these trees, almost as if by design, were oases of wild places where plants grew wild and thick. In those places, Millie told him, one could find hortmal, gumbnut, berries, and other foods. "They're not jungles. They're gardens," she said.

"Then what is all this?"

"I'm not sure," she said. Then after thinking for a moment, she added, "Roads and hunting lands."

"I see no road."

"The keepers of it have moved on," she said. "Or died. It's growing wild. That's why the grass is so high."

"Don't the animals eat it?"

"Nay. Famine is come. The animals are eaten or gone."

Millie stayed close to Dillon, but occasionally, at rests, would leave him to go and sit with certain of the colonists. The nice ones, as Dillon thought of them. None of the selects. There was Mr. Berrye and his son Ben, John Tydway, the widow Lawrence, Mrs. Pierce, Emme Mirrioth, and John Hemmington. To these folks, Millie spoke in whispers and in secret.

One night after mealtime, Aguirre noticed her talking to Mr. Hemmington.

"What are ye speaking of?" he asked, marching over with a perk in his step not even the other selects could match. He stood over Millie and the starving man and glared at them, his fingers thrumming on the butt of his pistol.

Even in the near darkness, Dillon saw Hemmington's face blanch.

Millie spoke. "We're reminiscing about our old lives on Enskari," she said. "We were neighbors in Vildeby."

"I'd think that conversation would be long spent," Aguirre said. "No need to think on such things as that. They're as useless here as daydreams. Concentrate on surviving. We'll need you in the new place."

"Aye," said Hemmington.

The next morning Mylton, Aguirre's own bodyguard, was found dead. He was found riddled with arrows, a dozen of them – short, barbed, and poisoned, protruding from all angles. Just like Millie's father. It had happened only thirty meters from the camp near the river that the band had used for toilet. No one had heard a thing all night. Emme Mirrioth had found the body at dawn and screamed them awake.

"They didn't take his gun," someone said.

"Of course not," said Aguirre. "The heathens don't know what it is. But by God, we'll show the next one what they do!"

Dillon gripped Millie's hand and shook with fear. His sister gave him a squeeze and a loving understanding smile that almost calmed him.

"How is it you are not afraid, sister?" he said.

"Of what?"

"Sparklers."

"Stop calling them that," she said. "Unless you mean it with respect."

"But they killed one of us."

"Aye."

Like the others, Millie scanned the forest, looking for enemies, but on her face there was not the fear so plainly etched on the others. Instead she had a certain determination and strength. Dillon was not the only one to see this. Dillon noticed that many of the planters watched his sister. At first it was only the ones she'd talked to. Emme Mirrioth and Mr. Hemmington. Then others. Then finally, the ones who she hadn't talked to noticed everyone looking at her and looked there as well.

Millie said, "I am afraid, brother."

"But not of the spar— The people here?"

"Oh, I am," she said. "But I understand them better."

"Better than what?"

"Better than us."

"What's going on here?" said Aguirre. "Why is everyone looking at Miss Dagney?"

The looks grew urgent among the watchers, particularly among the ones she had spoken to.

Ignoring Aguirre, Millie led Dillon by the hand to the creek. She helped him cross before bending down and taking a drink. When she looked up, she took a deep breath and then climbed atop a fallen tree.

The morning light glowed directly on her as the sun rose. There was a chill in the air and her breath came in quick puffs. These clouds hovered before her, but were pierced and broken through by circling bees.

She raised a hand to draw everyone's attention. The bees, three or four of them, rose above her head. They were small and Dillon didn't think anyone across the creek had even noticed them.

Millie cleared her throat and swallowed. "Those of you who want to live, come with me now," she said. "This is where we must break company."

The people she'd spoken to threw sidelong glances at the ones she hadn't. Those others looked at Millie as though she'd just sprouted wings and called them all to fly.

Aguirre was the first to speak. "What? Who do you think you are? What is this treason?"

"We're beyond Rodawnoc," she said, not to Aguirre but to everyone. "We've crossed into inhabited lands. The peoples here are strong and ready. And they are many. We are not half a hundred. They are millions across the entire planet. And they all know we are here."

"The girl's babbling. A correction is needed." Aguirre turned to his men. "Johnson, get her down and bind her. We'll drag her a ways until she comes right or we'll leave her to the savages."

"Leave me," she said. "And the others who would come with me."

Aguirre looked at the others and must have sensed the mutiny.

"Your treason has spread."

"We were on the right track, we Bucklers, but not here. We were right to flee our world but we were wrong to bring so much of it with us. For that they'll not accept us. They cannot. They should not. They'll not suffer us because we are backward and dangerous."

"Who've you been talking to, girl?"

Here Millie smiled. It was a strange knowing smile unlike anything Dillon had ever seen her wear before. It was at once wonderful and sad. Determined and resigned. It didn't waver and she didn't flinch when Aguirre raised his pistol at her.

"What must we do?" It was Mr. Berrye, with his son, Ben. They'd moved halfway into the stream and stared up at her as if she spoke from a pulpit.

"If we come willingly and openly, they may accept us on their terms. There is bad history. We may not overcome it. I wish I could promise you they would accept us. I wish I knew for sure, but I don't. I believe they might. I believe they'll recognize us as family. We are not so unalike. Not all of us need bees if we are willing to contribute. A desire to live and be useful should be enough."

"Satan's in you!" Aguirre fired his pistol.

Dillon screamed.

Millie didn't flinch. Her warm expression remained in place. The bees continued their circles.

The bullet missed, landing in the tree behind and splintering a bough into shards.

"Come now," Millie said. "Come across the stream to me and we will seek our Tirgwenian family and ask for help."

Aguirre stood with his gun still raised, outstretched and pointing at

Millie. With no shot and no charge it was an impotent gesture, but spoke of his rage when it began to shake in his unsteady hand.

A dozen people crossed the stream to join Millie on the other side. Among a handful of others came all the folks Millie had talked to save for John Tydway. None of the selects moved. One of the men, Richard Tomkins, who had been on guard duty when all this had begun and still held a charged musket, splashed across the water and faced Aguirre from the other side.

Tomkins adjusted his coilgun in the crook of his arm to point roughly where Aguirre stood and kept his eyes on their leader.

Aguirre looked at Tomkins and lowered his gun.

"Ye mutinous bastards! Go die in the wilderness," Aguirre said. "God will punish ye all. Ye are not worthy. Ye never were. Good riddance. If we see you again, we'll eat you."

Aguirre turned and marched back to camp. After a moment most of the others followed him. Mylton's dead body lay forgotten on the far bank.

Ms. Pierce said to no one in particular, "I left my things, my blankets and—"

"Leave them," said Millie. "Let's go. Before he changes his mind."

His chin trembling, Dillon looked up at his sister and said, "Where are we going?"

Millie took his hand and led him away. "To Bost and Lahgassi," she said. "To Pemioc."

CHAPTER TWENTY-SIX

And he shall take the two goats, and present them before the Lord at the door of the tabernacle of the congregation. And Aaron shall cast lots upon the two goats; one lot for the Lord, and the other lot for the scapegoat.
Leviticus 16:7-8

20, Fifth-Month, 938 NE – aboard Brandon's Blade, *Hyraxian Armada, 50 hours from Enskari*

Admiral Clelland was arguably the most hated man in the system but surely the most reviled on Enskari. He was hated more than Eren VIII, prophet on Temple, who'd ordered the assassination of their queen and raised an army of purgers to bring that world back to orthodoxy through torture and execution. Clelland was hated more than even his master, Prince Brandon, leader of the House Drust, sovereign of Hyrax, who poured the fortune of four worlds into the destruction of one, bent to subdue Enskari and conquer the system. These men were feared, but in the streets of Vildeby, in the shipping lanes between planets, it was Clelland's name that was spat with venom, and it was always linked with the *Pempkin*.

To his mind he'd done nothing wrong. Pirates were to be executed. The *Pempkin* had raided Hyraxian merchants and even harassed a corvette. When, as a captain, Clelland subdued it, he'd acted lawfully. He could have kept the crew, transported them back to Hyrax, and had them die slowly in prison cells or be hanged. True, they might have been ransomed or they might have escaped, but they would surely have been tortured. Was their fate so cruel? He could have hanged them himself from the top deck where the gravity would break their necks or lined them all up against a bulkhead and shot them with coilguns and crossbows. That would have been lawful and the same as the Enskari had done to them. Death was death. Dead was dead. The uproar amused him. It made so little sense. To his thinking still, he'd acted with expediency and resolve. Perhaps even mercy. He'd spaced the crew. He'd put them all in an airlock and opened the outer door. Dead and gone. Simple, elegant, effective, and yet what a row it had stirred. His own crew had nearly mutinied, his commanders had been horrified, the office of the prophet had voiced concern. Brandon didn't know whether to try him for war crimes, turn him over to the purgers, or promote him. In the end, he'd been promoted. He was the admiral of the armada. He'd been put in charge to subdue a planet of apostates, to be the hand that would unite the system. A noble task, the glory of which would eclipse any lingering stories about certain acts carried out against pirates in deep space.

He stood on the bridge of *Brandon's Blade*, the flagship man-o-war, and watched his fleet heading toward Enskari. Nothing in Saved history could compare to what he saw out his window. Four hundred ships armed and manned, soldiers, sailors and priests – war machines to subjugate a planet and overthrow a damned upstart woman from the throne. The armada would unify the system under a single church and for the first time, a single emperor. The Saved would be saved. The apostates punished and returned. A single voice to rule the worlds. His mission was holy, his weapons unstoppable, his fleet undefeatable.

"It's an amazing view."

Clelland turned to see High Purger Tarquin standing beside him. He was the highest-ranking official from Temple in the armada. He would oversee the purging of the planet after the Hyraxians subdued it.

"Your Eminence," said the admiral with a bow.

"Admiral."

Clelland cleared his throat. "I'm honored to have you here," he said. Clelland was not easily intimidated, but Tarquin had a reputation that rivaled his own, and unlike his, was probably understated and truly deserved. He was two and thirty, he knew. Younger than the admiral by seven years. His black-and-red checkered sash marked him as the disciplinary arm of the church, his crest and collar showed him to be on the prophet's own business. He was a man who kept to himself, betraying little in his eyes, and yet Clelland sensed a certain anxiety about him now.

Tarquin stared out the rotating window at the gleaming ships arrayed without.

Clelland tried to see them as what the minister might. Ignoring formation and tack, sail angle and firing arcs, he saw bright dots of gold and silver, lead, platinum, and crystal plate, more metal off-world than on, he thought. Sparkling ships as far as he could see, a constellation of warships, and in the far distance, the shining orb of Enskari, their waiting target.

"Looks like overkill," said the purger after a moment.

"Perhaps," said Clelland. "But it makes an argument. Enskari will probably surrender before we're even in orbit."

"Nay, they won't."

"Why do they say that?"

"Would you?" Tarquin's gaze stayed outward.

Clelland said, "I'm not your average sailor, High Purger. Most are not as loyal. Most would rather – not fight."

"You mean most would rather live."

"Aye."

Tarquin nodded.

"Bogey in Q-10 is not a friendly. Repeat – is not a friendly," announced the communications officer behind them.

Clelland turned to the officer. Tarquin remained watching the sky. Coronam crossed the window at the corner and filled the room with bronze-tinted light.

"Who calls the bogey?" said Clelland.

The officer consulted a chart on the wall. "Aye, let's see. Uhm, seven, three and twenty…that would be the *Deaver*, sir."

"The *Deaver*?"

"Aye, sir."

"That's but one squadron over. Verify."

They'd first met the enemy but eighty hours past Lavland. It was a small force, a dozen ships meant to delay and weaken them. Twelve ships, an even dozen, nibbling at their flanks. For three hours they hurled long-distance shots into the grouping, crippling five ships and wounding two and twenty, hitting about fifty.

Then they came too close, perhaps seeking to save ammunition after so many misses, or possibly, and more likely, to use their plasma cannons up close. In any event, at the fourth hour, they crossed the arcs of the man-o-wars and at distances where the enemy had hit one out of ten shots, four broadsides struck for eight of ten. Six ships, four broadsides, ten rails to a side. Each shot five tons. It had averaged a hundred tons per ship. In an instant, the twelve ships were flying debris. Every heretical soul aboard them dead from a single order.

Since then, they'd seen few ships and those far at their periphery. Enskari scouts would fly by at full burn, weaving and jerking at maximum distance, their plasma trails a zigzag of fuel scar against the blackness. They'd take a shot, maybe two, into the densest center of their formation and then run full burn for home, Hyraxian railshot chasing them out of sight.

The communications officer tapped a signal on his relay. A moment later a clicking indicated a response.

"Verified," he said.

"Dammit." Clelland took a moment to orient himself and then he walked to the back of the deck to a periscope. Tarquin kept watch out the window.

"Sir?" said the communications officer. "Should we alert the fleet?"

"Not yet." He pulled down a viewer for one of the stationary telescopes. He spun the wheels and peered in. "How'd it get so close? Right among us?"

"Don't know, sir. Shall I ask?"

"Nay, you idiot," said Clelland. "Call the captain."

"Aye, Admiral."

"Warm up the guns and give me coordinates."

As the communications officer relayed the information, Clelland searched the sky for the rogue ship. They were still days from Enskari and already this had happened.

From the beginning this had been his greatest fear, the weakness of a fleet this large: an enemy ship getting amongst them, turning their own firepower against themselves or worse, suiciding into a man-of-war. The complexity of managing so many ships would be chaos when the battle commenced in earnest. Inter-ship communication was tricky at best – focused light signals across vast distances. Compound that a hundredfold for four hundred ships and add enemy vessels signaling to each other or filling the void with noise to confuse the signalmen. The armada would most likely have to rely on standing orders and prepared battle plans with minimal inter-ship co-operation or adjustment. But Clelland wasn't worried. They were so many and they were so strong.

The big ships were the terror of the sky, more firepower than a dozen battleships. They might be slow and unwieldy, but when ranged and angled, a single one could decimate an entire formation with volleys of railshot. Once in low orbit over Enskari they'd rain hell upon planetside cities.

The Enskari had nothing like them. No one did. The man-o-wars were the achievement of the age and Clelland didn't plan on losing a single one of his twenty to a sneaky scout who'd passed their pickets.

"Tactical," called Clelland.

"Aye, sir," said the officer.

"Do you have him?"

"Aye, sir. Q-10, two and seventy degrees. Tacking into us."

"Guns ready?"

"Admiral?" Clelland recognized the captain's voice. Technically, this was his ship.

"Hello Sissard," said Clelland, turning wheels on the telescope. "Bogey. Got in really close."

"How?"

"That's what we'd like to know," he said.

"Gunnery Captain, take the mast," said Sissard. "We'll capture them."

"Nay," said Clelland. "Too fine a shot."

"We have the finest—"

"I'm sure you do, Captain. But a missed shot could easily hit one of ours at this range. Why do you think no one's fired at him yet? Crossfire."

Sissard cleared his throat. "Aye. Orders?" That was it. Having two commanders on a bridge was always tricky. Technically, Clelland was in charge of the armada, but Sissard ran this ship. Clelland knew the strain he was putting on Sissard just being there. He didn't want to step on toes, but needs must, and Sissard had given him command by asking for orders.

"Give me a firing solution for the hull. Mid mass. Five guns. No more."

"Aye, sir," came the gunnery captain's response.

"No prisoners?" said Sissard.

"Not my style." Clelland watched Sissard's face go white, recalling his reputation. "Captain." Clelland stepped back and offered Sissard the telescope.

Sissard peered in. "Damn," he said. "It's one of Sommerled's damn ships. How'd no one notice it?"

"I'm guessing it came out of the sun," said Clelland. "The angle would be right."

"Solution plotted," said the gunner.

Sissard made to give the command, but hesitated and looked at Clelland.

"Check it," the admiral ordered. "He's between us and the *Morrell*." The *Morell* was nearly as big as they were, another man-o-war. "I'd rather not scratch her paint." If there was one ship that could destroy a man-o-war, it was another man-o-war.

"Target has changed course," said the gunnery captain. "He knows he's spotted."

"They're firing," announced the communications officer.

"On us?"

"Aye, sir."

Clelland smiled. "Good. It might've hurt somebody otherwise."

The bridge crew chuckled, a nervous laugh.

The round hit and reverberated like a distant thunder shot.

Sissard beamed. Not only were the new man-o-wars the best armed ships ever to have been made by men, they were also the best armored. They had over thirty meters of armor. The flagship, *Brandon's Blade*, their ship, had six and forty meters of ablative metal. It would require a miracle to threaten their ship. Of course they could be flanked from behind, their mast and sails were vulnerable, but the bulk of the ship was an anvil. Designers joked that the biggest problem the ships might have during battle would be its gravity pulling debris toward it.

"New solution?" said Clelland, walking back to the window.

"*Deaver* requests permission to fire," said the comms officer.

"Clear shot?"

"Aye, sir."

Clelland looked at the logistics officer, who nodded. "Unless their gunner is an idiot it should be fine," he said.

Clelland reluctantly nodded. "*Deaver* has permission to fire. One time salvo."

The comms officer clicked a message to the beacon, which would give the flanking battleship its orders.

The gunnery captain spoke. "New solution."

"Check?"

"Aye, good for another twenty seconds. Even at full reverse."

"Fire," said Clelland.

Clicks from another station. From deep at the rear of the ship, along the gun platforms behind the bell, a slithery hiss could be heard, then another and another in rapid succession. Five shots fired. Clelland pointed to the left and put a hand on Tarquin's shoulder.

"If you would look there," he said. "The enemy ship should just be visible."

Tarquin looked.

"There," said Clelland, pointing to an orange flash of light.

"Oh," said Tarquin as another flash burst. "Good shot."

"Those aren't ours actually," said Clelland. "Those are from the *Deaver*."

Another strike on them. A better one. Thunder and a shudder.

Clelland looked to the damage control officer. Sissard was standing behind him. He shook his head, a smile on his face.

"Direct hit," he said. "No breach. No damage beyond ablation."

Back outside, a plume of yellow cloud erupted from the distant speck that was the enemy ship.

"Breach?" said Tarquin.

"No. He's trying to turn. He sees our salvo."

"Will he make it?"

"Nay," said Clelland.

They watched. A moment later, there was a bright white flash, then another. Then no more.

"Report," said Clelland over his shoulder.

Taps and clicks, messages relayed from observers.

"Two hits," came the report.

"Three misses?" said Tarquin. "We fired five times, did we not?"

"Aye, we did," said Clelland.

"Listing, sir," reported the comms officer. "*Deaver* reports catastrophic breach in the enemy ship. It's dead."

Clelland nodded. "Get everyone back on course and tell them to sharpen their lookouts."

"Aye, sir."

Sissard joined the pair at the observation window.

"Damn fast those ships," said Sissard. "My guess that they just ran into our formation, signaling urgent on their beacons. I'm sure everyone assumed it was a courier because of the speed, not recognizing the new design."

"But it's not a new design," said Clelland. "Sommerled's been flying his damned boat for years. It was an arrogant mistake. We mustn't underestimate those ships again."

The men fell silent and the bridge was filled with a low humming of glowglobes, background transmitter clicks, and the distant whirlings of unseen machines. Sissard returned to his station with a quick click of his heels.

"Are they really that dangerous?" asked Tarquin. "They hit us twice and there's nothing to show for it."

It was a good question, but not the kind of thing an admiral would necessarily answer. Tarquin however wore the prophet's crest. He was not a mere cleric, not even a mere purger. He was on the prophet's own business among his other duties. To deny him anything was to deny the prophet.

"Nay, not so dangerous," Clelland said. "Irksome is all. Annoyances." Clelland couldn't meet the purger's eyes. He turned to Sissard. "Battle summary."

"Aye. We took two hits. Half-ton gun. Scratched us."

"And our part?"

Sissard shuffled through a stack of communication slips. The comms officer handed him another. He scanned it at nearly arm's length before putting it at the bottom of his stack. He found a certain one and said, "*Deaver* hit three of eight, we hit two of five."

"Is that normal?" asked Tarquin.

Sissard said, "Most of their misses happened when ours did."

"When the enemy ship…moved?"

"Aye. It's a nimble thing and it threw off our calculations," said Sissard. "It's nothing."

Sissard was calm, but Clelland clenched his jaw, thinking of the implications. The regular calculation charts did not account for the maneuverability of the new Enskari ship. It was a warship, but it maneuvered like an armored courier, a ship between battleship and corvette. A ship that didn't exist before, or not in enough numbers to require a chart of its own. Normally, it wouldn't matter. A splatter pattern would do it in, like in the old days, but with so many friendly ships around, misses on the enemy were likely to be hits on friendlies.

"Friendly fire?" said Clelland. "What of the misses?"

"Nothing reported," said Sissard, glancing at the comms officer.

The man shook his head. "No reports, sir."

"Good," said Clelland. "An easy victory."

"Practically a suicide," said Sissard with a grin.

Clelland looked at the constellation of ships in the armada. The sheer number of them was breathtaking. A few would doubtlessly be damaged by friendly fire during the upcoming and glorious battle, particularly when things got close and plasma cannons were used. At those ranges, the man-o-wars would shred anything. The armada could trade with the enemy and win decisively. They could trade badly even – two or three to one, and still overwhelmingly outnumber the enemy. "Why did he do that?" he said to himself.

"I suspect, Admiral," said Tarquin, "that they knew we were aboard this ship."

Clelland looked at the purger and tried to read his expression. It was inscrutable.

"The church came down in support of my action with the *Pempkin*," he said.

"Aye, we did. Heretics mustn't expect the same treatment as Saved."

Clelland recognized the line from the official response. Tarquin quoted it like he knew it. He wondered if he'd read it, or possibly wrote it.

"They were pirates," Clelland said.

"Heretics." Tarquin's gaze was back through the window. "It's so big," he said.

"The most ships ever assembled," said Clelland.

"I meant the space around them. It's hypnotic. The spinning makes it doubly so."

"Aye."

Again, Clelland tried to see as Tarquin did, the way he once had, when the vast black nothingness of space filled him with terror and awe. He couldn't make himself see it that way now. It was just space. Nothing. Lots and lots of nothing. There were ships, a distant planet, and a sun.

The rest and the in-between didn't exist except in time and distance and problems to be solved.

The window turned to show the edge of Coronam again. It showed crimson-orange and stretched farther into his field of vision than it should.

Clelland stepped closer to the window. It was a solar flare, a long one. Bright and nasty. Rare for this time of year but not unheard of. He watched the plume of plasma spread across the sky, dim, and then disappear into a twinkling of hot coalescing debris that glowed for a while before fading. He mentally plotted the trajectory in relation to his fleet. No danger from that one.

The original plan had been for the armada to sail to Enskari in Eighth-Month when the weather would be more predictable, but things had been accelerated by four months. It shouldn't matter. They had more than enough ships, enough conscripts and purgers, crossbows and guns for the job. They had enough plasma bombs and railshot a dozen times over. He'd have liked the months to better prepare, season his green captains a bit, maybe get those new firing charts and more intel on the new ships, but with such an overwhelming force, the war was a foregone conclusion. The battle plan was as simple as a hammer hitting a nail. A monkey could direct it. He was that monkey.

At first he welcomed the change; the sooner he sailed, the sooner his glory. But as time went on, he worried more and more about the experience of his officers, particularly the captains. Some were impressed cargo captains who knew nothing of battle sailing. Others were fresh cadets who, though knew the physics and were eager to fight, knew nothing of actual sailing. The solution for all this was training and time. He went to see Prince Brandon himself to argue against the accelerated schedule at one point, citing preparedness and weather, but Brandon wouldn't have it.

"The prophet himself has asked that we move things up," he said. "And God knows I'd like this over and done with myself. The cost of the armada is draining the treasury – the metal and men. Food isn't free and we're barracksing a hundred thousand mercenaries and armoring an armada."

Clelland had been given a private audience with the prince. The usual court of over a hundred had been cut to a mere twenty, which felt as private as a parade to Clelland. There were many clergy there, he remembered. The Apostle D'Angelo, half asleep and smelling of drink, but also Minister Rendelle, who watched Clelland with a predatory eye that made the admiral feel hated and unwelcome. He was used to those looks after the *Pempkin* but still there was something more in his eyes, a worry perhaps, or an impatience at him for asking for the delay. He was angry. He remembered seeing Nicandus, Captain of the House Guard, positioned between the group of clergy and the courtiers, almost like a human wall. There was also the Lady Vanessa Possad who'd become a regular at court even though her house had been disgraced. Beautiful and young, there was something about her, too, that struck Clelland as unusual. With some surprise he realized that what set her apart was her obvious interest in the proceedings. Most women didn't have the brains or temperament for statecraft, he was told. Here was one who obviously did, or at least appeared to. He'd flashed upon an image of the sovereign of Enskari and gritted his teeth.

Brandon went on, animated and enraged. "And besides," he said, "the insult has been borne too long. That bitch Zabel must be brought down. Every moment a woman sits on a throne of a Saved world is an affront to me and to God. I'll have her head and her world. I'll set everything right, put it all back to its proper place, the way it should be. Let's get it done, Admiral. Don't argue with me."

"Aye, Your Majesty."

Five months later, four months ahead of original schedule, the final ships were commandeered – anything within reach, Lavlandian, Claremondian, even Temple traders. Into these conscripts were fed to round out a battle force. After a week of banquets and parades, prayers and ceremony, promotions and speeches, Clelland finally boarded *Brandon's Blade* and set the armada on course. A fortnight to Lavland in safe space and then slow to Enskari.

"When will the battle begin?" Tarquin asked.

"After what just happened, I'd say it's joined," said Clelland. "But I suspect the Enskari fleet will meet us within a day or two if they're coming."

"Why then?"

"It's a good distance from their planet. Close enough to retreat to, far enough to defend."

Another flare. Clelland watched it bubble up from the edge of the star and spread in an expanding ring outward.

Tarquin said, "And after the battle?"

"If they capitulate we'll begin landing immediately, soldiers and purgers. My people will subdue them, yours will clean it up."

"And if they don't capitulate?"

"Then we'll lower plasma bombs through their atmosphere and detonate them until they do."

The flare fire stretched across the window. Red-orange, pink. Undulating and darkening. Full of debris and heat. It appeared to be creeping across the sky, but Clelland could measure the distances in tens of thousands of kilometers per second. And it was a big one.

"See that, Captain Sissard?"

"Aye," said the captain. "Navigator, turn us in. Batten down."

By the exhaust clouds, Clelland saw other ships already turning, pointing their bullet noses into the oncoming flare, folding their sails behind them in their shadows to protect them.

"You will give that order?" Tarquin said.

"What's that?"

"The order to drop plasma on the planet," said Tarquin. "You will give that order?"

"Aye."

Light, hot, and streaming. Pink and burgundy. Another flare. Another big one. No. More than a flare. The beginnings of a storm.

"Aye," said Clelland, keeping his eyes on the light outside, watching it grow larger as the big man-o-war shifted and aimed its nose at Coronam.

Filters slid down over the window, dimming the hot light to amber.

"It's why I'm here," said Clelland.

"Aye. Exactly. That is exactly why you are here."

Something in the purger's voice drew Clelland's attention from the storm without. Another filter slid down. The room grew darker. Coronam an orange spot riddled with stripes and swirls like a flaming fingerprint.

"Politics," said Tarquin with a heavy sigh, a disgusted but resigned heavy sigh.

"What do you mean, Your Eminence?"

"Do you not understand?" said Tarquin. "You know that I am the anointed High Purger of Enskari. I'll oversee the reunification and reeducation of the planet."

"Aye. What? I'm sorry…I don't follow."

"I'm in charge of the purging. It is my name on the order."

The window filled with light, orange-pink in the filter. A final shield slid across the window, curtaining it entirely. The high purger looked at Clelland.

"When the landing happens, capitulation or not, there will be bloodshed on Enskari. Make no mistake, the streets will run red. The prisons will be filled with apostates and heretics and my purgers' fires will burn tall and hot for years. Reunification will not be quick or painless. Exactly the opposite, I'd expect. I'll do this, you see, so it 'makes an argument', as you said."

"I understand."

Tarquin raised an eyebrow as if he didn't think Clelland did. "The argument will be decisive," he said slowly. "The actors remembered. For years. For generations no doubt."

"I suspect they will."

Tarquin nodded knowingly, keeping his eyes on Clelland.

The purger's gaze made the admiral uncomfortable. He shifted his weight. "We're talking about infamy?"

"Aye. Actions have consequences. It is all politics, I'm afraid. The deed needs doing, and so it will be done, but it cannot be done anonymously or else it soils my prophet and your king. It imperils institutions. For history, someone must be sacrificed, left to take the blame, to have their name cursed for generations."

"You do only your duty, High Purger Thomas Tarquin."

"Aye. Of course. I know my purpose. I am the black and red that makes the white so bright," he said, gesturing to his sash.

Clelland didn't understand. He'd thought Tarquin was feeling sorry for himself, but he could plainly see he did not. The man was trying to explain something to him.

"I will be remembered on Enskari," Tarquin said. "History will take note of me for this. Thousands will die under my direction for the glory of God and the right of the prophet."

A snake of cold sweat pooled down the back of Clelland's uniform as he recalled the banquets he'd attended before leaving Hyrax. He remembered the many congratulations from nobles and officers who'd served longer and more prestigiously than he had. He recalled Admiral Mola, who'd wished him well and shook his hand. Not a drop of envy in his eyes, not a hint of jealousy for being passed over for the most important and significant command in the history of Hyrax – the history of mankind. A handshake and well wishes.

A plan that any monkey could carry out.

He was the monkey.

The first of the storm met the ship. The full strength of the flares he'd seen before were still some time away. This was just the invisible front wave leading the coming crash. The sound was familiar to every sailor. Nothing unusual. It was even pleasant. It sounded like the pattering of a light rain on a shingled roof, uneven muted thumps, steady and soft.

"We estimate the execution of upward of twenty thousand heretics on Enskari from purging," said Tarquin. "What was the fatality estimate if you lower your bombs to Enskari?"

The pattering grew louder, the wave stronger. Rain turning to hail.

"It'll be in the millions," said Clelland, understanding. "Three and thirty million was the conservative estimate."

"Three and thirty million," said Tarquin. "A memorable number."

CHAPTER TWENTY-SEVEN

When Coronam is orange-yellow,
She's apt to speed a happy fellow.
When pink, crimson, and red,
Hide or ye'll be dead.
Spacefarer Saying

22, Fifth-Month, 938 NE – aboard the Merry, *Fleet Command Squadron, Enskari defense line*

The ship jolted and veered. Men were pushed into their chairs or pulled to the extent of their straps.

"What was that?" called Sir Ethan Sommerled.

"Not the enemy, sir." It was Mr. Andrews, damage officer. "It was the storm. Push on the sails, damage on the third petal."

Ethan pulled his straps tighter over his bruised shoulders and turned his periscope rearward to inspect the damage himself.

"I can't see it," he said. His scope showed only light and glare, odd shadows he couldn't discern.

It was the second day of the storm, the worst Ethan had ever sailed in and he'd sailed a few. Coronam blew arcs of plasma across space at the battle as if the ships themselves were a magnet for it, as if Enskari herself had summoned it. The planet's shielding atmosphere sparked with it, and lit up from it like firecrackers. Aurora energy snaked across the sky below the fight in waves like ripples on a burning pond. Flashes of disintegrating meteors blended with stray railshot to give the battle a second sun: a white strobing planet on one side, an orange tentacled star on the other.

The shifting solar winds made navigation a nightmare. Gusts of fluctuating uneven energy caught the tops of sails and not the bottoms, cartwheeling ships into space. Masts were snapped, cables severed, sails lost outright. Streaking meteors, thrown from the sun or pushed from the winds, pummeled the ships like grapeshot, and waves of plasma in walls of heat burned down the ablative armor like a torch on a candle.

It was chaos.

Every able sailor, every smart captain knew they should run for cover. They should weather such a tempest in the lee of a planet, shielded by a whole world, hoping that the planet would defend them, forgetting if they could what Coronam had done to Dajjal, Ravan, and Kanluran.

Ethan had watched the storm come and cheered while his commanders quaked doubly for the size of enemy fleet and the wrath of their sun. Threatening to space any captain and crew who held back, he pulled the whole of his fleet – not a frigate left for reinforcements – and went right at the Hyraxian armada in the face of a solar storm that was guaranteed to decimate his fleet no matter what else happened.

The battle had been joined in earnest now for half a day. Their losses were more than five and thirty per cent if Ethan's observers were right. But the Hyraxians were suffering far worse. For each ship the Enskari defense fleet lost, Brandon lost five or ten. Percentage wise it might be close, but number wise, it was a slaughter.

All ships were purposed to resist Coronam. They were bullet-shaped bells of heavy armor and ablative ceramics trailing kilometers of sail and mast that could be folded behind them and protected in the shadow when the ship would turn its nose into a storm to weather it. Properly positioned, any one of these ships would stand a chance against even a storm like this one, but that presumed the luxury of facing the ship as you would.

The armada sailed into Enskari space ass-first, their sails retracted, their sleek noses hot and glowing from the storm, resisting Coronam to the best of their mettle.

Ethan's own fleet, at full burn, came out of the planet's shadow and rushed them, their sails open and overheating, meteors digging divots in their hulls, slashing sailcloth, and flaring visuals. Nevertheless, the Enskaran fleet found a shooting gallery of Hyraxian aft plating and took happy advantage.

Some saw them coming and spun to turn armor in time, to defend against the initial attack. But most were slow, at least at first, and when Ethan gave the order to fire at will – "For Zabel, for Enskari, for Glory!" – his ships turned their platforms at angle and let loose.

Red rings of molten gold showed where railshot penetrated weak sides. Hyraxian corvettes, transports, frigates, and even a man-o-war went silent in the first volley, spun out, or exploded in timed progression as the shots burrowed home.

Then they were among them, close enough to shoot fouling wire into their rigging, plasma cannon into their flanks and read the names of the ships in the crimson-orange light of Coronam's blessed hurricane.

Ethan's light ships were perfect for the battle. Small and sleek, they could fire and turn armor toward enemy one moment and storm the next. They could dart and weave amongst the sluggish monstrous man-o-wars and keep the range low and the arcs tight.

Ethan turned his periscope forward, toward the enemy, toward a cursed man-o-war. He watched a row of geysers erupt on its side, plasma-stream thrusters to rotate, steer its armor toward his rushing ship.

"We report but a few holes in the sail, Captain – I mean, Admiral. We lost two draw wires and ten per cent on sail number three. Navsails are fine. It was just a push," said the damage officer. "Nothing fatal."

"That remains to be seen, Mr. Andrews," said Ethan.

He could make out the name on the side of man-o-war. *Song of Hyrax*. The letters were as big as his bell while its sails as big as a star port. The huge glowing petals were in full facing, the ship obviously trying to catch storm flare to turn faster.

"Those sails look mighty clean," he said. "Change that, Mr. Paul."

The weapons officer clacked a signal key and called into his horn, "Grapeshot batteries and foulers, prepare. We're coming about."

"Might as well burn 'em while we're here," said Ethan.

"Plasma batteries, ready, aye," confirmed Mr. Paul.

"Hold up. How are the batteries?"

Clicks and whistles.

"Forty per cent." Then correcting himself, "Two and forty, Admiral."

"Belay the burners for now," said Ethan. He needed the plasma for maneuvering more than he needed to do damage to the *Song of Hyrax*. A meter of armor melted off that ship wouldn't account for much. If there was a breach, however, that was a different story. If that happened, he'd sidle right up to the cut and fill their decks with radiation. He'd gut it from the inside out.

Warning klaxons blared like tortured banshees.

"Incoming!"

"Evasive."

The ship lunged to one side. Ethan was pushed back into his chair.

"Phalanx defensive shot."

"Live and firing."

"Solution?"

"Calculating."

"Mr. Andrews?"

"Calculations complete."

A jolt of the ship. A shutter and a hiss. Silence.

"Who was it?" said Ethan.

"That wounded battleship aft, sir," said the nav officer. "The *Cuffly*'s on it."

"Damage?"

"Bell section six. Twenty meters. Bad, but it's holding. No breach."

Through his periscope he watched the *Cuffly*, his sister ship, strafe the big wounded battleship with plasma flamer. The Hyraxian warship's hull glowed red, orange, then white as the *Cuffly* rotated and brought its railguns to bear at the heated flank.

He was too far to see the shots, but he saw the hits. Red circles of molten metal on the slowly turning hull. One, two, three, four concentrically spaced rings of electromagnetically-propelled hot death.

The battleship shuddered and tossed. Ethan imagined the rounds ricocheting within the hull like a pellet ball in a can, tearing men and metal to shrapnel. Before it stopped, a wave of red arching plasma ran up the spine like a short-legged spider. Up the mast to the sails it went, overheating and melting them into a magnesium flash a moment before the rear hull breached and vomited the inside of the ship into the superheating sails.

"Aye, that was a thing of beauty," said Ethan. "Textbook. Never seen it done as well."

Above the fading orange cloud that had been the Hyraxian warship, a frigate streaked toward them, aft burners hot, sailing against the sun, its full sails quaking like someone was shaking them. It cut its engines, momentum in control, then fired pink-yellow thruster spurts from its side to slowly turn to bear.

"Do you see that, Mr. Kyle?"

"The new ship? Aye, sir?"

"Get us between this big bastard and that new little one. Stay sharp on the thrusters and angle the navsails for a dodge."

"*Astro* says we got another flare coming. A big one."

Ethan excused the imprecise alert. There wasn't time to calculate. He was otherwise engaged.

"I have solution," said Mr. Paul. "Taking control."

"Tear 'em up, weapons officer."

The *Merry* lurched, pushing Ethan to his right as the maneuvering thrusters fired to bring the guns to bear. Above Ethan, Mr. Paul was strapped to his station seat like a bat hanging from the ceiling. They were surrounded by the other bridge officers, also strapped in. A page floated in from an open hatch, swung around, and caught his toes in a hold to present a form to Mr. Andrews.

The zero-grav battle bridge was always disorienting, even for veterans like Ethan. He turned back to his relative horizon and put the periscope to his eye. He swiveled his chair to watch the port side, which swung into the arc of the man-o-war.

"Firing," called Mr. Paul, tapping the signal to the batteries.

From behind the bell on the gun pod a cloud of half-meter spiked shot flew out in a narrow but expanding cloud of sail-tearing steel. In the ship it sounded like an echoing slap, two giant hands clapping behind them as the magnets fired in push and pull to drive the shot along the rails.

In space, the sailshot looked like children's jacks tumbling to their target – shining spinning stars – before disappearing against the blackness to show again only as they hit the enemy sails. In a flash of pink-and-yellow lightning, they tore through the silk and spilled the collected plasma.

"Nice shot, Mr. Paul," said Ethan.

The fouling wire caught a moment later. It was a long tendril of nanocarbon and weights meant to cut or at least interfere with the nanofiber rigging that lifted and lowered the sail petals. Their accuracy was demonstrated by the sudden folding down of one petal against the mast, the loosing of another to where it flopped like a trailing ribbon behind the man-o-war.

"Excellent, Mr. Paul. Excellent."

"Aye, sir. My pleasure."

"Take us off?" asked Mr. Kyle.

"Nay. Line us up with that frigate. Arm sabot shot."

"Aye, sir."

The man-o-war's thrusters shifted its angle, attempting to bring gun platforms to bear.

The *Merry* slid along its axis and shifted to place itself between the two nearest enemy ships.

With the storm wave rising to crescendo and with momentum promising to carry it out of broadside arc of the man-o-war, the *Merry* turned its nose toward the coming flare. It was a smooth maneuver, not to be duplicated by even the smallest Hyraxian frigate.

"Where is the *Joshua* going?" said Ethan.

The fleet was arranged in squadrons, each capable of effective independent action should communication with the admiral be lost. Ethan was not one to lead from the rear and would engage the enemy with his squadron along with the other warships. The *Joshua* was a member of his eight-ship squadron. Five now. He'd lost three – rendered ineffective or destroyed outright. The *Joshua* had been ordered to reposition with the rest of his squadron, while the *Merry* and *Cuffly* drew the man-o-war's attention.

"I calculate he's running for the transports."

"He's taking the whole damn squadron! Call them back."

"Grapeshot incoming. Brace."

"The man-o-war?"

"Nay. The frigate."

"Where is the man-o-war?"

"Should have a solution on us in a few seconds."

"Are we reloaded?"

"Nay."

The hull resounded with the splattering of grapeshot. Sizzling hammers on a spinning anvil.

"Solid hit."

"We know that much already, Mr. Andrews. Find us a little more information please."

"Aye, sir."

The *Joshua* and his two wings headed for the rear of the Hyraxian formation. A handful of ships turned their sails and thrusted to follow.

The *Joshua* was captained by Lord Howells, the Earl. Ethan had met him at the queen's farewell. They'd had words. This was not as big a surprise as it could have been.

"I will be commanding the *Joshua*," Howells had told him.

"That's Captain Larsen's ship."

"Aye, well, I'll keep him on as first mate, but you must understand, my family has been in every meaningful battle Enskari has ever had. It's a requirement that I be there."

"What naval experience have you?"

"I am the Earl of Howells."

Ethan had stared at him, honestly wondering what that had to do with his question.

Howells stared back for a moment as if he'd answered it plainly before looking at the other punch-drinking dignitaries standing around them. "I come from a long line of naval officers and Enskari heroes."

"I've never heard of you," Ethan said.

"Nay," said the earl. "I don't suppose people in your...*circle* would have."

"The *Joshua* is one of the new ships," explained Ethan. "They're integral to our defense."

"Aye, of course."

"It's too valuable to be put in the hands of an amateur."

Howells looked at him with disgust. "I know its value, sir. I know what it cost. My family paid for it."

Sir Gael Aderyn, High Admiral of the Navy, stepped forward then and said, "And grateful is the Crown for your contribution. Of course you can captain the ship."

Ethan looked at his commander with some worry. The old sailor led him to a quieter corner. Howells and his friends watched them go with some amusement.

"Is it not my fleet to command?" asked Ethan.

"Aye, Ethan. You are in command of the defense fleet."

"Would you take it from me?"

"Nay, Ethan, I am not so vain. I do not need more glory. The queen is right in having chosen you. We are outnumbered and outgunned. Our hope lies in new thinking. I don't have that. I, and the queen, are confident you are the man to lead us through this danger. This will be truly a battle of the old versus the new. Thank God I recognized which side my thinking is on. With you at least, we have a chance."

Ethan was taken back. He'd received hours of praise just before, public speeches and royal edicts, and of course the months-long publicity tour Sir Nolan had sent him on, but none of that had struck him as deeply or as sincerely as what Sir Gael Aderyn had just said to him. As a young man, he'd admired the admiral. He was a legend, the first man to circumnavigate the system, and he'd done it twice. His was the first civilized foot to step on Tirgwenin. The patent for that planet had originally been marked for him. Ethan had always wondered if the old admiral had hated him for that or, as most of his class did, for taking glory beyond his station.

"Do you mean that, sir?" asked Ethan.

"Aye, Ethan – Sir Ethan, I do."

Ethan didn't know what to say. "Thank you," was all he came up with.

Aderyn chortled. "I don't know I've done you a favor with that, but let me do you one now. You must let Howells command that ship. It is politics and it is beyond us. For the sake of the queen and a peaceful court, allow him his ship. His house paid for it and three others like it."

"We have so few."

"We have enough. It'll not be missed and his vanity and his house will be assuaged."

"Has he sailed?"

"A yacht."

"Military?"

"Honorary, but he knows the forms," said Aderyn.

"Admiral—"

"It gets worse."

Ethan felt his shoulders sag. "What?"

"He has to be in the command squadron."

"Nay. Does he know I don't lead from the rear?"

"He knows. It's glory he wants."

"Dammit."

"Sorry Ethan, there are forces beyond our control."

"Are there other ships like this? Other nobles I didn't pick to captain?"

Sir Gael nodded. "A few. One in ten captains were assigned by noble privilege and a good number of general officers."

"Any of them any good?"

"If they were any good, you'd know about them and would have chosen them yourself."

Ethan raised his hand to his temples and rubbed.

Aderyn said, "The Hyraxian ranks are much more cluttered with this nonsense than are ours."

"I need grit and spit up there, not greasepaint and wigs."

"It's not just winning the war, Ethan," said Aderyn, "It's also how it's done and by whom."

"If we don't do the first, what matters the others?"

"You'll manage. I kept the worst of them out of the battleships and only Howells is in your squadron. Have faith, they are bred for this kind of thing."

The chronic elite defense that better blood makes better men fell flat on Ethan. He noticed that Aderyn had said 'they are bred' when he could have included himself in that and said, 'we', due to his own high lineage extending back to the Unsettling. It was a small thing, a courtesy to Ethan's modest ancestry or a veiled insult to it, but it was ultimately of little consequence in Ethan's mind as he knew only that his already outnumbered fleet had been effectively cut by a tenth before the ships had even set out.

Howells and the *Joshua* had been trouble from the start. They'd been consistently slow to acknowledge orders and outright questioned some of them. As if searching for a better dance partner, they moved sluggishly into formation. Ethan hadn't put them in the primary firing arc because he wanted to hit the Hyraxian bastards, after all. That the *Joshua* hadn't been damaged or destroyed already was a minor miracle and an irritant to Ethan as he watched it fly out of his formation like a fleeing cur.

"Signal them back," said Ethan, but he knew it was already too late. The *Song of Hyrax* blocked the necessary line of sight.

"Bell section seventeen," said Mr. Andrews. "A half dozen— Nay," he corrected himself, holding his headpiece tighter to his ear. "Eight five-meter craters, twice that, one-to-two-meter divots. Section eighteen, pocked a quarter meter or less. Seventeen at seventy per cent."

It was the first hit on that section of the bell. Had the same hit found section six, it would have breached them. He thought to ask for the best sections to aim against the enemy but remembered that a broadside of sabot railshot from a man-o-war would cut through any pristine section they had and probably the other side as well. "Very good," he said.

"Man-o-war should have solution," said Mr. Paul.

"Are we loaded now?"

"Nay."

"The frigate?"

"Closing for flamers, I'd guess."

"Get closer to him."

"Aye, sir."

"And the big bastard, what's he up to?"

"Guns tracking on us – no. Wait. Fired. Incoming broad—"

"Out of here, Mr. Kyle!"

The roar of full plasma thrusters at evasive vector threw Ethan to the ends of his restraints and snapped his head back. He felt like he was hanging from the ceiling, and relatively speaking, he was. The blood rushing to his head darkened his vision at the edges. Below him he saw Mr. Paul's face grow pale and then tilt to the side as he passed out.

Ethan grunted as he tried to pull his arms down to his sides. It was not comely for a commander to have his hands raised above his head in any gravity or orientation.

His nose bled, running in a gush into his sinuses, making him feel like he was drowning. His vision blurred as his tear ducts drained into his eyes. He tilted his head back to let the flow escape his nostrils and watched blood rush in a stream across the empty middle of the battle bridge and onto Mr. Paul's station and lap.

The thrust vector changed as the main burners fired. Ethan's blood ran down his chin and the front of his uniform. His arms were light enough to move. He pinched his nose and put his eyes to the periscope.

The *Song of Hyrax* was shrinking in the distance, her damaged sail outlining the bell like a black compass rose. To the side was the frigate, thrusters alight pushing its mass as it would.

Ethan rubbed his eye to clear the blood, but only made it worse. He wiped the eyepieces with his sleeve and looked again just as the man-o-war's broadside found the frigate and tore it to shreds. The little ship lit up in white, orange then crimson light; metal vaporized, atmosphere ignited, plasma released. A slurry of molten metal and men poured out the side like gore from a hemorrhaging wound, spewing rings of glowing and darkening death as the hulk rotated silent and dead.

"Who gets credit for that shot?" asked Mr. Paul, conscious again.

"Hyraxian on Hyraxian violence is the best violence," said Mr. Andrews.

"Damn obliging of that big bastard, but we'll take credit," said Ethan. "Nice maneuvering, Mr. Kyle."

"Thank you, sir."

"They'll not fall for that again," said Mr. Paul. "At least not the ones who saw it."

Ethan said, "What's our fuel?"

"Sixteen per cent, but a flare is here in two minutes."

"Turn the sails and catch it," said Ethan. "We might burn a bit of silk, but we need it."

"Heading?"

"Let me see." Still holding his nose, Ethan wiped the eyepiece with his other hand and scanned the sky.

Explosions and streaks, flashes of signal and decompression littered a crowded sky. It looked more like the Kanluran Cloud for all the ships than it did the high orbit of Enskari. He saw his world as a bright orb of light, flashing with debris, natural and manmade, defending the surface with ancient crystalline shields. A web of orange light from a solar flare stabbed out from his sun and slid across his planet like a shroud. Where it touched, Enskari glowed and folded the energies into slithering strings of living auroras. It was beautiful and awful.

A ship exploded red and angry, too big even for a man-o-war. The shockwave bubbled out like a flare, catching several nearby ships and blowing them up too, their smaller explosions dwarfed by the first.

"What the hell was that?"

"Stay to your business, Mr. Andrews," said Ethan, sticking tissue in his nostrils. "I suspect that one of ours got one of the Hyraxian bombers. Take a good look, gentleman. That's why we're here. They want to lower those horrors into our atmosphere and fire them off."

There was a moment of quiet as the real savagery of the threat settled in. Ethan let it, feeling it in his own heart, thinking of his beloved Zabel right now, imagining her pacing her courtyard beneath the sparking sky, fretful and proud, taking the whole fear of an entire people upon herself.

A storm wave hit the *Merry* and again the ship was jolted hard.

Ethan turned his periscope aft and saw his sails grow green-yellow, orange and hot.

Meteors slammed the bell in a fusillade of clicks become slams. He could only hope that his weakened panels wouldn't be hit straight on.

"The man-o-war is moving."

"Where's the *Cuffly*?"

"With us, sir. Sheltering behind our sails."

"Why?"

"She reports a damaged nose, sir."

"Ah."

He turned to see the *Song of Hyrax* growing larger in his view. At first he thought they were charging them, but then he realized that it was the push of the storm driving the *Merry* back into the thick of it.

"Where's the *Joshua*?"

"Q2," came Mr. Kyle's instant response.

Ethan checked the relative patching chart and changed periscopes.

There they were. His three other ships. One had sails up and was veering off, probably coming back. The other two ran with plasma burn directly to the center of the Hyraxian formation where the supply and support ships were being protected. Ethan's squadron had cut the deepest into the enemy group and everyone had secondary orders that should any of them get within range, to harass the less well-armed ships there, most specifically, the troop transports and the Temple vessels full of purgers.

"Tell me they're not going straight into them," said Ethan.

"Aye, sir," said Mr. Kyle. "But my best calculations say they are."

Back to his other scope. Ethan saw the man-o-war shifting to get a shot at them.

"*Astro* is warning of greater flares, Admiral."

"Tell me when I need to know."

"He says you need to know now, sir."

Ethan spun his station, grabbed, and filtered his other scope. Coronam was a big crimson ball of fire. He saw ships transit it, sails full and thrusters firing. Explosions and battle. Beyond it all was the star. He saw the spinning of its surface, the vortexes and surface storm that portended coming eruptions, some already sent out and more to come. He'd never seen so much motion there before. Shadow trenches bigger than worlds twisted around each other in circles and clashed like living forms, bacteria in a petri dish.

"By God...." he said.

"Man-o-war broadside on the *Joshua*."

"Dammit." Back to the other scope.

"Aye, sir. It is damned."

"Shut up, Mr. Kyle."

"Aye, sir. Shutting up."

He couldn't see the attack in the darkness, but he could guess the target trajectory between the two ships, the *Song of Hyrax* big in his scope, the *Joshua* and the rest of his squadron a twinkling beyond, moving in a predictable course.

"Move, damn you," he muttered. "Move, you noble idiot."

Late plumes of thruster gas, long and white, showed how they tried too late to scatter.

"Tell the *Cuffly* to peel off," Ethan said, getting an idea. "We'll see if we can't draw this bastard's shot. Tell them to be ready."

"Aye, sir." Clicks as the message was relayed. "Acknowledged."

"Good. Now, Mr. Kyle, bring us high around that man-o-war. When we've passed his arc fly round, about, and beyond those transports. Get in amongst them so they see us, but position to bring us behind them so we're on the home side. Give them time to turn."

"Give them time to turn, sir?"

"Aye."

"Aye aye, sir."

Clicks and taps and orders in horns were followed by cracks and pops as pulleys realigned the sails. The ship shifted as each came taut, was feathered and tacked. Thruster fire was felt as bumps as the ship came to.

He'd lost sight of the *Joshua* but found her again easy enough. Three red flashes showed where she was. Two more showed his other ship. The third he couldn't see.

The red spots grew from tiny bloody pinpricks to fill his scope in brightening shades of light. A single salvo obliterated his two destroyers, piercing their armor, turning its own metal against them just as it had the frigate. The earlier jubilation of that victory was sapped at the sudden loss of two of their own.

"Tell the *Cuffly* to go in at his stern. Do what he did before."

"Aye, sir."

The course plotted, the plan set, there was little for Ethan to do or say. He cursed Howells under his breath for his rashness, but pulled up short from calling it mutiny. Their lines of communication might have been cut; their watchmen might have missed the signals. He wanted to believe the best of the man because he was a kinsman who'd died in the defense of his planet and a sailor after all.

"The man-o-war will have solution on us again soon, Admiral."

"Keep the course. How're the batteries?"

"Eighteen per cent."

"Signal from the *Locust*, sir."

"So it was Captain Vorns who got away."

"Reporting the rest of the squadron destroyed."

"Tell him to head for home."

"What, sir?"

"You heard me."

"Aye, sir."

"Man-o-war should have solution on us."

"Keep a steady eye and a random vector," came the admiral's calm reply.

The *Merry* had put distance between them. A solution at this range could be broken by a quick maneuver before the shots landed. It became a guessing game; find a calculation to where you think the ship will be once they see you've fired. Not usually a problem with the physics of space flight, but Ethan's new ships had introduced it.

The enemy's best chance would be to fire at several of the most possible locations, but that many calculations were tricky. Ethan didn't think the *Song of Hyrax* would do that. It guaranteed several misses. Downrange of the *Merry* were the transport ships. They'd already have to answer for the frigate.

"*Locust* reports battle-ready. No need to return."

"Repeat it. Tell them to fly home now. Have them signal the fleet as they go to do the same."

"What? We're retreating?" said Mr. Andrews. "I thought we were doing well."

"Mind your station, Mr. Andrews. Communications, send the order now. Full speed, entire fleet leeward rally. Get in the planet shadow. Evasive as necessary, but get there now."

"Aye, sir."

"The *Cuffly*'s firing."

To the other scope.

The man-o-war was some distance away, a dark shape against the blazing sun. Plasma cannon fire identifiable only through filter. The shadow of his other ship. Then a silver streak of main thrusters.

"Signal them home as well," said Ethan.

"Aye, sir."

The *Song of Hyrax*'s rigging was tangled. Down several sails, it was even slower and more ponderous. He couldn't tell how close his sister ship had come, but he could imagine.

It flew into the rear arc, trying to nose right up its backside, close in to the end of the mast, ten kilometers. It'd burn the hull with forward plasma, burning the gun decks, testing the mast strength, torching rigging perhaps. It'd follow with grapeshot to peel the armor the more as it passed, then its rear weapons pod would unleash its railshot. With careful maneuvering, they might get off three or four of his six guns at the aft at near-point-blank range.

His imaginings played out in what he saw; the flamers, and the relative shadows showing terrible proximity. Then the flash and shockwave. The bastard had bombs aboard and the *Cuffly* had breached one.

Like an inflating bubble birthed from the dead man-o-war, a ring of energy spread outward in pops and flashes like some terrible pyrotechnic display. The little ones might well be debris, or flying shot or asteroids, but the bigger ones were certainly ships. There were many of those, most were Hyraxian, but at least one was his. The *Cuffly* was the second light after the first.

There were no cheers for the destruction of the man-o-war, though it was a glorious achievement. The men took note and fell silent, letting the room again fill with the sounds of engine machinery.

Through the front scope, Ethan saw the transports running scared.

"We want their asses pointed at Coronam," he said. "We're not in a fight now. We're in a roundup."

"Aye, sir."

For an hour the *Merry* maneuvered around the transports. With the Enskari fleet behind him, appearing to be regrouping for an assault, the Hyraxians turned their bells toward the planet while distant split-off warships flew at full burn to their defense.

The sides of the *Merry* rang with shot but none hit true enough to breach.

Ethan shifted from scope to scope, watching enemy sails swivel and turn through one, and the warships charge him in the other.

"Astronavigation, sir. They say—"

"I see it," said Ethan. "Mr. Kyle, we're leaving. Get us shadowed. Now." Panic had slipped into Ethan's voice and he regretted it, but he'd seen the burst that Astronav had called him about.

The flare had come from the center of the largest vortex. The moment of its birth was unnoticed in the maelstrom. Set against the light of Coronam, its early growth was invisible. Only when it had cooled enough was it recognized for what it was. The filters showed it to be apart from the surface, but not different – and already well on its way to them. The light preceded the wave by mere minutes. To the unfiltered eye it might appear as a nova, the light of the sun expanding out like the shockwaves of the genocidal bombs the Hyraxians had brought along. But Coronam had not moved. She was still there, angry but still there. She spat fire and fed the rushing clouds of energy that grew larger as they grew closer until they eclipsed the sun that made them and filled the sky with storm.

The *Merry* lurched, spun, and fired all thrusters. Warning sirens – gravity alert. Full burn. Long and hard. All they had. Enskari-bound.

"Batteries at five per cent."

"Turn us into the storm, full sail. Ride it out. Let it push us."

"Or burn us alive," muttered Mr. Andrews. Ethan was getting tired of that man's negativity. If they survived this, he'd have a word with his damage control officer.

The batteries were emptied by thrusters to turn the armored bell toward the sun, into the wind, so to speak. The ship filled with creaks and shutters as pulleys aimed the sails and the first debris splattered into them. Ethan doubted their sails would hold, but they might last long enough to speed them home around the planet, into the gravity well, to the harboring shadow of their home.

Against the backdrop of the roaring storm and spitting sun, Ethan saw countless ships tossed and twisted. In bursts of decompressions and colored explosions, the Hyraxian fleet was torn apart.

The solar wave smashed into the enemy ranks in a cascade of light. The man-o-wars were set aglow, their shields amelt but holding. Frigates, corvettes, and destroyers showed their navigators' skill by surviving. Or not. A degree off or a weakened shield and they were another fireball. The support craft fared worse. Much worse. Most of them were turned wrong by Ethan's maneuvers. Their crews were unseasoned and far from home, captains unfamiliar with the dangers of tempests and the realities of war. Fair-weather sailors. Nobility on a lark. Tourists on an unstoppable armada caught on the windward side of an enemy world in a solar hurricane.

Mr. Andrews called breaches as heat bent their weakened shields and tortured the rest. Bells and alarms; straining steel, snapping fiber core. Melting sails. The inner bridge grew hot. Sweat mingled with blood as Ethan watched through his failing lenses.

He still had ships out there. Many wouldn't survive. He himself might not. Probably would not. His ship, this valiant flagship, the *Merry*, patterned destroyer, was on its way to being slagged in the atmosphere, pushed by the storm and railshot to die over Enskari. Even knowing this, seeing his doom on one side, but scoping the destruction of the legendary Hyraxian armada on another, Ethan grinned.

CHAPTER TWENTY-EIGHT

Arrest and dispatch everyone on suspect list. Trials waived.
Defense of the Realm Directive,
Signed Archbishop Connor
16, Fifth-Month, 938 NE

24, Fifth-Month, 938 NE – Daven Estate, 890 km north of Vildeby, Enskari

Queen Zabel Genest, ruler of all Enskari, sat alone near a window overlooking a field of early green hay grass, watching the afternoon sky still lighting up like fireworks.

It was rare for the queen to actually be alone. There were no guards in the room, no handmaids to groom her or straighten her train behind her. There were no pages waiting by the door to run messages to anyone. There was only she, and the burning sky of her deliverance.

She'd been taken, nearly by force, from the palace in the depths of the night, covered and hidden, her courtiers unaware. She'd been loaded aboard a train into a nondescript carriage that was made comfortable for her but not opulent. It would pass for a merchant's car, and her trip just another weak and wealthy aristocrat fleeing besieged Vildeby as the Hyraxian fleet approached to lower plasma bombs onto the capital and wipe it out.

She'd been taken across the continent to Daven Keep far to the north. Lord and Lady Daven had been loyal during the troubles and Sir Nolan had secretly arranged for them to keep the queen until the danger was past.

When she'd arrived, the telegraph wires were not in place yet. The battle had been well met before the wires were able to bring them reports of it. No matter. She was in no position to help. Beyond a speech and a prayer, she was as powerless to aid her world now as were the sheep she watched graze in the Davens' meadow.

Once the wires were up, the clatter never stopped. She had waited with her Ears, Sirs Edward and Nolan, for reports in the communications room, which but hours before had been Lady Daven's own boudoir.

The Lady Daven had moved into her husband's bedchamber without a grumble or a word as the rest of the house was turned upside down. Zabel had taken the *royal room*, a remnant of an earlier time where noble houses, as a sign of their wealth and affluence, would keep a suite of rooms always ready specifically for royalty. It was a waste of space and had fallen out of fashion but the Davens were not so modern. To Zabel's knowledge, she was the first person to sleep in the hundred-year-old bed and probably the first royal to even visit this part of the planet.

She gave these things some thought as she waited and worried. The sky blazed above, sending her clear messages when the teletype would not. She read the fate of her reign in the flares and flashes of her sky.

The enemy numbers were staggering. Scout ships had started the alarm with ship counts that went beyond even the most doom-minded projections. "The sky's blotted out with Hyraxian sail silk," came an early report. Then the pickets reported and the message was the same. Orbital stations, elevator landings, and transports each sent the same dreadful news of the coming enemy fleet: cruisers, destroyers, frigates, transports full of purgers, more of soldiers, the awesome man-o-wars. Enskari would bleed.

As if in anticipation, the Enskaran sky itself turned a shade of red and the queen, far from her capital, hiding in the safest place within reach, had asked her advisors what to do.

"We can do nothing more," said Nolan. "The die is cast."

"Nay," said Edward. "We can capitulate, surrender now. Save millions of lives."

"Never," said Nolan.

"I'm surprised at you, Nolan," Edward said. "You are not usually so bloodthirsty."

"We could marry the prince," said Zabel. "That would stop the fleet."

In the silence that followed her offer, if that's what it was, she saw Edward's agreement. It was after all, the only bargaining position they had left. Sir Nolan, however, shook his head.

"Nay, Your Majesty. That might stop Brandon, for now, if he would do it, but I doubt it would move the prophet. Everyone who has been loyal to you would be lost to the fires of the purgers. And such a turn would defile the name of Genest forever. To keep your throne you must keep constant. We have placed you upon the altar to lead us in government and in faith. You mustn't fail."

Zabel snorted. "It's all poppycock. Pope or prophet, emperor or queen – what is the difference?" During the passage on the train, there had not been a stop, not an hour it had seemed, that she had not seen bonfires ablaze with human fuel. The smoke mixed with the petroleum exhaust and coal smoke giving the air a sweet and sour smell that scratched at the back of her throat. It was the work of Archbishop Connor and his Guard. They had orders to collect and summarily execute enemies of the throne by emergency order. He'd asked, she'd assented and now her people burned in their own fires. Hyraxian affiliation, Orthodox leanings, vocal opposition, or even pacifism were each now a death sentence. It was not her idea, but she had allowed it, knowing the skies would soon be blackened by ships and her lands by Hyraxian mercenaries and Temple purgers. When her nostrils filled with the sickly scent of human fat, it was difficult for her to see a difference between her and the prophet, his purgers or Connor's Guard.

"It is everything," said Nolan.

"What game do you have, spymaster?" said Edward. "How can you be so calm at a time like this? The enemy is vast and powerful. Have you found faith?"

"Nay," he said. "Not faith. Constancy."

"You could have played both sides, spymaster. Your calm today could bespeak a secret alliance you have with Brandon."

"Sir Edward!" said the queen. Such an accusation, such a suggestion, could get a man sent to Gray Keep.

"Nay, First Ear. If I had, I dare say, I'd have done better than this," he said. "I will take my fate with my queen. My allegiance is to you, Madam. It was made many years ago. It is my only constant. All I do, I do for you."

Sir Edward stared out the window at the flaring lights above them, battle debris they were told, railshot, armor, flotsam and jetsam, fired at or pulled into their world, igniting the atmosphere like fireflies in a cloud.

The queen took note of the flashes and sighed. "Can we stop them if they land?"

"Aye, of course," said Sir Edward.

"I don't know," said Sir Nolan. "It all depends on what gets through. Where they land. How long it takes us to react."

"And the bombs?" said Edward.

"Aye."

"And the prophet allows this?" said Zabel.

"I only wish we had some bombs. I'd send a ship to Temple now and leave our regards."

This stopped the queen. And she put aside indignity of the threat to Enskari and saw bigger things and bigger threats and felt ashamed. Edward's suggestion was only fair in this bloody and terrible war, but the thought of destroying Temple sickened her and she mourned though it had not happened. Temple was the sacred center of their civilization. She'd not given it much thought in those terms of late, but the thought of destroying the cities there with the weapon that she'd had described to her as the Devil's own fist, sent a terrible crawl down her back. It went beyond a few lives, beyond houses, cities, and worlds. This was the culture. This was all of history. All of their civilization.

"We shall see," said Nolan after she'd turned back to the window. "Your man Ethan is there."

"Our man," said Edward.

"Aye," said Nolan. "He'll do Your Highness honor."

His sentiment had a fatality about it.

★　★　★

The battle raged for days, the messages bad and terrible. The numbers insurmountable, Hyraxian broadsides gutting her ships, destroying entire squadrons in a volley. And Coronam throwing in, hurling radiation and meteors to add insult to injury, adding a solar arsenal to the terrible fight. God himself would have a hand.

The queen despaired and so had taken to her own company away from the messages that would upset her, away from her advisors, who could do little but lie to her. Those first days, she prayed like she'd never prayed before. She prayed for her life, and her people, her cities and planet. She prayed for Ethan, not just that he be victorious somehow against all odds, but that he return to her, or at least, that he survive. Not unlike her, he was the model of the age, the upstart from modest beginnings risen to glory. He was important. If they were to survive, he should survive. Or if not, she concluded, he should die well. God help him, he should die well.

What a hypocrite she was to pray though. She who'd cast an entire world away from the faith, she who'd been the center of an apostasy that had led to this moment. God might well throw meteors at her world. She had sinned. She longed for a confessor. She longed to repent to save her world from bombs and blood. She regretted the lives already lost to her, in her rise and her rule. In the war that came because she'd valued independence over unity, evolution over tradition, her mind – a woman's mind over a man's.

She spoke none of this to anyone but herself and the stars and God, if he were listening to a heretic these days. She kept alone and cared for herself, and found sanity in the daily grooming of her hair and the washing of her body. In the daylight she dreamed of a peace. She dreamed of an end of mistakes. At night, she dreamed of fire in the fields, of bonfires, human and wood, clouds alight in her nightmares. She'd dreamed of Old Earth, the bombs that had been left there, the strife and fall of it, cradle left to rot. She dreamed of Ethan and his lips, his hips and manhood. She dreamed of hope and love. And she dreamed, for a moment, of bees.

The third day, it all turned.

The first reports had come from far solar observers who'd seen the angry sun seething with storm. Messages were relayed from across the world. Some were hours old by the time they reached the queen, signals sent from space and down elevator cable to a military station who would send it on to another and then possibly another and then again until, if important enough, it'd land in Lady Daven's bedchamber.

Almost too late, Ethan had ordered his fleet into shadow, abandoning the battle, leaving the Hyraxians to the fate of their sun.

They took losses in flight, more in that hour than in the previous ten, but most had made it clear. The enemy had seen the danger and some Hyraxian ships had fled into the lee and were cut down by the massed Enskari fleet while signaling prayers of deliverance and surrender. Some were boarded. Some of these were captured and scuttled. Some crews impressed. Some spaced.

The storm blew vicious for a day and a half. Enskari lost a spaceport entire and five others were damaged. Ships too slow or too far out to reach shelter behind the planet were given up for lost though recent reports showed at least some, perhaps a third, had weathered it after all.

The enemy fared much worse. The carnage went across their entire fleet; only a tenth of their transports remained, a fifth of their tenders, a third of their battleships. The terrible man-o-wars fared no better than their smaller companions, perhaps worse. Bigger wasn't better when fending off solar-flung meteors. Bigger targets took bigger blows.

The remains of the mighty armada, what of them could sail, had left for home at full sail, their petals ablaze, their bells aglow, while the storm was still at its height.

And Enskari was saved.

That much had come from the station reports. It was modified and clarified by eyewitness accounts, interviews from crews evacuated from breached ships who'd dropped in life pods along evacuation strands while their ships burned in space. It was a miracle any of them made it, but a surprisingly high number had.

Now she just waited news of her admiral.

A knock on the door.

"Your Majesty, report from an Austen relay station. It's about Sir Ethan."

As calmly as she could, she rose from the window seat and straightened her dress. She took a deep breath and nodded to dismiss the page, confident she'd fooled him that she was intact, but taking another minute so as not to be so obvious to those who knew her better.

When she was ready, she left her sitting room and headed toward the telegraph station.

She passed Lord and Lady Daven at lunch and smiled to them as they stood and bowed. Their manners had been impeccable and their discretion admirable. They'd not asked to be included in any of the turmoil disrupting their house. They seemed happily ignorant, complacent perhaps by living so far from regular society that they couldn't imagine events so far away ever affecting them.

The queen entered the telegraph room and all rose and bowed. The first face she saw was Sir Nolan Brett's. He held a paper in his hand. She read shock in his face, disbelief. Her heart sank and she felt her knees wobble beneath her.

Sir Edward caught her and set her down. "Good news," he said, pulling the page from the Second Ear's grasp. "The *Merry* is fit and able. Admiral Sommerled is alive and well. He sends his glad tidings."

Looking at the other faces in the room now, she saw each one a picture of glee and happy surprise.

Edward laughed a rolling chuckle. "Listen to this, Your Majesty," he said, holding the paper out nearly to arm's length to read it. "He says, *To Queen Zabel Genest, sovereign of Enskari, leader of the people and the church. The enemy has been rebuffed, as per your request. Sincerely, your devoted servant, Sir Ethan Sommerled.*"

The room roared in laughter and rose in a cheer. "Hurrah! Hurrah! Hurrah!"

Across the room, by the window lit by flashing sky, she caught the eye of her Second Ear. Sir Nolan Brett smiled and nodded as if he had never a doubt things would turn out as they did.

CHAPTER TWENTY-NINE

By natural reason man can know God with certainty on the basis of his works. But there is another order of knowledge which man cannot possibly arrive at by his own powers: the order of divine revelation. Through an utterly free decision, God has revealed himself and given himself to man. This he does by revealing the mystery, his plan of loving goodness, formed from all eternity for the benefit of all men. God has fully revealed this plan by sending us his beloved prophet, who speaks with the Lord clearly and speaks for him to the people. His word is God's commandment.
Catechism of the Saved, Verse 15

28, Fifth-Month, 938 NE – Temple

Eren VIII knelt in earnest prayer at the altar of the prophet in the little anteroom connecting his personal chamber. It was not his usual time, not his usual posture, duration, or intent in this place. Normally, he'd visit once a day for form, twice if vexed looking for solitude. Usually he'd rattle off a quick devotion with half a thought and a third of his heart and enjoy the silence of privacy the little room afforded the most powerful religious leader in humanity. He'd stay ten minutes or an hour, knowing that no one would disturb him there. This was the prophet's personal sanctuary. This was where God would most likely communicate with his messenger.

In the eight years he'd been prophet, God had never spoken to Eren. Having served directly under the three previous ones and having living knowledge of four others, Eren wasn't sure any of them had ever actually spoken to God in this room or anywhere else.

From this, he'd come to suspect one of three things. First, that revelation wasn't real, that those who claimed it were crazy or conmen. This idea was heresy. Second, that revelation was a subtle thing easily missed and confused with normal emotional states and required interpretation. He must take good advice and trust his gut feelings, which was where God spoke. His opinion balanced, God would add grains of sand to weigh him one way or another. This is what he liked to believe, what he would tell his successor if he could. The third thing was that God had not intervened with him or the seven before because there'd been no reason to. Like a helmsman holding a rudder of a smooth sailing ship, the captain had not needed to be present at all for his wishes to be carried out. Nothing important enough had come up for him to intercede. Corollary to this was the idea that when God needed to speak he would and it would be clear. He prayed this day that this was the case, for he could not imagine a time or a decision more deserving of divine revelation than what he faced now.

There was ruin and doom on the horizon. A challenge to the very order of society. A secret and old terror, discovered and eradicated centuries before, but now again on the move. The true evil, the true danger.

Tarquin had sent a message through relay a day after 'the Battle of the Armada', as the system was now referring to it.

The battle is lost, he'd said. *The bulk of the fleet is damaged or destroyed. Enskari hit-and-run tactics played into the sudden storm. With no safe harbor, the fleet was cut down by Coronam. Enormous losses of life aboard the transports. Too early to tell, but would guess at above five and seventy per cent losses there; perhaps sixty among the warships.*

Heading back to Hyrax now. Admiral Clelland is arrested and held under guard by order of the prince. He'll surely be executed for this failure.

I'll remain on Hyrax until summoned home. I await instructions. For the glory of the prophet, for the glory of God. – Tarquin.

With the defeat of the armada, Enskari was nigh untouchable. The heresy of the queen, its intrinsic challenge to the order of society, must yet be tolerated a while longer. Civil war had failed, stealth had failed, and now invasion and war was orbital wreckage. It was as if some greater power watched over that damned kingdom. Knowing that God was with him, it was left to reason what was on the other side. But why had God let it come to this? Tarquin had not blamed anything or anyone, divine or mundane for the disaster, but everyone else had and the prophet could not but see a greater hand in that storm. Such a calamity would challenge the faith of the Saved and thus his throne. It would further weaken the threads of authority and hierarchy that held society together uniformly and wisely.

Before the Unsettling there'd been disunion and strife. Such dangers had been avoided in their new home by the strength of faith and the leadership of its elite, under the guidance of the prophets. Earth had been torn asunder when the natural order of society, its classes and castes, were questioned and overturned. The wars that came of that had nearly made their species extinct. God had saved them from those fires of that burning world by leading them to Coronam. God had saved them; their very name reflected that miracle. They were the Saved. To his glory, they'd built a firm and leveled society. Each to their place and station, all slowly working toward the ultimate unification of thought and order across all worlds. Eren had been sure that Brandon was sent to complete this task, a political unification upon which to build a spiritual one and then the next step toward the ultimate elevation of Temple as the government of all mankind. Hyrax was meant to subdue the worlds, but now, he realized, his hands shaking in clenched exertion over his private altar, this was not God's will. Not the time for it. It would have to wait.

He unlaced his hands and bowed to the altar, remembering its history. It had come aboard ship from Old Earth, carved by the faithful in a wood whose name was lost to time. A relic, modest, plain, and ancient.

He glanced upward at the tapestries, at the low glowglobes hanging from silk strands, his face upturned toward heaven but seeing only ceiling. He sighed in despair and closed his eyes and saw behind his lids a single image, a thing that had worried him, and vexed him, and taken his sleep, and now terrified him. That image he took then to be the word of God. This was the answer to his prayer. This was his direction. It was confirmation of his worst worry, the prophesy that his position had been made for. It was the face of the enemy. The danger to all the civilized. There was another threat to mankind greater than the Enskari apostasy. He was the first to understand it and it was his duty to save humanity from its evil influence.

He burst out of his cell, startling his palace guard.

Jessop, his first advisor, waited for him with a knot of other officials outside his chamber. Eren saw half his apostles among the group.

"Jessop," he said. "Bring me the archivist. I'll have all the records about the Brothers of Apis."

"What? Your Eminence, should we not discuss the armada and the war?"

"Affairs of men, brother Jessop. Affairs of state. Our charge is divine. We must look wider than this spat among our children."

Jessop looked at him as if he were speaking in tongues. He half thought he was. The rush of understanding, of threat and fear that his inspiration had filled him with made Eren feel for the first time as if his ascension was deserved.

"The Brothers of Apis, Your Eminence?" said Jessop.

"Aye, brother."

"They were executed to a man, burned alive. It's been centuries."

"Aye," said Eren as patiently as he could. "I'll see the records again."

"The records are sealed," said Jessop. "By the purgers."

"So bring me the archivist," he said, and then turned to face a page. "Bring me the high archivist. Immediately."

The page turned on his heels and ran. Jessop cast a glance back at the apostles and shrugged.

Jessop stepped in close to Eren and spoke softly. "Does this have something to do with your secret meeting with Tarquin last month?"

Jessop was always quick. It didn't surprise him that his first advisor knew of the meeting, nor that he'd not brought it up until now. The man was a pillar of discretion. "Assemble the Twelve," said Eren. "Within a week. I'll address them then."

"Aye," he said. "But what shall we do in the interim, about those 'affairs of men'? There is panic and worry now over the fate of the armada."

Always a pragmatic man. Jessop was good to have around.

"Announce it was a terrible and unfortunate loss of life," said Eren. "Announce a day of prayer and fasting for the dead."

"Aye. Any more?"

"And remember the losses from both sides."

"Your Eminence?"

"You heard right. Hyraxian, Templers, and Enskarans. Name them all Saved and brothers. It's time to mend some wounds."

"Aye." A half smile crept over Jessop's face. He'd surprised his advisor. "We have work to do. We start now with peace amongst the civilized to make war against the heathen."

Jessop's face blanched.

"What is it, Kendall?" asked the prophet.

"You've received prophesy?"

Eren looked at the apostles who'd been listening to it all. Their faces mirrored his advisor's awe. He was not sure before, but the looks on their faces confirmed his hope. God had spoken to him.

"Aye brothers," he said. "We have work to do."

The quorum fell to their knees in prayer of thanks while Eren thought of bees.

CHAPTER THIRTY

We leave to explore the way forward. For the species.
Jareth's last words to Earth before entering the wormhole to Coronam
November 7, 2345

1, Sixth-Month, 938 NE – Pemioc, Tirgwenin

Holding her brother's hand, Millie Dagney marched in the lead of the little band toward the walls of Pemioc.

Three and twenty souls had crossed the creek to join Millie, defying the last assistant. Millie had rushed them into the deepest parts of the forest to hide, knowing Aguirre's wrath was not spent. For two days Aguirre, his selects, and those who'd remained scoured the forest for them, shooting into shadows and cursing them before moving on.

Millie hid them in a secret cave and fed them from her own stores. When they had no sign of the others for three days, she allowed a fire and they prepared the hortmal and gumbnut she'd found. She showed them how as if she'd been making it her whole life.

The day after that, they set off.

The people asked her how she knew to find the cave, how she knew the way, how she knew so much about the place – guessed at rivers and knew the crossings, navigated in darkness by stump and glade, and so much more.

She told them to hush, to stay in line and keep a wary eye out.

She was but a girl, they said to themselves, barely sixteen. She'd been trapped like them within the fort, and yet she moved among the plants and places as if she'd been raised here. Even Dillon began to wonder. They'd all heard rumors that she'd snuck out of the palisade at night, but they were weeks beyond anywhere she could have explored from there.

When she would not answer their concerns, telling them only to wait, the worry turned to whispers of witchcraft and second-guessing their choice to come with her instead of staying with Aguirre. William Phevens jockeyed to usurp leadership away from Millie. He fashioned himself a new minister, acting as the new spiritual head of the group. Several times he'd tried to lead them in prayer but at each occurrence Millie had stopped him, saying only it was a bad idea.

On the sixth night out, two of their group disappeared never to be seen again. At breakfast when the defections were understood, Millie knew it could no longer wait. It was time to explain, at least a little.

She called them together.

"It is not witchcraft that has shown me these things," she said, "nor do I think it is God. I think it is a thing of this world, a unifying connection with the people who've lived here. It is manifested in a bee. See here how this little thing has made me its own?"

Plagued as they were by black flies and biting gnats, Millie was not surprised that no one had noticed one peculiar insect orbiting her. They bent forward to see it now. The creature swooped and landed on her shoulder, where it groomed itself serenely.

Since it began, Millie had searched for words to explain what was happening to her, knowing it would eventually come to this. She knew she alone was in a position to save some of these people, but her success rested on convincing them of the truth. It would have been so much easier to proclaim God's grace and summon the people around her like a prophet. That would have kept them to her, but it was not the truth. If they were ignorant or haughty, this world would not have them. They had to be open to its ideas. If they could do that, they'd have a chance. The test would be the truth of Millie's bee.

"Any one of us can have one," she told them. "We need only be ready for it to come. When it does, it will open knowledge, but only as much and what kind the host is ready for."

"Who determines who's ready?" said Phevens.

"The bees, I suppose," she said.

"It sounds like magic."

"It doesn't feel like it," she said. "It feels like a natural thing. To put agency to it beyond your own understanding is to misunderstand it. That I know. It is a thing of knowledge and enlightenment. It is a thing beyond prayer. It is not a subjection of will, but an assertion of it."

The others stared at her in confusion. Her vocabulary surely had left them behind.

"Sounds blasphemous," said Phevens.

She recalled a thing her father had once said when defending having a woman upon a planetary throne. "One needs to have a broader perspective," she said.

It was an idea that had helped birth the Bucklers at the start. The group recognized the sentiment, but some didn't like having it used on them now.

"It is different from what we're used to," she went on. "It is like electricity if you've never felt it before, or silk maybe. I've never felt that but I'm told it's pleasant and unusual. It's like that."

The faces told her that she was failing.

"Think of it like a telegraph wire to a library," she said, "but without the wire. Like to Old Earth perhaps, when radios worked."

"What do you know of that?" said Ms. Pierce.

It was knowledge beyond her education, beyond her class and sex. She was speaking against herself. She didn't answer right away.

Phevens said, "Who's sending you signals?"

Here she knew she must tread carefully. "I am convinced it is human agency. Humans are behind what I have seen. It is their knowledge. I see it like I'm seeing it in a lexicon, knowledge penned by countrymen."

"Humans? Just humans?"

"The knowledge I have sought has been of this place, so it comes from those humans who know it. I speak of the descendants of Jareth's ship from Old Earth."

"The sparklers?"

She cringed at the name, but said, "Aye."

"It is their witchcraft. You are possessed by their magic!"

"Nay, Emme Mirrioth. It may sound that way, but if it does, that comes from my failings of language. My inability to describe a state of mind that you have not achieved."

"So you're better than us?"

"Only insofar as I am more balanced. I have seen further than others of our band. I have access to more resources than you. But do you not see that I am here to share these things, not lord them?"

The people, so hungry and tired, victims of so much mishap and blatant cruelty, stared at her as if she was just another agent of calamity and not the savior she thought herself to be.

"We have a chance to live," she said.

"You're taking us to the sparklers?"

"Aye, to Pemioc. I know the way."

"You're delivering us to the enemy?"

"I'm taking us to people who can help us."

"We should have stayed with Aguirre," said Phevens. "He was going there too, but he would take us there as conquerors, not as slaves."

"Aguirre is lost. He doesn't know the way. He never did."

They all spoke over themselves then.

"Will the natives help us?"

"Will they kill us?'

"Will they enslave us?"

"Is there truth to what Phevens says?"

Millie knew that they might well be cast into slavery when they got there. They might also all be killed outright. The scars of the civilized worlds' affronts on Tirgwenin were not forgotten or forgiven. But she believed – no, she knew – that their only chance for longterm survival was to unite with the Tirgwenians. They were not bad people. She could not say the same about Aguirre's selects.

"If we are humble," she said, "if we are open-minded, if we can cast off the chains of ignorance, we can yet prosper here."

"She is insane!" cried Phevens. "Do you not see it? We were duped. We left our company to follow a mad girl, a delusional child who thinks she talks to bugs. We need to repent. First to God, for we have wandered far from his grace, and then to Aguirre, our kinsman."

"He is far from here," said Millie. No one asked her how she knew this.

"Then we will set out north and arrive in Placid Bay. That is the way we will go. We have listened to this girl too long."

Millie turned her back on Phevens and addressed the others. "Ye have to believe there is a better way," she said. "Ye have to have faith. New faith."

"Blasphemy!" called Phevens. "We will not listen to this girl any longer."

She bent down and gathered her things. "We are four days' march from Pemioc," she said. "I go there now with those of you who wish to live."

It was the way Phevens had said 'girl' that had told her it was time to decide. He'd evoked the ancient masculine right of leadership. It was as good a time as any to separate those with a 'broader perspective' from those who'd joined her just to get away from Aguirre but were unable to even try to change.

She took Dillon's hand and marched west. She kept her eyes forward, the bee telling her she'd done right, soothing the pain of human loss with a pleasant low drone. It was near on twenty minutes before she finally turned around and counted heads of those who still remained with her.

One hundred three and twenty souls left Enskari. One hundred eighteen arrived. After so many terrible days, three and twenty had crossed the creek to come with Millie. Then two had run off the night before and counting heads now, she saw that five had gone with Phevens. Sixteen souls were still with her. Sixteen souls marched with her to Pemioc.

★   ★   ★

The next day and for the days thereafter, they saw silent Tirgwenians working fields along the roadside. The tall natives watched them pass, their yellow skin shimmering in the afternoon light. Their faces were curious and bright, but none approached them. Millie let them be and kept the party on the path, which became a trail and then a road approaching Pemioc.

The colonists huddled closer and clasped dirty hands. They kept near to Millie and her bee, which buzzed and looped around her in speeding agitation. Forward they walked without talking. They kicked up dust with shuffling shoeless feet, their tattered rags blowing like banners in the warm alien breeze exposing cuts, sores, and bruises on their worn and tired bodies.

On they marched.

Until they saw the walls of Pemioc.

A kilometer out, soldiers fell in behind them. Marching in a mass, they matched Millie's pace and kept at range.

Half a kilometer out, painted soldiers appeared at the gate and fanned out along the sides of the road. They took up picket positions with lances and bows, spaced ten meters apart as if to watch a parade.

The walls of Pemioc rose before them and they saw tattooed yellow faces over the battlements, stern eyes watching them from turrets.

On they walked, slow and plodding, not breaking step.

The bee told Millie to be brave. To accept whatever awaited.

Dillon gripped her hand with both of his and tried to hide behind her torn skirt.

The gate swung shut.

Millie wanted to cry.

On they walked

Five meters, four meters. Two steps. One. They stopped before the gate.

In the shadow of the door the surviving colonists huddled together, seventeen men and women, girls and boys, lost settlers, dying and marooned.

Millie reached out and touched the wood that barred their way. It was a rich and interesting wood, mildly fragrant, bright-grained, and hard. Her father would have loved it, would have shaped it into marvels, cut it to plumb posts, shaped it to a chair, a table. A dowry chest. A door. She pressed against it. It did not move.

Tears poured down her face and splashed in muddy spots upon her weatherworn dress. Seeing her so, several others fell to their knees and wept also.

The Tirgwenian soldiers encircled them, barring retreat as if they had strength or will to go anywhere but there.

Millie turned her face upward and searched the battlements. Scanning the faces that looked down on them.

There, among them, a woman watched – a one-armed woman. Lahgassi. Millie knew her. She knew her name on Tirgwenin, and her name to the Saved, Lisa. Millie knew what she had endured, knew the loss of her arm, her breast. Her daughter. She knew it and felt it as if she herself had suffered those tragedies. The bee filled Millie's heart with Lahgassi's anguish and it mixed with her own. She wept and shook and could only look into that face and beseech another person for mercy.

"Please," Millie whispered up the wall. It was too far for her voice to carry and she was afraid to yell. She could think of nothing else to say. "Please," she whispered again.

When she was done, all was silent save for the droning of bees.

The gate swung open.

ABOUT THE AUTHOR

Johnny Worthen is an award-winning, multiple-genre, tie-dye-wearing author, voyager, and damn fine human being! Trained in literary criticism and cultural studies, he writes upmarket fiction, long and short, mentors others where he can and teaches at the University of Utah. Find out more on his website: johnnyworthen.com.

ACKNOWLEDGMENTS

This is a story of belief and hope and without those things and the support of those who have those things, this book would not exist as it does now. To that end, let me thank first my editor, Don D'Auria, who believed in this project and shepherded us across the voids. Thanks to Terri Baranowski for her constant belief in me and my projects. Thanks to Dorothy Diane, my first reader, my greatest fan, the font of all hope I possess. Gratitude and respect to Imogen Howson, who aligned the terms to historical accuracy instead of ahistorical bastardry. They both might have worked, but this is better. Her edits and insights are much appreciated. Last in order but first in rank, thanks to my children, who embody hope and my wife, who lets me believe.

FLAME TREE PRESS
FICTION WITHOUT FRONTIERS
Award-Winning Authors & Original Voices

Flame Tree Press is the trade fiction imprint of Flame Tree Publishing, focusing on excellent writing in horror and the supernatural, crime and mystery, science fiction and fantasy. Our aim is to explore beyond the boundaries of the everyday, with tales from both award-winning authors and original voices.

•

You may also enjoy:

•

Join our mailing list for free short stories, new release details, news about our authors and special promotions:

flametreepress.com